THE SECRET KEEPER HOLDS ON

(THE SECRET KEEPER SERIES #4)

BREA BROWN

WAYZGOOSE PRESS

Cover design by Keri Knutson at alchemybookcovers.com

Second edition ISBN: 978-1-938757-65-5

CONTENTS

For my husband, Clint.
Thanks for "holding on" with me all these years.

UTTER EXHAUSTION

"*D*o you feel guilty doing this?"

I stare at the ceiling liner of the Jeep from my reclined position and contemplate Brice's question.

"A little," I admit. "You?" I turn my head to look at his eyes, which are parallel with mine.

"No," he answers, unconvincingly.

If I look anything like he does, then we need this. His face alone provides a good idea of what parenting three babies under the age of two will do to a person. He carries off "tired" well, though, like he's happy to be zapped; like, *I'm exhausted, but it's so worth it. Look at my bewildered, shell-shocked smile and the cute bags under my eyes.*

I don't have cute bags under my eyes. I couldn't tell you exactly how I look, though. I haven't glanced in a mirror—I haven't *dared*—in days.

I reach across the center console and wiggle my fingers so he'll grab my hand. When he does, I squeeze his fingers and say, "Who's to say *how* we have to spend our 'us time'? Marianne and Clark wanted us to get away from the house and the kids. We're away from the house and the kids."

"We're less than a mile away," he points out, in case I've forgotten.

"So?"

"So I think they intended for us to go to dinner or a movie. Or both. Not hang out in our car. In a McDonald's parking lot."

"I'm too tired to get out of the car."

"Me too."

"Then be quiet, so I can get some sleep."

He smiles over at me. "Okay. Just a few minutes, though. Right?" Squinting at his phone, he grasps it in his free hand and pokes at some buttons on the screen with his thumb. "I'm setting an alarm. That way, we can wake up and actually do something. Or go somewhere. Or at least have a conversation."

I close my eyes, rubbing my head back and forth on the rest beneath it, trying to get comfortable. "Whatever," I mumble noncommittally.

"It'll get better."

"Mmmph."

I feel his lips against my hand. "It will. They're only a month old, still so little and helpless and—"

"Loud?"

He laughs. "Um, yeah. Sometimes. Well, Harris isn't loud."

He's right; Harris seems to be in the same boat with Brice and me, watching helplessly as Max and Brooks wreak havoc on the world. Max is nineteen months old, so his noises usually relate to playing or incessant babbling. Brooks, Harris's twin, is the quintessential fussy newborn. But Harris? He's so laid back that I asked his pediatrician if there was something wrong with him.

Dr. Baum simply smiled and said, "This is probably

exactly how it was in utero. Brooks jostled for more elbow room and was an all-around higher-maintenance fetus, while Harris was merely along for the ride. Personality is a powerful thing, and it develops earlier than we can probably even imagine."

"So he's not... slow?" I asked.

"Well, we won't know that for a while, but I wouldn't worry about it, based on his behavior so far. He's simply being himself. If he's not hitting his developmental milestones in a few months, we'll reevaluate. Till then, be grateful that you have one content baby."

He patted me on the knee and left me to bundle up two infants—one of whom was squalling, as usual, and the other sleeping as if he were in a silent, soundproof room—and their older brother, whose new favorite game is to make me chase him everywhere we go. That is, when he's not loving on his baby brothers—and nearly braining them in the process (he doesn't understand the concept of *gentle* yet).

Now I say to Brice, "You're right; Harris isn't loud. He's just always hungry."

He chuckles. "That's my boy."

"I know you're not being perverted."

"What?! Of course not. I meant it in the most wholesome way possible. Sheesh. Making me blush over here." After a short silence, he asks, "Wanna make out?"

"Not in a McDonald's parking lot!"

"So if I drive somewhere else, you'd be up for it?"

I turn on my side, away from him, facing the passenger door. "No. Leave me alone. Haven't you gotten us into enough trouble? We've resorted to sleeping in your car outside a fast food restaurant, because our house is a zoo."

After a big sigh, he says, "We have three kids. That's hardly a zoo. Although the twins *are* two little monkeys."

"Shhh. I'm sleeping."

"You have fifty minutes."

"My ass."

"Gerrrouchy!"

He can call me every name in the book, but I'm not budging from this car until I feel at least halfway human again.

Oddly enough, I wake up first, before the cell phone alarm, even. I stretch, then roll over so I'm facing Brice. He's on his back, one knee bent, his other long leg straight, disappearing under the steering wheel, where I imagine his foot is wedged between the gas and brake pedals in the floorboard. I can't resist smiling at how sacked out he is. He must have been even more tired than I was, which stands to reason, considering he's very much back into the swing of things at the church.

Harris and Brooks were remarkably cooperative to be born two weeks early, in mid-November rather than at the end of the month, nearer to their due date, so Brice got an entire week off with us, but he and I knew that would be the limit. It was only a matter of days before things ramped up again, and when they did, it was a mad dash to Christmas.

While the twins arrived early, the post-tornado church reconstruction wrapped up a full month later than planned, the week before Thanksgiving. Church staff members settled into their new digs in time for Advent, the season before Christmas, which is as—if not more—active than Christmas itself in the Lutheran Church. That meant midweek services, pre-Christmas toy and food drives, and all the church groups' Christmas activities had to be squeezed into an already jam-packed calendar, which also included the new church dedication as well as the grand opening and dedication of Peace Lutheran Daycare and Preschool.

Of course, Brice has had *some* help from Peace's associate pastor, Wayne Long, and our new assistant pastor, Wes Anthony. Unfortunately, Pastor Long prefers giving orders or pointing out perceived problems with orders already given by others. If you call that being helpful, he's given loads of input. He's made Lucy, the church secretary, cry more times than I can accurately recall, which is not at all useful when everyone's working twelve- to fourteen-hour days to ensure things are running as smoothly as possible before Christmas.

Pastor Anthony, on the other hand, has been a much better helpmate. When we called him to be the new assistant pastor at Peace, life was anything but peaceful. The church had recently been hit by a tornado—literally—but that didn't faze him. Fresh out of seminary, the twenty-six-year-old accepted our call and has been a quiet, calming influence throughout the rebuilding process.

Do I get a slightly strange vibe from him sometimes? Yes. But I'm sure that's only because he's so intensely quiet. Before meeting him, I'd never met anyone who commanded such a presence, often without saying a word. It feels like he can see into my soul. Let's hope that's not the case.

Despite his unnerving mannerisms, Pastor Anthony gets along well with Brice. The two of them have divvied up the workload according to each man's strengths. If something requires a more outgoing personality—like a wedding or baptism—Brice takes care of it. If the job calls for a more somber or quiet presence—like a funeral or hospital visit— Pastor Anthony steps up. All three pastors have devised a complicated (in my view) rotation to decide who preaches the sermon and who leads the liturgy each Sunday. The odd man out sits in the congregation during the service.

I'm still not sure how I feel about having Brice in the pew with me once a month. It's only happened once so far, but it was bizarre. Max loved it. I assume I'll get used to it, but for now, it's kind of unnerving.

I study Brice's profile now. He's been complaining that he gained a few sympathy pounds when I was pregnant with the twins, but to me, he looks like the same adorable, sexy pastor I married. Maybe a tad paunchier around the middle, but he hasn't had a lot of time to jog lately. And who am I to judge? I just had two babies and find extra, fatty appendages all over my body daily (or so it seems). At least he attempts to run now and then. The last time I ran was when Max made a wobbly break for the street while I was preoccupied with trying to get Harris and Brooks from their car seats. (From now on, he'll be the last child set free.)

Brice begins to stir, so I instinctively close my eyes and pretend I'm still dozing. My staring at him while he sleeps is one of his few pet peeves. I admit it's creepy, but sometimes I can't help it. We've only been married three years, after all. He still makes me feel like a stupid, giddy teenager.

Just as I'm trying to decide if I have the acting chops to pull off a full fake wakeup, his cell phone alarm chimes. Seconds after silencing it, he gently pokes my nose with his finger. I open my eyes and smile at him while blinking. All right, my cover's blown right there. I never wake up smiling.

He doesn't seem to notice the out-of-character behavior. "Hey. I feel so much better!" he declares in the middle of a stretch. Then he puts his seat in the upright position and looks out his window. "Wow. This place is nuts. Major run on Big Macs tonight."

"Christmas shopping makes people hungry." I too sit up. "Let's aim a little higher for our dinner, shall we?"

Pulling his wallet from his back pocket, he opens it and winces at what he finds—or doesn't find—inside. "I don't know. Somewhere with a dollar menu might be appropriate."

I wish I could pretend he was kidding, but money *is* tight right now. In spite of our medical and homeowners' insurance, the hospital and doctor's bills and roof repairs we had to make to our own house following the tornado took a huge bite out of our savings. Between that and the lower housing allowance we agreed Brice would take until the church paid for its new construction, my part-time job at the art gallery and boutique downtown isn't as fanciful or superfluous as it was when I started it a few months ago.

We're about to add a bigger car payment to the family budget, too, since I can't fit three car seats in the back of my full-sized sedan. I've been driving Brice's Jeep when I have to take all three kids anywhere, which is blessedly rare. As it is, we had to shell out quite a bit of money for narrow-profile car seats that would fit in *his* backseat. He's been commuting to work in my car until we have time to go shopping for something bigger for me to drive. *Not* a minivan. I'm not thrilled about it, but we're on the lookout for a deal on an SUV with a third row of seats. So far, nothing we've seen online has fit our shrinking budget or my requirement that I don't look and feel like I'm driving a tank that could single-handedly use up every nonrenewable resource our planet has to offer.

Despite all these financial worries niggling at the back of my brain, I smile cheerfully. "Well, if you let me super-size my meal *and* get a chocolate shake, I can easily pretend I'm in a Michelin-rated restaurant." That is, if I also conveniently disregard the town in which we live—I'm not sure Springfield, Missouri, has any of those.

His resultant grin stirs those familiar butterflies.

"Well, I believe we're going to be late for our reservation, then, if we're not careful." He hops down from the car and runs around to my side of the vehicle, so he can open the door for me. "My bride."

I giggle and simper, "Oh, my. Such a gentleman!"

Inside the eatery, I reluctantly order a Happy Meal and a small chocolate shake, instead of the heart-attack burger and the extra-large cup of happiness with a straw that I *really* wanted to get. I mustn't forget I'm nursing two babies, and empty calories won't do. Darn it! After savoring my last fry, I sit back on my side of the hard plastic booth and sigh contentedly.

Brice laughs at me but quickly sobers. "I do feel guilty eating this junk when we have a lifetime supply of casserole at home in the freezer."

"I don't. If I'd had to eat another casserole with ham chunks in it tonight, I probably would have cried."

"Oh, come on."

"I'm serious."

"Everyone's been so nice to bring us food. And to volunteer to stay with the kids so we have some time together alone."

Now he's making me feel like a jerk. "I didn't say they weren't nice. I just said I was sick of casserole."

He crumples the wax paper burger wrapper in front of him. "I don't want people to think we're not grateful."

I roll my eyes. "I'm not going to get up in front of everyone at church tomorrow morning and announce that I'm sick of casserole. Nobody's going to know we aren't tucking into one of seven billion combinations of meat, cheese, and cream-of-whatever soup at this very minute. Except Marianne and Clark. And hopefully, they're eating some of that stuff for us."

Finally, he stops denying he agrees with me and gives in to a hearty laugh, but his glance freezes at something over my shoulder, and he abruptly quiets. "Oh, Chicago!"

"What?" I turn around and follow his eye line. It's all I can do not to react physically when I see Pastor and Vivian Long headed our way. I turn back to Brice and quickly hiss, "What are *they* doing here?"

Defensively, he whispers back, "I don't know! How should I—Pastor Long! Vivian! How are you two tonight?"

The six-foot-five clergyman smirks down at me and puts his hand on my shoulder. I barely resist the urge to shrug him off.

Brice widens his eyes and smiles tightly across the table at me while Pastor answers piously, "We just finished shopping for the needy child we selected from the gift tree."

Vivian pats her helmet hair. "The real question is, where are *your* children?"

Before I can give them one of my signature sarcastic responses, Brice hurries to reply, "Home, with responsible adults. The Pryces were nice enough to give us a break."

Vivian blinks rapidly and smiles. "Oh. How nice! I remember the days when there was no such thing as a 'break' when it came to parenting." She punctuates this slam with a piercing laugh while I grit my teeth so hard I worry I may start a fire in my mouth.

"Now, now, dear," Pastor interjects. "Times have changed. Let's not get Pastor Northam started on one of his favorite topics."

Brice chuckles and rubs the back of his neck. "No,

you're absolutely right; we're blessed to have such wonderful friends."

How does he do it? I worry for his health. Someday, he's going to keel over from a stroke or a heart attack from restraining himself when around people like this. Right now, for example, he's begging me with his eyes to be the silent pastor's wife, to follow his lead, to hold my Irish temper in check.

My eyes respond with death threats when the Longs join us at our table, Vivian sliding into the booth next to me, Pastor next to Brice.

All joviality—even the faked kind—suddenly vanishes, though. Pastor levels a serious look at Brice, clamps his enormous, paddle-like hand on his shoulder, and says, "It's funny we should bump into each other here, now. Well, not funny, necessarily. I suppose God planned it this way, but in any case…"

I sneak a peek at Vivian to see if I can glean anything from her expression, but she simply looks constipated as she watches our husbands.

"What's on your mind?" Brice asks, zeroed in on his fellow clergyman's eyes. His forehead crinkles, and his hand lands on Pastor's unoccupied one on the table.

"It's time for me to retire."

My arms shoot up, like I'm starting "the wave" in the fast food joint, but halfway up, they realize that would be inappropriate. One arm redirects its hand to my neck, where it meets my shoulder, delivering a massage to the muscle there. The other hand lands on my hair, as if its intent all along was to merely tuck that wayward strand behind my ear. I clear my throat of its nearly escaped whoop of joy and simply smile mildly when Vivian turns her attention to me and my strange upper body contortions. I hastily fold both hands in my lap and assume an expression that I hope resembles the other three serious ones around the table.

Brice leans back in his side of the booth. Pastor folds his hands in the center of the table.

Why isn't anyone talking?

When I can hardly take another second of the awkward silence and aim to fill it, even if it's with something sure to be more awkward than the silence, because it's coming from me, Brice rescues us all, saying stiffly, "I see. Well. I take it you've already notified the Synod?"

"No! I wanted to tell you first, of course."

"Ah. Yes. I appreciate that."

"We're ready to enjoy our grandchildren more fully," Vivian says. "Iris has another on the way, due in the summer, you know."

With a tiny head shake, Brice replies, "No. I didn't know. But congratulations. That's... wonderful."

"You do understand, I hope?" Pastor queries. "Obviously, I'll stay until you call a new associate pastor, if that's what you want. Or need. The last thing I want to do is leave you in the lurch. Which is why I waited until now to tell you. I was going to announce my retirement months ago, but the tornado hit, and... Well, it didn't seem like the right time then."

Brice bites his lower lip before saying, "That was very thoughtful. I'm sorry you've had to postpone your plans."

Pastor waves his hand. "Bah. What plans? Like Viv said, we're ready to relax, but we're not going anywhere. Springfield is our home. Peace is our family. And you don't leave family when they're in need."

Blinking and half-coughing, Brice fidgets. A closer study

of his face reveals... Well, I'm not sure what's going on there, but he appears unable to speak.

That's *my* cue.

"Pastor, Vivian, we're so happy for you." *And for us.* "What an exciting, new chapter in your lives!" *And ours.* "And we're so glad you'll still be around. Peace wouldn't be the same without you." *No, it would be a lot more peace*ful.

Recovered, Brice seconds my verbal sentiments. "Absolutely. And please, allow us to plan a big send-off for you. I'll get Lucy started on it right away Monday morning." He turns to me. "We should be getting home."

"But—" I start to protest, before seeing the determined set to his chin. *Oh, boy. What fresh hell is happening?* "Yes. You're right. I didn't realize the time." *Time for the night to be ruined by these two buffoons.*

We say our goodbyes to the other couple, who stand up to place their orders, releasing us from the booth. We ride the five minutes home in silence. Brice is obviously lost in his thoughts, while I'm afraid to ask what those thoughts entail.

When we get home, Brice barely says thank you to Marianne and Clark before plunking himself down at his newly constructed desk under the stairs and shoving a pair of ear buds into his ears.

Marianne whispers, "Is everything okay?"

I honestly don't know how to answer her.

2

HIDDEN AGENDA

*K*ids have not only ruined my body, they've wrecked my skin. Every night in the winter, while Brice sits propped against our headboard, reading whatever boring nerd tome is his *book du jour*, I have to go about the tiresome and somewhat vain routine of oiling myself down. But it's not about vanity (well, not completely). My skin is so dry since having kids that if I didn't submit to this greasy nightly activity, Brice might wake up one morning to find himself a modern-day Lot, except instead of lying next to a pillar of salt, he'd be bedmates with a Peyton-shaped pile of dead skin cells. Gross.

Sometimes—but not tonight, since I still have another week before I'll be cleared for such shenanigans by Dr. Klein—Lotion Time evolves into foreplay. And other times, like tonight, it gives me the opportunity to studiously avoid eye contact with my husband while I discuss things with him that he'd obviously rather not discuss.

"Let's talk about it," I suggest brightly, knowing he knows exactly what "it" is.

"There's nothing to talk about."

I snort. "Right. I'll start. I'm effing *thrilled* that Pastor Long is finally retiring. Woot-woot!" I pump my lotion-slathered arms toward the ceiling in a 'raise the roof' motion.

Going back to rubbing moisturizer into my elbows, I continue, "I'm not, however, thrilled that his announcement —so wonderful on the surface—ruined our up-till-then fabulous date night." I blow raspberries to underscore my displeasure.

When he says nothing at the end of my delightful mono-logue, I look over to see him with his nose buried in his book.

"Brice!"

That warrants a distracted "Huh?" but nary a glance in his peripheral vision.

"Why are you so pissed off about Pastor Long retiring? This is a prayer answered."

Apparently figuring I'm not going to shut up until he says something on the subject, he sighs, tents his book over his crotch, and, staring straight ahead, says in a monotone, "I'm not P.O.'ed about it."

"Liar." My name-calling gets no reaction whatsoever, so I back it up with evidence. "When he first told us he was retiring, you looked like you could etch glass with your jaw. And you've been giving me the silent treatment ever since, as if *I* put him up to retiring. I wish!"

"I'm processing it."

"When we got home, you were practically rude to the Pryces, going straight to your desk and jamming in your earbuds."

"I said 'thank you' and 'goodnight.' I had some things to do for tomorrow's services. Now that my desk is in the middle of the house, I have to block out the noise somehow, or I'll never get anything done."

"It was your idea to have that desk nook built to free up the fourth bedroom as a guest room."

"I'm not complaining; I'm explaining."

"Anyway, what's to process? Big Bird's retiring! We can call an associate pastor who actually pulls his weight and works cooperatively and— and doesn't make Lucy cry!" I set my lotion bottle on my nightstand and wave my hands through the air, as if conducting an orchestra while drying the lotion on my skin.

"It's not that simple," he states quietly, then, "Ow!" when I inadvertently whack him across the side of the head.

"Sorry!" I lean over and kiss him on my way under the covers. "Okay, so it'll take a while to call someone. Maybe. But he said he'd stay on until we do. If you even need him, which I don't think you do. He might as well leave now. He doesn't do anything, anyway."

"He does... stuff."

At this lame declaration, I laugh and look up at his pouty face. "You're being weird."

He crosses his arms over his chest. "I— I can't *believe* him."

I wait, tired of dragging it from him. My patience pays off when, a few seconds later, he laughs mirthlessly, "Telling me in a flipping McDonald's!"

Flipping. Wow. That's as close to a real curse word as I've ever heard him use without actually saying the word. This is serious. Cautiously, I ask, "You're mad because of *where* he told you? They ran into us; the opportunity presented itself. I don't think it was part of a *plan*."

He rolls his eyes. "I'm not saying it was, but it was still

inappropriate. He's waited this long to reveal his big news. What's another couple of days?"

"The Spirit moved him."

"Maybe it was indigestion."

"They hadn't eaten yet."

"My point is, he's been sitting on this a while. A long while. Just waiting."

"Yeah. That's what he said. Waiting for things to settle down, waiting for the right time." *I can't believe I'm defending this guy!*

"Bull roar!"

I bite my lip to keep from giggling but only because I know he's really upset, and I don't want to upset him more. I pat his leg under the covers. "Hon."

"I guess I'm supposed to kiss his Adam's apple because he didn't go over my head and notify the Synod first."

Trying not to picture that, I reply, "No, I think he realized that was the right thing to do."

"And what's all this malarkey about Peace being his family? Well, they *are* our family! We know the real meaning of the word."

I gulp. "I don't know. I got the feeling he was being sincere, for once. For the first time *ever*, I can't find any fault with how he handled it. He waited until the reconstruction was over; he's offered to stay until the new associate pastor starts; he told you before giving his notice to the Synod. What am I missing?"

"I don't know, but I'm missing it, too. And it's driving me crazy." He moves to throw back the covers and get out of bed, but I hold onto his pajamas, nearly pantsing him.

"Hey. What are you doing? It's getting late, and there's church tomorrow."

He pulls up on the waistband of his bottoms, yanking them from my grip. "I can't sleep. I'll take the first feeding."

"You'll be dead in the morning."

"Don't worry about me. Get some sleep." With that, he takes his book—and his pants—and leaves the bedroom, turning off the light and closing the door softly on his way out.

I don't know what's going on, but I don't like it. When fussing from the baby monitor next to my head wakes me up this morning, and I realize I didn't dream the conversation between Brice and me last night, I half expect to look out the window and see the sky on the ground and the ground in the sky. *That's* how topsy-turvy the exchange was. Talk about role reversal! I was the one putting a diplomatic spin on something Pastor Long had done, while Brice railed against the associate pastor? Unprecedented.

I'm chalking it up to lack of sleep. I know only too well how it can make one do and say uncharacteristic things. That doesn't mean I'm not worried, though. We could have several weeks—or months—of interrupted sleep ahead of us. If Brice goes off the rails, we're in trouble. It can't fall to me to keep the peace at Peace. That will not end well.

Grayish, early morning winter light streams through the uncovered glass arch above the window in front of the kitchen sink. I grab two bottles of breast milk from the fridge and plop them in warm water to heat while I trudge upstairs to retrieve Screamy and Squeaky before they wake up Stinky. (Mental note: stop letting Brice nickname our offspring.)

I change Brooks's diaper first and shove a pacifier in his mouth, holding it for several seconds until he gets the hint that it's in his best interest to keep it there. Harris temporarily stops squeaking (his version of fussing) after he has a dry diaper and I nestle him in the crook of my left arm, but I know I don't have long to get a bottle in his mouth before he resumes his best impression of a car's worn-out serpentine belt.

On the return trip to the kitchen, Brooks decides he's had enough of the binky, and since nobody's holding the pacifier in his mouth for him, he unceremoniously drops his lower lip and lets it fall, skittering over the banister. It seemed a pretty deliberate act to me, but now he's acting like it was the biggest mistake of his short life, and he wants the whole neighborhood to mourn the lost pacifier with him.

"Oh, for crying out loud," I grumble, wishing I wasn't always so worried about falling down the stairs while carrying these two at the same time. It makes my descent agonizingly slow, especially when noise-stopping bottles await below. But you can't rush safety, no matter how much a screaming child can unnerve you to the point of forgetting that important fact.

Finally, I arrive in the kitchen, where I deposit the two obviously starving babies in their bouncy seats on the kitchen island, test the milk's temperature on my wrist, and plug a bottle into each blaring hole.

Into the resulting silence, I sigh. "There. Has it really been that long? Your dad fed you, what, four hours ago?"

I blow my bangs off my forehead, wishing I had a few more arms (long ones) so I could pour myself a cup of coffee from the pot that's auto-brewing on the counter behind me. Instead, I resign myself to waiting until breakfast is over for these guys, and I take a seat in the nearest bar stool facing them.

"It's a good thing I like monkeys," I say sweetly to them. "Because that's what you are. Itty-bitty monkeys with hairy little shoulders and long fingers and toes." I kiss Brooks's monkey toes, wondering where exactly his sock fell off on our way downstairs. Wherever it happened, I don't expect to see the sock—or his binky—again. Things like that manage to disappear around this house.

Harris is finished in record time, as usual. Someday, I'll be proudly watching from the crowd at Coney Island while he shoves a hundred hot dogs down his throat and dunks the buns in water to make them go down more easily.

Brooks likes to take his sweet time. For someone so frantic before feeding, he sure loses steam quickly. About halfway through the bottle, he's flicking at the nipple with his tongue, dribbling milk down his chin and neck, and casually looking around the room like he has no clue what gave me the idea he was interested in eating in the first place.

Already dressed for church, Brice enters the kitchen while I'm burping Harris and Brooks waits impatiently for his turn. I still haven't figured out how to burp them at the same time, considering that pesky problem I have with only possessing two arms. Harris is like Max was, and is typically easy and fast to burp, but this morning, he's not giving it up as readily as usual.

Brice steps over and grabs Brooks, placing him smoothly against his shoulder, which has a cloth diaper draped over it. "You guys finally decided you wanted to wake up and eat?" he asks.

I pause with my hand against Harris's back. "What do you mean, 'finally'?"

"I mean, they never got up for me. At two-thirty, I

checked on them to make sure they were breathing; then I went to bed."

First Pastor Long announces his retirement; then *both* twins skip their mid-night feeding? Oh, I *am* being rewarded for something. *Thank you, Lord.*

I blink away tears (of joy, pride, relief, rogue hormones?) and whisper, "Oh, gosh. That's such great news! Just in time for everyone visiting next week."

Brice shrugs and pulls a face in response to my near elation at this news. Like it's no big deal. Like it's not a Christmas miracle. After Brooks's dry burp, Brice settles him in his left arm and crosses to the coffeemaker, where he pours two cups and slides one across the island toward me. "It's only one night. I'm sure we still have several viewings of 'The Miracle Knife! It cuts through sheetrock!' in store."

"Don't ruin my moment," I plead, sipping my piping-hot coffee. "Just… let me fantasize."

He laughs at me. "It's only been a few weeks. Max didn't sleep through the night for months. Unless one of us was holding him."

As if I'd already forgotten. "I can't go through that again," I state emotionally. "I'm not as strong as I used to be. He took *years* off my life."

"I sincerely hope not."

We put the babies back in their side-by-side seats and look down at them for a while.

"Amazing," Brice finally says, spinning to return to his coffee. Before he steps away, I pull the diaper from his shoulder and snap it toward his retreating rear.

"Hey!"

"Were you going to wear this to church? Hot new pastor gear? The under-robe burp cloth?"

"Might come in handy during Communion." He tugs at

his shirt collar. "Good grief! My collars are even getting tighter! That's it. I'm making time to run every day. I don't care if I have to get up at four in the morning. Or if I'm out running at ten at night. I'm doing it. This is ridiculous."

"Or you could buy bigger shirts."

"No! I've been the same weight since— since forever, and that's not going to change now." He pulls a box of Raisin Bran from the pantry and shakes it at me. "Back to the 'Bran. It's never steered me wrong. It'll banish the fat."

"It's not obvious when you have clothes on."

He freezes mid-pour. "You can tell when I'm naked?"

I feel bad for him; I know exactly what he's going through. Times a hundred. Mmm… yeah. Not feeling so bad for him anymore. But still, I tread lightly, sensitive that this is the first time he's had to deal with that horrible thing called a grownup metabolism. "A little. I mean, not a lot. You just have"—I pull at the still-considerable ring of fat around my own waist—"love handles. Tiny ones!"

He plunks down the cereal box and pinches at his sides. "Oh!" Looking horrified, his head snaps up as he says to me, "I do!"

I laugh and join him on the other side of the island. "Honey, it's not a big deal. Everyone gets them." I affectionately nip at his.

"*I* don't!" He jerks away from me.

Chasing him around the island, I point out, "That's what happens when you eat Oreos for breakfast." I laugh harder at his caught expression. "Yeah, I saw that the other day. They're good with coffee, aren't they?"

"Not *that* good. Please stop buying them!"

"When did you become so vain?"

"I'm not vain; I'm health conscious! But with the construction and working out of temporary offices and the new babies and everything, I've let things slide. A lot, obviously."

I finally catch up to him and grab him around the waist. Rolling my eyes, I reassure him, "Cut out the cookies and the fast food and take a couple of runs a week, and you'll be back to your skinnier self in no time. Because you're a guy. And that's all it'll take." I kiss his upper arm. "Stop freaking out."

He twists his mouth to the side. "I'm not freaking out."

"Yes, you are. About love handles. I thought you were above such superficial nonsense."

"You're right; I'm being silly. But I really do need to take better care of myself. How am I going to keep up with those guys"—he nods toward the twins—"and Stinky? I'm not a couch dad."

"No, you're not. But you *are* about to be a late pastor."

He glances at the clock on the microwave and flinches. "Oh, no!" He rushes back to his bowl of cereal. "This is the last chance I'll have to eat until after noon."

I leave him with his flakes and sons and head upstairs to get Max up and dressed, shaking my head the whole way. *Who* is *that guy?* I'm suddenly wondering of my husband.

3

SECRET KEEPER SLIPS UP

*W*hat a fabulous day! I'm thrilled to be here at church with my beautiful children, listening to my wonderful husband preach a great sermon (I'm sure it is, anyway, even though I haven't *technically* been listening much to it. People are nodding their heads a lot and there have even been a few places where they've laughed, and I think that's what he was going for, judging by the smile on his face), knowing that this may be one of the last times Pastor Long leads the liturgy.

I can now openly (in my head) acknowledge that his delivery during certain parts is three parts pompous, one part mind-numbing, and I'll be glad when it's no longer his responsibility to stand up there and read the pastor parts. It seems like the service is so much slower when he's the leader, as opposed to when Brice or Wes leads.

Yes, even Wes is more animated, or at least he says his parts with more feeling. I guess "animated" isn't something Wes is capable of being. But I don't ever doubt his sincerity. He never sounds like he's just going through the motions.

Trust me, I know these are not the thoughts of a nice

person. I know it's seventeen kinds of wrong to sit out here and criticize and smirk at someone's service to the Lord. But the bottom line is, Pastor Long's days are numbered. And right or wrong, that's Number One on my list of blessings today (followed closely by babies who may be on the cusp of sleeping through the night, even though they're only five weeks old).

After the service, Marianne approaches me with a smile. "Well, I see Pastor is feeling better this morning," she says, leaning over and looking at the sleeping twins in their carriers.

"I guess," I reply noncommittally.

She straightens, one of her eyebrows arching. "Oh?"

Before thinking better of it, I blurt, "He's being so weird!"

"Early mid-life crisis?"

The inevitable crowd gathers around us, trying to get a look at the babies. Max crawls along the pew, wedging himself between the carriers and placing protective hands on his brothers' heads. *Slap, slap, slap.*

"Oh! Max! Buddy." I pull his hands up as quickly as I can without technically smacking them away. "Gentle! See?" I demonstrate soft strokes against the twins' velvety heads while Max earnestly watches, then mimics while looking up at me with his big, blue eyes. "That's right. Babies are fragile."

"Babies," he whispers.

I smile down at him.

Whap!

I guess a two-year-old has a finite supply of fine motor control, and Max has used his up for the day. Fortunately, his blow landed on Harris, who merely cringes in his sleep, gives a tiny squeak, and goes back to snoozing when the hitting isn't repeated.

It's not repeated because Brice swoops in and sweeps Max off the pew. "Whoa, Stinky. Why don't you give your brothers a break from all that lovin'? Smack on me for a while."

"Daddy!" Max wraps his arms around Brice's neck and smooshes his cheek against his dad's.

The ladies gathered coo and melt. I take the opportunity to step aside with Marianne.

"Maybe he *is* having some kind of midlife crisis," I reply to her suggestion, thinking back to our conversation this morning about his love handles. "But his reaction to Pastor Long's retirement wouldn't have anything to do with that."

Her eyes widen. "Pastor Long's retirement? What?!"

My stomach drops. "Oh, crap. I wasn't supposed to—"

"Did someone say Pastor Long's retiring?" one of the ladies nearer to Brice asks.

I'm afraid to look in that direction, but I'm also compelled to do so. My husband's staring at me with a mixture of disbelief, exasperation, and—there it is—disappointment.

I put my hand to my mouth.

He rolls his eyes and sighs.

"Is it true?" Marla McBrier asks him.

"Well. *Not that it's our place to tell you*, but… yes." There's general murmuring until Brice elaborates, "He's not going anywhere right away, but he's expressed his desire for us to call a new associate pastor to take over when he retires. Soon."

"Well, my heavens," Marla mutters. "He's still so young!"

If I weren't feeling sick to my stomach at my gaffe, I

would laugh at her comical relativism. I guess when you're pushing ninety, most people seem "so young."

Her daughter, Irene Whitney, scoffs, "Mom, he's about my age. And I retired two years ago."

Marla pulls a conceding face.

I'm superficially aware of all this happening around me, but my eyes are locked on Brice's, apologizing, pleading with him not to be mad.

He clenches his jaw, takes a deep breath, and relaxes his shoulders. I guess that's as close to a "You're forgiven" as I'm going to get for now. It's good enough that I don't worry about him making a scene when I stand next to him.

Max reaches for me. "Mommy!" As soon as I have him settled on my hip, he reaches back for Brice. "Daddy!"

"No," I say firmly. "It's time to go home. Lunch time. Eat."

"Eat!"

"I'm so sorry," I mumble toward Brice as the people around us continue to discuss and speculate about Pastor Long.

"I hope he's not sick."

"Their youngest is expecting another baby. I'm sure they're ready to spend more time with all those grandbabies."

"I know Vivian's always wanted to travel more."

Brice takes an infant carrier in each hand. "I'll help you load these guys up," he says, already walking toward the back of the sanctuary and the doors that lead out to the narthex and the parking lot beyond. I look over my shoulder at Marianne.

She winces and mouths, "Call me!"

I shoot her a shaky smile, loop the diaper bag over my

shoulder and say to Max as we follow his dad, "Let's go eat."

By the time we get to the Jeep, Brice has already strapped the twins into their car seats and is stowing the carriers in the cargo area.

I try to pretend like I'm not the biggest dumbass on the planet as I babble at Max while fastening his harness. "Tomato soup and grilled cheese. Doesn't that sound good?"

"Soup!"

I'm perfectly prepared to get into the driver's seat and drive off without a word to Brice—what can I say?—but he's standing so close behind me that I nearly trip over him when I go to close the back door.

He smiles gently when I turn and give him my most miserable look. Not expecting that, I almost cry with relief.

"I'm really so sorry," I repeat. "It slipped out! I'm so happy about it, and I'm already thinking about how much better life is going to be, and we talked about it so much last night that I forgot it wasn't something everyone knows yet. I really, really, really didn't mean to blurt it out. You know what a spaz I am!"

He doesn't say anything for a few seconds. Finally, he chuckles. "I know. You never *mean* to do anything that makes a mess for me to fix." Before I can protest or defend myself, he continues, "Don't worry! I'll find Pastor Long right away and tell him someone overheard us talking."

"But that's not technically the truth. And there are witnesses to what really happened."

He shrugs. "Who cares? If he calls me on it later, I'll tell him I was trying to spare you some embarrassment. That's my prerogative as your husband and pastor. Anyway, it serves him right." This last part comes out quite sullenly.

When I give him a questioning look, he explains, "He

started it by breaking the news at a fast food joint. If he had waited until tomorrow and told me in my office, we could have called the Synod together right away. Then there would have been no need for a day's worth of secrecy. It's all so unnecessarily dramatic. And you know if there's one thing I can't stand, it's drama."

I laugh at his rant. "You're a remarkably tolerant guy, except when it comes to that."

He kisses my forehead. "Well, I'd better get in there and find Wayne before someone else does. I'm tempted to let him be blindsided, but I'd rather he get my version of the story than Marla McBrier's."

"Marla's a sweetie."

"Yeah, she is. But she tends to be a town crier."

In response to my shocked look at his uncharacteristically semi-critical assessment of someone else's personality, he asks, "What? It's true," with a defiant lift to his chin.

I climb into the Jeep without further comment. I really don't know what to say, anyway.

I give him a weak smile as he closes the door and waves into the backseat at Max. I'm completely off-balance by everything he does and says lately. He's the same person— mostly—but what may seem to be subtle differences to someone who doesn't know him well are massive personality shifts to me. He's been under a ton of pressure lately. Does that mean these new traits are temporary, and he'll revert to his former self when things settle down? Or has he come to a sort of personal realization that makes these changes permanent?

As I watch him walk into the church, I'm not sure which Brice I'd prefer. Part of me has always thought it would take a lot of the pressure off me if he were a little less *good*. But now that he's showing signs of being just that, I miss the old

Brice. Anyway, who's going to keep me in check, if not him? I fear for our friends and family.

It's not a good sign when Brice comes home from work, pushes at the food on his plate, directs most of his conversation towards our not-yet-two-year-old, and retreats to his woodworking shed as soon as the bath and bedtime routines are over. I try not to take it personally or read much into it —he's weird lately, and I'm starting to come to terms with that—but after a half hour of my abysmal attempts at wrapping Christmas gifts, I hook the baby monitor to my waistband and set out the back door, my way illuminated by the gaudy competing Christmas light displays of our surrounding neighbors.

I ensure my imminent arrival is no secret by trilling, "Yoo hoo!" when I'm halfway across the yard. I hinted to him a few weeks ago that I'd like a cedar chest for extra blankets and quilts in our room. And by hinted, I mean I said, "For Christmas, please build me a cedar chest to put at the foot of our bed for extra blankets and quilts." If he's making it for me now, I want to give him time to hide it.

The overwhelming scent of cedar that greets my nose confirms I was right to give fair warning. When I arrive at the open double doors, I stand to the side and say without looking inside, "Is it okay for me to come in?"

"Yep," he answers. He doesn't sound overjoyed about it, though.

I step around the door and flash him what I hope is a charming grin. "Hey."

"Hi."

His back is to his workbench, which holds a large something covered by a drop cloth.

"Is that my Christmas present?" I can't resist asking.

"Maybe."

I rub my hands together. "Goody!" Suddenly I realize how cold it is out here, so I inch closer to the space heater. "Uh, I won't bother you long, but I wanted to make sure you're okay."

He sighs but seems to immediately regret it, straightening his shoulders and rearranging his face into a more pleasant configuration—not quite a smile, but no longer something barely on this side of tolerant. "I'm fine. Just busy."

"Okay." I start to leave it at that, but the nagging feeling inside won't let me. "But you haven't said anything to me since you got home, and… Well, I'm worried about you."

He pulls his head back, clearly surprised by this statement. "Worried? Why?"

Oh, gosh. He's going to make me come out and say it. Why, Lord, why?

I swallow loudly. I'm sure he can hear it from ten feet away. "Um…" I pretend to adjust the volume on the baby monitor and say, "You're kinda… *weird* this weekend."

At this accusation, he turns back to the workbench, but his project can't save him, since it has to remain covered in front of me. "I'm tired. That's all."

This matches up with one of my theories, and I want to grab it and run with it, so I step up to his back and thread my arms through his, wrapping myself around him, my ear against his back. "Come inside, then. Let's veg out together."

"I have to work on this if it's going to be ready in time for Christmas."

"I don't care if it is. Don't worry about that."

"I care."

"I know you do. And that's sweet. But I'd rather you relax."

"This *is* relaxing."

I step away and blink, stung at the implication that spending the evening with me isn't. I clear my throat, managing to smile before he glances at me over his shoulder. "Okay." At the doors, I turn and say lightly, "Oh, how'd it go with Pastor Long?"

His back gives nothing away, and his tone is bland when he replies, "Fine. Just fine. This forces him to call the Synod tomorrow, anyway, and get the ball rolling on that call for a new associate pastor. It's for the best."

"Is that what you told him?"

"No, that's what he told me." Now he turns and rakes his hand through his hair, rolling his head on his neck as if he has a crick.

"Oh, good. Then he wasn't mad?"

"No." Abruptly, he unplugs the space heater and walks toward me. My heart hops hopefully, until he says, "Hey. I'm going to go for a run before it gets too dark."

It's already pitch-black out there, if you don't count the flashing Christmas lights, but I don't point this out. On his way past me, he squeezes my arm and gives me a half-smile that I think is supposed to be reassuring, but it just makes me sad. "Yeah. All right."

He's already to the back door of the house when I offer my inessential blessing.

4

PERFUNCTORY PASSION

*A*t the risk of being crass, Dr. Klein has declared my lady parts road worthy once more. None too soon, either. Poor Brice has woken me up in the middle of the night more than once recently, groping me in his sleep. The first time, he was mortified when I woke him up and alerted him to what he was doing. The last few times, he's been more annoyed than embarrassed. Even I've been increasingly distracted by frustrating dirty thoughts, considering everything feels back to normal down there.

And how amazing is that, anyway? I won't go into graphic detail or dwell too long on this subject (ick), but the human body is incredible. When I think about what went on down there less than two months ago, it boggles the mind. Secret was so tiny, and I was so out of it, that I hardly remember feeling anything when I birthed her. I was unconscious for Max's C-section, so not only did I not feel anything during the delivery, but my nether regions never got involved. With the twins, Dr. Klein said there was no reason I shouldn't be able to attempt a more conventional birth, and although I was apprehensive about what could happen—and the pain, frankly—I was also not interested in recovering from another major surgery.

Plus, we have the technology to not feel pain. And I used it fully. I just forgot that I'd be able to feel the effects eventually. And did I. There was no mistaking that two things had traveled through a place typically reserved for a much smaller vessel. I thought I'd never be the same. But miracle of miracles! I'm back.

And I've been thinking, maybe Brice's recent personality changes are due to horniness. I've heard of stranger things. It also makes sense, considering that most of the changes boil down to him being crankier and angrier. I'd say most guys would admit that happens when they haven't gotten any in a while. Food or sex. And we've already established that Brice has been eating well.

Anyway, the point is, it's time to get back on that horse. And I can't wait. Literally. I stopped at the pharmacy on the way home from my appointment to pick up some supplies. Hopefully, all the children will be in some stage of napping when I get home. I know Brice is technically working from home, but a short (but not too short) break wouldn't hurt, would it? As a matter of fact, I think it could do nothing but *help* things.

When I arrive home, I toss my coat over the back of the overstuffed chair in the living room and continue through to the front of the house, where Brice is working at his desk under the stairs. Coming up behind him, I twirl my tiny drug store bag of goodies on my index finger. Then I place both hands on his shoulders, lean down, and whisper in his ear, "Hello, big boy."

"Hey," he answers dully and distractedly, swiping at his ear, as if I'm an annoying gnat, while he continues to stare at the text on the screen in front of him.

Undeterred, I glance at the monitor (surely, it won't be hard to compete with the latest online edition of *The Lutheran Witness*) and, while rubbing his shoulders, ask, "Did the boys recently go down for a nap?"

"About ten minutes ago," is his terse reply. "I don't know how you get anything done when they're all awake. Max is *obsessed* with the Christmas tree. I had to raise my voice at him, and he cried, and it was a nightmare."

"Have you seen the laundry hamper? I *don't* get anything done. I mean…" Discussing dirty clothes isn't going to get us anywhere, so I clear my throat. "Are you ready to take a break?"

"What? No. I just sat down."

"Oh. Because…" I get closer to his ear again. "You know, I saw Dr. Klein, and—"

"How's Dave doing? I haven't seen him at church lately. Everything okay?"

"He's fine. I didn't ask him about his church attendance." I take a deep breath and try to get back on track. "But he *did* give the okay on an early Christmas present for you." I suck his earlobe into my mouth.

He yanks his head away. "What the…? Peyton! I'm trying to wor—" He spins in the chair, his face full of irritation as he wipes my saliva from his ear.

I sigh, step back, and with a flick of the wrist, jerk open the plastic bag. I pull out the tubes inside. Waving them in front of me, I ask hotly, "Do you want to go fool around, or what?"

"What is that?" he asks, squinting at the moving targets.

"His-and-hers lube!"

He barely pauses to grab my hand on his way past me to get upstairs.

Eight minutes later (trust me, I clocked it), we lie side-by-side on our backs, panting at the ceiling. I kind of want my money back on the guys' gel. I mean, *that's* longer-lasting?

"That was—" Brice begins.

"Fast?"

"I was going to say 'fun,' but yeah, I guess it was a little fast." He turns on his side and props his head on his hand. With his other hand, he runs his fingers along my arm. "Was it not fun for you?"

Oh, boy. Must be careful. "Um, yes. It was." *Real convincing there, Peyton.* But it's all I can do not to say it was fun like a rocket launcher.

"But?"

"Over really soon. That's all."

He bites his lower lip. "Yeah. Well, it's been a while. Sorry."

"There's nothing to apologize about!" Now, he's making me feel like a major bitch. Maybe I *am* a major bitch. To make up for it, I cuddle up to him while pulling a throw over us.

But he rolls away and sits on the side of the bed. "I have to get back to work."

"What?! The kids are sleeping. What's the rush?"

"I want to take advantage of the quiet." He shrugs into his shirt, swiftly buttoning it. Then he pulls on his underwear and trousers and finger-combs his hair. Almost as if it's an afterthought, he glances over his shoulder at me. "You don't mind, do you?"

Flatly, I answer, "Of course not. Why would I mind?"

He gives me an "atta girl" smile, bends over, and kisses me on the cheek. "Why don't you take a nap or a hot bath? Relax."

I pull the throw up to my neck. "Good idea."

The door clicks shut behind him, but I don't close my eyes. I'd rather stare at the ceiling and fret.

~

"I've figured it out!"

I turn from the rum cake recipe I'm studying (and will probably botch tomorrow) to see a rosy-faced Brice enter the house through the garage, stomping the chill from his legs.

"Oh, good! I'm getting tired of resetting the microwave clock every time you blow a fuse turning on the Christmas lights."

If we had Griswoldesque displays like our neighbors, I could understand. But our modest roofline of white lights shouldn't be wreaking such havoc on our wiring.

He shakes his head, still grinning. "Not the fuse. I'll have to get an electrician over here to fix that."

"Well, call one now! My family will be here tomorrow for Christmas! I want the house to be perfect."

"We have three boys. The house isn't going to be perfect for— Well, it's never going to be perfect. Sorry."

"Call the electrician."

After a distracted wave, he says, "Whatever. Later. What I meant was, I figured out what's bothering me with Pastor Long and this whole retirement business."

This is almost as interesting to me as the fuse issue, especially considering how animated and Brice-like Brice suddenly is for the first time in nearly two weeks. "Do tell," I urge, grabbing my mulled wine (that's right; it's Christmas!) and leaning my lower back against the counter.

He pulls off his hat and gloves and shoves them into his coat pockets. "Well. Remember how altruistic he made his intentions sound when he described waiting to tell us about his retirement?"

"Yes. I almost liked him for a second." Must have been the cheeseburger afterglow.

"That was a load of dookie."

"You already suspected that, though."

Shrugging out of his coat, he drapes it over his arm. "Yes. But I assumed the act he was putting on was about his motives for holding back the information. The real act is that he was holding back any information at all."

I swallow a mouthful of fruity deliciousness. "Huh? You lost me."

"He hasn't been considering retiring since before the tornado. No way. He only wants us to think that."

"What? Why?"

He looks like a kid who's figured out there's no Santa Claus—and has proof. "Because the last thing he would ever want to admit is that I'm right about something."

"Still lost," I mutter into my nearly empty wineglass.

He pulls on my hand, dragging me from the kitchen to the living room, where he sits me on the sofa. Quickly, he goes into the foyer and hangs his coat in the closet. He's practically running when he returns, plopping down next to me. I drain the rest of my wine and set the glass on the coffee table.

From the light of the Christmas tree, he looks even more boyish as he explains, "About a month before we ran into him at McDonald's, he and I got into it about this year's Christmas events schedule. I told him we should keep it low-key, considering the tight budget and the extra strain on the schedule with the construction, dedication, and nursery school grand opening. He gave his usual, 'This is what we always do' argument, completely ignoring the fact that we spent a sickening amount of money rebuilding the church and the preschool and hiring a new assistant pastor."

This all sounds sadly typical, so I merely nod, even though I'm somewhat surprised he never told me about this at the time.

He continues, "So I said, 'Maybe we should put it to a vote, your proposed schedule versus mine, and see which one the elders and board of directors prefer.' He blew up, saying I was trying to put a price on tradition. I suggested that if he was more worried about tradition than fiscal responsibility and the future of the church, then perhaps it was time for him to retire."

"Why didn't you tell me about this?" I finally can't resist asking. "This sounds like a major confrontation."

He shrugs. "I don't know. The twins had just been born. Plus, it was one more thing for you to hold against Pastor Long." He says the last part a bit too casually.

"Aha!"

"Well, you do hold grudges. It's not healthy. Or Christian-like."

Ignoring those observations, I ask, "And this brouhaha between the two of you didn't immediately spring to mind when he told you he was retiring, because…?"

Again, he looks unconcerned with that detail. "I wasn't operating at peak performance. No sleep, no… other things… I felt like I was walking through a haze. I mean, it obviously set off some alarms in my low-functioning brain, but I couldn't quite make the connection. And not to keep bringing it up, but I'm *not* a grudge-holder, so after Pastor Anthony stepped in and suggested a few compromises that would serve to keep all the usual events on the schedule but with more financial support from participants, I let the Christmas thing go. I mean, if I stewed about every instance

Pastor Long and I butted heads, I wouldn't have time to think about anything else!"

"That's sad."

"Isn't it?" His bright tone makes it sound like we're discussing something as benign as the declining popularity of the lime Jell-O salad.

I stare at the Christmas tree for a few minutes while I review everything he's said and take stock of the many questions I still have. Finally, I ask, "Why, again, would Pastor Long make up all that stuff about postponing his retirement?"

"Because he knows I'm right that he *needs* to retire. It's not about what he wants to do. But he'll never cop to it, especially because I was the one to point it out to him. He wouldn't give me the satisfaction of knowing what I said led him to his decision."

"And you want him to give you credit for the decision?"

He snorts. "No! I don't give a Chicago-style pizza about that. It's galling that he'd lie, though, thinking that I *would* care. I've worked with the man for how long? We've been through a natural disaster together! He's baptized two of my children. Yet, he can't sit down with me, like a man, in my office and say, 'Brice, I've been giving what you said a lot of prayerful consideration.' He could have even said he didn't agree with my assessment. Fine. Whatever. I said it in the heat of the moment, anyway. But to *lie* to me. To my wife! In a McDonald's!" He says this last thing with the most disgust, his nose crinkled, his mouth pinched.

"You are so hung up on that."

"It was really inappropriate."

"Who's holding grudges now?" I grumble, lifting my wine glass and rising to go into the kitchen for more.

He snatches the glass from my hand and pulls me back into the cushions, then onto his lap.

"Hey! C'mon now. I want more wine." In reality, as long as he's hugging me and smiling, and we're sitting here in the soft, twinkly glow of the tree, I don't need or want more of anything.

Squeezing me even more tightly to his chest, he puts his chin on my shoulder. "I'm sorry if I've been short with you lately."

"'If'?" Since when have I made any apology an easy one? He's going to be damn sure of what he's apologizing for by the end of this evening.

"Okay, not 'if.' I'm sorry I have been. You're not going to hold it against me for the rest of our lives, are you?"

"You mean, like when you called yourself my 'fruit inspector'? Or when you said I was ridiculous? Or when you tattled on me to my dad for being selfish?"

He laughs. "Yes. Like that."

"No. This is nothing. Although, you did have me worried. I thought you were going through a midlife crisis."

"I'm not *that* old!"

"Well, the other explanation was a brain tumor, and I didn't want to go there."

Sighing contentedly, he declares, "This has been nagging at me for weeks, and now that I've figured it out and see how silly and insignificant it is, I don't give a fig about it." His warm breath tickles my face as he turns his head and whispers against my cheek, "I'm sorry."

"I know how you can make it up to me in the next eight minutes."

He pushes me from his lap. Laughing, I nearly land on my face on the couch cushion next to him.

"I explained that!" Lying on top of me, squashing his chest into my shoulder, he covers my face with kisses.

"There's only one way to prove it was an isolated instance." I slide out from under him and sit on the rug on the other side of the coffee table, holding out my arms to him.

He looks around. "Here? In the living room?" he whispers, pulling a face eerily similar to the one he wore when criticizing Pastor Long for his McDonald's announcement.

I roll my eyes. "Your window of opportunity is closing quickly, Reverend Adventure."

Joining me on the floor, he pulls me tentatively to him. "If you say so…"

Oh, I do.

5

HOLIDAY CHEER

The kitchen is jammed with people, cooking, loitering, laughing, and talking. After pulling my (slightly lopsided) rum cake from the oven, I place it on a cooling rack on the counter and watch the flurry of activity around me, feeling content, feeling like this is what my entire adult life has been leading up to, feeling like the cheesy female lead in the final scene of a made-for-TV Christmas movie. The pastor's wife who finally figures out what life is supposed to be about. Whatever. It's probably just the mulled wine.

Someone familiar, yet foreign to this setting, enters screen right from the garage. Howard, one of our church's younger trustees, takes off his ball cap upon coming into the kitchen and walks straight up to me. "Pastor told me you'd write me a check for the electrical work?" he says uncertainly into what must appear to be mayhem to him.

I snap out of my reverie. "Hey, Howard. Oh. Okay. Um, follow me." I lead him to Brice's desk, where I pull open three drawers before finding the checkbook. I haven't written a check in forever. That's Brice's territory. Which leads to me wonder, aloud in this case, "Where *is* Brice?"

Howard twists his hat. "He went around the back of the house after he told me to come in here and find you."

I roll my eyes. He's been obsessed with my Christmas present, putting the "final touches"—which apparently include hovering over it like a nervous expectant father—on it over the last day-and-a-half.

I think he's also slightly miffed (though he'd never admit it in a million years, because it would make him look petty and ungrateful) that my sister stole his Christmas gift's thunder by handing me the keys to her SUV when they showed up earlier this morning.

"We know you need a vehicle with room for three car seats, and I've wanted a smaller car for a while now, so… Merry Christmas," Nicole said casually while I stared at the shiny, mahogany-colored vehicle in my driveway.

Brice laughed, thinking she was kidding. "And what are you guys going to drive home?"

As if it was the most normal thing in the world, she said, "Lonnie and I are picking up my new car at one of the dealerships here in town the day after Christmas. We'll get directions from you guys later." With that, she walked into the house before we could properly thank her.

Brice didn't look like "Thank you" was on the tip of his tongue, anyway. I thought he'd gotten over it, but if he's spending more time in his woodshed, then maybe not.

I agree with him that it's slightly awkward, having such a huge gift bestowed on us, but we can't afford to be proud. It's a prayer answered. I have to go back to work in a little over a month, the first week of February. With our schedules, we'll need two cars that can accommodate all three children. Safely.

We can sell my car, which is still like new, pay off what's left on the loan, and pay off our hospital bills. Our lower monthly housing allowance from the church won't sting as much. I know he'll recognize all this eventually; at the moment, I think he's more focused on the injury to his provider's ego.

Now, I say to Howard, "How much do we owe you? And no skimping. It's Christmas Eve, and you should be with your family. Brice was supposed to have called you a week ago. Make him pay for it."

He chuckles nervously. "It wasn't anything. Really."

"Howard."

A blush spreads across his cheeks. "A hundred will do it."

"You're full of it," I say, but I write the check, because I can tell haggling over the amount is making him uncomfortable. Nobody can say I didn't try.

Taking the check with a small smile, he says, "I'll ask Pastor to make something for Gracie for her birthday."

"Make it something big," I suggest. "A rocking horse."

His laugh signifies he's still not sure if I'm being serious. "I don't know about that. Doesn't seem like a fair trade."

"Okay, something *slightly* smaller. The rocking horse would probably be a disaster, anyway." I walk him to the front door. "Merry Christmas."

He steps onto the porch and puts his hat back on. "Merry Christmas. Oh, and I'll see you at church tonight?"

"Yes. We're going to the midnight service."

"Us, too. It's a tradition, you know?"

As if on cue and following precise scripting, Brice clomps up the front porch steps, grinning at Howard. "Did the missus settle up with you?"

"Not really," I answer. "You owe Howard some wood things."

Brice laughs. "Deal." From the corner of his mouth, he

reveals to Howard, "I'm not skilled, though, so keep it basic. Boxes. I can do boxes."

Howard chuckles and ducks his head. "Merry Christmas, guys," he says before escaping down the steps to his panel truck.

Brice waves at him from the front porch as he backs away. "Nice guy."

"So shy!"

"Uh, have you been in our house today? It's kind of overwhelming for the uninitiated. I remember when you weren't one for big groups of strangers."

I glare at him. "I used to prefer strangers to my family."

"There ya go. Imagine if your family were strangers. Double-scary." He puts his arm around me on the cold porch and gives me a side-squeeze. I'm glad to see he's at least pretending to have gotten over the shock of being the proud new owner of a free car. "You wanna stay out here for a while, catch your breath?"

My answer is to turn back toward the house. "Still too much to do inside before dinnertime. Speaking of, when is Pastor Anthony supposed to be here? I'd like things to be less hectic by the time he shows up."

"I told him dinner was at one o'clock, so I'm assuming he'll be here any minute now. He's a punctual guy."

"Well, I told Ben the same time, but he said to start without him if he's not here when dinner's ready," I say of our friend, Peace's youth minister.

I say "our" friend, but he and I haven't reverted to our original easygoing companionship since he found out about Secret last year. Actually, I think it has less to do with that information than it has to do with some of the things he said to me in the aftermath of finding out. With Brice's help, I've come to understand that most of Ben's problems with my past have nothing to do with me at all and more to do with his own issues as the son of a single mother who was abandoned by his father. And it hurt him that I didn't trust him enough to tell him myself.

Brice also has a theory that Ben's embarrassed and ashamed of the things he said to me, but he doesn't know how to apologize. It's going to be up to me to put the conflict behind us, and I'm probably going to have to do so without Ben or me saying anything else about it. I'm trying, but it's turning out to be more difficult than I hoped to let go of my hurt feelings.

Now, concerning Ben's attendance, Brice predicts, "He'll be here on time, too. It's going to be a full house. I guess I'd better think about getting those tables set up."

Back inside, Mom looks up from helping Dad carve the ham when we walk into the kitchen. "There you are! We wondered where you guys snuck off to."

"Nobody's sneaking anywhere," I say, suddenly reconsidering Brice's offer to stay on the porch for a few more minutes. "Had to pay the electrician."

"That's a new one," Lonnie mumbles with a lascivious smirk.

Mom, either not hearing him or ignoring him, cries, "But this house is new! I don't understand how it can have electrical problems."

"Shoddy construction," Dad suggests shortly. "Nobody makes anything worth a damn anymore."

Nicole, feeding Brooks and overseeing ten-year-old Sadie, who's feeding Harris, laughs. "Oh, no! Don't get Dad started!"

Brice's mom, Mary, looks on with a smile, running her hands through Max's fine hair as he sits quietly on her lap. She's always had the touch with him, and she knows that loud kids frazzle my nerves, especially in situations like this, so she quickly took command of him when she arrived this morning. I've hardly heard a peep from him as he's soaked up Grammy Mary's attention.

"Well, it's true!" Dad huffs.

Mom tuts, "This is a nice house!"

"Everything's designed and built with profit in mind. It's all cheap, no matter how much you wind up paying for it," he grumbles.

"Sweeping generalities, as usual," Brice mutters. Then in a louder voice, he addresses Lonnie, my brother, Jason, and his partner, Dustin. "Guys, you wanna help me set up some tables in the living room?"

"We're eating in the living room?" Mom asks, obviously horrified at the prospect.

Brice and the guys see this as their cue to leave as quickly as possible.

Knowing that nonchalance is the key to keeping her inner Martha Stewart calm, I focus on testing the tenderness of the potatoes boiling on the stove when I answer, "Yes. It's the only place we can fit enough tables so we can all eat together." It's no oversight I haven't mentioned the seating arrangements before now, either.

"What's wrong with having the kids eat in the kitchen and the adults in the dining room?" she questions, her voice becoming shriller.

"Mom, there are fifteen of us. Moving the kids to the kitchen leaves eleven. The dining room table seats six. And there's no room for another table in there." I drain the potatoes in the sink, shaking them in the colander. Transferring them back to the stock pot and setting the pot on the counter, I say in the most reassuring voice possible, considering I'm starting to lose my patience with her refusal to accept that I'm a legitimate adult who can problem-solve, "Trust me, Brice and I have thought it through."

"But the carpeting!"

"It's survived worse," I mumble, with a private smile.

"What?"

Clearing my throat, I speak more loudly. "Mom! We're rolling the rug out of the way, moving the living room furniture into various other rooms, and putting the dining set and some other tables and chairs from church in the living room. Period. Don't worry about it." I take my frustrations out on the potatoes with the masher, then decide a loud hand mixer would be better.

Before I turn it on to discourage any further argument, Mary pipes up. "I think it'll be nice in there, near the tree. Festive."

I shoot her an appreciative smile and turn my attention to the potatoes, careful not to splash myself with butter, milk, and sour cream as the beaters turn the lumpy, grainy spuds into silky mounds of starch and fat.

Cooking. Just one more thing for which I have Mary to thank. I used to hate it. Well, fear it, is more accurate. But since she's taught me a few basics, and I've learned to try other things without being afraid of failure, I've come to enjoy it. In times like this, it's especially useful. It's a great distraction. *Sorry, too busy cooking to deal with your histrionics about proper entertaining.*

The doorbell rings, but I pretend I don't hear it. Someone else can answer it, especially if it's Pastor Anthony. It's not that I don't like the guy, but my continued unease around him tends to make me say even stupider things than normal in one-on-one contact with him. And if it's Ben... Well, I'm not necessarily good at interpersonal communication with him, either.

I'm starting to think I'm the problem. Maybe. I *am* the common denominator, after all. Brice doesn't seem to have issues with either guy.

The ham carved, Mom takes charge of setting the tables in the *gasp* living room. When I turn off the mixer, I hear her out there, asking Brice where the "good table linens" are. He'll have a harder time locating them than I did the checkbook, namely because they don't exist. She'll figure it out soon enough, though, when he shows her to the linen cabinet in the dining room, and she sees her choices. The clashing, worn tablecloths will go well with the mismatched dinnerware we'll be using (my set wasn't big enough for this group, so we had to borrow some place settings from the church kitchen, and she's already complained about that).

As she bustles back into the kitchen to retrieve the hodgepodge stacks of plates and wide variety of glassware and flatware, I smile into the potatoes. She's maddening, but I always know what to expect from her. And I love her. If she were any other way, I wouldn't know how to act around her.

Nicole interrupts my affectionate reverie when she sidles up to me, sans babies and says, "The twins were falling asleep with Sadie and me, so I changed their diapers and put them in their cribs. I hope that was okay."

"Yeah! Thanks!"

Without my asking, she scrapes the potatoes from the stock pot into serving dishes (yes, this is my concession to fine dining, serving dishes) while I hold it with both hands.

"Is Mom driving you crazy?" she asks *sotto voce*, nudging her head in the direction of the woman herself, who's muttering about the shame of using paper napkins at a holiday dinner.

I chuckle and shake my head. "Maybe, but that's how I

know she's around. Anyway, if Dad didn't complain about everything and Mom didn't fuss about everything, I'd worry there was something wrong with them."

Mary sets Max on the floor and offers to help Mom set the tables.

Mom accepts with a piquant, "if that's what you can call it," tacked on.

As soon as both women leave the kitchen with the dishes, Nicole and I dissolve into giggles.

Max toddles over to see what's so funny. "Eat!"

"Yeah, yeah, we're working on it," I grumble good-naturedly. To Nicole, I say, "Let's get the food on those low-class tables."

The children have scattered, leaving us adults to sit around the table, nursing cups of coffee, staring at pieces of cake, and groaning about full bellies. I soak up the compliments on the cooking but always give credit where it's due for the dishes I didn't prepare, which were admittedly few. I was up late into the night and out of bed early to make sure everything was ready to go in the oven, according to a precise schedule. Needless to say, I'm exhausted and need the coffee in front of me. I have no idea how I'm going to make it to the midnight candlelight service at church. Maybe I'll volunteer to stay home with the kids.

Feeling someone's gaze on me, I glance down the table at the usual suspect, but Brice is focused on Dustin, who's telling a colorful story about trying to rescue a dog from a locked car in a shopping center parking lot a few weeks ago. My eyes travel warily to the right, until they run into Pastor Anthony, who doesn't attempt to hide that he's staring at me. I'm oddly ashamed of it, though. I quickly look away, pretending to listen to Dustin. He has everyone else in stitches, so it's conspicuous that I'm not laughing. It's less odd that Pastor's not laughing, since I don't think anyone's ever seen or heard him do it.

While I give my best impression of an amused sister-in-law, I sweat under the assistant pastor's study. What's his deal, anyway? Do I have food on my face? I swipe at my mouth with my napkin, in case there are cake crumbs there. I know, though, that his staring has nothing to do with my appearance. He's analyzing. And it's not the first time. When I'm around him, I feel like I'm one of those Magic Eye pictures he's trying to figure out. He does everything short of tilting his head and squinting his eyes in an effort to get a clearer picture.

I complained about it to Brice after my first few encounters with Pastor Anthony, but my husband laughed and said, "He's an intense guy. Half the time, I bet he's not even really looking at you. You just happen to be in his line of sight when he's thinking about something."

I bought that explanation for about a month. But I've never noticed him inadvertently staring at anyone else while supposedly deep in thought. And you know what? It's starting to piss me off. It's like he's knows there's something about me that's not up to snuff, and he's trying to put his finger on it. *Well, cut it out, Wesley! I'm not a dirty riddle. I'm a person. And if you have any questions about me, ask. Because I'm not shy about admitting I have faults. Lots of them. You're young and probably won't understand half of what's happened to me in my life, but I'll use small words.*

I wish I could say that to him.

While I'm delivering my mental chewing-out, everyone else around the table stands up. I closely follow suit, catching up to the idea that it's time to clean up. We divide into pathetically traditional gender roles, the guys mobilizing to return the living room to its original state and the women heading into the kitchen to put away the leftovers and clean dishes.

Brice snags my hand on my way past him. "Hey. Everything okay?" he asks quietly.

Now's definitely not the time to tattle on Pastor Creepster again, so I simply smile and give him the other honest half of the answer. "Fine. I'm tired, that's all. I'll get my second wind soon."

He accepts that explanation with a sympathetic noise and lets go of my hand, joining the other men as they dismantle the two temporary, folding tables, move the dining set back where it belongs, and reassemble the living room.

While we're still rinsing dishes and loading the dishwasher, Ben and Pastor Anthony hover in the kitchen doorway.

Ben says, "I'm going to head home. Thanks for having me. It was nice to see everyone again."

"Same here," Pastor seconds with a slight wave. "This was really nice."

I wipe my hands on a dish towel and approach the two men, assuming the role of gracious, dutiful hostess. Hugging each of them in turn, I smile and say brightly, "We were so glad to have you. Thanks for coming."

The odd thing is, I mean it. I *am* glad they joined us for dinner. Despite the baggage I have with Ben and the increasingly weird vibe I get from Pastor, I like both guys, and I'm glad we could host them. They were a welcome addition to the family dynamic.

Ben looks surprised by my hug, but he returns it warmly with a "Merry Christmas" for good measure. Pastor, on the other hand, acts as if he's never been hugged before in his life. He keeps his arms straight down at his sides, and when I let him go, he looks like he wishes he were anywhere but here. I feel like an idiot.

To cover my embarrassment, I prattle, "I guess we'll see you both tonight at church. Unless you're skipping, Ben. Which is your prerogative. Or you could be going to the earlier service, led by Pastor Long, I guess. But we're all going to the midnight service, so we won't see you if you're at the early one. Except Brice. He's doing the sermon at both services. Of course. Pastor Anthony, you're leading the liturgy at the candlelight service, right? Good luck with that. Not that you need luck. You're very good. And the choir does most of the work in the midnight service. Of course, you work hard, too, and are important. So... anyway."

The kitchen is suddenly stiflingly quiet.

Nicole eventually says, "Well! It was nice seeing you guys. See you later!"

They each wave one more time before turning and leaving.

I remain in the same spot several seconds after they're gone.

"What was that about?" Mom asks, a nervous laugh serving as the question mark at the end of her sentence.

I rub my face, suddenly feeling faint with humiliation. "I don't know."

The moment quickly passes, though, and I shake it off as I return to my post at the dishwasher.

6

HELLO, PASTOR!

*I*t's Sunday morning, but something out of the ordinary is happening. Brice's arm snakes around me. His hand cups my armpit, his grip tightening as he pulls me against him in the bed. His hand wanders lower, massaging my breast through my nightshirt.

"Um…" I utter sleepily and uncertainly. It's not that morning sex is out of the ordinary, in general, but *Sunday* morning sex is something we haven't done in years.

The rule—if you can call it that—originated the first week we returned to our real lives after our honeymoon. Like most newlyweds, we couldn't get enough of each other. Every day began and ended with lovemaking. Sunday morning rolled around and seemed like it would be no different than the six other mornings preceding it.

Something *was* different, though. I reached my destination, but Brice kept going… and going… and going, and he didn't seem to be enjoying himself. He was sweating and sighing and grunting. There were prolonged pauses between thrusts.

Finally, he collapsed on top of me, buried his face in my neck, as if he were hiding, and said, "I can't."

Those two words confused me. "You can't... what?"

"I can't *do* it," he said in an anguished tone, as if he were admitting the worst thing in the world.

I tensed. "Oh." Immediately, I figured it had something to do with me, but I couldn't bring myself to say anything to confirm it or to ask if there was something I could do differently... or better.

He rolled back to his side of the bed, panting as he stared at the ceiling fan above us. I pulled the covers protectively over myself and lamented our first dysfunctional encounter, less than a month into our marriage. I'd never even had this problem with drunk guys in my past, so I was wondering how I could let down such a robust, healthy, sober guy.

Just as I was starting to panic, he stated hoarsely, "I can't stop thinking about church."

"What?!"

He turned toward me, adjusting his head on his pillow, looking miserable. "I couldn't stop thinking about church. The whole time we were... I... At first, it started with me worrying about the time, but that led to thinking about everything I need to do to prepare, and..." He blushed, and I felt horrible for him. But relieved for myself.

Snuggling up to him, I said, "Oh, hon. It's okay."

"It's embarrassing."

"It shouldn't be! You have a big responsibility on Sundays. Like— like a quarterback. You need to focus all your energy and thoughts on the job ahead of you. I'm sorry I didn't think about it."

"It's not your fault." He relaxed against me. "I— I didn't think it would matter."

"Well, now we know. No Sunday morning nookie for you."

He laughed. "But every other morning is still fair game, right?"

"Absolutely." I paused to think, then sticking with the football player analogy, added the caveat, "Unless it's my Bye Week." This made him laugh even harder.

The rules still stand today.

That's why I'm so confused now as his efforts become more concerted, and he whispers, "Good morning," against the back of my neck, letting me know he's not putting the moves on me in his sleep as the result of a dream.

"It's Sunday." I feel like I have a responsibility to point this out, before either of us gets too excited. It's the Sunday after Christmas, after all, so he could be confused or have forgotten the day, due to the change in routine.

"I know," he replies, yanking at my underpants. "We need to hurry."

Remembering how dejected he was the one time he couldn't finish the job and wanting to avoid a repeat of that, I say, "We don't do this on Sundays."

He pushes me onto my back. "I'm sick of that rule."

"Oh. Okay. But—"

Putting his finger to my lips, he says, "Shh," and laughs at my widened eyes, knowing how much I hate being shushed. "It's my Sunday off. From preaching, that is."

"I see," I say against his finger before pulling it into my mouth and biting it gently. "That's for shushing me."

Much longer than eight minutes later, he gives me one more lingering kiss before heading for the shower, whistling. Shortly after, I hear him singing an extremely un-pastoral song as the water slaps against the tile floor.

Oh, my. Some parts of New Brice seem to be sticking around, and that's fine by me.

When he emerges from the bathroom in a towel and sees I haven't moved, he smirks. "You all right?"

I grunt something that sounds affirmative, so he grins and crosses to the closet to pull out the clothes he ironed the night before.

Finally, I muster the energy to move. Sitting naked on the side of the bed, I say, "Now I have something to feel self-conscious about when Pastor Anthony looks at me this morning like he's reading my mind."

As if it's the first time he's heard this complaint, Brice freezes while tying his tie. "What?"

I wave dismissively toward him, not in the mood to talk about Pastor Anthony minutes after having sex with my husband.

"No, really." He walks to the bed and sits next to me. "That's still happening?"

"What do you mean? You tried to convince me it *wasn't* happening, that it was all in my imagination." I move away from him and retrieve my robe from the back of the bedroom door.

"Maybe I was wrong about that."

"You think?! Did you see him staring at me Christmas Eve, after dinner? It was creepy! Then in the kitchen, when he came to say goodbye, I gave him a friendly, innocent hug, in front of a bunch of people, and he nearly came out of his skin. It was humiliating."

Brice laughs but quickly catches himself. "Really? How did I miss all this?"

"I don't know! It was after you guys moved the furniture back. Both he and Ben were leaving."

He looks into space, trying to remember. "Oh, yeah. I

was putting Max down for a nap. He was in Whine Mode." Focusing his eyes on my face again, he asks, "But why didn't you tell me about that?"

I shrug. "I was exhausted, so I came up here to nap. When I woke up, you were getting ready to go to the church. Then, when we got home after the candlelight service, I could barely think straight. The next day was busy with church and presents and my family. By the time everyone left yesterday, I figured it wasn't worth mentioning."

He nods. "Well, I wouldn't worry about it. Are you worried about it?"

"Sort of," I say with a sigh. "The guy treats me like I'm a sideshow oddity. Do you think Ben told him about Secret?"

Brice rolls his eyes and goes back to getting dressed, pulling his shoes from the closet and sitting down on my new cedar chest, which he outfitted with a simple molding along the top to keep a seat cushion in place. "Here we go again. Nobody's talking about that behind our backs. It's not an issue."

"What if it is, though? What if Ben accidentally told him, thinking you'd already told him?" I cinch my robe's belt too tightly, undo it, and tie it again.

"How would that come up in conversation, even?"

"I don't have all the answers! All I know is that he stares at me. A lot. And it makes me uncomfortable. Like he's judging me."

Patting the cushion next to him after he finishes tying his shoes, he says, "Come here."

I do as I'm told.

"Listen. He's a genius. He gets lost in thought in the middle of a sentence sometimes. He stares off into space—"

"I've heard this theory before, so save your breath. Have you ever noticed him staring at other people, besides me?"

Reverend Honesty looks loath to admit, "No."

"See? It's something about *me*!"

He bites the inside of his cheek and seems to consider whether to respond to my claim before saying, "I don't like to speak unkindly about people, but…"

"Yes…?"

"Wes is… Well, he's socially awkward. Based on some things he's told me during unguarded moments, I don't think he's ever had a girlfriend."

"I'm not shocked by this news."

My shoulder receives a nudge for that one. "Be nice. He's a nice guy. He's a little rough around the edges, that's all. He can translate Biblical text from Latin, Greek, and Aramaic, but he gets flustered around pretty women."

"Puh-lease! Tell me this has nothing to do with *that*!"

"Maybe it does!"

"No way. He's not staring at me in that way. He's staring at me like he's trying to figure me out. Reconcile something in his head with what I'm doing or saying. It's— I can't describe it right!" My inability to get Brice to understand is frustrating me to the verge of tears. I quickly stand and walk toward the bathroom. "Never mind. It's dumb. Whatever. I don't care what he thinks about me or what he knows. I'm just going to avoid him."

"That's not a solution! Come on. Maybe the three of us should meet in my office later and discuss—"

I spin in the bathroom doorway. "No! That's about the only thing that could make this worse! Please, don't say anything to him."

He puts his hands palms-out in front of his chest in a

defensive gesture. "Okay. Fine. I'm sure it's nothing more than him having a bit of a crush on you."

"I think I'm going to be sick."

"But if his behavior changes or escalates in any way, I want you to tell me right away."

Exasperated, I groan, "I'm sorry I brought this up." Entering the bathroom, I turn on the shower and hold my hand in the stream, waiting for the water to warm up.

Brice comes up behind me, puts his hands on my upper arms, and kisses my cheek. "He wouldn't be the first pastor to find you irresistible."

"You obviously don't think that's the case, or you wouldn't be joking about it."

"Darn right. Cut the guy some slack. Continue to be your charming, friendly self…"

"Are you being sarcastic?"

"…and everything will be fine," he says through his laughter. Sobering slightly, but still grinning, he says while taking hold of the robe I'm shedding, "Anyway, I'll be right next to you today, to protect you."

"From what? It's nothing, remember? I wish you'd make up your mind."

"It's nothing. That's my final answer."

I shut the shower door in his face. Why do I have a bad feeling his naivety is setting us up for trouble?

"Ah-booga-booga-boo! Yes! Are you going to talk to me, Brooks, now that you have a full tummy? Ah-boo! What about you, Harris? You gonna talk to Mommy?"

I check the time on my cell phone one more time. All three boys have been fed and washed and are ready for bed.

We're on the floor in the middle of the twins' room. Harris is on a blanket, lying on his back and kicking his feet. Brooks is in my lap, using my criss-crossed legs as a hammock. Max is standing next to me, looking down at both babies.

And still, I wait for Brice. I wonder what's keeping him. Usually, he texts me when he's going to be late so I know if I should keep the kids up for his goodnight kiss or put them to bed. And since Christmas is over, he's keeping saner hours and hasn't been home late in a while.

"I talk!" Max interjects.

"Yes, you do. A lot. Tell your brothers something funny."

"Where Daddy?" he blurts unhelpfully.

"At work."

"Chutch?"

Tucking the phone in my pocket, I reply, "Yes. Church. Very good! You're such a smart boy, Max."

Overcome with affection, he grabs my arm and buries his face in my neck.

"I love you," I tell him, pressing on the back of his head and kissing his hair.

"Yuv you."

Blinking away tears, I sniff. "Aww! I can't wait to tell your daddy you said that. To me. First."

It may be childish, but Brice and I have an unofficial contest going when it comes to getting Max to say or do certain things for the first time. "Daddy" was his first word, so Brice got that point, but I got the first step, and now I've gotten the first "I love you." Ha! That'll teach him to work late. (That logic makes sense to me, at least right now.)

"Well, guys, I hate to do this to you, but it's bedtime."

Max clumsily dances around the room while I stand and put Brooks in his crib.

"Nigh-night time! Nigh-night time!" he chants like Brice always does with him.

"Watch out for Harris," I warn him when his stomping comes dangerously close to the infant on the floor. "Max! Careful!"

Quickly, before there's a disaster, I snatch Harris from the floor and hold him to my chest. As my heart pounds from the close call, Max continues his oblivious bedtime dance/chant. I close my eyes, wondering when I'm going to get the hang of keeping track of all three of them at once. I'm either terrible at multitasking, or it's nearly impossible to make sure they're safe—from each other and the environment.

I say in a weak voice, "Max, you have to be more careful around the babies."

"Babies, babies, babies!"

I hear a door bang downstairs and freeze.

"Max. Shhh!"

Before I can worry too much about who's in the house with us, I hear Brice's voice. "Honey? Where are you?"

"Up here, in the twins' room!" His raised voice and running footsteps make me hold Harris more tightly. When he rounds the door frame, I immediately ask, "What's wrong?"

He grins, sidestepping Max, who's trying to greet him by hugging him around the legs. "Hey, Bud," he says distractedly. "Just a second." To me, he directs, still grinning. "Put down the baby."

"What?"

Instead of repeating himself, he takes Harris from me and puts him in his crib. Then he picks me up and spins me while hugging me.

Caught off guard—and worried about knocking over Max—I protest, "Hey! What the heck?"

"What da hack!" Max parrots, giggling at us.

"I have such good news," Brice says, finally stopping and setting me on my feet. Dizzy, I wobble but catch myself on Brooks's crib rail.

"Okay. I kind of got that impression."

His joy is contagious, so I'm already smiling when he drops, "Peace is going to call Jared to be its associate pastor."

"Jared? Vicar Jared? Our Jared?"

He laughs. "Uh, I guess. More like Mitzi's Jared. Jared Laszewski."

"But... but how? I mean, what? I mean, Jared doesn't want to be called. And how did you convince the call committee to call him?"

Max refuses to be ignored another second. "Daddy! Yuv you!"

Brice closes his mouth just before answering me, looks down at his son, and blinks. "Stinky! I love you, too, Bud!" He picks him up and smirks at me. "Ha! Did you hear what he said to me?"

"He said it to me right before you got home."

"Sure he did."

"Don't even accuse me of lying about that."

"You have a point," he grumbles. To Max, he says, "Let's get you in bed, Big Guy, so I can talk to your mom."

The bedtime chant resumes, this time in stereo, Brice singing the bass line.

"I'll meet you downstairs," I tell my husband through the ruckus. I kiss Max on their way past me to the door, check on the twins one more time before turning out their light, and head down to the kitchen, where I pour two large glasses of red wine.

After what feels like an hour, Brice joins me in the living room. I'm already on my second glass of wine, sipping it on the couch in front of the fireplace. He accepts the glass I'm holding for him, thanks me, and takes a long, smooth swallow before asking, "Where was I?"

"You were about to answer a whole lotta questions about this supposed plan to call Jared."

His smile returns. "Oh. Yes. That's right. Well, we had a call committee meeting tonight, as you know."

"Which was three hours ago," I point out.

He flinches. "Is it that late?"

"Yes. But proceed."

Shrugging off his shock about the time, he continues, "Anyway, we looked through the list of candidates the Synod sent us, and nobody seemed right. One guy is already the associate pastor at a large, contemporary church in Arizona; another guy has only been the assistant pastor at his current church for about the same amount of time Wes has been with us; there's a kid straight from the Sem who has less experience than Wes but would have more seniority if we called him—that didn't seem right. And on and on and on.

"Some things were more about personality, too. You know, Wes is... Wes. And I'm a centrist, but I'm laidback, sort of low energy, although Wes makes me look like Mr. Personality. We need an associate pastor who will up the energy, especially after Pastor Long leaves. We need someone who's going to make us think more about how things could or *should* be, not how they always have been."

"I thought that was you."

"It can't be me."

"But it *has* been you."

"Right. And that has to stop. I have to be a more stabilizing influence."

I shake my head, confused. "But don't you want changes, too?"

"Yes. In some cases, I do. And I'll be selective about implementing the changes I think are most important. I need someone—Jared—to show people that I'm not about change for change's sake. I'm counting on him to propose some radical things that I then veto, showing I'm on the side of the traditionalists, too."

With my nose buried in my wineglass, I mutter, "This is exhausting."

"It *is*! But it's an act Jared and I have already perfected."

He's so excited that I'm almost afraid to potentially poop on his party by prompting, "So I take it you threw Jared's name in the running and talked him up as young, enthusiastic, fun, and likable, leaving out words like, 'radical,' 'clumsy,' and 'ineloquent' in your description. I also take it you neglected to mention some of the finer moments of his vicarage at Messiah, like when Mrs. Peretta got the alcoholic Communion wine, fell off the wagon, and drunk dialed him?"

"That wasn't his fault! The altar guild set up the Communion trays incorrectly!"

I try to hide my grin while taking another sip of wine.

"It's not funny! And anyway, you're not supposed to know about that."

"Just answer my question: did you mislead the committee into thinking he all that and a bag of Communion wafers?"

"'Mislead' is a really unfair characterization. I truly think Jared would fit in well at Peace. A lot better than he did at Messiah." He sets down his glass on the side table next to him. "Anyway, what's all this resistance? I thought you loved Jared."

"I *do* love him! He's my best friend's husband. He's one of my best friends, in his own right."

"So, what's the deal?"

I avoid his eyes, tracing a seam in the leather sofa. "I don't love when you and Jared work together. It's ten kinds of stressful. I don't think you remember how much he gets on your nerves when you have to run interference for him all the time."

He waves that away like it's the most insignificant detail in the world.

"And what about what Jared wants? His plan was to avoid the ministry, at least for a few years. I think it would be best if you and the committee reevaluated the other candidates from the Synod. Interview one or two of them. They may be just as enthusiastic and fun, without the potential for disaster."

Now Brice looks sheepish. "Oh. Well, it's too late."

"What do you mean? Surely, you haven't notified the Synod of your decision. You'd have to wait until tomorrow, at the earliest."

He bites his lower lip. "Um. You're right; the Synod is still unaware of our wish to call Jared. But Jared isn't."

"You've already told Jared?! Isn't that against the rules?"

With a wrinkle of his nose and a shake of his head, he answers, "Not that I know of. As such. I'm sure the Synod would prefer to be the one to notify him, but I didn't want to bother the Synod with our request if Jared wasn't interested. I actually called Jared before tonight's meeting to ask him if it was okay for me to put forth his name, since I know he's not on any call lists."

"And he agreed? Did you pressure him?"

"Yes, he agreed, and no, I didn't pressure him!"

"No need to get defensive."

"I thought you were going to be overjoyed. If the Synod approves this call, and Jared doesn't change his mind, Mitzi will be moving here, to Springfield, to live. Permanently."

I refuse to get that far ahead and raise my hopes. This situation sounds shaky, at best. But I don't want to hurt Brice's feelings, so I say, "That *would* be great. I miss her a lot."

"And you *love* Jared," he repeats. "And he loves you. You guys are great friends. I think having him and Mitzi around will be wonderful for you. And wonderful for Peace."

"And what about you? Are you ready to be on Jared cleanup call, 24/7?"

"If I weren't ready for it, I wouldn't have asked him. And the timing is perfect. He's between semesters in his master's program, which he can continue here. After all, he has two major universities to choose from in this town." He pauses, grabs my hand, and searches my face. "Please, tell me you're happy about this."

The worry in his eyes breaks my heart. "Of course, I am! I want you to be happy, too, though."

"Making you happy makes me happy."

I hope he remembers that the first time he has to fix one of Jared's messes.

7

THE TRIPPIN' TRIO

"*T*he Trippin' Trio is back."

Okay, that was never a thing, but I tried to get it to catch on when Jen, Mitzi, and I were in college. I was drunk when I came up with the name, but for a full week afterward, I mercilessly hounded them about making that our collective nickname.

Now, as we drape ourselves on a loveseat that's not technically big enough for the three of us but that is currently the only piece of furniture in the living room of Mitzi and Jared's adorable new house, I listlessly try to revive it, as I do every couple of years.

"Don't even," Jen says.

Mitzi laughs. "Why are you so obsessed with that stupid name?"

I shrug and giggle at myself. "I don't know. I think it's cute."

"It's hideous. Stop trying to get us to call ourselves that." Jen places one of her spike heels into my side to underscore her command.

"Ow! But think about it! When we get together, we tend

to drink—you know, we like to have fun—but when we drink, we've been known to be a little clumsy."

"A little?" Mitzi sits up straighter. "Remember when you stabbed yourself in the hand with a corkscrew?"

I hold up my hand and splay my fingers so we can all get a look at the scar in the webbing between my thumb and forefinger. "Yeah. And what about the time when Jen twisted her ankle outside that nightclub, when she was trying to convince the bouncer that we were the Hiltons? That was classic."

Jen laughs but quickly sobers. "Even so, we're not the Trippin' Trio. End of discussion."

"You're no fun," I pout. After a few seconds of the three of us sitting without saying a word, I gripe, "What's taking the guys so long backing up the truck? How are we supposed to tell them where everything goes if they never show up with the stuff?" It's a gray, cold, damp late-January Friday. None of us want to go outside to see what the holdup is.

Without moving, Mitzi answers, "Jared was worried some of the stuff wouldn't fit through the front door, and they'd have to bring it around back to the sliding glass doors off the kitchen. And take the doors off the track."

"Humph. That sounds like a pain," I observe, also not moving.

Suddenly from the street, we hear several raised voices and the sickening creak of scraping metal.

Jen sighs. "Maybe we should see if they need help."

Again, none of us move.

"Yeah, you should do that," I say sarcastically, my tone teasing. "In your four-inch heels. Well-played, by the way. You wore the perfect shoes to ensure you wouldn't have to do a damn thing today."

"It wasn't a sinister plot. I figured us girls would be inside the whole time. I plan to take them off when we start unpacking stuff. Anyway, these are the shoes that go with this outfit."

Mitzi snorts. "Yeah, it's too bad spike heels are the only things that go with jeans."

"They are, in my book. You guys are married and can afford to dress like frumpy slouches." Jen sits up, clomping her heels on the hardwood floor. "I, however, am still on the market and must look fierce at all times, ready for my Meet Cute moment."

Mitzi and I shoot each other outraged looks at our friend's insult, but I quickly give up the act. "Yeah, whatever. If I tried to chase after a toddler in those shoes, I'd kill myself. If I tried to carry two babies down our stairs in those shoes, I'd kill all three of us, probably."

"Just who are you trying to attract with those shoes?" Mitzi asks.

"Not a pastor," Jen snips.

"You could do a lot worse than a pastor," Mitzi says defensively.

I struggle to keep a straight face when I add, "Yeah! Mine sometimes makes sex last a whole eight minutes."

"How's he do that, by reciting the books of the Bible in his head, in order?"

"You two are nasty," Mitzi scolds.

"Uh-oh. I think Jared only lasts seven minutes," Jen whispers toward me.

"He loses his train of thought after Leviticus," I quip, straining not to burst into laughter. "But he's new at this pastor thing. He'll be powering through the New Testament in no time."

That gets all three of us giggling hysterically, gasping fragments of thoughts:

"Never hear 'Leviticus' again without losing it!"

"Tantric Tips from Pastor Brice!"

"Seven minutes!"

Something grabs Jen's attention through the front window, and she shushes us, "Oh, here come the Lutheran Lotharios now."

"Baaaaaaaaaaaah!" I shriek, falling onto the floor in front of the couch.

Jared, Brice, Ben, and Pastor Anthony come to the threshold of the front door, taking turns wiping their feet on the welcome mat Mitzi's already placed on the porch.

"What's going on in here?" Brice wonders, taking in the sight of me on the floor. "Have you guys started drinking?"

Ben says, "Sounds like they're already finished!"

"Pipe down, Eiffler," Jen flirts, pretending like she's going to throw one of her shoes at him.

Pastor looks on with an unreadable expression, not necessarily disapproving, but again, he looks like he's an anthropologist studying the behavior of a newly discovered tribe.

I sit up and wipe my eyes. "Nothing's going on in here. What's going on out *there*? We heard an awful noise!"

"The noise you heard," Jared says, "was me, rubbing the side of the moving van against the tree in the front yard. I thought they should be friends. I guess."

Mitzi covers her mouth to try to hide that she's laughing.

"There goes that deposit," Brice states matter-of-factly. "On the plus side, the truck is backed right up to the porch, so we should be able to get most stuff through the front door in record time."

"Then what are you guys waiting for? Chop-chop." I clap my hands to underscore my obnoxiousness.

Brice lowers his chin and raises his eyebrows at me.

"I'm just saying, we have free time away from the children that we're wasting on drudgery. Let's move on to the fun."

"Pretty sure you already skipped to that part," he mumbles on his way back out the front door.

When I challenge, "What was that?" he merely calls over his shoulder, "Nothing, my bride!"

"That's what I thought." After the men have cleared the room to get back to work, I drag myself from the floor and bow to my friends. "And that, ladies, is how you train a pastor."

Jen snorts. "Whatever. He has *you* trained so well that you think it's the other way around. Genius."

Mitzi giggles. I turn on my traitorous friend and say, "What?! You and Jared lived with us. You *know* it's my way or the highway to Heaven."

She puts her hands up. "I'm not saying a word."

Trying to recall anything happening that would suggest Brice has me wrapped around his finger, I think back on the past three weeks, while Mitzi and Jared stayed with us as they looked for a place to live, and I come up blank. Not that it matters.

Well, it sort of does. For some reason, it's important to me that they see I haven't turned into some meek, mild, subservient pastor's wife with no personality of my own. Mitzi was born for that. Me? No way! I'm a rebel, not a "prude," like Jen once accused me of being.

Now she challenges me, "When was the last time you cursed in front of him, Miss Big Talker?"

"I don't know! It's not a conscious thing. That doesn't mean anything, anyway."

"You used to be so defiant about it. 'I'm not changing the way I talk for him. They're only words,'" she says, mockingly.

"I don't talk like a doofus."

The guys twist and turn the larger sofa from the living room set three different ways to try to get it through the front door. Finally, I yell helpfully, "It's not going to fit!"

Jared shouts back, "Thanks, Mrs. N.!" before grumbling something under his breath to the others, who shuffle with him as they retreat from the porch. Minutes later, they appear at the back sliding door, which is *barely* wide enough to accommodate the overstuffed piece of furniture.

"Yay!" Mitzi cheers, pointing to a spot in the living room. "Put it right there. No, wait! Maybe over there. No… Oh, gosh. I'm not sure where it would look best!"

Jared seems willing to hold the couch forever or until she makes up her mind, but Brice sets down his corner. The others follow suit. He wipes sweat from his brow with his shoulder. "You three can figure that out yourselves. There are sliders in the back of the truck, so you can move things around to your hearts' content."

Jen widens her eyes at me and sucks in her upper lip, perfectly conveying a non-verbal "I told you so" that makes me want to punch her.

It also makes me laugh. Who cares what she thinks? I know the truth, and that's all that matters. And the truth is… Well, it's somewhere in the middle, I guess. Neither one of us has the other trained. At least, I hope not. What's the fun in that?

∼

It's nearly 9:00 by the time Brice and I drag ourselves home, both of us physically and mentally exhausted from the moving experience, which was equal parts work and fun. After seeing Marianne to her car, I reenter the house and lean against the wall next to the front door. Brice stands at his desk, thumbing through the mail, separating it into piles for junk, bills, and other.

I watch him for a while before getting the nerve to ask him what's been on my mind all afternoon and evening: "Which one of us is the boss of us?"

He sweeps the junk mail into the trash can under his desk and looks up at me, clearly not understanding my question.

Admittedly, it was phrased childishly, so I clarify, "I mean, who wears the pants? Around here."

"You're not a fan of dresses, so I'd say we both do," he says with a half-smile.

"You know what I mean."

He sighs, taking up a position against the stairs, his head level with the banister. "We're a team. Equals."

"I know that's the 'correct' answer, but is that really the case with us? Does one of us have more control?" I cross my arms over my chest, anxiously awaiting his perspective.

He scrapes his lower lip with his teeth as he seems to think about it.

When he takes too long to give me the answer I want, I say, "Because I don't think so."

Looking visibly relieved, he quickly agrees and adds, "Neither one of us is a controlling person, anyway."

Before I can suppress it, "Well…" slips out.

He narrows his eyes at me. "What? You think *I* am?"

"You can be. Maybe not *controlling*. That word is so negative. But you like things to be a certain way."

"Says the woman who will not let us put the bed on any other wall in our bedroom, despite the fact that the dormer ceiling requires me to duck to stand next to the head of the bed."

"Why would you ever have to stand there?"

"To get into it? To make it?"

I dismiss his complaint. "That's the only logical place to put the bed. I'm talking about important stuff, like... the boys' names."

"What are you talking about? We chose their names together."

"It was a major pain, because you're picky."

"They're going to have those names forever. I think it's worth some thought."

"Yeah, but..." I tick off on my fingers, "...you didn't want common names; then you didn't want names that were too odd and would be difficult for people to spell or understand or pronounce; then you didn't want anything that sounded too unisex; then you didn't want anything that rhymed with bad words or words that bullies could use to make fun of them. It was an ordeal."

"If it had been up to you, they would have all sounded like English lords. Or Leprechauns!" Before I can protest, he holds up a hand and takes a deep breath. "Never mind. Okay. I agree that I was picky about their names. But I didn't make any unilateral decisions. We chose their names together."

"After much ado."

"Well, you're obsessed with making love in odd places!" he blurts.

I tilt my head and raise my eyebrows. "Like where?"

"Like"—he points toward the living room—"there. And in the kitchen. That's just untoward."

"You've never refused. And *untoward*?"

"Perverse."

"I know what it means," I say through gritted teeth. "And if you're so against it, then I'll never ask you to have sex anywhere but our bed ever again."

"Good! We have kids now. They could walk in on us and be scarred for life."

I laugh at that, considering two of them can't walk, and the other is still confined to a crib. The laugh bears little amusement, though.

"Forget I said anything," I tell him.

"Well, why *did* you?"

Pushing away from the wall, I go toward the stairs. "I don't know! It bothers me that everyone thinks I don't have a say in anything anymore. Like I became a pastor's wife and stopped having a personality."

"I don't think anyone who knows you thinks that."

"They do! They think you call the shots, and I merely nod and smile at everything—"

"If they only knew," he mutters.

"But seriously. What was the last major decision I made?"

"Uh, going back to work?"

I snort. "That was hardly—"

"It was a big decision! And it was up to you. Completely."

"It only affected me, though."

"I beg to differ. It affects our whole family."

"All right," I concede. "I made that *one* decision."

"You accepted your sister's car without so much as a glance in my direction to see if I was okay with it."

And there it is.

"I *knew* it."

"Knew what?"

"I knew you were pissed off about the damn SUV. The *free* vehicle that we desperately needed, that was handed to us like a gift from above."

"I'm not *mad* about it. It would have been nice, though, if she'd told us about it privately. What if we had already made other plans?"

I climb the first two steps so we're eye-to-eye. "Then we would have told her, and she would have taken her car back with her. But we didn't have other plans. And we needed that car. And it's awesome."

He shrugs sullenly. "I guess."

His stubbornness makes me roll my eyes. I make my way up the rest of the stairs, until he stops me with, "You know who calls the shots around here?"

"You?"

"No. God. God does. Or He should."

I groan at the pastor answer, even though I know it's going to annoy him.

"It's true! For me, at least."

I let that dig slide, knowing I started this and have pushed him to this point. When I say, "let it slide," I mean I don't say anything in response. I do level him with a toxic glare before continuing up the stairs. I wish I could stomp, but I don't want to wake up the babies.

Unfortunately, he follows me. We silently and tensely get ready for bed, careful not to brush against each other in the bathroom or make eye contact as we change into pajamas and slide under the covers on our respective sides of the bed, where we lie stiffly, lest our elbows or feet accidentally touch.

I feel like an idiot for even bringing it up. I half meant it as a joke, even if I was curious how he viewed the decision making in our household. When I pondered it myself, I counted silly things, like who chooses the kind of food we eat and toilet paper we use and clothes the boys wear, and it came out remarkably equal.

Then I had to go and blow everything out of proportion and make it about "big things." Whatever that means. Only then did I start to feel slighted, like I don't have as much say as I thought, like maybe Jen's right.

Relaxing slightly, I edge my foot over so it bumps his. He tetchily moves further onto his side of the bed.

"I'm sorry," I mumble into the dark.

"It's okay," he says coldly, making me wonder if he knows that I'm not apologizing for nudging his foot.

"About our argument."

"It's fine." Still, it feels like there are icicles hanging above our bed. I'm worried about being impaled.

"It's not fine." I scoot against him and lift his arm to put it around me as I rest my head against his shoulder. He's a stiff and unyielding pillow. "It was a dumb, immature thing to bring up. I like the system we have. If you relied on me to make more of the super-weighty decisions around here, I'd hate it. I trust you. I'm glad you know what you're doing. Someone should." When I can feel him relax a bit, I say, "Why do you always have to play the God card, though? That's so unfair."

"Who says you can't play it?"

I laugh. "Oh, I *know* I can't play it. I don't have the qualifications." He sighs, so I quickly steer him away from a potential sermon about worthiness with, "I really just wanted you to say, 'Peyton, you're the boss of me.'"

"Peyton, you're the boss of me," he says, in a monotone.

"Forget it now. It's not the same."

He combs his fingers through my hair for a few seconds,

so I'm good and relaxed when he says quietly, "I don't like when you get that way—the way you were downstairs— after you've been around Jen. What do you have to prove to her?"

"I'm not proving anything," I say a lot less defensively than I would have fifteen minutes ago.

"You guys hang out, and suddenly you're convinced you're a prude or too boring or not fun enough or— or too submissive. And I wind up with a headache. Or mashed googlies. It's exhausting."

I think about it for a while and weigh my words, then say, "When I'm with her, I see myself from a different perspective—and I usually don't like what I see. She makes me feel inferior."

His rarely used sarcasm makes an appearance. "Because she has it all figured out?"

"No, because she makes me realize *I* don't have it all figured out. I can usually fool myself into thinking I do most of the time. Then she holds up the mirror and forces me to take a long look, and I realize I don't know anything."

"None of us do, hon."

"You do."

"I know less and less every day."

"Well, that's not comforting. I'm counting on you to know what the hell's going on."

He grunts. I'm not sure if it's in protest to my language, amusement at my joke, or a combination of both. As I'm analyzing the timbre of his grunt, he asks in a musing tone, "Why do you think Jen's still single?"

Now I do get defensive, this time for my friend. "She hasn't met The One. And maybe she doesn't want to be married."

"Do you really believe that?"

"Which one?"

"Both. Either. Whatever."

Grudgingly, I have to admit, "No. Well, maybe the first one. Or if she's met him, it wasn't at the right time. But she told me once that she does want to be married someday. She was drunk when she said it, but you know how some of the truest things come out when you're looking at the bottom of a bottle."

"I'll have to trust you on that one."

I thread my fingers through his, which are resting on his belly. "Now, now. You may not know it for yourself, but you've been around enough intoxicated people—mostly my family—to know it's true."

"My point is, you say Jen makes you feel inferior, but I bet the opposite is just as much the case."

I scoff at that. "She thinks my life is lame."

"Did she say that after a bottle of wine?"

"She's never said *that* exactly. I just know. It's in every comment about my clothes and my hair and my ratty fingernails. It's in the way she looks around at the toys all over the living room. It's in her raised eyebrows when she looks in our refrigerator and sees the only cheese we have comes in individually wrapped, rubbery squares."

"I like American cheese. Sue me."

I giggle at his defensiveness. "See? You can't help but feel like a rube when you look at our life through her eyes. It makes you question everything."

"Not me. Nobody's asking her to eat our cheese."

"Forget the cheese for a second."

"She's done it now, insulting my cheese slices. I can tolerate a lot of things, but she's crossed the line. See if I ever make her one of my special grilled cheese sandwiches with bacon and tomato. Uh-uh. No grilled cheese for her."

"Stop it!" I swat at his tummy.

"Am I making you hungry?"

"Yes."

"I'll make you a deal: I'll stop talking about my ooey, gooey, delicious grilled cheese sandwiches if you stop letting Jen get to you. I want you to see yourself through God's eyes, not Jen's eyes. And in His eyes, you are magnificent. Mine too, by the way."

"Okay, but…" When he makes a loud, frustrated noise at my perceived stubbornness, I put my hand over his mouth and say, "I really want you to say that other thing. With feeling."

I feel his lips smile against my hand, so I lessen the pressure against them, grinning in anticipation of those wonderful words. And he doesn't disappoint.

"Peyton, you're so the boss of me."

8

EYE CANDY

'm feeling smug. I've been back at work for two weeks, and we've already settled into a nice routine. Brice goes to work in the morning, while I get the boys up and ready. After an early lunch, I take the boys to the church, where I drop them off in the capable hands of the staff at Peace Daycare and Preschool (two corridors and a covered walkway from Brice's office), then I go to work at Eye Candy Art Gallery and Boutique and typically work until 6:00. Brice brings the boys home and feeds them dinner. I start dinner for Brice and me when I get home, while Brice bathes the kids, brings them to me for kisses, and tucks them into bed. Then he goes for a quick run, and we eat after he returns and showers. The evening routine is a bit hectic and could use some tweaking, but the rest of it runs smoothly.

And that's good, because I *need* this job. Not simply to get out of the house for a few hours a week, either. I need it so we can live comfortably without worrying about money all the time. At this age, I don't want to pinch pennies, clip coupons, or deny myself my addiction to pricey caffeinated beverages. We're not wasteful; we're not over-indulgent; but we don't live like college students anymore, and I don't plan to start, even with the increased population in our house. We may eat American cheese like college students, but I will *not* purchase any cups of Ramen. This, I most solemnly swear.

Anyway, as long as I have my part-time job at the gallery/boutique, I also have a legitimate reason (a.k.a., "excuse") to limit how involved I can be at the church. I still volunteer at the Pregnancy Crisis Clinic, although I've had to switch my hours to Friday mornings, when Brice is home with the boys, but I no longer have time in my schedule for Parents of Peace or in leadership roles with the Lutheran Women's Missionary League. Oh, darn.

Well, technically, I could go to PoP before work on Tuesdays, but I've wiggled out of that with a sincere, "I'd rather spend that time with my boys, now that I'm back at work." That satisfied the PoP Nazis, even if Brice saw right through it and has teased me mercilessly about it since he witnessed my saying it to Paul Vitely, PoP's self-appointed Parenting Guru.

As for my job, my co-workers were glad to have me back after my twelve weeks away and have made being away from the boys a lot easier than I thought it was going to be. They've been so nice, shielding me from all the less-desirable jobs (dusting the merchandise) and yielding to me on the more fun tasks (setting up window displays). In fact, keeping me busy seems to be their primary goal.

Carrie, the Amazonian hippie who owns the shop, announced my first day back that she was putting me in charge of a local artist's first opening.

"You've done stuff like that before, right? At your former job in Chicago?"

"Y-yes. But…"

"If you don't want to do it, that's fine. I thought it would keep your mind off baby withdrawals, though."

Quickly, I assured her, "I *want* to do it," but I wasn't sure I was telling the truth.

Part of me—the good, accommodating employee— wanted to agree without hesitation. Another part of me wanted to do it to recapture something of the me I used to be, the single, carefree woman who was in touch with all the latest trends and knew the names of every new up-and-coming artist in the industry.

But a louder, more insistent part of me wanted to run away from the responsibility—and the potentially difficult artist I'd be working with. A certain cretin's face kept flashing in my head.

"But?" she prompted while I contemplated all these things.

I scratched my head and smiled self-consciously. "I'm not sure I have the time to devote to this person. You know, when I'm not here, I'm off the clock."

She laughed. "And that won't be a problem. The person whose show you'd be organizing isn't a prima donna. None of our local artists are. They're all really cool, down-to-earth people. You've met some of them."

"Do I know this one?" I asked hopefully.

Shaking her head, she answered, "Not from here. That's not to say you don't know him from some other place. It's a small town, after all."

Her words made me want to break out in song, but I held back. Barely. Instead of singing, I asked, "Is he a Lutheran artist? Because that's about the only other way I'd know him. Unless he works at the grocery store near my house. I don't get out much."

"I don't know his religious background, but I do know

he's not employed by a grocery store," she said with a grin. "I believe he's a therapist by day. Sculpts and sketches by night to relieve stress."

Warning, warning! Potential nutjob alert!

But I smiled and said, "If you think I have time for it, in addition to watching the shop in the afternoons, then I'm willing to give it a go. But I... I can't do late nights, you know?"

She placed a comforting hand on my arm. "Trust me; it's not going to require that." Then she left me to my shift, the boutique smelling of patchouli in her wake.

By the time I got home that night, I wasn't as frightened of the possibilities. After all, we live in Springfield. I haven't met a single person even close to Stefan's caliber. I doubt this Matt Benson is going to be a problem. I trust Carrie. And based on the few phone conversations we've had so far, he seems pretty normal—for a therapist.

Plus, I'm already settling into a rut at work, so it'll be good to have something different to do.

Jared seems to be making himself at home at Peace, too. That's been a huge relief to Brice, who has the most at stake, considering he so highly recommended him. I keep waiting for that to blow up in his face—this is Jared we're talking about, after all—but so far the congregation loves him.

He appears to be in his element, too. He's not nearly as unsure of himself as he was as Messiah's vicar. I think he's learned a lot about himself in the past couple of years, and marriage suits him, too. He's still eager and energetic, but there's no nervous energy about him. He doesn't strike me as always looking over his shoulder, second-guessing everything he says and does.

Today, he's in Brice's office when I stop by to say hi on

my way to work after dropping off the boys in the nursery. I give him a hug before going around Brice's desk to get my pre-work kiss.

"You two slacking off, as usual?"

Jared, taking me seriously, replies, "Not really. We're discussing Vacation Bible School."

"Oh? What's the theme going to be this year? Sorcery?"

He narrows his eyes at me. "Very funny. *Harry Potter* isn't anti-Christian, you know."

I laugh. "I'm a major Potterphile, so you don't have to convince me. But you sure got some people's panties in a twist that year when you wanted to split the VBS age groups into the four Hogwarts houses."

Brice chuckles. "The best thing about that is that I think everyone here at Peace would really like that idea. But we haven't gone as far as discussing a theme yet."

"Oh."

He lowers his voice, keeping his eyes on his office door to make sure nobody walks in when he says, "Now that Pastor Long is out of the picture, I'm going to propose—again— that we hold VBS earlier in the summer, before it gets so blazing hot, and that we hold it in the evenings, when more adults are available to participate."

"Most churches are doing it that way nowadays," Jared confirms, holding up a sheaf of papers in his hands. "I've done the research."

"You guys are quite the pair," I state. "The traditionalists won't know what hit them."

"We're not out to get anybody." Jared widens his eyes and pushes his glasses higher on his nose. "But it's not fair that some people can't participate because they're at work during the day. And their kids are at daycare and have no way to get here. VBS is fun! Everyone should be able to join in."

Oh, yes. It's great fun. That's why I'm glad my children are still too young to take part, so I have a reason to stay home and not join in the fun.

I don't say any of this to Jared, though. Instead, I smile and edge toward the door. "Well, you two have fun revolutionizing VBS as Peace knows it."

"There's no need to be sarcastic," Brice says sullenly. "Baby steps, you know."

"Who's being sarcastic?" I ask innocently, backing into the doorway and nearly colliding with Pastor Anthony as he creeps over the threshold. "Oh! Sorry!" I sidestep him to avoid further contact.

He stands completely still, looking like someone who's been told that a fierce predator can't see him if he doesn't move. Not acknowledging me at all, he says to Brice, "I got your message that you and Pastor Laszewski wanted to discuss Vacation Bible School plans?"

"Prepare your mind to be blown," I mutter, edging past him.

"Pardon?"

"Don't listen to her," Brice orders, shooting me a fake scowl. "She was just leaving. Love you!" he calls toward my back.

I blow him a kiss over my shoulder. To Lucy on my way through the reception area, I say, "Try not to let those guys get too excited in there."

I haven't been this nervous in a long time. Probably since my wedding day, if I were being honest. But making a lifetime commitment to not only a person but also to a lifestyle that I knew didn't suit my natural personality was something to sweat over. It didn't matter that I loved that person more than I thought possible; I knew myself enough to worry that my fickle feelings might betray me with little notice, especially if and when things became difficult. If it hadn't been for my inability to hurt Brice, I probably wouldn't have gone through with marrying him, simply because I didn't think I was good enough to be his wife.

But today, meeting artist Matt Benson, is hardly worth the dry mouth, shaky tummy, and frayed nerves I'm experiencing. My reaction is utterly ridiculous and baseless, which makes it even more annoying. He's just an artistic person, like hundreds I've worked with in the past (well, hopefully *not* like some of them), with whom I'll work for this short period of time and maybe never see again. After all, these small-town artists tend to produce enough art for a show—as a hobby—then fade into the background, having marked the experience from their Bucket List. During our many phone calls, Matt has had that earnest, eager-to-please demeanor that signifies he fits into that category.

I tell myself I'm anxious because I haven't done anything like this in a while. I've become sheltered, complacent, allowed to encourage my introverted nature. My extrovert muscles have atrophied—clearly evident in the way I interact with half the people at church. If Matt's okay with my conversing in baby talk, we'll probably get along just fine. If not, I'll have to beat back the butterflies and remember I have nothing to prove to him. In fact, it's the other way around.

Nothing is helping, though. The only thing that's going to put my fears at ease is meeting this guy in person and finding out for sure—if that's possible—that he's *not* Stefan two-point-oh.

Because that's really what this is about. I can kid myself and try to come up with a hundred other explanations, but it's really all about Stefan. Just when I think that guy can no longer have any effect on my life, something like this proves me wrong. He scarred me. And I hate that he has that power over me. Still.

Plus, I feel bad for people like Matt who have to prove they're *not* arrogant, selfish, emotionally abusive bastards who use sleeping with women as sexual experiments and get off by psychologically terrorizing them about it for years afterward. It's not fair to paint every artist with the same brush. But I can't help it. Dastardly until proven decent. Or something.

I chose a Wednesday afternoon for our meeting, because it's our slowest afternoon in the shop, so we'd have fewer distractions and interruptions. Plus, he doesn't see patients on Wednesday afternoons, so it worked out well for him, too.

Unfortunately, I didn't consider that every man who walked past the front window in the twenty minutes before our meeting time would be a potential Matt who would elicit a near panic attack. I'm not sure my heart can take another passerby. And I wish I'd done a crappier job with the window display so fewer people would slow to look at it. As it is now, it's difficult to ascertain who's simply walking past and who's going to enter the shop, potentially to wreak havoc on my newly placid—albeit sometimes dull—life. I like dull. Dull is good. Dull is…

The bell on the door makes me jump, but I hide the flinch by hopping from the stool on which I'm perched behind the shop counter.

In the seconds it takes the tall, dark-haired guy who's entered to walk toward me with a nervous—although rather disarming and, frankly, gorgeous—smile, I think, *Can I do this? Do I look "artsy" enough, like I know what I'm talking about? Do I really know what I'm talking about? Have I forgotten everything I learned at school and at Smart Art? Please Lord, don't let this guy be an asshole. I'll simply quit if he's an asshole. I'll tell Carrie something came up at home, and I can't do this. Maybe I'll do that, no matter what. I don't think I can do this!*

The visitor extends his hand and closes one gray eye. "Peyton? I'm Matt Benson."

Great, Lord. Thanks for making him hot. That's not *helpful. If this is one of Your stupid tests, we're going to be in a fight.*

"Hello," I reply stiffly to his introduction, pumping his clammy hand once before quickly taking mine back. "Thank you for agreeing to come in today to take a look at the showcase area." Even though I'd rather keep the counter between us, I know it would be weird and unnatural, so I come around and stand at the end of it, nodding toward the room through the archway to my right. "Would you like to see it? The showroom, I mean?"

He swallows audibly. "Yes. Thanks. Although, I've been here before for other shows."

"You have?"

He follows me. "Yeah. There aren't that many galleries in this town. This is one of a handful where my friends occasionally have openings."

We come to a stop in the middle of the showroom. An installation by another local artist is still on display, but it will come down and be replaced by Matt's in two weeks' time.

I motion to the walls. "Well. Here we are. It's a small room—but you know that. You just said that. Do you know this artist, Yazeel Winters? His work is…" I stop, because I suddenly can't think of a complementary word. Truth is, I hate this current display, and I can't wait to get it out of here. Even Matt's stuff—sculpted metal, which is slightly strange, and of which I've only seen pictures—will be an improvement over this dreck, which I lamely call, "...unique."

Matt chuckles. "Yazeel's a strange character. But an okay guy. Maybe he thinks he needs to be 'unique' to be a true artist."

His candor relaxes me somewhat. "That happens. So, anyway, based on the pictures you sent, I think your largest... thing... should go on the back—"

He laughs loudly this time. "'Thing,' huh? I guess you'll be describing my work to the next artist as 'unique,' too?"

I blush. "Uh, sorry. I— They're not technically sculptures. Although, I guess they are. But—"

"Pieces. Let's stick with that description, maybe."

"I'm sorry. I didn't mean to make it sound like I think your art is bad. It's just not my... thing. See? I use that word for everything. I'm not an eloquent person."

After staring at me, looking amused, for a beat past "comfortable," he says, "Lemme guess... middle child. Used to be wild but have settled down in adulthood, although sometimes you rebel against it. Constantly worried about doing what's 'right' in any given situation and concerned more about what other people think about you than how you feel about yourself."

I bristle at his disturbingly accurate psychoanalysis but maintain eye contact when I say primly, "Maybe we should stick to discussing your 'pieces.'" Unfortunately, my unintended double entendre makes me blush an even deeper shade than I already am.

He appears chastened but unabashed. "All right. Didn't

mean to make you uncomfortable. Sometimes it's hard to turn off the therapist in my head, that's all."

The self-conscious people pleaser that he's already recognized in me brushes off his half-apology. My diplomacy skills are a bit stale, but they're still hanging around here somewhere, albeit packed in moth balls.

Pulling an expression that lands somewhere between rueful and amused, he breaks eye contact and looks around the room. "Anyway! Um, yeah. I think you're right about the largest *piece* going on the back wall. We can scatter some of the others in the middle, too, so it's not just stuff pushed against walls. I'd like to highlight my favorite piece in the center. Maybe even put a spotlight on it."

We talk about nothing personal for the remainder of his visit, although he does drop rather casually that there's a particular piece he's most eager to sell, since it was inspired by his ex-wife and brings back awful memories every time he looks at it.

"I keep it covered in my shop, actually. So if there's anything I'd like you guys to get rid of, it's that. The others… It'd be nice to sell them, but I don't do this to make money, so there's no need to kill yourselves with any hard sells."

"We're not really about the hard sell here, anyway," I say. "The art either speaks to people, or it doesn't."

"Looks like Yazeel's isn't speaking to many people," he mutters, referring to the full walls of mixed-media framed art.

I smile sheepishly. "Uh, no. Not so much. But he'd probably do well at a gallery in a bigger city. I think Carrie's been in touch with a few places in St. Louis and Kansas City on his behalf."

We spend the final minutes of his visit discussing the

logistics of getting his pieces to the gallery the day before the opening. Then I show him some fliers and other marketing materials I've drafted, including the Facebook messages I'll be strategically posting the week before the show.

"Sounds like you have everything under control," he says, jamming his hands into his coat pockets. Almost immediately, he pulls his right hand out again and nervously runs it through his dark hair.

His sudden, inexplicable unease makes my nerves jounce once more. I'm no longer worried he's a jerk—although he really does need to learn to keep his psychobabble to himself when he's met someone for the first time—but now I *am* worried he's about to drop a bomb on me. The fact that I have no idea what that bomb could possibly be only makes it scarier.

"It was, uh, nice to meet you in person finally, Peyton."

"Likewise," I reply warily, sensing a major "but" to his niceties.

He opens his mouth as if to say something else, but then he closes it, smiles tightly, and says, "I almost did it again."

"What?"

"Never mind," he answers enigmatically, his gray eyes twinkling.

His smile broadens, and I notice again how beautiful his teeth are. I'm talking, *beautiful.* And I've never before given teeth much aesthetic weight, as long as they're not gross or hideous. "Nice" is about as far as I've ever gone when assessing an acquaintance's choppers. After that, a tooth is a tooth is a tooth, in my book.

What's wrong with me? I'm fixated on this guy's teeth, of all things.

I must be staring, because his grin falters, and he rubs his tongue across his pearly whites. "Do I have something…" He trails off, trying to feel out the situation with his tongue.

"What? No! Sorry! I was staring into space. No. Your teeth are…" *Magnificent, glorious, amazing, gorgeous, stunning.* "…fine. Sorry." I laugh nervously and busy myself with straightening the pens and small stapler and notepad next to the cash register. "I have three small boys, and…" *Where the heck am I going with this??* "…don't get much sleep!" *Yes. I'll milk that until the children are in college. Covers all manner of sins. Not that it's a sin to admire a man's smile. Even if he's not your husband. Looking is okay. Lusting is another matter. But I wasn't really lusting, was I? No…*

His face relaxes again. "Oh. How old are they?"

"What?"

"Your kids. How old are they?"

"Oh! Um, Max will be two next month, and the twins are three months old."

"Newborn twins, huh? I bet you *are* tired. I should probably go and let you take a nap in the back room, since this place is quiet."

In more comfortable conversational territory, I regain my composure and ask, "Do you have any children?"

"Nah. That's about the only thing my ex-wife and I agreed on. Neither one of us was ready to be a parent. She wasn't ready to be a spouse, either, apparently. But, you know, live and learn." He looks sorry he said so much but turns the conversation back to me. "What does your husband do for a living?"

My husband. Oh, yeah. That guy. "He's a pastor."

Matt's eyes widen. "Wow. For, um, some reason, I wasn't expecting that answer. You don't hear that often."

"This town has a lot of churches; I bet you hear it more than in some other places."

"Which church?"

"Peace Lutheran."

"Isn't that the one that got hit by the tornado last year?"

"That's the one."

"Wow," he repeats. "Then I saw your husband on the news once or twice afterwards."

"He *was* on TV a few times, yes. The community was good to us during our recovery."

Before he can say anything else, the bell chimes on the door, and two women—a couple of our regulars—enter the shop. I greet them by name and tell them to let me know if they need help with anything.

Matt takes a deep breath. "Well, I'll leave you to it, then. I'm sure we'll be in touch between now and the show."

"Absolutely. If you think of anything I need to know, give me a call. I'm here Monday through Friday, in the afternoons."

"Yeah. I will. Thanks." He gives me a breezy goodbye and strides to the door, beaming and nodding at the other customers on his way out.

He's hardly gone for ten seconds before Shelly appears at the counter, wondering, "Who was *that* and what can I do to see that smile again?"

As I tell her about his upcoming show (hey, you gotta get the word out any way you can) I feel less guilty about my own preoccupation with his mouth, since it's obviously not just me. Whew.

9

THE CRUSH

*B*rice doesn't know about Matt. I mean, he *knows* about him, because I mentioned before I met Matt in person that Carrie was putting me in charge of an artist named Matt Benson's show. But he doesn't *know* about him. If you know what I mean.

Maybe I haven't talked more about Matt because I'm worried I can't do so without blushing. I mean, I do think he's cute. And that's definitely not something you dish with your husband about, no matter how innocent and harmless the attraction is. It's not that I've never admitted my attraction to another man to Brice, but it's one thing to ooh and aah over a picture of Ryan Gosling and another thing altogether to get all starry-eyed about a personal acquaintance's smile. That's a bit too… real.

Not that it is. It's not. Real, I mean. I'm merely admiring the scenery. I love my husband with all my heart (well, most of it; some of it is reserved for our offspring), and there's no man—not even Smiley Benson—who comes close to making my heart flutter like Brice does. But I'm not dead. And Matt reminds me a lot of Brice when we first met:

unsure of himself in some ways but comfortable in his own skin in other ways. He knows who he is and isn't ashamed of it. I find that so attractive. Plus, they're physically alike with their tall statures and dark hair. So, what it boils down to is that Matt's my type. Period. Big deal.

It doesn't help—or hurt, whichever way you want to look at it—that he *knows* me so well already. After only a few phone calls and three brief face-to-face meetings, he seems like someone I've known for a long time. Again, chalk that up to him being a lot like Brice, probably, as well as the fact that he analyzes people's personalities and motivations for a living. I mean, he had me pegged when he said those things to me at the gallery about being a middle child and a people-pleaser.

And how did he know about my "wild" past? Not that it was wild. It wasn't, by most standards, but I had my moments. If I'm being honest—and I think I'm being painfully so, at this point—it was a relief that he could see that about me, like my younger self isn't as dormant and hidden as it sometimes seems.

Since his first visit, we've been in touch several times through email, and he's stopped by the shop on two other occasions. In both instances, there were several other people around. Even our electronic communications have all been above-board and professional, not even a hint of cyber-flirting, but I do get a tiny thrill when I see his name in my inbox. Chalk that up to leading a boring life, though.

Well, that's not entirely true. It's gratifying that he's contagiously excited about his show. Plus, he's so impressed with my marketing efforts—I've lined up the Arts and Entertainment reporter at the local paper to cover his opening— that it makes me feel good. Not even the nicest artists I worked with at Smart Art were this appreciative of my work. I guess I've been starving for approval, and I didn't even realize it. Now, I can't get enough of it.

Anyway, it's just a silly little crush.

The biggest reason I don't talk about him more with Brice is that Brice is too busy to listen to me ramble on and on about a local artist. As a matter of fact, when we talked at dinner the night after Matt's visit to the gallery, Brice made it pretty clear it wasn't an interesting topic to him, after I reassured him that Matt's not a jerk and that he's not going to bring any added stress to our life. He said something dismissive like, "That's nice," and rushed to change the subject to something church-related.

Of course. Heaven forbid we talk about *my* work for a change.

Since then, I haven't talked about work at all. Tonight, though, I have to break my silence.

Casually, at dinner, I drop, "Next Friday is Matt's opening."

His mouth half-full, Brice asks, "Who's Matt?"

I want to cross my arms over my chest and harumph, but I maintain my cool and answer, "You know, Matt Benson. The artist whose show I've been working on."

Still giving me a blank look, he swallows and says, "Oh. Have we talked about this?" He seems ashamed to admit his ignorance—and he should be—but it still annoys me that he's so disengaged from my career.

"Yes! I told you about it when Carrie first asked me to organize his show."

He takes a drink of milk, obviously stalling, then says, "I guess I didn't know his name. Matt Benson, huh?"

I will myself to remain detached, calm, and unflushed as I continue eating my lima beans. "Yes. That's his name."

"Is he a painter? A sculptor? A candlestick maker?"

"He's a sculptor. Welder. Person."

"A sculptor-welder-person, eh?" He chuckles down at his plate as he cuts his chicken breast. "That's a new one."

"You know what I mean. He welds metal things together to make pieces. Of art."

"Sounds artsy."

"He's talented." I'm not sure I really believe that but wish Brice would stop being so condescending. No longer hungry, I stand abruptly and take my plate to the sink, uncomfortably aware that my husband's staring at me.

"Okay. Sorry," he offers lightly. "Didn't mean to strike a nerve."

"You didn't."

"Could've fooled me."

I slide my dirty dishes into the dishwasher and close it with my hip. "What I was getting at is that I'll have to attend his show, since I'm in charge of it. I was trying to let you know I'd be home late next Friday."

"How late?" His tone is mild, merely inquisitive, but his question annoys me nevertheless.

"I don't know! Late. Don't wait up."

With exaggerated calm, he sets down his knife and fork on the edges of his plate. "What's your deal?" He leans back in his chair and crosses his arms over his chest.

"Nothing! I'm trying to tell you about something, and you're being a smart ass."

He laughs. "I'm not!"

"Yes, you are. 'Sounds artsy,'" I mock him, which makes him laugh harder. "Forget it. I told you; now, you know. That's all I wanted to say."

I make a break for the doorway to the living room, but he stops me with a loud, "Wait a second!" When I whirl, he says more gently, "Hey, I'm sorry. I didn't mean to make it sound like I was making fun of your job… or your friend."

"He's not my friend."

"Well, whatever. I'm sorry." He abandons his dinner at the kitchen table and crosses the room to me, wrapping his hands around my upper arms. Bending his knees so he can look me in the eyes, he repeats, "I'm sorry."

Suddenly feeling ridiculous and like the conversation has run away from me, I look at the floor and mumble, "It's not a big deal."

"It is, obviously. I wasn't meaning to be a jerk."

"I know."

"Are you sure? Because—"

"I'm fine!" I shrug my arms from his grip. "You're making this into something bigger than it is. It was stupid for me to be so touchy."

"I wouldn't say it was stupid."

"Can we just drop it? Please?" I walk to the table and gesture to his plate. "Are you finished with this?"

He stares me down for a few seconds before nodding. "Yeah. I guess. I'm not really that hungry. Are you sure you're okay?"

I scrape his leftover food into the trash and smile tightly at him. "I'm fine. I lost my temper when you didn't remember my telling you about Matt's show, that's all. Sometimes it seems like you don't listen to me, like you're too busy worrying about church stuff to hear me when I tell you things."

He leans against the wooden molding of the kitchen doorway and crosses his arms over his chest. I see his pec twitch under his soft, gray t-shirt. "I hear you. But you don't seem to like to talk much about work. And it's been a while since you mentioned anything about the show. I just forgot."

"Well, I don't forget about your work. I'm not allowed to." I toss his silverware into the dishwasher with a clang.

He sighs.

"Don't sigh at me." His plate still in my hand, I slice through the air with it while I rant, "I know everything from the inventory of the Communion supplies to Lucy's favorite kind of candy. I know who's had a baby, having a baby, trying to have a baby, and can't have babies. I know who's having marital problems but I also know not to let anyone know that I know. Ditto goes for addictions and mental illness. I know who's lost their job and who's looking for a job and who's found a new job, as well as those who have retired from their jobs. I know who *is* sick, may be sick, or who feels sick all the time, because they're hypochondriacs."

"Do you want me to stop telling you things? Because when I don't tell you things, you get angry that I don't tell you things."

"I just want you to retain the things *I* tell *you*, even if they don't seem that important or interesting. It's not like I ask you to remember much." As I'm bending over to put his plate in the dishwasher, it slips from my hand, bounces off the side of the dishwasher door, and hits the floor at the perfect angle so that the impact against the wooden floor snaps the plate almost directly down the middle.

I gasp. "Oh, no!" Picking up and holding the two pieces in front of me, I press them together along the clean seam, as if I can will the broken plate to be whole again. "Damn it. This is part of the set we got from my parents for our wedding." My throat tightens, but I'm determined not to cry about something so petty.

Brice steps forward, holding out his hands. "Here. Let me see it." I reluctantly hand it over, biting my thumbnail as I watch him inspect the damage. "It's a clean break. I can glue it. I'll let it set overnight, and it'll be good as new in the morning."

"Let me clean it first," I say, reaching for the pieces.

While I wash and dry the halves, he goes to his wood-shed, returning with a bottle of ordinary white glue and a small paintbrush. Then he grabs a box of rice from the cabinet and fills a large, shallow pan with the grains.

"What's that for?" I ask.

Taking the clean, dry ceramic semicircles from me, he smiles reassuringly. "You'll see. It's an old trick I've seen my mom do a few times."

I watch, engrossed, while he paints the broken edges with a fine coat of glue. He presses the two halves together. "I need to hold these like this for a minute or so..." His tongue peeks out of the corner of his mouth as he concentrates on keeping the halves perfectly still and firmly together.

I stand on my tiptoes to look at the bond. "Doesn't bacteria grow in cracks? I mean, is it going to be safe to eat off that in the future?"

He shrugs. "I've never gotten sick from eating off any of my mom's repaired plates. If it makes you feel better, we'll put it at the bottom of the stack and only use it when the others are dirty. But at least you'll still have a full set."

When he seems confident the glue is setting, he gently rests the plate on the bed of rice grains in the pan. "The rice allows for cushion and air flow, so the glue can dry, but it prevents the plate from shifting and re-breaking."

My eyes snap to his. "Oh. That's actually really smart!"

"Mom's a smart cookie." He twists the cap to close the glue bottle. Turning to the sink, he rinses the paintbrush under the tap and washes his hands.

I look down at the hairline fracture in the dish resting on

the rice. It's hardly noticeable, unless you know it's there. But I do know. I can clearly see it bisecting the wide, chocolate-brown rim at the top and bottom, even though it's nearly invisible in the white center.

He did a great job putting it back together, but it'll never be as good as new, like he promised. I'll always know it's flawed.

I study the layout chart to make sure each of Matt's pieces is where we agreed they'd go for tomorrow night's show. I want—no, *need*—everything to be perfect. He'll be by in a few minutes, after his final appointment of the day, to check on things, make suggestions, and give his final approval.

Satisfied there's nothing more I can do regarding the setup of the artwork, I return to the counter, where my shift replacement, Kimi, is sitting, thumbing through a magazine. She looks over at me while I dig through my purse for my lip balm. (Okay, it's tinted, but it's not lipstick or lip gloss. My lips really *are* chapped. I'm not *primping* for Matt.)

"Nervous about tomorrow night?" she asks mildly.

"No!" I quickly answer, wrapping my fingers around the elusive tube of lip balm near the bottom of my bag. "Why would I be nervous? I've done hundreds of these before."

She points out matter-of-factly, "You've been fluttering around since I got here."

"The movers we hired to deliver Matt's stuff were clumsy oafs. I was worried they'd broken something," I lie.

Her nod lets me off the hook, but I know she's skeptical of me. *I'm* skeptical of me. As a matter of fact, I'm sure everyone can see right through me. They know I'm not worried about a small-town art opening; they know I have all the details for the show in hand. The only thing I could possibly be uneasy about is the artist himself.

Kimi confirms my fears when she says too casually, her eyes on her magazine once more, "That Matt Benson's hawt. And his sculptures are bad-ass."

It would be odd not to acknowledge Matt's a good-looking guy—all of the female gallery employees have treated flirting like an Olympic sport when he's around—but I remain noncommittal when I say, "He's attractive. And his artwork is growing on me. It looks much better in person than in the pictures."

She laughs. "You don't like it?"

"I don't have to like it to promote it."

"Does he know you don't like it?"

I rub my earlobe and scan the front window to make sure the man himself isn't about to walk through the door. "Uh, I may have slipped and said something to that effect. But like I said, my opinion of it is irrelevant. Anyway, I'm pretty picky. Just because it's not my thing doesn't mean it's not good."

"Well, I think it's awesome. I wish I had a chance to tell him that… in private." She wiggles her eyebrows, her line of piercings doing something resembling "The Worm."

Tossing my lip balm into the bowels of my purse, I say lightly, "He'd probably like that."

"I doubt it," she mutters.

Before I can ask her what she means, I see Matt jaywalking toward the gallery. It's a chilly late-winter evening, but he's wearing no jacket, his hands jammed into his khaki pants pockets, his head bowed against the brisk wind that's fluttering the lower hem of his untucked dress shirt, the sleeves of which are rolled to mid-forearm.

Rushing through the door, he stomps his feet on the mat

and gives a self-deprecating laugh. "Leave it to the pseudo-scientist to disregard the effect of the sun—or lack thereof—on the temperature this time of year. I guess walking here from my office without a jacket after sunset wasn't very bright. No pun intended." He rubs his arms as he walks further into the shop, towards us. "It feels good in here, though."

"It does now," Kimi says with a smirk and a wink.

His grin falters, but he seems to catch himself after reassessing Kimi in her form-fitting, off-the-shoulder sweater. I see his eyes land on the cherry blossom tattoo that climbs her neck from her exposed shoulder to right behind her ear. I'm pleasantly surprised (and relieved) that their mutual attraction doesn't bother me any more than most overt exchanges as inappropriate as this one. See? I'm cool.

Since it *is* inappropriate for Kimi to be talking to him and looking at him like that, though, I pull his attention away from her with a subtle clearing of my throat and a bright smile. "You ready to see everything?" I ask, leading the way to the showroom.

"Yes!" He follows closely on my heels without as much as a backwards glance at Kimi. "This is exciting! I can't believe this is happ—"

When he abruptly stops talking after we enter the room with his displays, I turn to face him, my heart dropping, sure he's displeased with something. But as soon as I see his expression, I can tell *dis*pleasure is not the root of his speechlessness.

"You like?" I ask quietly, hesitant to interrupt the moment he's obviously having.

He swallows visibly and audibly before letting his jaw go slack. He turns in a circle to get a view of the entire room. Finally, he comes to a rest in his original stance and points to the banner on the facing wall, above his largest piece. "'Heavy Metal.' It's perfect. Did you come up with that?"

I nod eagerly. When I asked him about a week ago for a name for his collection, he laughed and said he'd never thought about trying to label his entire body of work. Then, after several awkward minutes on the phone, he admitted he couldn't think of anything and would have to get back to me.

"No pressure," I said, "but I need to get the information to the printer before they close tonight so they can have the banner ready in time." It was the one detail I'd let slip, and I felt bad, but, assuming he had a name in mind, I hadn't thought it would be a big deal.

An hour later, I received an email from him that said, *I'm blanking. Call it anything. Would "Untitled" work? I don't even care. Just name it something and surprise me. I trust you.*

Honestly, I picked the first thing that popped into my head. It seemed to work on more than one level, and I didn't have time to be choosy, so I called the printer and told them to use a dark blue, masculine font on a metallic gray background, and I called it good. I've been stressing about my impulsive, unilateral decisions ever since.

Beaming at him, I say, "I'm so glad you like it. I wasn't sure if you'd think it was corny, and I almost called you to clear it with you, but I really didn't have time. As it was, I only got in touch with someone at the printer because my contact there goes to my church, and I have her cell phone number."

"What a godsend."

Okay, so I guess I didn't have to worry about him disliking *corny*.

"How about the placements? This is what we discussed, but now that you see it in real life, what do you think?"

He shakes his head. "I can't think well at all. It looks great. This is unreal."

I love that he's not trying to play it cool and hide that he's overwhelmed by the experience of seeing his art all in one place, spot lit and on display for the general public. I put a supportive hand on his arm but quickly remove it when my fingers brush against his bare skin.

"You did it. This is happening," I assure him, trying to pretend I didn't touch him. I take a step to my right to put more space between us, but he follows, pulling me into a crushing hug that lifts me off the floor.

"Thank you!" he breathes against my hair before setting me down as quickly as he picked me up.

I'm not too caught in the moment to feel uncomfortable. He's already moved on, though, striding across the room to look more closely at the placards I had printed with each piece's name and story.

I smooth my hair and focus on breathing to get my heart to beat normally again. I try to block out the sensory memories that are trying to take root in my brain—the way he smelled (like fading aftershave and generic, office-grade hand soap) and the way his arms felt around me (warm and solid)—as I look through the archway toward the shop counter to see if Kimi witnessed what just happened. I'm oddly disappointed when I see she's still fixated on her magazine. I wish someone could confirm for me that I didn't imagine it. Then I shake it off and tell myself I'm, of course, relieved that no one saw something so *wrong*.

Well, maybe the hug wasn't wrong, but the way I felt in the middle of it sure was. Really wrong. I choke back guilty tears and breathe away the sudden nausea in the pit of my stomach as I think about Brice and twist my wedding ring on my finger.

Matt turns to me once more, flashing me the biggest, most amazing grin I've ever seen, but it almost immediately disappears. "Oh, my gosh. What's wrong? Are you okay?"

I nod rather unconvincingly, sniff, swallow, and take a deep breath. "Yes. Of course, I'm fine."

"You look horrible."

My laugh falls flat, but I manage to choke out a characteristically sarcastic, "Thanks."

"No, I mean— You look like you, I don't know, found out some really bad news. Or something."

Claiming a sudden headache, I wave off his concern and limp through the rest of the pre-show checks with him, but the whole time, I can't stop thinking, *I did find out some really bad news, the worst news: I'm an unfaithful, awful wife.*

*S*ilence meets my ear after I've finished pouring out the whole disgusting, sordid story to Jen and Mitzi on a three-way call from the gallery parking lot not two minutes after I've said goodbye to Matt, until tomorrow. At first, I think the call's been dropped, and I want to cry harder—in frustration—at the possibility of having to repeat any of my confession.

But when I check the line with a desperate, "Hello?" Jen responds by laughing. Hysterically.

"It's not funny!" Mitzi and I say together.

"Thank you, Mitzi," I mumble. "It's *not* funny," I repeat to Jen, who's trying to stifle her laughter but keeps emitting these little giggles that signify her mirth is just under the surface. "I feel like I cheated on Brice."

"Now, now," Mitzi soothes.

Jen lets loose with a more strongly worded, "Oh, for fuck's sake!"

"I *liked* it. I cheated in my heart."

"Listen, Jimmy Carter. Cut the bullshit, all right?" Jen demands, no trace of amusement in her voice anymore.

"A hunky guy hugged you, and your body did what bodies do, and it reacted. Big whoop. You didn't hug him back—"

"Well, I sort of did. I held on."

"Another reflex. It's not like you guys kissed or made out or— or had sex!"

"It's a slippery slope. A really slippery slope."

Mitzi speaks up. "Honey, I know you feel guilty because you have a teensy crush on this guy, but it wasn't your fault. He grabbed *you*, right?"

"Yeah, but when he let go, why didn't I speak up and tell him it was wrong for him to do that? Because I *liked* it. Because I was too busy trying to commit to memory how good it felt. I... I'm horrible!" I sob into the phone, covering my eyes and hoping nobody walking by can see well enough into my dark car to know what a wreck I am.

"She can't be reasoned with," Jen says, obviously for Mitzi's benefit. "If she wants to feel bad about it, then let her feel bad about it."

"I have to tell Brice," I whimper.

"NO!" is the overwhelming consensus from my two best friends.

"Uh-uh," Jen adds. "Do *not* do that."

"He deserves to know."

"Why? Do you hate him?"

"What?! No! I love him. And he deserves my honesty, since I can't give him faithfulness, apparently."

"Would *you* want to know?" Mitzi asks. Her quiet, calm tone gets my attention much more effectively than Jen's heated words.

I sniffle and answer immediately, "Yes."

"Really? Think about it."

"Yeah," Jen interjects. "Let's say Lucy—"

"Oh, my." I roll down my window an inch to get some air, since I suddenly feel faint, on top of feeling nauseated.

"Lucy gives Brice a hug in the office one day to thank him for... for visiting her mom in the hospital, and Brice gets a semi-, because, you know, he's a guy. And she smells good, and she's young and cute, and her gratitude makes him feel good."

"A semi?" I question, despite feeling sicker than ever and knowing I would probably rather not fully understand what she's saying.

"You know, a half-boner."

Mitzi sighs. "Jen, come on. This isn't helping."

"Please," I say faintly.

Jen ignores both of us. "Anyway, he immediately feels bad about it and shuts himself in his office for the rest of the day. Then he goes home and tells you what happened. And how he doesn't have *any* feelings like that for Lucy, but he had a physical reaction. And he didn't go any further than that, and he's disgusted with himself, but he felt you should know. How do you react to this information?"

"But I *do* have other feelings like that for Matt. Maybe."

"No, you don't."

"What if I do?"

"Have you pictured him in your head while having sex with Brice?"

"No! I mean, that's none of your business, but... No!"

"Then stop worrying. And think how you would feel if the tables were turned. It's useless, hurtful information. Unless you *want* to make him jealous."

I cry harder. "No. I don't want to do anything like that. I don't want to hurt him at all."

Mitzi coos, "Then you need to keep this to yourself. Trust us, sweetie. It's for the best. You're not going to pursue anything with this guy, and you're going to be extra-careful when you're around him from now on—"

"I never want to see him again!" It's mostly true. I don't. Because I don't trust myself. Even as traumatic as this has been, I'm afraid my "body will do what bodies do" again and betray me. And Brice. "I don't know how I'm going to get through the show tomorrow night. And what if he keeps coming into the shop? Or has another show?"

"Maybe you can tell Carrie he makes you uncomfortable, and you don't want to work with him anymore," Mitzi suggests.

"Then she'll know something happened."

"Nothing happened!" Jen explodes. "Listen to me, Half Pint. I know in your *Little House on the Prairie* world, this seems like something, but it was nothing. He gave you a thank-you hug. Period. You love Brice. You guys are solid. This guy just made you forget for a second that you're a pastor's wife. And you liked it. Cut yourself some slack."

"There's nothing wrong with being a pastor's wife," I reply sulkily.

"Who are you trying to convince?" she retorts. "Now go home to Brice and make *him* forget everything, including his name."

Mitzi giggles. "Yeah. Put those babies—and your worries—to bed. Then see to it that Brice doesn't even get past Genesis before he loses his train of thought."

They're right. I've somehow allowed myself to become distracted by a pretty set of teeth (*Nonono, don't think about those damn teeth!*) and have lost sight of the most important thing in my life, but that all ends now. It's been a long time since I've felt attraction for anyone other than Brice, and it was so foreign that it was scary. That's all. And that fear woke me up.

I'm awake. I'm refocused. I'm—what did Brice call me? —*magnificent.*

~

It wasn't easy at first. I had to give myself a major pep talk in the garage. But knowing that Brice was waiting for me inside, thinking he was going for his run as soon as I hit the door, motivated me to keep it short.

"Get ahold of yourself, woman. You're not just any pastor's wife. You're *that* pastor's wife. And he's a damn good one. And a good man. And a great husband and father. And he gives good hugs, too. *Better* hugs. So snap out of it. You dumbass."

After a final look in the rearview mirror to ensure I don't look like I had an emotional breakdown in a downtown parking lot, I take a deep breath, crunch the remaining pieces of peppermint Lifesaver between my back teeth, and enter the house through the kitchen.

As I suspected would be the case, the house is quiet, considering it's forty minutes past the boys' usual bedtime. I swallow down the guilt at not only missing their bedtime routine but... well, never mind. *I'm not thinking about that anymore*, I remind myself sternly.

Along with the silence, the smell of a hot, buttery skillet, melted cheese, and crunchy bacon greets me, as does the sight of Brice manning the spatula in shorts, a hoodie, and running shoes.

"Hey!" he greets me with a broad grin over his shoulder. "Perfect timing. I knew you had to be home any minute, since you hadn't called to say you'd be later, so I started making your sandwich, and... here you are!" He slides what appears to be one of his signature grilled cheese with tomato and bacon sandwiches onto a plate. "And here this is!"

I will not break down. It's only a sandwich. A beautiful, perfect sandwich made with love and timed so that it would be waiting for me when I came through the door, but… a sandwich.

That's when I notice something that makes my heart lurch even more. "Oh, that plate," I blurt.

He looks down at the plate in his hand. Wincing, he says, "Oops. Sorry. I guess I forgot to put it on the bottom of the stack after I washed the glue from it the other morning." He looks as if he's expecting me to blow up at him or flog him.

Before he can retrieve another dish and transfer the sandwich to it, I grab the cracked one from him. I take a quick bite of the sandwich, as if it commits me to using the damaged plate.

"It'll be fine," I say with a full mouth, realizing too late that I'm not at all hungry and that I'm not sure I'll be able to swallow this bite of sandwich, no matter how delicious it is.

He laughs at my antics. "Okay, then. Well, I'm going to squeeze in a run with Jared—"

The bread sticks in my throat, but I croak, "What? No!" before finally managing to swallow it with a cough. I set the plate onto the counter next to me and grab the sleeve of his hoodie. "Wait. I need to talk to you about something."

Oh, Lord. Why did those words come out? I don't need to talk at all. No talking.

He tilts his head and bites his lower lip, giving me a proud smile. "I remember that tomorrow is Mike's show."

I don't correct him on the name, because—frankly—I'm not sure I can say his real name without breaking down.

"That's why I need to go on this run with Jared. I told

him I'd meet him at the commuter lot down the street, so can it wait? I already had to cancel on him once this week when you were working late. And with mid-week Lenten services, Wednesdays are out."

Trying not to sound as frantic as I feel, I keep hold of his sleeve's cuff. "I know. You're busy. And I've been gone a lot this week, and I appreciate that you remember about the show, but that's not what I need to talk to you about."

"What is it?"

Yeah, Peyton. What is it, nimrod? Now you've done it. Think of something, quick! Something he'd be willing to forgo running for. You know what it is…

"Umm, I'd rather talk in the bedroom," I say coyly, remembering his aversion to lovemaking in other parts of the house, especially the kitchen. I wouldn't want to be accused of being "untoward."

He chuckles at me. "Oh-ho! Well…" I think I have him, but then he whines, "Honey, I really, really, really need to go on this run. I haven't run all week." He detaches my fingers from his sleeve and picks up my plate, thrusting it at me. "Here. You eat this while I go on a short jog with Jared. I'll come back, and we can… you know."

Realizing I'm assigning a sense of urgency to this that isn't natural or logical to someone who doesn't—and will hopefully never—have all the background information on the situation, I force myself to smile, nod, and acquiesce.

"Of course," I say quietly, accepting the sandwich from him once again. "I'll be waiting for you."

"I'll run really fast, knowing that," he says with a quick kiss to my forehead on his way out the door.

As soon as he's gone, I chuck the food into the trash and clean up the kitchen before deciding to take a hot bath and give myself a more prolonged pep talk.

11

STUFF OF NIGHTMARES

I promised I'd be waiting for him when he got back, so waiting I am, doing my best Eve impersonation, albeit under the covers in our bed. Granted, he's not holding up his end of the bargain (running really fast), or if he is, the distance he's running is canceling out his speed. Whichever the case may be, I've been waiting an hour now, and idle time is not my friend. Gives me way too much time to think.

In the past, on the night before an art opening, I'd relish the quiet alone time and use it to make lists of last-minute preps and day-of to-do's, but the last thing I want to think about right now is *his* show. Or him. At all. My brain is being typically contrary, though, and the longer I wait for Brice, the more often my thoughts wander to that damn hug.

I keep remembering new details about it. Like how he pressed his face into my hair. And how he muffled "Thank you" with his lips against my head. And how the muscles in his shoulders felt under my hands.

He felt so *different* than Brice. And I know it seems

obvious that it would be so, but they're built similarly, so I always imagined—not that I do that much imagining about it—that it wouldn't feel much different to be held by him. I guess I've been out of the game so long that I forgot that no two men are alike.

And maybe I've been blurring the two in my head. Maybe that's how I've allowed this to even happen.

Grrrr. What's taking Brice so long?

I check my phone for the umpteenth time, only to see that it's five minutes later than the last time I checked my phone, but there are no new calls or texts. Of course, there aren't. I've been holding the phone the whole time.

Now, I send him a flirty text to entice him: *"Hurry up, Rev Hot Stuff. You don't want me to start without you."*

Snuggling further under the covers, I close my eyes and will myself to think about Brice and nothing—or no one— else. I picture him jogging, his baggy shorts brushing against his inner thighs with each long, powerful stride. Sweat slowly slides from his hairline down the side of his face and neck, collecting in a wet patch at the base of his throat.

Once, when we were newlyweds, I cornered him after a run, before he could hit the shower, and I licked that spot. Up until then, he had been protesting my getting so close to him when he was sweaty and stinky, but he didn't stink. He smelled male and alive. He tasted even better. When I licked him, he finally stopped resisting.

It's been a long time since we've done anything that spontaneous. As soon as I hear him arrive home, I'm going to get up and block his way through the bathroom door, lick that spot, and show him that I can still be spontaneous, that I still love him and want him now as much as I did when we were first married. Yes. That's what I'll do. As soon as I hear him…

My phone wakes me.

"Shit, shit, double-shit!" I hiss, fumbling for the device, which has slipped from my grasp and lies somewhere in the bed clothes. Then I realize it's Mitzi's ring tone, so I stop my furious search. I don't want to talk to her. I want to make love to my husband. Well, really, I want to go to sleep, but I wouldn't mind taking a detour to a happy, happy place before then. Man! How did I fall asleep so quickly? What time is it?

The phone stops ringing as it goes to voicemail, but I wrap my hand around it and pull it close to my face. It takes several blinks for me to comprehend what the numbers are telling me. 10:23. 10:23? 10:23?! I sit up, remembering at the last second that I'm naked. I clutch the sheet to my chest and stare at the phone some more, trying to process what it means that it's 10:23, and I'm still alone in bed.

Oh, damn! He must have come home, saw me passed out, and took a shower before going downstairs to work or watch TV or something that wouldn't disturb me. Well, screw that!

I toss my phone onto the center of the bed and cross to the door, where I grab my bathrobe. As if in protest to being treated so roughly, the screen on my phone lights up, illuminating the bed. But it's just Mitzi calling me again.

Can't she take a hint? I'm sure she wants to check on me, make sure I'm okay after I've had a chance to calm down, but it's after 10:00. Nothing says "Something's up" like a call from your best friend at an odd hour.

"Leave a message!" I grumble while pulling open the bedroom door. "Sheesh."

I trot down the stairs, leaning over the railing on my way down. Brice isn't at his desk, and he's either watching the TV on mute, or he's not watching TV at all, because the house is silent. I round the newel post at the bottom of the stairs and notice there's no flickering light coming from the living room.

"Honey?" I call out loudly enough for him to hear me but still softly so as not to wake up the babies. No answer.

Hurrying through the empty living room, I go into the dark kitchen and stand, staring at the garage door. I yank it open to see both of our vehicles parked in their stalls, silent and cold. When I turn to reenter the house, my eye catches a glimpse of the edge of his woodshed through the window and across the backyard.

"Really?" I mutter, annoyed that I'm competing with hunks of wood and clumsy tools. But as soon as I open the back door, I can tell he's not out there. The padlock is secured on the shed's double door, and there's no light spilling from the small, uncovered windows on either side of the doors.

"What the…?" I trail off, reaching into my robe's pocket for my phone. I curse when I realize I left it upstairs on the bed. As I approach the stairs at a near-run, worry gripping my guts, I hear Mitzi calling me again. I immediately know something's wrong.

"Oh, no. Oh, no. No, no," I whisper, taking the steps two at a time, not caring how loud my footfalls are on the bare wood. In our room, I lunge for the bed, grappling with the phone, trying to pick up the call before it goes to voicemail.

"Hello?"

Nothing.

Damn it. I immediately hit the button to connect to the last caller and don't even have to suffer through a full ring before Mitzi picks up.

"Peyton. I've been trying to call you."

"What's wrong? What happened?"

Her voice shakes when she tells me, "There's been an accident."

I start to cry before she can even tell me what's happened, my mind immediately springing to worst-case scenarios. And if it was a worst-case scenario involving Jared, Mitzi wouldn't be calling me; Brice would. But Brice isn't calling me. While she says what I've already surmised, I struggle to breathe.

"It… It's Brice. He's hurt."

I fall against the bed but catch myself on the bouncy mattress. "H-hurt? H-how hurt?"

"Pretty bad, sweetie."

All I can do is blink at the wall directly across the room from me while she tells me something about our husbands jogging in the dark and crossing the street to get back to the commuter lot where Jared had parked his car. Brice was in a hurry, she said. He crossed the street after only looking one way and ran directly in front of a car driving without its lights on. The car hit him. Hard.

My voice is hollow when I say, "Is he… Is he…?" I can't make myself ask, one way or the other.

"He's alive. Oh, gosh! I thought I already said that. Oh, sweetie, I'm so sorry you thought maybe— Oh, geez! I'm not good at this. Yes, they think he's going to be okay. They just took him into surgery."

I nearly collapse as I take my first full breath since hearing Mitzi's voice. "Surgery?! Why am I just now hearing this?" Now that I can breathe, the oxygen is helping me process details, but I still don't understand what I'm being told. "This must have happened *hours* ago! Which hospital? I need to get to him. I have to wake up the boys, get in the car, and get to him. Now. Why didn't someone call me?"

"He told Jared not to call you right away. He said to wait."

"He was talking?"

"Yes. He stayed conscious right until they took him back."

"Oh, Mitzi. Oh, shit. Oh, Lord. Don't do this to me, Lord. Don't. I'm sorry. I'm so, so sorry!"

"I'm on my way to get you," Mitzi says calmly. "I'll call Marianne on the way and ask her to stay with the boys. Don't try to drive yourself to the hospital."

"I don't even know which one!" I sob. "I'm not dressed. Oh, Mitzi! What if he... he...?"

"He's going to be fine," she says firmly, finally sounding as confident as I need her to sound. "Get dressed. I'll be there in ten minutes."

The waiting was the worst. At least, it *was*. Until the wait was over. Now I've decided seeing whatever I'm about to see is a definite tie for worst. I'm shaking. But when Mitzi offered to come with me, the nurse gently vetoed that plan.

"Family only. And one at a time, until we move him to a private room."

Mitzi gave my hand a supportive squeeze and shot me a sweet smile. "It'll be fine. Jared said this"—she motions to her face—"looked okay."

Yes, Jared. Well, I have a bone to pick with him later, when I don't feel like I'm constantly on the verge of passing out. For now, I have to follow this nurse and pretend my legs don't feel like something one of the ladies from the LWML made for a potluck dessert. Then I have to smile and—no matter what he looks like—hold it together. No crying allowed.

I have to be strong, because this is about *him*, not me. He's the one in pain. He's the one who's been through a terrible ordeal, both physically and emotionally. He's the one who's waking up from surgery and won't be able to function normally for a long time.

The nurse doesn't even give me a chance to take a deep breath before pulling the curtain aside and saying quietly, "Someone's here to see you, Mr. Northam."

"Pastor," I correct, like it matters. Any distraction, no matter how inane, will do, apparently.

She looks down at his chart and laughs. "Oh. So I see. Reverend. Sorry about that."

He groggily replies, "Don't worry about it."

While she asks him about his pain level and if she can get him some water, she takes his vitals, and I take a minute to absorb what I'm seeing. Other than some slackness in his face, which I attribute to having recently woken up from the anesthesia, he looks about the same. There's a scrape on his forehead, near his temple. It's shiny, like it's covered with salve or liquid bandage. His hands are wrapped in white gauze bandages that resemble fingerless gloves. The third knuckle of his left middle finger is cut and raw. It has the same shiny, clear ointment on it as the scrape on his forehead.

My eyes travel downward. I'm somewhat prepared for what I see, because the doctor (or was it the surgeon?) came out and told me that the impact broke Brice's lower left leg in multiple places. That leg is now full of pins and is wrapped in a stabilizing cast that will have to be replaced by a harder plaster cast once the cuts and abrasions on that leg heal enough that there's a decreased risk of infection.

There are less visible injuries, too: a few broken ribs and toes, most notably, as well as road rash on body parts that dragged against the pavement when he finally hit the ground. Oh, and he has a partially reconstructed hip, although I also can't tell that from where I'm standing, mouth-breathing, while the nurse wraps up her ministrations.

She gives me a supportive smile and nods on her way past me. "I'll be right back with that water for you, hon," she tells Brice.

"Hey," he says to me when she leaves. His head flops back on his pillow, like it's too heavy and he's too exhausted to hold it up to talk to me.

I rush to his bedside and adjust the pillow to give his head and neck more support. "Are you hurting? I'm sorry; I didn't hear what you told the nurse. I'm sorry," I repeat.

He blinks and looks away. "No, as long as I don't move, I don't feel much of anything."

I search for somewhere safe to kiss him, but I can't seem to find anywhere. His hands are obviously in bad shape. The part of his forehead closest to me is gory. His lips are turned away from me, and they're trembling. Eventually, I settle for planting one on the cheekbone pointed in my direction.

Someone on the other side of the curtain across the way moans. A chime sounds in the distance, somewhere in the direction of the nurse's station I passed on my way in here.

He looks tortured as he turns his head to meet my eyes. My encouraging smile falters when I see the tears on his lower lids. He gulps and whispers, "I'm so sorry."

"What? Why?"

No, no, no. Don't cry. I can't hold it together if you cry.

All he can do is shake his head. I want to hug his head to my chest, but I imagine every muscle in his body hurts.

Finally, I decide I can't put him in much more pain that he's already in, so I give into the urge and wrap my arms around his neck, leaning into him, careful not to move anything below his shoulders. I kiss the top of his head, inhaling the faint smell of dried blood, antiseptic soap, and his sweat, which still lingers in his hair.

"Don't be sorry," I tell him, fighting to keep my voice steady. "There's nothing to be sorry about. You're okay."

"No. I was stupid. And careless."

"My text to you was stupid and careless. That driver was stupid and careless. Please, don't upset yourself."

My heart knocks against my breastbone. *This* is what gets my adrenal glands pumping. Not violence, not danger. Fierce protectiveness of a different sort. I don't want him to blame himself. I don't want him to suffer any guilty anguish. Or fear. I'm afraid enough for the both of us.

"I hate that I'm putting you through this," he says when I let go enough to smooth his hair and separate his head from my chest so he can't hear my frantic heartbeat.

"I'll gladly go through this, as opposed to... something worse. I'm just glad you're okay."

Oh, gosh. I can't even think about the alternative without hyperventilating.

"But I'm not okay. Look at me!"

I take a step away from the bed to do as he says. "You look pretty good to me. I'm amazed you're still in one piece."

Abruptly, his voice full of trepidation, he asks, "Are the boys here?"

"No, they're home with Marianne."

"Oh, good," he says on a breath, catching his lower lip in his teeth when he becomes emotional again. After he recovers, he explains, "I don't want them to see me like this."

I tilt my head. "Oh, hon. They're babies. They don't—"

"No. They know this isn't normal. They know their dad, and this isn't him."

Deciding to table that argument for a time when he's not overwhelmed and weepy and half-drugged, I ask in a mock-scold, my throat aching with pent-up tears, "So, why did you make Jared wait to call anyone until after you were in surgery? If I hadn't fallen asleep waiting for you to get home, I would have been worried sick, wondering where you were."

He blots his eyes on the back of one of his bandaged hands. "You didn't need to hear what was going on."

"Yes, I did. I'm your wife. Remember?"

"It was bad. I was— I wish I had passed out. I wished at the time it was happening that I could either stay quiet or lose consciousness, but I didn't have any control. And I was worried about you. I... I didn't know what was going to happen. I didn't want that to be your last memory of me."

I suck in a sob. "Oh."

He reaches for my hand, curling his fingers around mine. "I made Jared promise to wait until there was no way you'd be able to hear or see me that way."

"He should have disobeyed you."

After kissing my fingers, he clears his throat and gives me a knowing look through his eyelashes. "Don't be mad at him and hold this against him for the rest of his life. He was honoring a dying man's wishes. At least, it felt like I was dying."

"If you had—" I can't finish. "Anyway!" I say overly brightly. "Where'd that nurse go? I thought she was getting you some water. And when are you going to be moved to a room?"

He pushes his head into his pillow and closes his eyes. "I don't know," he says wearily. "I'm so tired."

I don't want to leave him, but I'm afraid I *have* to. I can't keep it together much longer.

I kiss the tip of his nose. "Rest for a few minutes. I'll hunt down that nurse and get some answers. And your water."

After I find a place to fall to pieces.

At his weak nod, I push through the curtain and stand on the other side, pressing my hand so hard against my mouth that I can feel my teeth making impressions on the inside of my lips.

I don't deserve him. I know this. Everybody knows it. Most importantly, *God* knows it.

Message received.

12

COOLING OFF

"So you'll be okay? I only have to be gone for a few minutes. Jen might even be here before I get back. But we're completely out of diapers—I don't know how I let that happen!"

Brice waves at me from his "command center" in front of the TV. "We'll be fine. The boys are napping. I've peed. I have the remote and my phone. And if I do have to get up for some reason, it's not a biggie. I can do it." He taps the walker next to his chair. "As a matter of fact, I might go for a walk around the block."

"Don't you dare."

"I'm kidding! I would never leave the boys home alone. Now, go." He tosses a snack-sized packet of pistachios at me. They hit me in my butt when I turn defensively away from him.

"Okay. I'm going." First, though, I pick up the nuts and toss them on the TV tray next to his chair. "There. You might want those."

He rolls his eyes. "The only thing I really want isn't happening for a few more weeks." Grabbing my wrist before I walk toward the kitchen, he pulls on my arm. I work hard to maintain my balance so I don't fall into his lap or knock against his cast. I brace my free hand on the arm of the chair, leaning down for the kiss he's obviously angling for.

"You're bad," I tell him. "And you need to be more careful." I press my lips against his, anyway, to reward his carelessness.

It's been three weeks since his accident, and everything is mending remarkably well, but I still feel like he's so fragile, despite his hardly ever complaining about the pain. As a matter of fact, he hasn't shown any weakness since his emotional revelations in the recovery room.

Not that his statements were a sign of weakness. They were, as it turns out, a sign of the effects really strong drugs can have on one's mental state. And from what I can tell, based on numerous conversations since then, he doesn't remember a word of what he said.

Not a word.

The next time he woke up, we were in his private room, and when he saw me sitting next to his bed, he visibly flinched before grinning—and wincing—and saying, "Hey. I, uh, had a little accident." Then he asked me when I'd gotten there. And he asked about the boys.

Gently, I asked, "Don't you remember talking to me in the recovery room?"

He laughed, cringed again at the pain in his ribs, and replied, "What recovery room? This is the first time I've been awake since surgery and the first time I've seen you since I left the house to run… into a car. I meant to do that, by the way."

I glossed over the details of our post-op conversation, merely telling him we talked, to which he matter-of-factly responded, "Don't remember a thing about that. Did I say anything funny?"

I told him no, that we were simply happy to see each other, and left it at that. I knew I wouldn't be able to repeat what he'd said without blubbering like a pysch ward escapee. He's seen me do enough of that in the past. During this entire ordeal, I've been determined to be strong, upbeat, and un-blubbery. At least, around him (I don't care what the walls in the shower think of me).

And he's made it easy, for the most part. He's been the perfect patient, other than trying to do too much too soon. But even his physical therapists have encouraged that with their obvious admiration of his recovery work ethic. In one breath, they'll tell him to take his time, but in the next, they'll cheer him on for being able to do something most patients with his injuries still haven't mastered weeks later than him. And he soaks it up like an approval-starved puppy in obedience classes.

"You should see who's in charge of the church while I'm out of commission," he said the other day to a perky therapist named Jacie. "You'd be trying to recover in double-time, too."

He has a point there. So far, nothing major has happened, but we all know it's only a matter of time before Jared and/or Wes run up against something way over their heads. If it didn't affect my life, I'd be waiting with gleeful anticipation to see what it is. It *will* affect my life, though, so I dread the backlash.

I stand straight and adjust my purse on my shoulder. "Okay, then. I'll be right back."

"You already gave that speech."

"Right. Leaving." I know the garage door won't even be fully closed before he'll be on the phone to Jared or Wes or

Lucy or Ben or one of the elders, trying to catch up on what's going on at the church. He's been virtually cut off, ordered to relax and focus on healing, and it's driving him slightly batty.

We've had a rotation of friends and family members helping us with the boys while I take Brice to physical therapy and doctors and specialists in the mornings. Mary was with us for the first two weeks. Then my mom came to stay. And now Jen's about to arrive for a week's visit. They also help out in the afternoons, while I'm at work, since we can't afford for me to take any more time off without pay. But I go straight to work, then come straight home. No detours, no errands, no staying late... for anything. Or anyone.

Obviously, I missed Matt's show in March, considering it was the day after Brice's accident. I've delegated all responsibility related to him to Kimi, who was more than happy to take over for me. She didn't have to do much, anyway, other than show up the night of the opening, answer a few questions for the newspaper, and make sure Matt was happy with how everything went. I think she enjoys making Matt happy.

And he hasn't sought out my advice or company at all, other than to drop me an email to thank me for my hard work on the show and to express his hopes for Brice's speedy recovery. I'm beginning to stop tensing every time the bell rings on the shop door.

As I hustle through the automatic doors at the grocery store, the internal stopwatch in my head tells me I have ten minutes, tops, to get what I need in here and get back to the house. I don't care how much my husband insists he can be alone or if he craves the solitude. I'm terrified something else is going to happen to him. What, I don't know. But I never imagined he'd be mown down by one of this town's godforsaken, infernal idiot drivers, either.

"Diapers, wipes, tampons, chocolate…" I mutter to myself as I make a beeline for the diaper aisle. "Oh, and eggs. Eggs, eggs, eggs." Easter wiped out our supply, and I promised Brice I'd make him some brownies. "Brownie mix," I add to the growing list.

I have most of the items I need when I round the corner into the baking aisle, the buzzer going off in my head, telling me it's way past time for me to check out and get home. I'm praying I don't run into anyone from church. I'm actually shocked it hasn't happened yet. It's a personal record.

Then who should I see studying the dessert kits… but Matt Benson?

"Oh, fuck," I blurt, killing any chance of him turning and leaving the aisle without seeing me.

He glances up, then back at the shelf of cake mixes, then quickly at me again.

Don't smile. Don't do it, you sexy bastard.

"Hey! How's it going?" The corners of his mouth inch upwards, and I have to fight the instinct to turn on my heel and run away from him.

"Fine," I say, coming to a stop with my cart between us and facing the shelf, pretending my profane greeting had to do with the store being out of the brand of brownies I wanted. "How are you?"

"Great! Better than great. Awesome."

I refuse to look at him. I can hear the smile, which is bad enough. I don't need to see it or its cute, accompanying dimple. "That's good. I'm glad."

He edges closer to me, coming around my cart so that he's standing next to the handle. I will myself to hold my ground, because stepping away would seem strange—and possibly rude—but I'm fully prepared to bolt if he makes a move to touch me. There will be no more inappropriate contact, as long as I have something to say about it.

I'm also tempted to keep my eyes averted from him and somehow pose myself so that I'm shielding the contents of my cart from his view, but I do neither unnatural thing. Rather, I try not to care about the economy-sized box of tampons on top of the mountain of diapers as I turn both my body and my head and steel myself to face the teeth.

He punishes my socially acceptable behavior with a mega-watt grin. Yep, they're as pretty as I remember.

"How's your husband doing?" he inquires. "I felt so awful when I got to the gallery for my show and Carrie told me what had happened. What a miracle he's okay, though!"

I grip the handle of my shopping cart with both hands so they can't betray me by doing something coquettish like tucking my hair behind my ear or fiddling with my necklace (*Which was a gift from Brice on our first Christmas as a married couple*, I remind myself sternly).

"Yes. He's doing really well, considering."

That's it. I've reached my limit on visual exposure to his annoyingly handsome, friendly face. It's disarming me, and we can't have that.

I return my attention to the store shelf, grab a package of standard brownie mix, then quickly exchange it for the deluxe, gooey fudge-filled kind. *Brice deserves the top-of-the-line brownies. Brice. Let's talk more about him. Let's keep him as the focus of this conversation, a reminder to both of us.*

"He's home right now," I state, "probably doing a bunch of stuff he's not supposed to be doing."

Matt laughs. "One of those, huh? Can't sit still?"

"He's going stir crazy. I told him I'd bake him some of

these if he stopped trying to rush his recovery." I drop the brownies in the cart and resume my death grip on the basket.

"Do you think that's going to work?"

"No." We both laugh at that. My giggle is pathetically nervous and over the top. I want to use my grocery cart handle to jab myself in the ovaries.

Trying to steer things to even less personal territory, I say, "Sorry I had to kind of drop you at work, but I take it Kimi's been taking good care of you?"

"She's very attentive," he replies enigmatically, suddenly becoming the eye-avoider in this encounter.

I immediately decide not to ask him what he means. Nothing good can come from that, surely. If she's attending to his *every* need, I don't want to know. If she's merely offering that service, and he doesn't appreciate it, my knowing about it only obligates me to do something about it, and I don't want to get in the middle of anything like that. No. I'm going to take his words at face value, as a testament to her commitment to client-centered service, and move on.

"Good." *The word of the day, children, is "good." It's a good word, because it has a way of politely ending uncomfortable conversations. And manners are important.* "Uh, I'm glad your show went well. And I noticed the other day that we've sold a few pieces."

The smile that faded when I replied so shortly to his comment about Kimi returns full-force. "Yeah! I mean, the show would have been better if you'd been there. But I totally understand why you weren't there. You know what I mean, though. You put a lot of hard work into it and didn't get to see the result."

I'm not subtle about digging my phone from my purse to

glance at the time while I respond dismissively, "It's fine. It wasn't about my work; it was about yours."

"But we had a great showing, thanks to your marketing and publicity efforts."

Keeping my phone in my hand, I smile tightly. "It was really no big deal. Your show wasn't my first rodeo, ya know?" As if it's a gift from above, my phone chimes to alert me to a new text message. I nearly cry from the giddiness the distraction produces. "Oh!" I quickly read it, not caring how rude it is to do so in the middle of our conversation. It's from Jen.

I'm at your house. What side of driveway should I park?

"A houseguest I'm expecting," I tell him. I quickly tap back, *Left. I'll be home soon.*

He takes a deep breath. "Oh. Well, I should let you go, then. It's— it's been really good to see you!" He reaches out for my arm, but I pull it away. The move is subtle, yet the message is clear.

Since I can't honestly return his sentiment, I simply smile and nod. "Yeah."

"I'm glad your husband's okay, or at least well enough to be giving you a hard time and requesting junk food." He side-steps away. "I'll, uh, see you around. I guess."

"Yeah."

I mean, no; I hope not.

If I weren't so rattled after seeing Matt at the grocery store, the scene that greets me when I open the door from the garage to the kitchen would crack me up. Brice and Jen are standing in the kitchen, facing each other. Brice has one hand lightly on his walker, and he appears to be demonstrating a lateral leg lift, showing off the range of motion with his new(ish) hip. When I come through the door, he freezes, leg in midair, eyes wide, as if he's been caught putting the moves on my best friend.

Jen, not knowing he has anything to feel guilty about, glances at me and says, "Look at this guy! Can you believe he can do this already? I'm telling you what, he's a walking advertisement for clean living. And milk."

I hoist my grocery bags onto the counter island and reply drolly, "Yes. But he's a horrible listener."

He drops his leg and bends it at the knee so his cast doesn't drag on the floor. "Jen was my spotter," he defends himself. "And if it wasn't for this stupid broken leg and my dumb ribs, I'd be walking with a cane by now. And back to work. It's not like you caught me in here doing my exercises alone." His eyes flicker to Jen.

She catches his pleading expression and innocently bats her eyelashes at me.

I sigh. "He was in here doing this alone when you got here, wasn't he?"

"You don't have to answer that," Brice says to my friend with a mischievous twinkle in his eyes. "We shouldn't put you in the middle of things. That's awkward. Forgive us."

I laugh in spite of my frustration, but I do say while putting away the groceries, "Fine. Fall down and die. Or whatever."

"I'm not going to die!" He hop/scoots over to me and gets as close as his walker will allow. Letting go of the metal frame, he uses the edge of the counter for support, then grabs me from behind and puts his chin on my shoulder. "Don't be mad at me. I'm going crazy here. Oh! Brownies!"

"Not that you held up your end of the bargain."

"But I'm trying. I'm being as good as I can be. For every time I give into the urge, I've resisted it twenty other times."

"This is starting to sound like something you'd hear in the confessional booth," Jen mutters.

"Wrong denomination," he and I say together and laugh.

"We're getting predictable," I tell him, turning my head and smooching his cheek.

"I like it." He lets go of me and cruises along the counter to get back to his walker. "So, you gonna make me those brownies?"

"Of course," I reply in a defeated tone. I quickly flash him a smile so he knows I'm not upset with him.

I love his determination. I've been as proud of each of his recovery milestones as I've been with our boys' developmental skills. I'm so glad he's alive and healing and happy that I'd make brownies for him every day while standing barefoot on hot coals and listening to "Feliz Navidad" on a loop.

Just thinking about how much I love him and how close I came to losing him forever requires me to sniff back tears.

"Are you *crying* over there?" Jen demands to know, as if it would be the most heinous crime in the world.

"What? No!" I deny, keeping my back to both of them and pretending to read the instructions on the brownies kit. I blink rapidly and inject sunshine into my voice. "Why would I be crying?"

"That was going to be my next question," she answers.

"Well, I'm not. See?" I turn to face her, confident that all signs of my errant emotions have disappeared.

Brice looks back and forth between the two of us. "What's wrong with crying?"

"Nothing!" Jen and I say in unison.

"Okay." He hobbles from the kitchen and returns to the living room.

As soon as he leaves, I hiss at her, "Stop calling me out in front of him."

"What?" she whispers back. "I wasn't. What the hell are you talking about?"

While pulling from the cupboards the baking pan, mixing bowl, and measuring cups, I say quietly, "I don't want to cry in front of him."

"You said you weren't."

"I was lying. A little. Just a little. I was crying a little."

"How much?"

"Shut up. I was having a moment, if that's all right with you."

"It's fine with me. Why isn't it okay with you?"

"He doesn't need me to be all weepy."

"He seems okay with his and other people's emotions."

"Well, I'm not going to burden him with mine, for once. He has enough to deal with. He has cabin fever, and he's still in a considerable amount of pain—"

"He's in a good mood today. Is that unusual?"

"No."

"I think you need to chill out."

I scowl at her while cracking the eggs into the mixing bowl and pouring the dry mix on top of them. I retrieve the vegetable oil from the cabinet above the stove and drop in the required amount, then collect some water in the same measuring cup and pour it on everything else.

As I pull a whisk and a rubber spatula from the wide, flat utensil drawer in the kitchen island, she contends, "He probably wouldn't be so bored if you'd let him walk around his own house."

I say nothing to that. I don't want him to overhear us in

here talking about him. Instead, I busy myself whisking the brownies, greasing the pan, and pouring the rich, chocolatey goo into it, spreading it with the rubber spatula to make it smooth and even. After I've scraped every last bit of batter from the sides of the bowl, I hold out the spatula to Jen, who, hugging the decorative wooden column on the corner of the island with one arm and peeking around it at me, takes the utensil without hesitation and begins licking it.

While I'm sliding the glass baking dish into the oven, I hear Brice turn on the TV in the adjacent room, so I feel safe to say as I close the oven door, set the timer, and turn to face Jen once more, "I ran into Matt. At the store."

"Oh, dear," she says, sounding unimpressed, continuing to lick at the batter. "I'm sure you made that as awkward as possible."

"I had tampons in my cart."

"Crap. Now, he knows you have a period."

I laugh. "Shut up! That's not what I'm worried about."

"What *are* you worried about? Did he come onto you in the cereal aisle? Are you so irresistible?"

Taking the licked-clean spatula from her, I place it and the mixing bowl in the sink, filling the bowl with soapy water and tossing the whisk in. With a kitchen towel, I swipe at a smudge of fudge in the corner of her mouth. "Okay, I get it. I'm being stupid."

"Not 'stupid,' really." She grabs the towel from me to clean her own face. "I was thinking more along the lines of 'arrogant' or even 'silly.' But 'stupid' would work in a pinch."

I do just that to her upper arm, which is discouragingly firm.

"Ow!"

"I know guys throw themselves at you all the time, but—"

She tosses her head back and gasps at the ceiling. "Where did you get that idea? And if that's the case, please direct me to these invisible men."

"You know what I mean. You've always been the party girl, the flirt, the popular one."

"Maybe ten years ago. But P, we're too old for stuff like that now, don't you think?" She's suddenly serious, looking intently at the towel she twists between her fingers.

I consider her question before answering, "I know *I* am, but I'm married and have three kids and have no choice. You're still young and single and free."

"And alone. And too old for most of the decent single guys out there who don't have the baggage of an ex-wife and a brood of kids. I don't want a ready-made family." She looks up at me and grins playfully. "Plus, all my friends keep moving to this podunk town called Springfield, Missouri. After they marry pastors. I don't have anyone to go clubbing with me anymore."

"You miss the Trippin' Trio," I state softly and mock-sympathetically.

"So help me, God, Peyton, if you don't stop calling us that…"

I pull her roughly away from the column and against me in a silly hug. "Now, see? You'd make a wonderful pastor's wife. You asked for God's help and everything!"

The thought of her married to a pastor and dealing with all that it entails, including the varied personalities of congregation members, makes me chortle, which turns into a giggle, which morphs into full-fledged belly laughs. I let go of her, bend at the waist, and lean against the counter. She joins in, better containing her mirth but shaking with the chuckles next to me.

When we recover, she says, "I don't know. That Pastor Anthony dude is kind of dark and mysterious and smexy."

I stare at her, dumbfounded, for a moment, until she smirks at me and says, "You know, smart and sexy. Anyway, just kidding. Of course."

"Of course," I raise one eyebrow. "You had me going there for a second."

"Gotcha."

From the other room, Brice calls, "Yo! How much longer on those brownies?"

13

RECOVERING

*I*t took some begging on his part, but I've taken Jen's observations to heart, and I know she's right about my anxieties getting in the way of Brice's full recovery, so in addition to placing an extra walker at the top of the stairs for when he can attempt climbing and descending alone, I've agreed to accompany him outside the house. Tomorrow, he's going to return to church for the first time since the accident (as an observer, not to work). And this afternoon, he and I are taking a halting walk around the neighborhood.

It's a beautiful, sunny spring day, the smell of blooming flowers and new grass swirling around us in the breeze.

Brice squints and grins into the sun. "How long before Jen sends us a mayday call?"

I try to pretend like I'm not clenched and ready for disaster with each hop-step he takes next to me when I reply, "She'll be fine. She's at Mitzi and Jared's. They'll help her out. The biggest challenge will be getting them all strapped into their car seats when it's time to come home."

He inhales deeply. "This is so nice. I needed this."

"I know. I'm sorry I've been so controlling."

"You're scared. And I understand it's hard to trust my judgment, since I ran out in front of a car to get this way." Smiling over at me, he adds, "But I can do this. I need to do this. Every day."

"Okay."

"As soon as this frame comes off my leg, I'll be able to do a lot more. I'm pretty worried about bumping it on things right now. It still hurts quite a bit."

I can only imagine what it's like to have pins and bolts *inside* my leg as well as connecting an apparatus on the outside of my leg to the inside. I try not to imagine it, as a matter of fact. It makes me queasy and weak.

"Just a few more weeks," I say, encouragingly.

He wiggles his eyebrows. "Trust me, I'm counting down those weeks for a lot more than that."

I clear my throat. "Yeah. Well. Let's not allow that to distract you again."

Churlishly, he replies, "I don't have much else to think about."

"Think about healing and— and being alive and—"

"I have. I am."

"That's all you need to worry about right now."

"Hmmm."

We walk without saying anything for a while. He seems to be concentrating on every move, making sure he's using the proper motions, watching out for potential tripping hazards. I encourage his caution and attention to detail, ready to catch him at the first sign of a stumble.

When we get to the end of the block, he stops to catch his breath. "Stupidly out of shape," he grumbles at himself. He lifts one of his hands from the walker frame to hold his side. Sucking in, he grits his teeth and holds his breath, his eyes squeezed shut.

"Are you okay?" I check.

"Fine," he says on his exhale. "Stitch in my side."

"Let's turn back."

"In a second."

So that I'm not staring at him and making him feel self-conscious, I look around at the blooming dogwoods in the neighborhood and enjoy the feeling of the sun warming my hair.

Less out of breath, he asks, "Are *you* okay?"

I quickly turn my attention to his face and say, "Yeah. What do you mean? I'm fine."

He purses his lips and chuckles. "Real convincing."

"I'm not the one with half the left side of my body in pieces."

"I'm not talking about physically. I mean, you've been *different* lately."

"Almost losing your husband will do that." I lean in for a kiss.

He pulls his head back. "Is that all?"

"All?! Yeah. And I'd say that's plenty." My second attempt at a kiss fails, so I quit trying. Feeling rejected, I put my hands in my jacket pockets and step away from him, on the edge of the curb.

He returns both hands to the walker but doesn't continue our walk. Instead, he stares at his knuckles and states, "I'm worried about you."

"You never worry."

"I am now. Worrying. Just a tad."

"Why? I'm fine. Better than fine. Tired, maybe. Worried about *you* and wanting to make sure you have what you need to recover, but I'm really okay." I put my hand on his arm. His muscles flex under my touch.

"You were crying yesterday. In the kitchen. When you came home from the store."

His gentle tone makes me feel okay admitting it, although I qualify, "I didn't really cry. I just got choked up. I'm so thankful that you're still around. And proud of you for being so strong."

"Why do you try to hide it, then?"

"I don't! I'll tell anyone who hasn't started avoiding me, because they're sick of hearing me brag about you."

"No. I mean, why do you hide your crying from me?"

"It was one time."

"Peyton. It's been more than one time. I've heard you in the shower. And other times, when you think I can't hear you. What's wrong?" He wraps his hand around my fingers and squeezes. "You can tell me. I won't get upset. It's more upsetting to know you feel you can't let go in front of me. We've always been able to laugh and cry together."

I sniff and in a no-nonsense tone explain, "I don't want to be a cry baby, when you're the one going through so much, but you know, it's an emotional time. It's hard to see you like this, even though you're doing so well. I worry that I'm not doing a good job of supporting you."

"You're not crying about… something else?"

"What else would make me emotional right now?"

He shrugs and avoids my eye contact. "I don't know. That's why I'm asking. I'm not sure why you'd cry at all, really. I'm fine. Going crazy without being able to work, but fine. You, on the other hand, seem far away."

"I have a lot on my mind," I say truthfully. "But I'm right here. For you."

"I know."

I tug on his shirt sleeve. "Come on. Let's go home."

He signals his acquiescence by turning the clunky walker to face the opposite direction. "Can I have brownies for dinner?"

"Sure. With a side of chicken and broccoli and rice."

He sighs. "No fun. What happened to the rebel I married?"

I know he's half-joking, but that means he's also half-serious. Part of me thinks she was run over by the same car that hit him. Pancaked. Ground into the pavement. Gone for good.

I shouldn't be worried or scared or—as is the latest—annoyed. I shouldn't be any of those negative things. I should only be feeling relief and gratitude and joy. That's what everyone else seems to be feeling today.

We've been surrounded since we entered the church building this morning. Brice has been hugged, kissed, fussed over, and cried on. He's returned their hugs, allayed their worries, and wiped their tears. He's answered every question, often multiple times. He's smiled and laughed and made jokes about everything from the extra hole in his rear —from his hip surgery—to road rash to remembering the rules you learned in kindergarten about looking both ways before crossing the street.

I know everyone's happy to see him, and I've been so thankful to them for respecting his need for peace and quiet for the past month, while he's recuperated in the hospital and at home, but I wish they'd all back off a bit. It's not like I haven't been keeping people informed. I've been at church nearly every Sunday since the accident, and I've answered all of their sometimes-intrusive questions.

Today, they're making it sound as though I've shut them out. I've had to bite my tongue several times to stop myself from saying, "I told you that, [fill in the blank]!" And why do they need to know the name of his pain medications, anyway?

Since the conversations are only making me mad, I've stopped listening. I have my hands full with the kids, in any case. Five month olds are not patient when they're ready for lunch and naps, which means Brooks is restless, and even Harris is beginning to break out his cranky squeaks.

Jen has control of Max—in a way. He was quiet and still during church, but now that it's over, he's full of pent-up energy. While the crowd continues to gather around Brice, she chases Max up and down the center aisle. He squeals when she gets close to catching him, so she falls back a few steps and pretends he's too fast for her.

I hope I'm sending Brice a strong enough hint when I strap the babies into their double stroller and inch my way toward the exit.

Jen catches my drift. "Yo, Max-Man. Time to go home. Your mom's leaving without us."

That brings the two-year-old running. "Coming, Mommy!"

Brice glances at me, but he's still surrounded by at least ten people. He shoots me a helpless reply with only his eyes.

My eyes convey, *I'm over this,* while I flash a tight smile.

As Brice starts to make extricating statements, Pastor Anthony emerges from the vestry and approaches Jen and me.

"You're quite a natural with children," he says quietly to Jen with a smile that looks rusty but sincere. For the first time, I notice he has laugh lines around his eyes. *How does someone so young get those if he never smiles or laughs?*

She snorts at his observation. "I have no idea what I'm doing. But Max likes me anyway."

"He understands you're trying."

With a skeptical look, she says, "He's two."

Pastor chuckles. "You're right; he probably likes you *because* you don't know what you're doing. My nieces and nephews are the same way with me. They know they can get away with murder when I'm in charge."

"Murder, Pastor?"

"Figuratively speaking, obviously."

Brice's conversations this morning may be tiring, but this one is decidedly fascinating, so I continue to tune in while pretending to fuss over the twins.

Jen picks up Max. "I have to admit, I do spoil this one."

"He's easy to indulge," Pastor concedes and pardons in one sentence. He chucks Max under the chin and is rewarded with a grin and Max's outstretched arms. "We're buddies, aren't we?" he asks the toddler.

"Buddy," Max confirms. "Candy."

Pastor laughs (who *is* this guy?) and puts his hand lightly over Max's mouth. "We should probably keep that on the sly," he mutters from the corner of his mouth.

I stare openly at him now. He catches my gaze and smiles sheepishly. "Uh. It's never been a lot of candy. Just a few M&Ms from the dish on my desk."

"It's okay," I mumble, not giving two craps about the secret candy exchange. I'm sure Brice was there, anyway, and kept the consumption under control. To explain my staring, I say carefully, "I didn't realize you and Max were friends."

He hands Max over to Jen and shoves his hands in his

pockets. "Ah. Yes. Well. It took him a while to warm up to me, but I'm sure the candy helped."

Said every pervert in the history of pervs.

Not that I think he's a perv. I don't. I don't know why that even popped into my head. But smiling and laughing and being nice to kids seems so out of character. He's usually so somber. Not unfriendly. But not a cuddly candy distributor, for sure. He's actually more like the guy who turns out to be a serial killer, and all his neighbors say, when interviewed, "He seemed to be a nice guy. Kept to himself. Never caused any trouble." Other than with the seven bodies covered in lyme in his crawlspace.

Brice, suddenly at my elbow, interrupts my unkind musings. "Ready to go?"

I blush, as if everyone may have been able to hear my thoughts. "Um, yes. I am. Have been. Sorry I couldn't rescue you, but the people demand to know your showering strategies."

He laughs. "Yes. That was an odd question, but you know, I guess the information will come in handy if Mrs. Whitney ever has hip surgery. It's possible. She's getting up there."

I marvel at his ability to put the best construction on everything but shake my head and smile. "Sure. Anyway."

"Where are Jared and Mitzi?" he asks, looking around the sanctuary.

"They left right after the service to do hospital rounds," I tell him, trying to keep my tone neutral.

The truth is, I find it hard to hide that I envy Mitzi her ability to so fully immerse herself in this lifestyle. She's been a bona fide pastor's wife for all of two months, and she's already better at it than I am. Not that I'm surprised. She's inherently good-hearted and doesn't have to work as hard at it as some of us do. But witnessing her seamless transition still makes me feel like I'm lacking a requirement for this job that I'll never have.

Brice nods at my answer and says to Pastor, "Great sermon today."

If "terrifying" is "great," then yes, he hit the mark. Of course, it's a good thing he's willing to preach about Hell and the heavier things, since Brice practically refuses to do so. And Jared. Nobody would take seriously a sermon from him about the wages of unrepentant sin. He's never been able to deliver bad news, anyway.

Pastor bows his head humbly. "Thank you. I meant it for Lent, but after your accident, our preaching rotations became a bit jumbled, so I had to improvise."

"Sorry about that," Brice says with a grin. "The consequences of my stupidity are far wider-reaching than I'd have imagined."

"Not at all! I only meant..."

"It's okay." Brice chortles. "Really."

"We praise God you're okay. And we're ready to have you back."

"I'm ready to *be* back. "I miss this place. And everyone in it. Even you, Wes."

They share a quiet laugh about that before shaking hands and saying their goodbyes. Pastor gives me a slight wave, but he makes a special point to say goodbye to Jen.

"It was good to see you again, Jennifer. Safe travels back to Chicago."

Darned if she doesn't blush and stumble over her own goodbye.

"Good night!" I call over my shoulder at Kimi, still laughing at an observation she made about a new stock of designer notepads we received today: "They look like someone stood over them, crying, letting her mascara drip in random patterns on each page." She's right, too. They do look like that. And they'll sell. People love crap like that. I mean, art. Art like that.

The smile hasn't yet faded from my face as I turn the corner to enter the lot where my vehicle is parked. The light above it flickers on for the night, spotlighting an unwelcome person, like something from a cheesy, poorly written stage play.

Matt hops down from the hood of his car, which is backed into the spot right next to mine.

My first thought is that he's been waiting out here for my shift to end so that he can speak to Kimi about whatever they may need to discuss without my being there. Surely after our encounter last week in the grocery store, he's picked up on my discomfort around him. He's an intuitive guy. The unanswered emails he sent me earlier this week would dispel any remaining doubts.

But when he stays between my car and me, it becomes clear he's not waiting for the end of my shift; he's waiting for me. And that's weird. And puts me on my guard.

I stop several steps away, cringing at a gust of chilly April night wind. "Hello," I begin the exchange, anxious to get to the bottom of what's happening.

"Hey," he replies, shuffling his feet and shooting me a nervous half-smile. "Do you have a minute to talk?"

"Not really." I inject a hint of regret so I don't sound like the biggest bitch on the planet. Then I add for good measure, "They're waiting for me at home."

He keeps his distance, leaning against his car, pushing his hands in his pockets, pinning his eyes to his feet, and taking a deep breath. "I'm making you uncomfortable. Again."

For some reason, I feel the need to deny this. "No. Why would I feel uncomfortable?"

"This was a mistake," he states, not really answering my question. He looks around, seemingly glad when he verifies we're the only people hanging out in this parking lot, and the building next to us is shielding us from sight.

This behavior sets off major alarm bells in my head. My intuition is suddenly buzzing, trying to tell me to get out of here. I clench my keys between my fingers, ready to use them as weapons to poke out his pretty gray eyes, if necessary.

I laugh nervously. "I can't really disagree or agree, since I don't know what 'this' is." I wish my pounding heart would shut up so I could better hear myself think.

He looks up sharply. "I wanted to talk to you about something that's been on my mind."

"Okay." My mouth dries out like someone's just poured an entire can of powdered cocoa into it.

"I often advise my clients to speak face-to-face with people when they need to address something between them, but I may have to rethink that in the future. Now that I've actually done it myself, I realize it can be confrontational. And creepy."

"Yes. And yes." At this point, he would know I'm obviously lying if I keep trying to convince him I think this situation is perfectly normal, so I give up the charade.

He smiles broadly. "I knew it. I'm sorry."

For the first time since seeing him, I take a full breath, but I don't move any closer to him. "So, what's going on? Is something wrong?"

"You tell me."

"I don't understand."

"'Obtuse' isn't really your thing, but if you insist, I'll spell it out."

"I really have to get going," I say, changing my mind about hearing him out and stepping toward my car before he can say any more. The lights blink and the alarm system chirps as the doors unlock when I hit the button on my key fob.

"I don't like guessing or putting words in your mouth, but here goes," he says in a rush, coming around the back of my car and standing next to me. "I think I crossed the line last month when I hugged you the day before my show opening."

He doesn't do anything to stop me from opening my car door, getting in, and driving away, but I find myself turning to face him, anyway, my left shoulder against the driver's door.

He must read the affirmation in my eyes, because although I say nothing to confirm this, he says, "I'm sorry."

"It's not a big deal," I tell him what I've been trying to tell myself for weeks. "You were excited. I was there. You hugged me. Your way of saying thank you. That's all."

"Do you really believe that?" His expression tells me he wants me to say no.

My stomach feels like a mass of writhing worms when I answer, "Yes."

His shoulders slump. He takes a step back. "Oh. Okay. Because I— I get the feeling you've been avoiding me." He chuckles mirthlessly at himself. "I mean, I *know* you have been, since you haven't answered my emails or—"

"My husband was hit by a car, Matt. I've been slightly busy."

"Yeah, but I could tell by the way you acted in the store last week that you were uncomfortable around me. You were even more awkward than usual. Which I think is adorable, by the way." He edges closer and drops his voice. "There's a lot about you that I find adorable. And sexy. And amazing."

My heart hammers like it's going to explode at any second. "Matt, I'm marr—"

"Yeah, I know."

Cutting me off to say something so blasé infuriates me. Suddenly, I'm enraged by this entire situation. "Do you? Do you *really* know? Because in that case, all of this is even more inexcusable!"

"I know. I'm sorry."

"You know, but to Hell with it?"

"No."

"That's the message I'm getting. 'I know you're married, but I'm going to make you say no anyway. Because maybe you won't. Maybe you'll give in. Because you miss your wilder days.' Is that what you think?"

"No, I—"

"That I'm some pathetic pastor's wife who's been waiting for someone like you to come along and pay some attention to me, to make me feel young and wild again? To smile at me and flatter me and make me forget I have a husband and three kids at home?" I yank open my door and toss my purse across to the passenger seat. "Screw you!"

"It's not like that."

"Well, only a jerk would admit to it after being called out on it," I spat.

He galls me even more by laughing. "No. Really. I respect that you're married."

"This conversation implies the opposite."

"And I don't think any of those things about you. Maybe you think those things about yourself."

"Excuse me?!"

His hands fly up in front of his chest. "Just a theory."

"You can take your theories and shove them up your—"

"Okay, okay. I didn't come here to insult you. I came here to— I... I wanted to clear the air. That's all."

He holds the top of my door so that even if I were to get in, I'd have to risk injuring him to close it. So I stand there, assuming my most mulish, discouraging expression, the one I usually reserve for the likes of Pastor Long.

"Peyton, I can't stop thinking about you."

Oh, man. I'm going to puke.

I swallow down the bile. "Stop."

"I can't!"

"No, I mean stop talking. Just stop." I quickly get into my car, prepared to slam his fingers in the door if he doesn't have the sense to back off.

But he inserts his entire arm into my car and grabs my forearm. Not roughly, not aggressively, not threateningly. Just a gentle, warm cuff.

"Quit touching me."

"I will. But I need to know you understand. I love you."

"Have you lost your fucking mind?" I blurt, then answer for him, "You have. You're not right. You're crazy."

"I'm perfectly sane. Well, as sane as someone can be when they're in love."

I shake off his hand. "That's not a good enough explanation. You're *not* sane. A sane person doesn't fall in love with someone after only knowing them for two months, especially considering we've barely interacted, other than by phone and email. We've met in person less than half a dozen times!"

"So? I feel like I know you. Like I've known you my whole life!"

I refuse to admit I've often felt the same way, regarding the familiarity. I don't want him to think we feel the same way about anything.

He doesn't give me the chance to say anything, anyway, because he rushes on, obviously knowing he's running out of time, that I'm seconds away from calling for help or macing him or calling 911.

"When I held you that night before the show... Didn't you feel that? I felt it. It felt..." He blushes. "Well, it felt amazing. Like you were always meant to be in my arms. I didn't want to let you go. And I know love at first sight is corny, but I guess I'm corny, because I honestly think I fell in love with you the first time I saw you. So it doesn't matter that we haven't known each other long or been around each other much. Because all it took was the first time."

There's ice in my voice when I say, "You need to let me

leave right now." He compliantly steps away, but before I close the door, I beseech him in something that sounds more like a groan than a word, "Why?"

He looks bemused by the question. "Why do I love you?"

"No. No. Please, don't say anything else about that. I mean, why did you tell me this? What am I supposed to do with this information?"

He shrugs but, looking tortured, holds my eye contact. "I don't know. I guess I thought you needed to know. Plus, I can't keep it to myself anymore."

"Tell your therapist."

"I don't have one."

"You should."

I slam the door, put the key in the ignition, and start the car. I'm disappointed when the further from the gallery I drive, I feel no closer to a solution to this problem.

∾

"You have to tell Brice."

"What?!"

"You have to tell him."

Stunned, I stare at my friend. We've been whispering in the master bathroom since I got home twenty minutes ago. I gave her an oddly unemotional account of what happened in the parking lot—at this point, I don't even know what the appropriate emotions would be—while she stood with her mouth agape throughout the entire story. And now she's telling me the exact opposite of what she advised after the hug.

"But before, you said—"

"That's when all that had happened was an ambiguous hug. This… this is major."

"But what's Brice going to do about it?"

He's been decidedly testier this week, with Jen as a witness, than in previous weeks since the accident. I'm not sure what's behind it, because he hasn't been talkative. My number one theory is that he's annoyed with Jen in general. Or not her, but more accurately, she and I together.

I was hesitant to take her up on her offer to come help us, because I know how he feels about the way the two of us are when we get together, but she had that tone of voice that indicated she would have been crushed if I'd turned her down. And she does love Max to pieces and is a huge help as an extra pair of hands with the twins.

So I've been careful not to let her good-natured needling push me to say or do things that irritate Brice or lead him to believe I agree with her that our life is lame or that we're goody-goodies. But that's not as easy as it seems. And maybe I'm not doing as good a job as I think I have been.

Pushing all those thoughts aside and dealing with the problem at hand, I ask Jen, "How am I going to explain not telling him about the hug weeks ago?"

"Yeah, that might be awkward. Just leave the hug part out."

"How the heck do I do that?"

She taps her lips. Finally, she says, "I don't know. Do I have to think of everything?"

I sigh. "No." Now the tears push through. "I should have told him when this whole thing started. I should have—"

"Just tell him the truth. About everything," she says, backtracking on her earlier counsel to leave out the part about the hug. "He hugged you; you tried to act like nothing happened; he sought you out and confessed his undying love for you."

"It wasn't like that. This isn't a Jane Austen novel."

"How did you feel when he told you he loved you?"

"I was disgusted." When she looks unconvinced, I say, "Really! I felt sick to my stomach."

Ironically enough, it's the only part of the whole thing I feel good about. It's one thing to have silly daydreams about a person, but it's quite another when he's seriously professing sentiments I can't, won't, and don't return.

"I don't feel that way about him. I knew it as soon as he said those words to me."

Jen smiles and folds me in a hug, rubbing my back. "Aw, P. I'm proud of you."

"You are?" I whimper.

"Yes. I am. You were strong. You didn't back down from your feelings. You told him the way it is, the way it has to be, the way you *want* it to be, and you didn't worry what he would think of you for saying it."

I dab at my eyes. "You're right."

"I know I am." She pushes me away and holds me at arms' length, looking down into my face. "Now, you have to tell Brice."

"Awww…" I whine.

"The man made a move. A serious move. That's something you and your husband need to face together." She laughs when I bite at my fingernails. "C'mon. It's Brice. What are you expecting? He'll be supportive. He's not going to go all caveman on you and knock down the guy's door. As a matter of fact, tell him now, while he's in no physical condition to do anything in the heat of the moment."

When I continue to bite at my lips and grunt uncertainly, she offers, "I'll stay with the kids tonight, so you guys can go out somewhere and have a private conversation."

"No," I say, immediately rejecting the idea. "Not tonight."

"Why not? Get it over with."

"No. I'm still trying to believe it happened. *I'm* still too mad about it. If I tell him tonight, I'll wind up crying, and he won't care that he only has fifty-percent use of his body and is a man of God who can't act like a Neanderthal and has to have respect for all human life. I need to be calm when I tell him. And I can't be calm about it tonight."

"So you think you can pull off acting completely normal —or what passes for normal in your world—until you can tell him without losing it?"

I jut out my chin. "Yeah!"

She laughs and mutters, "This oughta be interesting," as she opens the bathroom door and motions for me to exit ahead of her. "After you."

"Promise you won't say anything."

With her hand to her chest, she pulls back her head and says indignantly, "Me? I'm not saying a word."

"No snide remarks under your breath. No meaningful looks. Nothing."

"Would you like me to wear a bag over my head?"

"Maybe."

"Peyton, trust me. I don't want to be around when this conversation takes place. That's why I tried to get you out of the house tonight."

"I'll wait until you leave on Saturday, then," I say, walking past her into my bedroom. I glance at myself in the mirror on the dresser, relieved my outward appearance doesn't resemble the wreck I am on the inside. I can do this.

My resolve wavers a tad when Jen and I enter the living

room to find Brice buried in sleeping babies on the couch. Keeping someone so sweet and trusting in the dark seems more than questionable; it seems downright cruel.

At first, I think he's asleep, too, but when we pause to look down at them, he opens his eyes and whispers, "Help."

Jen and I rush forward to relieve him of Brooks and Harris, leaving two sweaty patches on his t-shirt, one in the center of his chest, the other on his left side. He shakes his arm as soon as it's free and pulls his t-shirt away from his body to provide some ventilation.

"Two hot boxes," he murmurs.

Max nestles more firmly into his dad's other side, against the back of the couch. Suddenly, his hand shoots up and lands on Brice's face. Jen stifles a snort while Brice blinks but casually moves his son's hand to a more convenient position. Max moans, smacks his lips, and bangs his heel between Brice's legs.

"Uhn!" Brice grunts when his defensive reflexes bring his legs up, and his leg frame jars against the couch cushions. "Mother Hubbard, that hurts like a sunbeam!" he growls, his eyes squeezed shut.

Jen runs from the room, ostensibly to avoid laughing in his face at his pain, but we can hear her giggling all the way up the stairs. I stay by his side, feeling helpless with my arms full of baby and not sure what I would be able to do to ease his suffering, even if I had both hands free.

"Did he kick you where it counts?"

Brice shakes his head. "Missed, barely." He opens his eyes and looks sideways at me, grimacing. "His aim isn't as good as yours. But my leg! Aghhhh! And my hip!"

I laugh at his allusion to *The Nutcracker Seduction*, relieved that he feels well enough to joke. "Oh, hon. Let me put Harris to bed, and I'll be right back. Okay?"

He nods, his eyes still clamped closed. On my way back downstairs, I pass Jen on her way up, carrying Max. "Ugh. This one's a lot heavier."

"You want me to take him?"

"No, I think you'd better get to your husband. He's not looking so hot."

I rush to the living room and kneel next to the couch. "What did you damage? Or re-hurt? Can I get you anything? Pain pills, water?"

"Shh! It hurts more when you're talking."

I know exactly what he means, so I don't take it personally. I remember, before my epidural with the twins, every word that came from his mouth sent shockwaves through my body, like my ears were hardwired to the nerves in my back and abdomen.

But his excitement prompted him to verbalize everything. "I should have eaten more than that granola bar for breakfast." "Are you thirsty? I'm thirsty." "I wonder what that button over there does. Better not push it, huh?" "It's a bit warm in here, don't you think?"

Finally, no longer caring if I sounded like a laboring woman cliché, I said through clenched teeth, "If you can't be quiet, please go out to the waiting room with our parents."

He'd looked heartbroken for a second or two, but he quickly recovered with a sheepish, "Sorry. I'm nervous."

"I know. I don't mean to be mean, but you're annoying me."

That made him laugh, pull out his journal, and settle into the chair next to my bed. "'Nuff said. I'll sit over here and keep my lips zipped."

"Thanks."

Now I take a page from his book. There will be plenty

of time later to determine if he re-injured himself. I go into the small powder room opposite the stairs and wet a washcloth with cool water. Returning to the sofa, I kneel next to it and swab Brice's sweaty forehead with the cloth. He jerks his head away.

Hissing through his teeth at the pain in his hip, he gingerly sits up and inspects the sites where the pins enter his leg. I look away, too squeamish to participate in the post-trauma evaluation.

He mumbles, "Looks fine. Just hurts. I can't wait to get this stupid thing off!"

"A few more weeks," I encourage for what feels like the hundredth time.

I help him swing his legs over the side of the couch. He leans back, sighing with relief as he situates his upper and lower body at a 130-degree angle to each other.

"Okay," he whispers, probably more to himself than to me. "I'm okay. It's okay."

His profuse reassurances scare me, but I remain quiet.

After a few minutes, he moves to rise from the couch.

I jump to my feet. "What do you need? I'll get it. Water, pain meds?"

He resolutely shakes his head and stands. "I've got it. I need to do things for myself."

"Normally, yes. But you're hurt."

He snorts ruefully, grabbing his walker on his way to the kitchen. "I've been hurt for a month. And I'm sick of it. I can't even hold my kids."

I stare after him, gripping the wet washcloth as I sit back on my heels. I listen to him crashing around in the kitchen, opening a cupboard to get a glass, then another cupboard to get his prescription painkillers. Both cabinets close in quick succession with loud bangs.

I slowly follow him as far as the kitchen entryway and stand there, watching him power down the pills and water.

"Be patient with yourself," I say quietly. "You're doing so well. Everyone says so."

With exaggerated calm, he sets his glass in the sink and stares through the window into the backyard. After a long pause, he says, "They don't see me struggling to do the most basic of things every day. They don't have to feel the pain every time I do something as simple as sitting or standing."

"It's not simple, though. It's stuff we all take for granted, but it's *not* simple."

His back still to me, he says in a controlled voice, "I don't need you to coddle me."

"I'm not!"

"You baby me more than you do the boys."

The accusation knocks the wind out of me. Eventually, I manage to reply, "Oh. So now I'm a bad mom, too?"

He jerkily turns to face me. "That's not what I said!"

"Just what you meant."

"No."

Summoning my inner robot, I say coldly, "Whatever. At the risk of babying you, we should get you upstairs before that medication kicks in. Unless you'd rather stay down here, on the couch, tonight."

It's the lamest bluff I've ever dealt, not to mention it's cruel to suggest he sleep anywhere less comfortable than his own bed, so when he asks, "Do you want me to stay down here?" I immediately fold and answer, "No. Of course not."

"Because I might as well, I guess."

I roll my eyes. "Don't be a dumbass."

He hobbles toward me. "My butt *is* dumb. And it hurts. And I'm sick of being an invalid with houseguests babysitting me." When he arrives at the doorway, he finds he can't fit past me. "Excuse me, please."

I keep the way blocked so I can tell him, "I need people's help. *We* need people's help. It's hard enough keeping track of three babies, but when I have to take care of you, too—"

"Because I'm just another helpless infant?"

I refuse to acknowledge his self-pity. Instead, I remind him, "This is only temporary."

He looks away from me, over my shoulder and into the living room. "I know that. Do you?"

Before I can answer, he takes advantage of my limp stance and pushes past me. I stumble backwards but quickly regain my balance by grabbing onto the molding around the doorway, bending back one of my fingernails in the process.

I know better than to utter a single protesting "Ouch."

15

LIES AND MISCONCEPTIONS

Someone's not as proud about accepting help when
he needs a shower before his morning occupational therapy appointment. Having settled him under the
stream with the instructions to text me when he needs help
getting down the stairs, I pad into the kitchen to find Jen,
already seated at the kitchen table, curled over a cup of
coffee.

"Awkward!" she trills.

I'd laugh if I weren't so annoyed at the entire situation.
Coldly, I say, "Sorry. He insisted on sleeping on the couch
last night. He didn't want me to help him up the stairs."

"You could have mentioned that before I went to bed.
What happened?"

"Just a little argument," I answer vaguely.

"Really? Everything seemed okay last night after I came
back down here: he worked at his desk while you and I
watched that awful Lifetime movie—when are we gonna
learn, anyway?"

"It was the Hallmark channel."

I can feel her glare through my back while I pour my

coffee and supervise my bagel's toasting progress. "Whatever. My point is, I wasn't expecting him to sit up on the couch as I was walking through the living room this morning, picking a wedgie. I about pissed my pants."

Picturing it, I snort into my coffee mug but quickly sober when I remember what led to his sleeping arrangements. I tell her what I told myself over and over again as I lay in bed alone last night: "He's losing patience with his recovery."

I retrieve the cream cheese from the fridge and focus all my attention on spreading it on my warm bagel.

"I left you guys alone for fifteen minutes, tops," she recalls.

"Apparently, that was long enough for me to get on his nerves. I hover too much—which I already know, but I can't help it—and he was in too much pain last night to be diplomatic while expressing his frustration about it." I join Jen at the table.

She smirks at me. "Wow. Didn't know he had it in him to be so blunt."

"He's a normal person."

"No, he's not," she says with a laugh, then reconsiders. "Well, he's a normal person from a time when people were a lot more polite than they are now. Rude is the new normal. And he's never rude."

"That's a sad commentary on modern society," I grumble, knowing I'm a lot more a part of the "new" normal than I am Brice's brand of it.

"In any case, he must have been pushed pretty far to be so upfront."

"Yes. I dared to offer to get him a glass of water and his pain pills."

Looking down into her coffee cup, she says, "Oh. So, I

guess now's not the time to tell him about... you know... since he's so prickly."

"Definitely not," I concur. Just the thought of it makes my insides jiggle. "I can't wait too long to tell him, though. I mean—"

"Tell me what?"

I actually feel my face fade to the color of the cream cheese on my bagel when I turn my head to see Brice entering the room.

In addition to appearing neat and clean-shaven, he looks emotionless as I fumble for an answer and finally settle on the question, "How'd you get down here by yourself?"

He replies vaguely, "I managed. What are you waiting to tell me?" He stands at the island counter and looks expectantly at me. When I drink my coffee to stall, scalding my tongue in the process, he raises his eyebrows at Jen, who jumps from the table.

"Better get dressed before the boys wake up," she says unhelpfully, practically running from the room. Not that I blame her. I don't expect her to get in the middle of this or —worse—lie for me.

As soon as she's gone, and we can hear her footsteps overhead, he says bluntly, "Out with it."

Before I even know I'm going to lie, I blurt, "My period is late."

The transformation to his countenance is remarkable. The skin around his eyes relaxes, his jaw unclenches, his mouth falls open, and he tilts his head. "Really?" he says at a near-whisper.

Since the lie and his reaction bring on a fierce wave of self-loathing, I don't give him a chance to do the math or myself a chance to get in any deeper. "No. Not really."

He blinks rapidly. His lips whiten. "What the funnel cake, Peyton?"

"I panicked! I'm sorry. It was the first thing that popped into my head."

"The first thing wouldn't be the truth, for Heaven's sake." Visibly disgusted, he turns away from me and busies himself preparing a bowl of cereal and pouring a cup of coffee. When I stand to help him carry everything to the table, he snaps, "Don't bother. I'll eat standing up, right here."

"Don't be mad at me, please. And sit down to eat."

His reply is to remain exactly where he is, leaning over the kitchen island like an uncouth, sulky teenager.

"I need to tell you something, but now's not the right time," I say to the top of his head. He gives me no signal he's listening, but I say anyway, "It's not important, it's just something you have the right to know. But it makes no difference to your life. Or my life, even. Well, kind of. But not really."

Without looking up, he pauses his cereal shoveling to ask, "Why bring it up, then? So I can have it hanging over my head? So I can wonder what it is?"

"I didn't bring it up; you overheard me talking about it to Jen."

He throws his spoon into his bowl, causing milk to splatter into his face. He flinches and blinks, straightens, and swipes at the droplets with his sleeve. "That's right; Jen knows. But I don't. Even though I deserve to know, according to you. I just don't deserve to know right now?"

"*This* is why I'm afraid to tell you!" I cry, blinking at the tears that always threaten when I know he's not happy with me.

Pointing his finger at me, he bellows, "Don't cry! Don't

you dare cry about this! *I'm* the one being kept in the dark about something. So you're not allowed to cry." Momentarily, he loses his balance but catches himself before I even have time to gasp at the idea of him falling. "Darn it," he mutters, frustrated.

"Are you okay?"

He shakes his head and chuckles mirthlessly. "Oh, my goodness. What a question."

"I mean, physically."

"Don't worry about it."

"But I do!"

"I wish you'd worry more about *this*." He taps his chest. "Because if you did, you'd stop being so clinical. You wouldn't believe that something could affect your life and not affect mine. You'd tell me *everything*. You'd tell me the truth. And you'd trust that I could handle it." Leaving his breakfast dishes on the counter, he scoot-hops to the garage door. "Please let Jen know I'm ready to go to therapy."

"But—"

"I want Jen to take me."

His walker doesn't allow for dramatic exits, but he painstakingly maneuvers himself so he can open the door to the garage. At the top of the three small steps, he tosses his walker to the concrete floor below and demonstrates—to some extent—how he "managed" to get down the stairs after his shower.

After Brice and Jen left for Brice's physical therapy appointment, I tried to be strong for the boys. That lasted all of ten minutes. Even Max wasn't convinced I was really crying over the episode of Sesame Street that was playing, like I tried to tell him. "Sometimes Elmo makes me sad" makes no sense to a two-year-old (or any other reasonable person). Lies are all I have, though. I'm glad the twins aren't old enough for me to lie to them about anything.

I've just settled everyone down on the floor for some playtime when the doorbell rings.

"Naturally," I hiss under my breath, jumping up and practically running to the powder room to make myself semi-presentable. As soon as I look in the mirror, I know it's not possible in the amount of time I have to answer the door, get rid of the person, and get back to the kids.

My chagrin deepens when I look through the peephole to see a fidgeting Pastor Anthony. I swing the door open to him and try to pretend like everything's normal. If nothing else, I hope he'll take my behavior as a cue to ignore my appearance.

"Pastor," I greet him neutrally. "Come in."

He blushes. "Oh. Peyton. I, uh, was expecting someone else."

Leading him into the house, I state dully, "Brice is at the occupational therapist." Upon reaching the living room, I'm relieved to see the boys are exactly where I left them, for once.

I sit on the floor among them and smile weakly up at the young pastor. That's when I notice *his* appearance. I've been so wrapped up in myself that I didn't notice how he's dressed: jeans, casual brown shoes, and an un-tucked, dark blue button-up shirt. NOT a pastor shirt. No clerical collar. This is *not* a professional visit.

Immediately, I'm wrong-footed. "Uh, sit down. Please. I mean, you don't have to, but you should. If it will make you more comfortable."

He accepts my invitation, perching on the front edge of the couch cushions. Max runs up to him. "Candy!"

Pastor laughs and returns Max's hug. "Not with me. Sorry."

"Um, Brice is at occupational therapy," I repeat. "Which I already said, didn't I? The boys and I are hanging out."

"I see that. I expected someone else to be hanging out with the boys." Again, his cheeks redden. "Jennifer," he clarifies when I simply stare at him.

"Oh!" I blush, too, for some reason. His color deepens. At this rate, the living room will be on fire in sixty seconds.

He manages a tight laugh. "Yes. 'Oh.' I'm sorry. I didn't mean to make you uncomfortable. See, I thought you'd be at the doctor with Brice... er, Pastor Northam... and I'd drop by to see Jennifer before she goes back to Chicago. You know, a social visit."

"Of course."

Of course, there's no "of course" about it, but it seems a much more appropriate reply than, *"For reals?! You and Jen?! Hahahahahahahahaha!"*

Since Pastor doesn't have candy, Max quickly loses interest in his company and goes back to playing with his favorite wooden car on the floor. Brooks and Harris continue to do their best blob impersonations, although every once in a while, they kick and grasp at each other, as if they're still in the womb. Not for the first time, I wonder if they remember that time or if those memories have already faded. I'm sure I could look it up somewhere, if I weren't too lazy.

While I'm scrambling for anything else to say, Pastor turns his head to the side, narrows his eyes, and asks, "Are you okay? I feel like, maybe, I'm intruding on something."

I sniffle and give him a self-deprecating smile. "What gives you that idea?"

"Elmo make Mommy sad!" Max explains from his side of the room.

At my mock-sober nod, Pastor says, "I see. Do you want to talk about what Elmo's done to upset you?"

My first instinct is to shut him out, but I surprise myself by saying, "Oh, he's just so stinking honest. And right all the time. Well, not all the time, but most of the time. And even when he's being a meanie, he's justified. At least, more justified than I am."

We both glance at Max, who seems to be ignoring us, but Pastor continues with, "People like Elmo can be difficult to live with."

"But I *love* Elmo. Don't get me wrong."

"That goes without saying."

I pick at the rug. "I don't want to badmouth him. I probably shouldn't say any more."

Pastor sits back further into the couch cushions and rests his ankle on his knee. "I won't tell anyone. And I won't think less of either of you."

"How can you not? Maybe you don't think less of people after they tell you personal things, but you think differently of them, for sure."

He shakes his head and says solemnly, "No, I don't. It's hard to explain."

"Brice says the same thing," I state. "I've never understood how it's possible. I thought he was the only person on the planet who could do that, though."

"He's not as odd as you think, maybe," he says with a wry smile.

"Is it something you learn at Seminary?"

He coughs. "Um, no. I mean, there's no course for it. It's

something you train yourself to do. Or not, rather. It's about not judging."

I sigh. "Well, I stink at that."

Now he doesn't bother hiding his laugh. "Like I said, it's a state of mind one cultivates. An attitude, for lack of a better way of putting it."

I look up miserably from my study of the carpeting. "Wes—Can I call you Wes?"

"Absolutely."

I plunge on before I lose my nerve. "What if someone told you they loved you? Like *love* loved you. Someone who's not supposed to love you. Or at least, they're not supposed to admit it or act on it."

He blinks rapidly, and his posture becomes rigid. His foot slips off his knee, his shoe hitting the floor with a thump. Following what looks like a painful swallow, he croaks, "Is this hypothetical?"

I want to answer positively. Based on his reaction, even he's having trouble conjuring the attitude of non-judgment he was seconds ago so proud of having cultivated. I shake my head, my eyes filling again.

He stands. "I should go."

I rise with him. "No. Please, don't. Don't look at me like that. It's not my fault. It was the hug's fault. I didn't *want* it to happen."

"Probably not, but…" He edges toward the entryway.

"You have to believe me." The panicked look on his face makes me feel sick and ashamed all over again, like I'm standing in that parking lot with Matt. "Oh, gosh. If this is how *you're* reacting, how am I ever going to tell"—I peek nervously at Max—"Elmo?"

"You should *not* tell Elmo," he says loudly and adamantly. "No. Definitely not."

"But he already knows I'm hiding something. And he has the right to know, right?"

He shakes his head, his face mint green. "Uh-uh. No. You should pray about this. And discourage such thoughts. And you should never, ever tell Elmo about these feelings. They're wrong."

"I know they are! I *have* discouraged them. But I don't have any control over them!"

"Yes, you do. You most certainly do."

Confused, I ask, "How? I've already said I don't approve of the feelings."

"That's a start. Listen. Hey. I, uh, really have to go. I shouldn't be here." He fumbles behind him for the front door, but it's still several feet away, which he sees when he glances over his shoulder. He closes the distance and grips the doorknob as if his life depends on it.

Mortified that I told him so much about Matt and that he so obviously disapproves, probably thinking I asked for it, that I led Matt on (Did I? Perhaps I did...), I blather, "I'm sorry. I'm so sorry. I shouldn't have told you this. It puts you in an awkward position, but you said— Never mind. Just pretend I never said anything."

"Oh, I'm going to try."

"Thank you." I wish he could give me a more definite promise, but I'll take what I can get. "And I'll tell Jen you—"

"No! Please. Don't. It's probably best if nobody knows I was here."

I don't understand the need to go *that* far. "But—"

He finally manages to turn the doorknob and pull the door open. "Really. Don't tell them I was here. Please. You should forget it, too."

"What? Hang on!"

"No. I'm leaving."

I follow him as far as the front porch, but I can't leave the house with the boys inside, unattended. "Wes!"

"You should call me 'Pastor,' now that I think about it," he says at the bottom of the porch steps.

"Wait! What's the ma—"

"Goodbye!"

He practically dives into his generic-looking gray sedan. His tires squeal on the street as he shifts from reverse to drive and stomps on the gas.

"Be careful!" I implore him at a normal volume, as if I'm putting it out in the universe, since I know he can't hear me. I stare at his brake lights as he comes to a rolling stop at the sign at the end of the street before speeding off again.

What the heck is the matter with him? From the look on his face, you'd think he was personally involved in what I was telling him. As a matter of fact, he looked like I *felt* when Matt told me he—

No. He couldn't. He doesn't.

I close my eyes and grip the door frame for support.

I replay our conversation in my head, wanting to smack myself for being so ambiguous. Just one word, "him" or "his," would have made things so much clearer. But I don't think I used it. I think I only said "feelings," making it sound like they could be anyone's feelings, including mine. For whom?

I bang my forehead against the wooden jamb when I realize who he must think I meant.

I'd cry, but I'm fresh out of tears this morning.

16

CONFESSION

I feel like I've been jumping from one unsavory situation to another all day. By the time Brice and Jen returned home from therapy, I barely had time to say hi and bye to them in the same breath as I headed out the door for work. At work, I held my breath all day—at least that's how it felt—praying that Matt wouldn't come in and force another uncomfortable conversation. Now that work is over, I can't even savor the relief that he didn't show up, because I'm headed home to a talk I can no longer put off with Brice. I still haven't decided how much I'm going to tell him, but I'm running out of time to plan it. I'm going to have to do what feels right and pray for the best.

And—oh, yeah—I have to tell him that our assistant pastor thinks I'm in love with him.

After Wes left, my two attempts to call him failed—and obviously only served to make him think I was obsessed with him, because when I called the third time, hoping to leave him a voicemail to explain myself, a curt recorded message told me the caller was unavailable and didn't give me the option of leaving a message. I've never had my number blocked before today. So many lovely firsts.

That means that even at this hour, Wes Anthony is laboring under the misapprehension that I harbor a forbidden desire for him.

Actually, that thought makes me laugh out loud in my dark car as I turn onto our street. I don't think I'll ever run out of ways to humiliate myself and those around me.

I'm no sooner through the door into the kitchen than Jen is pressing Brice's Jeep keys into my hand and pushing me back out.

"I can't stand another minute with you two like this," she says. "You guys are going out, to talk."

"Can't I kiss my kids goodnight?"

"No. You can kiss them later."

"Where's Brice?"

"I'll bring him out to the garage in a second. He's using the bathroom."

"Seriously? Can I—"

"No." She pushes more insistently on me when I try to get past her. "If you guys don't clear the air, it's going to be weird and uncomfortable tomorrow night when Jared and Mitzi and the Pryces come over to hang out." She grabs my coat sleeve to hold me in place.

"Let go of me!" I say through gritted teeth. I hear the powder room toilet flush on the other side of the kitchen wall.

"No. Wait for him in the Jeep. You guys are going to talk it out. Somewhere else. You're harshing this house's mellow with your bad 'tudes."

"This is *my* house, in case you've forgotten. I can harsh its mellow if I feel like it."

Brice enters the kitchen to see us engaged in something

only a hair more dignified than a slap fight. He smiles quietly at me. "I've been told we're going on a date."

"More like a forced peace summit," I grumble.

Jen steps aside so Brice can get through. "I don't care what you two call it, as long as you don't come back until you're that sickening couple I used to know, who makes goo-goo eyes at each other across the room. I love you two, and even though I feel like you're my brother and sister, I expect you to *not* fight like siblings. Because that's gross and wrong."

Brice laughs and rolls his eyes. "I already got this lecture earlier, so can we please go?" he asks me. He accepts my help down the stairs and into the passenger seat of his car.

As I round the front of the Jeep to get in the driver's side, I say to Jen, "We won't be late."

"Don't care!" she sings. "Just come back happy."

Brice is completely apathetic about where we should go, but it suddenly seems like a no-brainer to me, so I say, "Let's grab some Chinese food and eat in your office at church."

He wrinkles his nose at me, "Really?"

I back from the garage. "Yes. It's perfect. Even if someone happens to be at the church, we can close the door and have some privacy. Plus, you miss it, right?"

He nods.

"It's settled, then. Let's go."

Less than thirty minutes later, we're seated on either side of his desk, dividing out portions of noodles, rice, and gravied chicken onto paper plates.

It's not the same office in which he took my very first confidence years ago, but it has the same feeling, the same atmosphere. When he's in this room, he's more than my husband or even my friend. He's my pastor, the Pastor Northam to whom I can tell anything. It's a safe place, containing familiar objects. Even if I'd been led here with my eyes closed, I could tell you where I am. It smells like him. The air feels somehow lighter in here, the temperature perfect. The lighting is neither too bright nor too dim. It's the interior design personification of moderation. It exudes Brice-ness.

And he's at home. While we eat, I study him through my bangs. The pinched lips and flared nostrils that have become his resting expression at our house this week are absent from his face now. The sparkle is back in his eyes, and his eyebrows don't look like they're constantly trying to hold hands. His shoulders sit inches lower, no longer bunched up around his ears.

A few bites in, he taps his chopsticks on the edge of my paper plate to get my attention.

I look up as if I haven't been watching him the whole time.

"I'm sorry I've been awful this week," he says matter-of-factly and takes a drink of his iced tea.

I shake my head. "You haven't been."

A hint of the now-familiar, perturbed lip pursing occurs. He sets down his tea. "This is only going to work if we're honest."

I nod, acknowledging his thinly veiled accusation. "You're right. Okay. I forgive you for being 'awful.' I also understand—somewhat—why you have been."

"Thank you," he replies, not elaborating further.

I have to say, I'm disappointed he's not compelled to offer a better explanation. I mean, I know he said a lot last night and this morning, but I'm still hazy on why he's been so crabby all of a sudden this week. It's like someone flipped a switch. Maybe it *is* as simple as losing patience with his physical recovery. But if it's something more, I want to know. I understand if he doesn't want to talk about it, though. Anyway, this tête à tête isn't about *him* spilling *his* guts. I guess I should be grateful that he was willing to apologize at all.

We eat in silence for a while, but I'm finished after a few more bites. Knowing what I have to say next—and not knowing how I'm going to say it—is killing my appetite. I put down my chopsticks, wipe my mouth, and take a drink of water.

Since he's set the tone with apologizing, I start with an apology of my own. "I'm sorry I lied to you this morning. Especially about *that*. I just—" I stop, catching myself before I go into the same excuses he's already heard. "It was wrong. If I had thought about it for a single second, I would have never said it."

His mouth goes up on one side. "It was terrifying." When my chin drops at his admission, he laughs. "Don't get me wrong; I'd love him or her just as much as the others, but the thought of another baby, especially now… My heart's racing just talking about it."

It's the first time he's ever come out and said he doesn't want more children. It's a topic we've quite handily avoided in the past few months. I've avoided it because I thought it would lead to an argument, with me on the "Anti" side and him on the "Pro" side, so to hear that he's on *my* side on even one thing brings such heady relief that I have to fight back hysterical giggles. And it makes me hopeful that he'll see other things my way, too.

I grab his hand on top of the desk. "Me, too. It hasn't been as bad lately, because we've had so much help, but when I'm alone with them, it's overwhelming. They're my kids. I shouldn't feel that way, should I? Or at least, I should be over it by now. They're five months old!"

"It's fine. You're fine." He says it so confidently that I believe him as if he's a doctor giving an objective diagnosis.

"Oh, good. I worry sometimes, that's all."

He licks his lips. "I'm, uh, sort of tired of being cut on, but maybe we should think about taking permanent measures to prevent future issues?"

I study his eyes and answer carefully, "If that's what you want."

"Not right away, maybe. But soon."

"Oh. Sure. I mean, my pills should suffice for now, though."

He pulls his hand from mine and wipes his mouth with the thin, white napkin that came in the plastic wrapper with his chopsticks. Clearing his throat, he raises his eyebrows and says, "Anyway. That's a bit off-topic."

His discomfort with the subject elicits a tenderness I haven't felt towards him in a long time. Throughout his recuperation, he's been so strong, too strong to elicit the poignant tugging beneath my sternum that I'm feeling now. As he's recovered from his injuries, I've felt more proud of him than anything else. His strength has been inspirational.

Now it's my turn to show the same fortitude.

"I have something hard to tell you," I begin while I'm still feeling safe and connected to him.

He pushes our food to the side of his desk so it's no longer between us. Then he sits back in his chair and assumes the Pastor Pose: hands folded across his belly, face placid and unreadable, eyes sympathetic and completely focused on my face. I smile at its comforting familiarity.

"Go on," he prompts.

I take a deep breath. "I have a problem. Someone at work told me he has feelings for me." Brice doesn't move. As in, he suddenly looks like a wax figure of himself. I go on, despite my thudding heart trying to tell me to stop talking. "Actually, he, uh— He told me he loves me."

"What?" No more Wax Pastor Pose. His hands grip the edge of his desk as he leans forward. All placidity is gone. I can read a lot of emotions on his face, and none of them are positive.

I try to wave it off like an insignificant detail. "Yeah. I mean, that's what he *said*."

"I think he—whoever *he* is—would know. Who is he, anyway?"

As if we're talking about something completely commonplace, I say lightly, "You know the artist whose show I—"

"Matt Benson?"

I gulp. "Yes." I hadn't counted on him remembering his name.

He bites his lower lip, rolls his eyes, and says what suspiciously sounds like, "Sonofa—" something under his breath.

"Actually, I've never met his mother," I take a stab at levity to dilute the terror brought on by hearing a swear word on my husband's lips.

"This isn't funny."

"No, it's not. I'm pretty freaked out by it, actually."

"Why? What has he done? What has he said?"

"He told me he loves me. That's sufficiently freak-worthy."

Standing, he hobbles around the front of his desk and sits on the edge of it. Or tries to. Immediately, he winces on a sharp breath, and moves to the chair next to me. Once he's settled, he continues his inquiry. "How did he tell you this? In an email, on the phone, in person?"

"He was waiting for me after work yesterday." I instantly regret my choice of words.

Brice's nostrils flare. "*Waiting* for you? Outside? At your car?"

I nod. "But it wasn't scary. I mean, it was scary when he said it, but he wasn't trying to intimidate me or threaten me."

"What *was* he trying to do? What did he expect to happen?"

In trying to give my husband the most accurate answers possible, I have to relive the confrontation, which makes my hands shake and my eyes water. "To get it off his chest, I guess? I don't know. He said he thought I should know."

"Why would he think that? How would that information be useful to you?" Suddenly the intense anger in his eyes falls away, to be replaced by what looks like fear. And sadness. "Did he think you— *Do* you…?"

I should be indignant that he's even posing the half-question, but I know, unfortunately, how legitimate it is. Still, I'm careful not to answer too vehemently. I want him to know I'm speaking the truth when I say, "No. Absolutely not. And I told him in no uncertain terms that I don't feel the same way."

He lets out a breath so gusty that it moves my hair and leaves him slumped in his chair. "Oh, Peyton," he mutters, rubbing his hand across his face and pressing it against his eyes.

"I didn't do anything wrong!"

He lowers his hand. "I didn't say you did."

"I know. I want to make sure you know, though. I didn't lead him on or pretend I was single. I talk about you and the boys all the time!"

Grabbing my fingers, he squeezes them reassuringly. "I believe you."

"No. Wait. That sounds like I'm feeding you a line that

you need to decide to believe or disbelieve. There's no question. It simply *is*." When he kisses my knuckles, I start crying in earnest. "I'm so sorry! I should have told you sooner."

"Shh… It only happened yesterday. When you got home, I was dozing on the couch with the boys; then I got hurt, and we argued. You didn't have a good opportunity. And this morning… Well, anyway. I don't blame you, okay? You're telling me now."

"No, I should have told you weeks ago!"

His lips halt against my hand, which drops from his grip and bounces off the arm of his chair. I shake it and place it in my lap on top of my other hand.

Dangerously quiet, he asks, "Weeks ago? What was there to tell me weeks ago?"

"I didn't think it was a big deal at first. I'd catch him looking at me when we were in a group of people, or he'd say something that could be taken two ways. You know, some people are flirty. It doesn't mean anything."

"But?"

"But then hugged me, and—"

Brice shoots from his chair. "Agggh!" he cries out in pain after the sudden, seemingly involuntary movement. Refocusing quickly, he growls, "He *hugged* you?! What the— When? And why didn't you tell me?"

"It was the night before his show. The night of your accident."

He breathes deeply. "Okay. So, you were going to tell me, but I got hurt before you had the chance?"

Oh, gosh. I wish I could fudge this. I close my eyes, unable to face his reaction to my next words. "No. I wasn't going to tell you."

"Why not?"

Keeping my eyes closed is the right decision, I can tell from his tone. "I… I didn't think it was worth the drama."

"Because you thought it was platonic?"

"Not strictly, no. But…" Now I open my eyes. "I don't love him. I don't. But I love you. And I didn't want to hurt you—"

"Why would it hurt me to find out someone else hugged you? It would only hurt if you *felt* something for that person."

"I don't love him," I repeat in a whisper, scratching at the tickle brought on by a tear sliding down the side of my nose.

He nods curtly. "I see."

"No, you don't."

"Oh, I do."

"Brice." I stand and step toward him, but he tenses.

"Don't. Touch. Me. Not now."

"This is why I didn't tell you. It's stupid. It's pointless. It's — it's useless information."

He seems to be ignoring me as he puzzles out, "So he hugged you, and you felt… whatever. Then you came home and… and you wanted to… But I—"

"I wanted to be with the man I love, to remind me—"

"You needed a reminder?"

"Not like that!"

"You needed to feel the difference between love and lust, to make sure you had it straight?"

"Please, stop putting words in my mouth!"

"I'm trying to understand!" he shouts, then abruptly mumbles, "I have to get out of here," before grabbing his walker and heading for the office door.

"Where are you going?"

"Away from you. Just for a few minutes."

He pulls open the door, only to come face-to-face with Wes, who turns chalk-white at the rage in Brice's eyes. The blood then rushes to the assistant pastor's cheeks when he sees me, distraught, in the background.

"Sir, it's not what you—"

"Move, Wes," Brice demands coldly.

He gladly does what the senior pastor says, but as soon as Brice is clear of the outer office and clanking down the hallway, he turns to me and asks, "What have you done?"

17

SORRY

"*I* haven't done anything!" I snap at Wes, frustrated that I've turned into the villain of this drama.

He seems to take that as the end of the conversation and moves to leave, but I stop him. "Wait!"

After looking as if he's not going to comply, he reluctantly steps further into the office, but he makes sure there's nothing between him and the door.

I sigh and roll my eyes. "Wes, I think you misunderstood what I was telling you this morning." I don't know how to say it without offending him, but considering he's not making it any secret that he's horrified about my supposed feelings, I feel justified simply saying, "I wasn't talking about you."

His brow furrows, and I can tell he's not sure I'm telling the truth when he checks, "You weren't?"

"No! I mean, no offense."

He reaches back for the wall, which he uses to support himself. "Oh." He blinks, and his face relaxes. "But you said —" He pinches the bridge of his nose and squeezes his eyes shut, as if he's trying to remember my exact words. "You said, 'It was the hug's fault.'" He opens his eyes and looks at me. "The hug."

I stare at him as if to say, *"So?"*

Impatiently, like I'm the one who has it all wrong and needs to be corrected, he throws up his hands and yells, "The hug!"

"What do *you* know about the hug?"

"I was there!" he cries. Now I can tell he thinks I've lost my mind. I believe I recognize something akin to fear in his eyes.

"What? No you weren't. Matt and I were alone."

"Matt? Who in Hades is Matt?"

"The guy who told me he loves me!"

Finally, the penny drops. "Oh." But just as quickly, he snatches it back up. "Wait…"

I really don't want to tell him the whole story; otherwise, I would have done so already for the sake of clarity. He caught me at a weak moment this morning, when I needed to talk about it. But now I feel like I've already said too much.

He taps his chin. "You hugged this Matt person, too?"

"He hugged me." That's an important distinction I'm determined to take with me to the grave. "And what do you mean, 'too'?"

"You hugged *me*. At Christmas Eve dinner."

I have to reach way back in my memory for it, but after a few seconds, I realize, "You're right. But it was Christmas! That doesn't count. And it most definitely wasn't a romantic hug!" The thought that he's considered it inappropriate all these months makes me sweaty. "And anyway, until recently, you're the one who's always staring at *me*, like I have a permanent booger stuck to my face."

It's his turn to blush. "I— I—" he stammers.

I wave him away. "Never mind." Gathering the trash from my dinner with Brice, I say, "I simply wanted you to know that I wasn't trying to tell you about inappropriate feelings I had for you when we talked this morning. I was alluding to an issue with the guy I just mentioned, Matt. I was looking for advice about how to tell Brice about it. I *needed* advice. Because now I've told him, and you saw the result. I botched it, as usual."

He quickly transitions from our conversation to my problem, striking his version of the Pastor Pose: elbow rested in one hand, other hand on chin, legs slightly spread, contemplative look on his face. The Thinker Pastor. "Do you want to talk about it?"

"No. I don't. I've talked about it enough today, and it's caused enough trouble."

"Do you want me to go find Elmo and see if *he* wants to talk?"

I freeze in the middle of stuffing a folded, dirty paper plate into the paper sack that's holding our trash. I turn my head to look at him and laugh, even while the grateful tears are marshaling and threatening to overflow. I nod. "That would be nice. Thanks."

He gives me a serious return nod and matter-of-factly leaves the room without further comment.

After an interminable twenty minutes, I can't sit still any longer. I leave Brice's office, intending to roam the church campus, hoping I find something—but not someone (I really hope I don't bump into anyone who wants to chat)—to occupy me and take my mind off what Brice and Wes are currently talking about. And, okay, if I happen to stumble upon the two of them, I might accidentally-on-purpose hear what they're saying. But that's not the primary objective to my walk, even if I do make a beeline for the sanctuary, knowing that would be Brice's first choice when looking for a quiet place to think outside his office.

When I walk past there, however, the only lights on are the ones that stay on continuously, illuminating the cross and the altar. The sanctuary appears empty. I rethink my not-so-subtle search and take a seat in one of the rear rows. Brice said he wanted some time away from me; I should respect that.

Sitting on the front edge of the pew, I brace my arms on the back of the row in front of me and fold my hands. I'm emptying my mind—not that hard to do, as it turns out—and settling in for some much-needed reflection when I hear something closer to the front of the sanctuary.

I crack one eye and look up, but there's nobody there. Chalking it up to an overactive imagination, I close my eye again, only to hear the sound—a low humming—once more. Only this time, it's louder. And it's definitely not my imagination. I stand and walk quietly down the center aisle, looking into pews as I get closer to the altar. About three rows from the front, my glance lands on something that my brain can't immediately process, so I keep walking. Then I backtrack. And stop.

Brice, prone, looks up at me from the pew. His eyes are red but dry. His casted leg hangs alongside the pew while his shoeless right foot rests on the seat, his leg bent slightly at the knee. The buzzing culprit is his phone, which is lying on the pew under his leg. Every few seconds, it lights up and vibrates, as he receives a text, Facebook notification, or email, all of which he appears to be ignoring.

"Hi," he says miserably.

"What are you doing?"

"Thinking."

"Praying?"

"Not really."

His answer surprises me.

"Did you already talk to Pastor Anthony? He was looking for you."

"He came by here earlier. I'm hiding from him. I don't want to talk to him."

I slide into the pew, lift his head, and place it in my lap. When I drape my arm along the back of the pew, he reaches up and grabs it, pulling it down to his abdomen. I take heart that he's receptive to my being here with him, but I worry I'll spook him or set him off if I say anything, so I wait for him to initiate further conversation.

Fortunately, he doesn't make me wait too long. Unfortunately, what he says baffles me.

"Justine."

Immediately, my hackles rise. "What about her?" I ask, heavy on the attitude.

I don't like where this is going. Maybe he's wishing he'd married her after all. Justine would never let biology get the best of her. She'd never allow herself to think of another man besides Brice. Heck, she's not even married to him, and she probably doesn't allow herself to think of any other men.

"She was in love with me," he says simply. It's the first time he's ever admitted it so bluntly.

I nod. "Yep. Still is, I bet."

He neither agrees nor disagrees but swallows. "Anyway. She hugged me all the time. She named me her son's godfather. She—" He stops, and I can practically see his logical brain working it out, making the comparison. "She never told me, 'I'm in love with you,' but she didn't need to. Everyone knew it. I pretended like I didn't, because I felt if I ignored it, I was discouraging it, but I wasn't. I... I've never had the guts to tell her unequivocally that I don't feel the same way about her and that her feelings are disrespectful to you. I even went so far as to ask you *not* to say anything to her about it. I was wrong."

"You were kind," I say, spinning it differently.

"And you were incredibly tolerant. And now I'm getting a tiny taste of what you put up with for years. Only you told him no. You didn't allow him to disrespect me by encouraging his feelings. Thank you."

I blink rapidly. "I didn't even think about Justine. I still don't think of it as the same thing. And I don't somehow think we're even because of this. I wish I'd never met him."

He sits up, scoots closer to me, and puts his arm around my shoulders. I rest my head against his shoulder as I blot the hot, lazy tears that pool at the corners of my eyes.

"You met him for a reason."

"A test, to see if I'd screw up?"

Chuckling, he answers, "No. That's not how it works. Life isn't an obstacle course."

"It sure feels like it most of the time. And I'm stumbling through, knocking things over and making a huge mess of everything."

He kisses the top of my head. "Everything's about you, isn't it?"

I laugh through my tears.

"Seriously, though." He pulls away and looks down into my face. "Who says he was even meant to be *your* 'test,' as you put it? Maybe he was *my* wakeup call." I shake my head, but he insists, "Yes."

"You're a wonderful husband. Stop fishing for compliments."

I expect him to laugh, but he asks earnestly, "How did it feel?" When I shake my head to signal I don't understand him, he clarifies, more quietly, so I almost have to strain to hear him. "When he held you. Did it feel… *better* than…?"

Concentrating on not puking or bawling, I whisper, "No."

"But you felt *something*. What did you feel?" He angles his body so that he's facing my profile.

I turn so we're face-to-face. "Brice, I don't want to—"

"No. I need to know. Just, you know, so I know."

Although I wish he'd ask me to describe or talk to him about nearly anything else (*Would you like to see my episiotomy scar?*), I still feel like he deserves for me to answer any and all of his questions about this, no matter how squirmy they make me.

I close my eyes and take a deep breath, the air hitching on a sob. "Um. Well, at first, it was surprising. He just grabbed me. And it wasn't romantic. It wasn't an embrace. Just a joyous squeeze. My feet came off the floor, so I had to hold onto him. I felt out of control. I felt small. Dainty. Pretty. I was happy that he was happy. Proud that my efforts made him happy. Then I felt guilty. And a little rebellious. Maybe defiant. Then sick. Just sick."

When I open my eyes, Brice is watching me with his mouth slightly open. He quickly sweeps a tear from his cheekbone with his thumb and gives me a shaky smile. "It hurts," he says, his voice catching. He looks down at his lap and nods. "I know you would have never done it if he hadn't taken the choice away from you, but it still hurts."

"I'm sorry."

"I forgive you. Not sure I forgive myself yet—and definitely not *him*—but I forgive you. You didn't choose it."

A small part of me wants to argue that there's nothing for him to forgive if I never had a choice, but deeper down, I know the "harmless" crush I harbored for Matt before he ever hugged me or told me he loved me requires forgiveness, as do my feelings during and after the hug, and possibly even keeping it from my husband, although I still think it was more correct to try to spare him this hurt. At the very least, I'm sorry he feels betrayed that I kept it from him.

"Do you forgive *me*?" he asks, looking beseechingly at me.

"For what?"

"For requiring you to look elsewhere for affection."

"No, you didn't!"

"For taking you for granted."

"That's not—"

"For letting you think that someone else could feel a fraction of what I feel for you."

"I'm pretty sure you're the only one patient enough to go there."

"For not sweeping you off your feet more often."

"We're married!"

"For not taking more of an interest in your career."

I snort at the word *career*.

"For letting you think I'd be angry if you told me what happened. For proving you right when you did." He finally stops, his shoulders slumped. "I'm sorry. Please, forgive me."

"I do, hon. I really, really do." I lean over to kiss his cheek.

He turns his head and brushes his lips against mine. Then he holds my face in his hands and kisses me harder.

I pull back, my eyes flicking to the towering cross behind the altar. "Uh, not really comfortable making out in the Lord's house."

He smiles, his eyes glued to my lips. "We're not making out. I'm kissing my bride."

18

GAME NIGHT

"Tell me again why we're inviting Wes to this thing tonight? Isn't he going to be the odd man out?" Brice asks from the living room, where he's arranging plates of finger foods for our upcoming evening with Jen, Jared and Mitzi, Marianne and Clark... and Wes.

"Not as much as you think," I mutter before saying more loudly so he can hear me from the kitchen, where I'm stocking the fridge with assorted beverages, "I think he'll be fine! I get the impression he doesn't have much of a social life, and I feel bad that we haven't had the chance to help him get to know more people."

Brice appears in the kitchen doorway, slightly out of breath, sweat shining on his forehead. I resist the urge to "coddle" and ask if he's okay, but when he complains about the temperature of the house, I suggest, "Why don't you take off that sweater vest? I'll crack a window in the living room when everyone gets here."

While he peels off his outer layer of clothing, he says, "Anyway, I thought Wes gave you the creeps."

I laugh. "I think I give *him* the creeps, so we're even."

"What?" His head reappears from under the sweater, which he drapes on his walker.

"Never mind." When he grins and seems like he's not going to drop it, I promise to tell him later.

In all the hubbub last night, I didn't have a chance to tell Brice about the misunderstanding between Wes and me, but I don't think now's the time to bring it up. It's not that I'm keeping it a secret, but it's not exactly an "Oh, by the way…" conversation.

I was exhausted by the time Pastor found us sitting quietly (really, just sitting) and told us he was leaving and we'd be the only two people left in the building. First, though, he made sure we were okay, and his genuine concern prompted me to rather impulsively invite him to our house tonight for the gathering we've had planned for Jen's last night in town. Ben had already begged off, having plans with the Youth Group, so we were facing uneven teams for the games I'm sure Mitzi will force us to play.

Plus, I felt bad that his efforts to pay "Jennifer" a "social visit" yesterday were thwarted by all the drama in the Northam household.

Anyway, "Jen doesn't seem to have a problem with him," I add before lowering my voice, in case she comes downstairs while we're talking about this. "And I think he has a thing for her."

Brice laughs loudly but quickly puts his hand over his mouth. When he's finished laughing, he says, "Really? Oh, the poor guy."

"What do you mean by that?" I ask, equally amused but feeling a duty to defend my friend if he's making a dig against her.

He widens his eyes. "She will eat him alive."

"I think he might be hoping for that."

Throwing his sweater at me, he protests. "Hey, now. Keep it clean."

I snatch the clothing from the air before it hits me in the face. "You're the one who brought it up!"

"I didn't mean it that way, and you know it." He shakes his head and shivers. "Oh, man. *Not* the mental picture I ever wanted to see."

Jen startles us both by striding confidently into the room, sliding her peep-toe stilettos onto her feet and modeling them for me. "What are we cringing about? Talking about Pastor Long again?"

I know Brice won't lie, so I jump in and do the dirty work for him. "Yes! Pastor Long. Ew." I turn my attention to her shoes, trying to change the subject. "Nice kicks."

"Thanks. What brought him up?" She turns her leg sideways so I can get an enviable look at her long, toned calf. "Is he about to return from his vacation? I'm surprised he didn't rush back to help when you had your accident," she says to Brice.

He merely shrugs, but I say, "I'm not surprised. He's one of the least-helpful people I've ever met. As a matter of fact, he's worse than unhelpful. You should have seen all the things he did to 'help' Jared get acquainted with his duties at Peace. Weasel!"

"Now, now. Don't tell me you've started holding grudges on behalf of other people, too."

"You don't like him, either, so stop being all Jesus-y over there," I demand.

He holds up his index finger. "Wait, wait, wait. I never said I didn't like him. I don't like some of the things he does or says, but that doesn't mean I don't like him. I try to accept him for who he is, recognizing that he's different than

I am and that he reacts differently to situations than I do. But so do you."

Jen laughs. "Are you seriously putting your wife on the same level as Pastor Long?"

Grinning, his eyes sparkling, he says, "Okay. I'm not quite that good. I have degrees of acceptance."

"Nice save," I tell him. "You were dangerously close to physical harm there."

"Well, I do want to go on record that I don't *dis*like Wayne Long. That's an assumption you've made based on some uncharitable things I've said in weak moments. He's my brother in Christ."

"Buh-rother is right," I grumble, but with a smile. Brice sticks his tongue out at me.

"It's nice to see you two are back to semi-normal," Jen mentions casually, fussing with her clothes, straightening what's already perfectly straight. She walks over to the microwave and checks her reflection in the shiny surface of its door. Pressing her lips together, she then dabs at the corner of her mouth with her pinkie to rub away some lipstick that dared to stray outside the lines.

I shoot a knowing look at Brice, who raises his eyebrows and shakes his head. I think he's discovered yet one more reason to be glad Jen's leaving in the morning.

"I win!" Mitzi says for the third time. If she weren't so cute, she'd be obnoxious.

We've wrapped up our third game of Apples to Apples, and most of us are pretty loose. By that, I mean Jen's slurring her words, Mitzi's giggling at everything, Marianne's volume level has increased threefold, and the guys are watching all of us with expressions of amusement (Clark and Brice), bemusement (Jared) and curiosity (Wes).

I've been careful not to overindulge for an assortment of reasons: 1) I have to help a 200-pound man up the stairs at the end of the night; 2) I've said and done enough disastrous things this week to last me a lifetime; 3) I want to attempt to keep Jen in check; 4) I don't want Wes or the Pryces to think we're out-of-control drunkards when we get together with our friends; and 5) I still have to get up and function with three children in the morning.

Wes's cheeks are rosy from the beers he's had. I haven't counted them, but he's had more than a couple. Jen keeps bringing them to him. Not that I care. Actually, I've been studiously avoiding interacting with him. I underestimated the awkwardness of having him over here a day after all that family drama he witnessed. Yet another impulsive decision gone wrong. I don't think it's obvious that I'm uncomfortable around him. Or at least, not any more uncomfortable than usual.

After Mitzi beats us for the third time (I think she's stacked the deck on her own game), we scatter throughout the ground floor of the house, Brice and Clark taking bathroom breaks, Marianne, Mitzi, and Jared wandering into the kitchen for beverage refills, and Wes and Jen stretching their legs in the living room. I don't need to use the bathroom, and I'm not imbibing, so after spending a few minutes in the kitchen with the Laszewskis and Marianne, getting a refill on my water, I return to the living room, hearing first Brice's, then Clark's voice.

No sooner have I sat on the sofa, though, than Brice and Clark abandon me to get more beers from the kitchen. I'm stuck with nothing to do but loiter uncomfortably on the periphery of Jen and Wes's conversation. Is it my fault they're talking loudly enough for me to hear them all the way over there by the fireplace?

"How old are the three of you in this picture?" Wes asks Jen of the framed photo of Mitzi, her, and me that sits on the mantle.

"That picture was taken last year," Jen lies boldly.

Gullible, earnest Wes replies, "Oh. It's just, your hair is so short in that picture. It must grow fast."

"Yes," she simpers. "It does. I'm a healthy girl." Then a smile breaks through, followed by a laugh.

He half-smiles nervously. "What? Oh. It's an older picture, isn't it?"

She nods. "Uh, yeah. Like ten years old."

After a short chuckle, he asks, "Why'd you lie?"

She shrugs. "Dunno. I thought it would be funny. Then I realized it would only make you think I've aged a lot in the past year."

"I didn't even—"

"Whatever. That picture was taken way before… a lot of things. When we were young. And idealistic. And thought the worst that would ever happen to us was a hangover. Or a bad date. Or a failing grade on a term paper. We were so naive. Life hadn't shown us exactly how cruel it could be. Bad things happened to other people. Mostly old people. And by old, I mean over thirty."

Wes laughs. "Mmm. Ancient."

"Yeah, well, you're still well under that mark."

He puffs out his chest. "By a couple of years. Just."

"I guess what I'm trying to say," she says wistfully, fingering the frame on the picture of us, "is that I didn't know anything when that picture was taken. And look at me there. It's obvious. I'm clueless."

He regards the picture for a few seconds, finally saying, "I think you look happy. And beautiful."

"Yes, well. Age was on my side."

"You're still young!" When she rolls her eyes, he adds, "Plus, I think experience has added a dimension to your beauty."

"Oh, my gosh!" she snorts, fanning herself. "Nice line."

He blushes and is about to defend his statement when she turns to me and calls into the kitchen where the others are still loitering, "Hey, guys! We totally need to play that one game where we have to tell whether we've done—or not done—certain things, and whoever admits they have or haven't is the idiot."

"Loser," I correct, quickly appending, "And I don't think that's a good idea, considering."

"What? Because there are so many pastors in the house? Even better! It'll be hilarious."

Brice practically sprints into the room like a man in a three-legged race whose partner fell down at the starting line. "Yeah! That game's fun!"

Mitzi and the others follow close behind him. She says while clapping her hands, "I love that game! I didn't bring it with us, but we can make up our own scenarios."

"I've never played," Marianne says. "Explain it again."

Jared does, ending with the example, "'If you've never been to a rock concert, take a letter.' Like HORSE. Only, with the letters spelling out "loser." Only, let's not call each other losers. That's mean."

"How about LAME-O?" Clark suggests. "Same number of letters, but less harsh."

Brice laughs. "I love it. All right. Let's go around the room and come up with scenarios off-the-cuff. Honey, go get some paper and a pen from my desk. We'll keep track of letters that way."

"But—" I linger between the living room and the entry-way, torn between being a party pooper and going with what the majority seems to want (even though the majority has no idea how humiliating this game can get). Eventually, I go for the paper. Who am I to stand in everyone else's way?

When I get back, Brice says, "I'll start us out. If you've ever cried about a grade on a test, take a letter."

Jared glares at his friend. "Wow. See if I ever confide in you about anything again."

"Write one down for Jared," Brice crows.

"No matter. As if I don't have plenty of dirt on you," Jared retorts.

"Bring it."

Jen's sitting to Brice's left, so it's her turn next. After thinking about it for a long time with an evil smirk on her face, she opens her mouth to let loose with something I can only assume is going to cause me to get my first letter on the board. "If the only cheese in your refrigerator comes in individually wrapped slices OR if the 'cheese' in your house doesn't even need to be refrigerated (a.k.a., Velveeta), take a letter."

"What do you have against our cheese?" Brice says with a playful scowl. "You've been here a week. It's just as much your fault there's no 'real' cheese in this house."

She directs at me, "That's a letter for you and Brice, in case you need help with scoring."

"That's something Peyton's never needed help with," Mitzi says with a cackle.

I close my eyes for patience while giving both Brice and me "L"s.

Marianne, laughing at Mitzi's dig, says, "Post some letters for Clark and me, too. Must be a married-with-kids thing."

Now to Wes, who doesn't hesitate for second before tossing out, "If you've never made out in a church, take a letter."

The room nearly explodes with indignant responses.

I wait, pen poised, trying to act as casual as possible.

Jen leans toward Wes. "Uh, you're supposed to say things that don't require *you* to take a letter."

He scrapes his thumb against his temple. "I don't have to take a letter this round. Do you?"

Her mouth drops open.

Marianne says, "Who does that? *Everyone* has to take a letter, except you, apparently."

Wes points to Brice and me with the first two fingers of his right hand. "Not those two."

I'd blush, but my brain is too busy trying to pick what to blush about for my face to actually do it. Brice looks caught but not particularly embarrassed about it.

Jared pipes up. "Wait a minute. You told *Wes* about that time in your office in Chicago?"

"What's this?" Wes asks, laughing. "I was referring to last night, when I walked past the sanctuary while minding my own business."

"Thanks, Jar," Brice mutters, definitely blushing now.

Sheepish, Jared nonetheless defends himself. "Consider that payback for outing me about crying over that grade. I studied hard for that test!"

"You and Jared made out in your office in Chicago?" Clark jokes.

"No!" Brice quickly answers. "Peyton and I did. I mean, it was only once. And I felt awful about it."

"Thanks," I mumble, laughing at the reaction his confession is receiving.

Jen closes one eye and leans forward to look at me. "And now again last night? I see why you two were so late getting home."

"It wasn't like that," I say, not wanting anyone to think Brice and I have some kind of sick fetish and routinely sneak around churches, "christening" sanctuaries and pastor's offices. "It was a few kisses. Not even first base."

"Uh-huh," Mitzi says skeptically. "And the time in Brice's office? Equally chaste?"

I glare at her. I expect this from Jen, but what's her deal tonight?

"She was pregnant," Brice says, wrongly believing that will explain everything.

"This keeps getting better and better," Clark says.

"You know how pregnant women are," Brice digs deeper.

Marianne wrinkles her nose. "I didn't want anything to do with sex when I was pregnant. I felt like a whale."

Brice frowns. "Oh. Well, Peyton's not like that. She's—"

"Okay, enough!" I demand, equal parts mortified, amused, and ready to move on. "Mitzi, Jared, Jen, Clark, and Marianne, none of you have shamed yourselves in this way. Good for you. But you have to take a letter." I write down their respective letters and point to Marianne with my pen, since she's next in the circle.

Jen, however, isn't done. "Wait, wait, wait. Hang on. We're letting someone else off the hook too easily here, especially considering he opened up this unholy can of worms. Wesley, when did *you* defile God's house?"

He waves away her question. "Oh, that. I was a stupid teenager. Snuck up to the choir loft with the pastor's daughter during a youth group gathering and messed around. Nothing serious." His forehead wrinkles. "Incidentally, I was teasing about them." He gestures to Brice and me. "They weren't doing anything wrong. At least, what I saw." He blushes. "I shouldn't have said anything."

"Oh, yes, you should have. Now everyone knows they need to keep an eye on those two," Jen says with a pat on his knee and a wink at me. "Moving on."

19

RECONNECTING

"**C**heck out my sweet new duds," Brice crows as he walks into the waiting room, his lower left leg encased in a clean, shiny cast that looks like plastic, much nicer than the plaster one he went into the doctor's office wearing less than an hour ago.

"What *is* that?" I ask, setting aside the months-old issue of *People* and tapping his cast with my fingernail.

"Fiberglass," he answers. "But you're missing the most important part."

I raise my eyes from his leg and lock onto the instrument in his hand. "A cane, huh?"

He wiggles his eyebrows. "Oh, yes. How debonair am I? Now I need a monocle and a top hat."

I laugh. "I don't think those things will go with your shorts."

As we check out and make his next appointment, he shows off his cane maneuvering. "See, if I hadn't worked so hard with my hip therapy, I would have had to use crutches. But since my hip has healed so well, and I've developed those muscles, I only need the support of the cane. I had to promise to bear most of my weight on the cane, though. No cheating and walking around without it."

"Am I supposed to enforce this?" I ask as we exit the clinic and walk across the parking lot to my vehicle.

"Yes."

"In other words, they have no clue how little influence I have over you."

"I told them you ruled the roost."

"I see. How convenient."

"It's true, half the time." He grins cheekily.

I narrow my eyes at him. "It's amazing to me how someone as unfailingly honest as you are can suddenly lie with the best of them when it results in you getting your way."

"It wasn't a lie, per—"

"Don't say 'per se.' I'll take away your cane and leave you stranded in the middle of this parking lot."

"As such," he amends quickly.

"Get in the car."

When we're halfway home, he breaks the easy silence between us by asking casually, "The boys are at Peace already, right?"

His question puzzles me, since he knows they are. When Jen left six weeks ago, he put his foot down about having anyone else stay with us to "babysit" him, so we've devised this routine on his doctor's visit and therapy days, to save me the trip later, before work.

I'm starting to think he hit his head on the pavement harder than they think he did, but he continues before waiting for my answer, "Because— Well, that means we have the house to ourselves for an hour or so, right? Before you go to work?"

"I guess. But I thought you were going to get straight in

your car and drive yourself to work. You can drive now, right? That was part of today's visit, was it not?" The thought of continuing to be his chauffeur makes my stomach drop.

He nods. "Yep. I'm cleared to drive. And other things."

Braking at a stoplight, I look over at him. He shoots me a meaningful look. "*Other* things. You know?" He winks at me. "I'm ready."

"Oh!" I feel the heat travel up my neck, and I laugh nervously. "Yes! Of course. I knew that." I inadvertently squeal the tires when I stomp on the gas too hard at the green light. "Um. Sure. I mean, are you *sure*? Maybe we should wait until tonight, when we can take our time."

"I won't need a lot of time." He clears his throat and looks out the window, assuming his more familiar demeanor when talking about things of this nature.

"I just mean, we should be careful. If we're in a rush, you might get hurt."

"I won't get hurt. But if you don't want to…"

"No! I do! Totally." I reach over and pat blindly for his hand as I keep my eyes on the road and the lunch rush traffic around us. Finally, my fingers brush his. I grasp them and squeeze. "I do. But I have to go to work. You have to go to work. Are you sure you want to be all sex-grungy? I mean, I don't mind. But have you thought about that?"

He laughs. "Have I thought about it? Um, only nearly constantly for ten weeks. And yes, I'm okay with being 'sex-grungy.' Definitely okay with it."

"Okay. Just checking."

I turn into our neighborhood and flash him what I hope is an encouraging smile. Truth is, I'm more nervous than I was after resuming sex with him after having the twins. What if I break him? I mean, he still has to use a cane to walk. He's not fully healed. How am I going to get in the right frame of mind to do this with all these worries? I'll be all seized up down there.

We barely get into the house before he's pulling at my clothes. I duck away from him.

"Let's go upstairs," I suggest.

He reaches for me again. "But you like it down here."

"You don't, though."

"Today, I don't mind." He pulls me against him and kisses my neck. "This is special."

My mind races. "Which is why we shouldn't, um, sully the moment. You were right; doing it in the kitchen is pretty debased. I mean, people eat in here. And cook, too." Plus, I can almost imagine the sound of his hip crunching against the hardwood floor.

"Relax," he whispers against my neck, raising goosebumps.

My eyelids flutter closed. "Mmm. Well, I'd be more relaxed in bed. You know, a softer surface."

"Too many stairs," he continues to breathe along my hairline, behind my earlobe. "The living room has softer surfaces."

I sigh. A few months ago, this would be a huge win. I'd be pulling him down onto the couch so fast, the potato chip crumbs under the cushions would be crushed to dust. But today, no. I need a large, stable, flat, soft surface with pillows and covers and plenty of handholds, or this isn't going to work. And subtlety is getting me nowhere.

I push away from him and speed walk to the kitchen doorway. "I need a bed. I'll meet you upstairs in five minutes."

Two minutes later, I hear him come to a breathless rest next to the bed, where I'm naked under the covers, trying to think of anything sexier than crunchy hips, canes, monocles, and top hats.

He says to my back, "Are you okay?"

I nod but don't roll over, because I don't want him to see the tears in my eyes. "I'm fine," I manage to say in a normal tone of voice. "And I'll be better in a few minutes, I'm sure." I sound like a first-time porn actress reading cue cards.

I hear his clothes rustling and his cane clinking as he props it against his nightstand. The mattress shifts under his weight, after which there's more fabric sliding against skin. He slips under the covers and presses himself against my back. He doesn't feel as ready as he did downstairs, but he's warm to the touch.

Oh, no. Is he feverish? Maybe he has an infection.

"What's wrong?" he asks, his lips on my shoulder.

I shake my head and lie, "Nothing." The pillow under my head dampens with my slow-leaking tears as I ask as casually as possible, "Do you need to keep your leg elevated?"

"No." He pulls on my shoulder and forces me onto my back. Rising up on his arms, he looks down at me. "Hey." He tilts his head and smiles sadly. "What's going on?"

"I don't want to break you again!" I croak, covering my face with both hands, trying to hide my ugly crying from him.

He laughs. "What? You won't break me. Really. I'm fine!" As if to prove it, he presses himself harder against me. "See? Me strong like bull." He pulls my hands away from my face, wiping the tears with a corner of the sheet. "Come on. I can't do this if you're crying."

I sniff mightily and blink. "I'm sorry. I'm ruining this for you."

"It *is* sort of emasculating that you think I'm too fragile to make love to you, but your concern is touching. Just not the right kind of touching." He kisses my lips and palms my breast. Smiling against my mouth, he says, "Don't worry. I'll go really slow, like the grandpa you think I am."

He doesn't look like any grandpa I've ever known. And he feels pretty young and virile. Even his hard fiberglass cast is reinforcing his argument.

I rest my arms on his shoulders and twine my fingers in his hair. "You'll tell me if it hurts? You'll stop?"

"It's not going to hurt. It's going to feel…" He buries his face in my neck, too overcome to finish his thought as I finally relax.

And he's right. As usual.

"*I* feel like we've hardly seen each other since Jared and I moved here!" Mitzi gushes over the rim of her wineglass a month later.

Her statement doesn't sound at all like a criticism, but it puts me on the defensive, anyway. Instead of saying something snarky—for once—I look around the dimly lit, trendy tapas bar and reply offhandedly, "You know, it's been a bit hectic at home. But getting better now that Brice is more mobile. His cast came off last week, thank God. He's like a new man. With mismatched legs. But he doesn't care."

"Yes, he modeled his albino leg for me the other day when I was at the church. And Jared's so glad to have him back full-time. He was stressed out when he was in charge of everything."

Again, I swallow a defensive response along with a good-sized gulp of red wine. "Brice is glad to be back, too," I simply say. "So! How are you settling in? You getting to know everyone? Sorry I haven't been more available to introduce you to people. Helping a grown man shower and dress himself is—as you can imagine—time-consuming."

Her smile tightens. "Don't worry about it. Marianne and Clark have been super-helpful."

I nod. "Aren't they great? They were really welcoming and sweet with us, too. Still are. Marianne's saved my butt more times than I can count when it comes to babysitting. And being there when I needed to talk."

"She's kept me company a lot when Jared's been busy."

I feel the urge to apologize once more, but I stifle it. Neither of us should be sorry for supporting our husbands, even at the expense of our friendship. That's what happens when life gets crazy. And none of us would have ever chosen for Brice to be hit by that car. The person apologizing to both of us should be the driver of that car, but they never did catch him or her.

I can't think of anything else to say, so I keep sipping.

The silence drags on until Mitzi finally says, "We need to have a game night again. Maybe Jared and I can host now that it's not such a hassle for Brice to get around."

I smile. "Yeah, that would be fun. We'd have to get a babysitter, but…"

"Maybe Lucy?" Mitzi suggests.

I laugh. "Uh, no thanks. I'm not sure Lucy has the hang of taking care of herself, much less three babies." I try to picture the church secretary in charge of my little ones, and my laughter turns to shivering. "She once tried to give Max a stapler to play with when we were waiting for Brice to finish up a meeting in his office!"

Mitzi winces. "Yikes. Okay, not Lucy. Well, I'm sure you could find someone. Everyone at Peace loves you guys and your kids."

"Not everyone," I mutter. "Have you met the Longs? What about Paul Vitely? That guy can't stand me. He was relieved when I finally gave up the pretense of wanting to attend the PoP weekly meetings."

She finishes the last of her wine and raises her glass to our server to signal she'd like another. "I've only met Paul and his wife—Crystal, right?—in passing. Aren't they the ones with the two girls who make a bunch of racket during church?"

I point at her. "Bingo."

"Yes. He seems… hands on."

"You're too nice."

"And, of course, I've met the Longs." She abruptly stops, although she looks as if she was about to say much more.

"And?"

She waits for our server to replace her empty glass with a full one and step away, then gives me a wide-eyed innocent look. "And nothing."

"You're almost as bad a liar as Brice." I reach across the table and poke her shoulder. "C'mon. You're not going to say anything about them that'll hurt my feelings."

She doesn't respond to my teasing as I would expect, by giggling or coming out with her bluntest observations. Rather, she squirms on her side of the table and refuses to make eye contact with me. "I don't want to gossip or cause trouble."

Dread builds in the pit of my stomach, but I continue to keep it light. "Oh, my. Did you discover something truly juicy about those two? Ew, wait. Maybe I don't want to know."

She shakes her head. "No. Nothing like that. But they're… not nice people."

"No shit," I say with a snort. "Who did they trash-talk in front of you in the name of 'Christian concern'?"

I know I'm red-hot with this guess by the panicked

expression on Mitzi's face when she swiftly lifts her eyes to mine.

"What did they say?" I ask, no longer idly curious.

"It was nothing. And Jared set them straight right away."

"Why did Jared need to set them straight? *How* did he set them straight?" I'm not sure I'm comforted by the thought of Jared clearing anything up by talking. He tends to achieve the opposite.

"I wanted to tell you right away," she says, her eyes pleading with me to believe her. "But Jared said we weren't even going to dignify what they said by repeating it to you or Brice."

"Mitzi."

She bites her lower lip. "Oh, man. Okay. But you did *not* hear this from me."

"Whatever!"

She sighs. "You know when we first got here, Brice downplayed our association with you two, because he thought it would make it easier on Jared if Pastor Long didn't think we were friends?"

I nod eagerly. "Yes. He figured Wayne would be more helpful that way."

Mitzi snorts. "I wish that had been the case. I don't think that guy knows how to be helpful, but… Anyway, it did work in that he and Vivian were nice to us, socially. They invited us to their house several times for dinner, introduced us to other people in the congregation, and showed us endless pictures of their numerous trips to the Grand Canyon— they're obsessed with that place!"

"Buttering you up. Trying to get you on their side."

She shrugs. "I guess. It didn't seem like it at first, but after a while, they started saying things, dropping hints, ya know?"

"Like what?"

"Like that Brice wasn't the pastor they were led to believe he was when Peace called him. Just stupid, petty stuff that they backtracked on when Jared would seem uncomfortable. Then they started fishing for information, asking Jared how he got along with Brice during his vicarage."

My body temperature feels like it's rising a degree per second. "Did you ever figure out what they were trying to learn?"

Shaking her head, she says, "No. Jared gave them generic answers like, 'Pastor Northam means well,' and 'We didn't always see eye-to-eye, but Pastor Northam's fair.' Stuff like that. They seemed to get the hint that Jared either didn't have any dirt on Brice or wasn't willing to dish it."

I breathe easier until I see from her wringing hands and continued lip-chewing that she's not finished. She sits forward, pinching the stem of her wineglass between her thumb and forefinger. That's when I know—I just *know*— she's about to tell me something I will detest, something I'll wish she never told me, something that will seriously ruin my day.

"I think Vivian got mad that we wouldn't badmouth Brice, so… she moved on to you."

I want to tell her to stop talking, but I can't. My mouth won't open. My teeth are too tightly clenched for my jaw to move. She takes my silence as her cue to continue.

"It started out fake-innocent, like, 'That Pastor Northam sure has his hands full with Miss Peyton. Hardy-har-har.'"

I roll my eyes.

"Then Vivian was like, 'I worry about her, though. She doesn't seem happy here. And there was a time I thought she was getting a little too chummy'—yes, she used that exact word—'with Ben Eiffler.' That's when Jared spoke up a lot more definitely and said you were his friend—*our* friend —and he didn't appreciate what Vivian was insinuating. And Pastor Long laughed and accused him of being awfully protective and added that, anyway, you'd moved on—to Pastor Anthony."

"Please, tell me you're kidding," I mumble.

She shakes her head and grimaces. "No. And there's more."

"Oh, my go—"

"He said he warned Wes that you could be flirty and overly friendly when Brice wasn't looking."

I rub my neck, my hands creeping around to my hot cheeks. "That bastard!"

Quietly, she concurs, "I know. Jared told Wayne, 'I'll pretend you never said that, because I'm sure you've never shared such vile gossip with anyone besides Pastor Anthony and us.' Wayne swore he hadn't, but c'mon. We all know he probably has."

I nod, cursing the mortified tears that I can't stop from forming. It's not just that I'm embarrassed, either. I'm enraged. And scared. Scared that there's some truth in what the Longs observed.

Mitzi grabs my hand. "We had your back. I told them you wouldn't dream of looking twice at anyone other than your husband, much less act on any impulses."

Her statement makes me cry harder.

"Oh, honey. They're miserable old farts. And who cares what they think of you?"

"What about Matt?" I abruptly ask her, dabbing at my eyes with the square napkin from under my wine glass.

I can see she's forgotten all about that until I mention him. I wish I could forget as easily.

She swallows. "Well, this conversation with the Longs happened before—"

"So? I made liars out of you and Jared. I looked way more than twice at Matt. Probably a hundred times."

"It's just a figure of speech."

"And he hugged me. And I liked it. Doesn't matter that I regretted it or wished it hadn't happened. I liked it while it was happening. And I had to tell my husband that. And it made him cry. Have you ever made your husband cry?"

She doesn't answer, which I take as a no.

"Well, I have. Mine, I mean. And it sucks. So thanks for sticking up for me, but, unfortunately, I think Wayne and Viv have me pegged." I hiccup while searching through my purse for my wallet. "They were wrong about Ben and Wes, but does that really matter?"

"Yes, it does!"

Thankful I have cash for once, I toss some bills on the table and hop down from the high chair. "I have to go."

"You're not leaving like this."

"I'm fine. I want to go home."

"I'd sooner let you drive drunk. Come with me." She pulls on my arm and leads me into the nearby bathroom, where she immediately wets a paper towel and pushes it into my hands.

While I mop my face, she says sternly, "Now, listen to me. You're going to stop beating yourself up for that silly hug. He forced it on you, and it doesn't matter what you felt during it. The fact is, if it had been up to you, it never would have happened. And like you said, you wish it never *had* happened. So who cares how you felt for two-point-seven seconds, or however long it was? How many seconds have you spent hating it?"

Uncomfortably aware of the pair of feet in the nearby

stall, I nevertheless blubber, "I encouraged him. I made him feel like it was okay to do it. And afterwards, I didn't say anything to let him know it wasn't okay. I was complicit with my silence. That's why he felt it was okay to tell me he loved me."

"What?"

I drag the coarse, bleached paper towel under my eyes and nod. "A few weeks later. Jen didn't tell you?"

"No! I'm so out of the loop!"

"She only knew about it, because she was staying with us when it happened. I wasn't purposely keeping it from you."

To try to make up for the oversight, I tell her about Wes thinking *I* was in love with *him* (something Jen doesn't know), confessing all to Brice, and our pew peccadilloes, which were nothing about sex but more about forgiveness, no matter how Wes made it sound. By the time I'm finished, my tears have long since dried.

The woman in the stall emerges, shooting me a sisterly smile. I'm sure she lingered in there longer than necessary to hear all the sordid details, but I don't blame her. It does sound like something on a reality TV show.

After the woman washes and dries her hands and leaves, Mitzi smiles sympathetically at me. "You poor thing! You've been through the wringer."

"I've put Brice through it. And now he's obsessed with having sex in weird places—I think to prove to me that he can be exciting. I don't want to tell him no, because I used to complain that we were boring, and I don't want him to think I don't want him. But it's exhausting."

"Oh, boy. I could've done without that," she mutters before throwing up her hand and quickly requesting, "Don't tell me if you guys have done things in parts of the church I see all the time."

"No! At our house, only! Oh, hell. I'm never playing that LAME-O game again." That reminds me of the game night at our house and some of the things that Mitzi said that baffled me at the time but that make more sense now, in light of her story about Wayne and Vivian. Shyly, I say, "Please be honest with me. Did you believe anything the Longs said about me?"

"No!"

"Because at game night, you said some things. Things about my not needing help scoring—"

"I was drunk, Peyton! Seriously drunk."

"Still. The truth comes out in times like those."

Her eyes widen. "I swear. I meant in the old days. Our Trippin' Trio days." We laugh together for a second, but she quickly sobers. "I didn't mean now. I wasn't referring to Ben or Wes or Matt."

"Oh, my gosh! The list is so long! How did I become this person, this sad, sad married mom who gives people the wrong impression because she tries too hard to be something she's not anymore, young and cool?"

"You've never had to try to be those things. You *are* them. And some jealous people can't stand it. And they try to twist it to make it sinister. And others are drawn to it. They want to spend more time around it. They love it."

I groan into my hands. "I'm going to lock myself in my house, where my husband can have his way with me in every closet, on every stairway, in every woodshed…"

"Really?!"

I peek through my fingers. "Splinters like you wouldn't believe. Yes. But the point is, I'm never again going where people can observe and judge me. Or misinterpret my intentions. Ever again."

"That's not very practical," Mitzi regretfully informs me.

I sigh. "I know."

"And P?"

I drop my hands so I can look at her earnest face.

"Please stop going into detail about your sex life. He's my pastor now, ya know?"

I laugh. "Yeah. Mine too!"

FILLING IN BRICE

J've calmed way down since leaving the tapas bar
and arriving home, where the nightly routine has
kept me occupied and focused on something other than
myself—imagine that. As soon as I hit the door, fresh-from-
the-bath, naked Max ran full-speed at my knees, smelling
like milk and honey soap and looking like a true clone of his
father, with his neatly combed, dark hair, wide grin, and
sparkling blue eyes. Brice was calling to him from upstairs,
where I could hear the other boys, squealing and splashing
in their bath, the noisy highlight of the eight-
month-olds' day.

I was slightly worried about how Max got down the
stairs by himself, and how long he'd been wandering the
main floor alone in the nude, but seeing that he was in one
piece and nothing looked amiss in the house, it seemed
pointless and a little late to spend too much time dwelling on
it. We've been working for quite some time to get him to
scoot down the stairs on his bottom; apparently, he's
mastered that skill.

I called up to Brice that I, not a random stranger with

degenerate motives, was the one entering the house and currently nibbling our naked two-year-old's toes. Then I carried the toddler up the stairs, fully intending to tell Brice what Mitzi had revealed when we met for drinks, as soon as I put some clothes on our child.

But you know how it goes. I had barely come to a stop in the bathroom doorway when I was sent on a mission to grab more towels, as Brice had used the ones he had originally brought into the bathroom to mop up the splashes the twins had sent over the side of the tub. After I delivered the dry towels, Max brought me a book—a long book—to read to him before bedtime, which I did, after taking charge of getting Brooks dressed in his pajamas and settled in his crib, then kissing Harris goodnight, then saying a proper "Hello" to my husband for the first time all day, then dutifully retrieving the three specific stuffed animals Max wanted to cuddle with during story time.

By the time Max grew tired of listening to the story and started turning the pages before I could read the text they contained, Brice had long wandered off to do whatever he wanted to do, so I ran a hot bath after tucking in Max and checking one last time on the twins.

The bathtub has always been my favorite place to reflect on things, and tonight, without fear and self-doubt clouding my judgment, I came to the conclusion that Mitzi is right about a lot of things, chiefly that Wayne and Vivian Long are jealous old farts who like to stir the pot.

The second thing she's right about is that I've done my time over the Matt thing. I've regretted and fretted away enough hours of my life. I've suffered the consequences of my actions. And I've learned a lot of lessons from the experience, too. Not just about my marriage, but about life in general and human nature. And myself.

I'm *not* a flirt or a tease. I'm not. I've never made advances to a man who wasn't a prospective boyfriend, even in my wildest days. I don't know what the Longs imagined they witnessed with Ben or Wes, but they are either out of their minds or straight making things up. Even with Matt, I didn't lead him on in the slightest. The worst thing I did in that situation was that I failed to be more assertive when it came to *dis*couraging him. But I didn't overtly *en*courage him.

So *phbbbbbbbbbbbbbb*, Wayne and Vivian!

And I'm not sure Brice needs to get involved with their shenanigans. Why burden him with more of what he already knows about them: they don't like me. Wah. It's not the end of the world. And there's nothing *he* can do about it, anyway.

When it's clear that Max has succumbed to sleep, because I can no longer hear him singing in his crib, I pull myself from my cooling bath and dress in a comfortable night shirt and cotton boy shorts. My plan is to flip through my latest issue of *Entertainment Weekly*, goof off on Pinterest, and call it a day.

"Check your Facebook wall. I just wrote something," Brice says to me from his spot on the couch when I enter the living room.

I pull my phone from my purse and sigh. "Really? Are we *those* people?"

"What people?"

Before answering him, I curl up in the corner of the other couch and check to see what he wrote: *You're the best!*

"Ugh!!" I cry in disgust and embarrassment.

"What?" His question suggests innocence, but his accompanying laughter proves he knows he's being a goober.

"What does that even mean? It sounds like something on a candy heart. I hate when couples talk to each other on Facebook for everyone to see! You're sitting ten feet away from me. Why didn't you just tell me that?"

His only response is continued laughter.

"You know the couples I'm talking about, right?"

He nods through his wheezing.

I assume a sultry tone. "'Hey, baby... I love you so much.' 'Me, too, baby. I can't wait until we eat some ice cream later and watch *Honey Boo Boo*.' 'Aw, yeah, baby, it's gonna be so good!' 'Did you get the toppings I like?' 'You know it, baby.'"

"Stop it!" Brice begs, pinching at his watering eyes. "You're killing me."

I drop my act and giggle more at his reaction than at my contrived online conversation. "Well, that's how you make us sound when you post something like that on my wall. I'm deleting it."

"No!" He lunges for my phone, trying to knock it from my grip.

"Watch your leg!" I say around a chortle, not really worried about his newly de-casted limb. Really, I'm trying to distract him so he won't get my phone.

"What's there to watch?" he sasses back. "It's white and skinny and disturbingly hairless."

"I'll write that on *your* Facebook wall. 'Nice gam!'" I wrap my fingers around my phone and pull it to my chest with a tiny shriek as he towers over me.

"You should do it!"

"No! I said it to your face. I don't need to put on a show for our Facebook friends."

He plops next to me and rests his chin on my shoulder. "Come on. It'll be funny. Let's see if anyone responds."

I narrow my eyes at him but navigate to his Facebook wall and tap out a message, only not the one about his leg, and I hide the screen from him while I compose my public love note.

Grinning, he glances down at his phone when I finish typing and nearly drops it when he reads, *My, what big feet you have!*

Immediately, a comment pops up directly below it. *Has Peyton been hacked?* asks Jen.

Ben chimes in next. *Whoa, there!*

Mitzi adds, *Ummm, I think you forgot to make this a 'private' conversation.*

Oh, dear, Mom contributes.

And in a matter of minutes, there are about twenty "likes," including one from Wes.

I quickly type, *You all are pervs. He really does have large feet.*

Mom "likes" my comment and confirms, *He really does.*

We collapse against each other on the couch. After we get our breath back, I say while wiping my eyes, "You're right. That was fun."

He checks his phone one more time. "Meanwhile, nobody has 'liked' or commented on my wonderful compliment to you."

"Because they're embarrassed for you."

"Oh, wait! There's one. From Geoffrey Billmeyer. He's a good kid. Let's see what he says. 'Pastor, you're a dork.'" He presses his lips together, trying to suppress his smile. "Nice."

I laugh and type into my phone under Geoffrey's comment, *Thank you, G-Man.*

No problem, Mrs. N., is his prompt reply.

"'No problem, Mrs. N.,'" Brice imitates the high schooler. "Whatever. He has a crush on you."

The teasing, off-handed remark hits a freshly exposed

nerve, but before I can react—or hide my reaction—Brice is pushing me down on the couch cushions, nipping at my lips.

"Not a peep from the boys for about an hour now," he whispers. "That usually indicates the all-clear."

"Mmm," I murmur, rubbing my hands against his chest. "Good. Let's head that way, then."

"What way?"

I glance toward the ceiling. "Upstairs."

"What's wrong with right here?"

I take a deep breath and sit up, gently pushing him away in the process. "Do *not* take this the wrong way," I begin, which I can tell immediately puts him on his guard, "but can we please just have sex in bed?"

He opens his mouth, closes it, and reopens it to say, "But I thought you liked—"

"*Once in a while*, it's nice to do something a little different, slightly naughty. But if it's every time, it's not different. Or naughty. It's just... uncomfortable."

"Oh."

"Don't get me wrong; it's fun. I always enjoy myself. Well, usually—the woodshop was a mistake." I stare off into space, remembering the discomfort. Snapping back to the present, I blink and smile at him. "But now that we've done it pretty much everywhere in this house and within the bounds of our property lines, I think I can safely say, I prefer our bed."

"You do?" He looks deflated.

"Yeah. Don't you miss it? It's so soft and warm. And private. And it has covers. And pillows."

He grins sheepishly. "I miss it, too. But I thought this was what you wanted. Spontaneity. Excitement."

"I did. I thought I did. But now I realize we were doing it right all along."

No longer looking disappointed, he jumps to his feet and pulls me up by the hand. "Race you up the stairs?"

I start running before agreeing. In spite of everything, I still need a head start against him.

Much later, as we're cuddling in our cozy, comfortable bed, neither of us picking splinters from unmentionable areas or rubbing at bruises on pressure points, I sigh contentedly. "Yes. Put *that* on your Facebook status."

He laughs. "Mrs. Whitney would stroke out."

I look up at him. "Is *she* on Facebook?"

"Everyone's on Facebook."

"Well, she's not friends with me!"

"Hmm. Umm... Well... Huh. I don't know what to tell you."

I settle my head on his chest once more, adjusting my position to get more comfortable. He puts his hand on top of my head.

"Maybe she's in the Long camp," I grumble without thinking.

He tenses beneath me. After a fussy-sounding sniff, he asks, "What's the 'Long camp'?"

Casually, as if I don't really care, I say, "You know, the people who—like the Longs—think I'm an inferior pastor's wife and who aren't picky about who they tell."

"There's such a camp?"

"Apparently."

Dropping his hand to my lower back, he strokes it with his thumb until I squirm ticklishly. "That's unfortunate," he states dully. "And how do you know about this?"

I backtrack somewhat. "Well, I don't. I don't know if

there are other people who share the Longs' low opinions of me, that is. But I do know how they feel. Because they were dumb enough to say something to Mitzi and Jared."

"Jared hasn't mentioned any of this to me."

"Jared didn't want to upset us."

"Did you get any specifics from Mitzi?"

I gulp. I can tell by his quiet, economic speech patterns that he's taking everything in, he's not pleased, and he's not going to let this go. "Yes. Yes, I did. Evidently, I'm an unhappy person who likes to flirt with church staff members behind your back."

"They said that?"

"Yes."

"I see."

Suddenly, a laugh bubbles from me. I'm almost as surprised by it as Brice, who startles at the sound. "I'm sorry," I say, covering my mouth. "It's just… those two!"

"You don't seem upset by this."

"Oh, I was," I assure him. "When Mitzi told me at the bar, we had to move our conversation to the bathroom, because I was making a scene at our table. But the more I think about it, the more ridiculous it is. Do they really have nothing better to do than sit around, analyzing my level of happiness or studying my interactions with guys like Ben and Wes? When the twins were born, did they compare their features to Ben's, to see if maybe he was their father? Do they think this is an episode of *Jerry Springer*?" Again, I giggle.

His hand returns to the crown of my head. "I don't think it's funny," he says calmly. When I stop laughing, he repeats, "It's not funny. It's malicious gossip-mongering, and I won't tolerate it."

"What are you going to do about it? People are going to gossip. I'm not the only one they gossip about."

"This is different. These are *lies*. Bold-faced, out-and-out lies. It's one thing to hear something or witness something and talk about it to someone else. Bad, yes. But 'Did you hear that the so-and-so's are getting a divorce?' is a lot different than 'Pastor Northam's wife sneaks around behind his back with the youth director.'"

"Oh, and Wes," I add, so he's not surprised by that if he hears it from someone else.

"Wes Anthony? Our assistant pastor?"

"That one."

"You have to be kidding."

"Listen." I prop myself on my elbow and look down at him. "There's more."

"More? Please, make it stop."

"Okay. But I'm just going to tell you this one last thing. Don't freak out."

"You're worried I might freak out? That's freaking me out."

I simulate taking deep, even breaths and invite him to follow my lead. After he humors me, I say soothingly, as if I'm narrating a children's fairy tale, "Once upon a time, Wes thought I was in love with him, based on some things Wayne said to him, warning him about my alleged propensity to go after single, church-employed men." Brice's nostrils flare, but I rush ahead, "And it didn't help when I sought Wes's advice before telling you about, um, that one thing, and he thought I was confessing my feelings for *him*." I stifle a laugh at the memory of panicked Wes running from our house.

The left side of Brice's mouth twitches upward. "Say what, now? You somehow led Pastor Anthony to believe you were telling him you loved him?"

"The seed had already been planted by Bizarro Cupid Long! Wes misunderstood what I was saying, because he thought he already knew what I was saying, but he wasn't expecting what I was actually saying."

A bark of laughter escapes Brice's chest. He tries unsuccessfully to resume a straight face but can't and has to resort to grasping his lips in his hand. The facial acrobatics make him look slightly deranged. "H-how did he react?" he asks after pulling himself together and removing his hand from his mouth.

"He burned rubber out of our driveway."

"Baaaaaaaaaaaaaaaaaaaahahahahaha! Nuh-uh!"

"Yes-huh. At the time, it wasn't funny, because... Well, I hadn't told you about *that* yet. And we had argued just that morning. And at first, I thought he and I were talking about the same thing, so when he was having such a strong reaction to what I was saying, I kept thinking, 'How am I going to tell Brice about this, if someone this removed from it is freaking out?' and he kept saying, 'Don't tell Brice! Reject these feelings!' and I was like, 'I *have* rejected them.' Then he said I shouldn't tell anyone he'd been here—it was that morning Jen took you to therapy, you know? And he had stopped by to see her. I was like, 'Okay...' and then he was gone, running the stop sign at the end of the street, and it hit me that he thought I was talking about having inappropriate feelings for *him*."

Brice rolls onto his belly and buries his face in his pillow, his shoulders shaking with laughter.

I lean on him, contemplatively nibbling his shoulder. "And now, knowing what Wayne-O told him, a lot of things make sense, not just that crazy morning. Now I get why Wes was always staring at me, always uneasy when we were alone in a room together. I know why he got all stiff and twitchy when I hugged him on Christmas Eve—"

"Stiff!" Brice muffles into the pillow, banging his hand next to his head.

I slap his shoulder. "Not like that!"

"Doesn't matter. Still funny!" His giggles reach an octave I've never heard from him, not even that time he overheard me fart in the bathtub.

"Yeah, well, he didn't think it was funny, especially when you opened your office door that night, looking like a charging bull. He thought you were going to kill him."

He turns his head to the side, wiping his damp temple on the pillow. Finally, after a few more seconds, he manages, "I take it you cleared things up with him then."

"I'm not sure he would have come looking for you otherwise," I reply. "He doesn't seem like a masochist. Or particularly brave."

Sniffing, Brice tries keeping the corners of his mouth from rising, but he ultimately gives into his amusement and goes on another jag that lasts nearly a minute, pausing only once to say, "I keep picturing him running from you, peeling out on the street!"

"Laugh it up," I drawl, but I'm relieved he thinks it's funny. I'm glad he's not mad I didn't tell him right away or even in the nearly three months since then. I still feel the need to explain, though. "I would have told you before now, but I've been trying to forget about it, honestly. Plus, Wes seemed pretty embarrassed about it, almost to the point of anger, so I knew he wouldn't be in a hurry for you to know. Not that what he wants is more important than what you want or need to know. But, you know, I'm trying to be sensitive, since he has to work with you, and the misunderstanding wasn't his fault. Mostly."

"At all!" Brice goes even further. "The poor guy."

"Well, maybe 'the poor guy' should put less stock in gossip and give people the benefit of the doubt until they do something to him personally to influence his opinions," I assert.

Blinking the last of the tears from his eyes, Brice says, "Okay. I'll give you that. But he thought you *were* doing something that day, acting on the feelings that—" He can't finish for his sputtering.

I wipe his spit from my arm. "All right. I get it."

He lays a hand on mine and smiles. "Hey. Don't take it personally that he was horrified by it. I mean, think about how awful that would have been for him, if it had been true!"

"Yes, I know. I'm scary."

"No! But you're his colleague's wife. And he's a man of God. Trust me, it's a horrible position to be in. It happened to me once."

"Another pastor's wife came onto you?!"

He pushes himself onto his elbows. "Not a pastor's wife, but a married congregant."

"Who?! You never told me this!" I sit up straight, fold my legs, and spin on my butt to face him squarely.

"It was before I ever came to Chicago. In Kansas. I was a couple of years older than Wes is now and probably not nearly as naïve as he is, but still green. She and her husband invited me over for dinner, but when I got there, her husband was still tied up at work—not sure if that was the plan all along, or if it simply worked out that way—so we sat down on the couch to talk and wait for him, and she, you know…"

"No! What? She put the moves on you right there, when her husband could have come home at any time?"

He blushes. "Yeah. She put her hand on my leg, really high on my inner thigh, and told me that she didn't love her husband anymore and that she knew I was single and probably had 'needs,' too."

"Oh, my gosh! Who does that?! Did she research porno scripts for this idea?"

He chuckles nervously. "I don't know. I was too shocked to appreciate the absurdity of it at the time."

"Did you run away?"

After an eye-roll, he answers, "No, I didn't. I moved to a different chair, told her I wasn't at liberty to take care of my 'needs' in the way she was suggesting, and asked her if she needed to talk to someone about her marriage."

"What did she say?"

"She was embarrassed and asked me to leave. I never saw her or her husband again. They transferred to the local Methodist church."

Now it's my turn to crack up as I picture Brice handling this awkward situation.

He shrugs. "It's funny now, but at the time, I was traumatized."

"You still blush when you talk about it."

"She was… attractive."

"Oh, really?" I lean forward and press my smiling mouth against his. "Did you get aroused when she touched you?"

I can feel the heat from his face when he says, "A little. Like I said, she was nice looking. And it had been a while. Maybe a few years earlier, I wouldn't have had the self-control to tell her no."

"Big talker."

He sits up and pushes me onto my back so my head's at the foot of the bed.

"I'm not proud of it."

"I can tell."

"I'm just saying, as funny as Wes's reaction was, I'm proud of him for doing the right thing. I'll let him know that next time I see him."

"Oh, to be a fly on the wall… You gonna tell him your story?"

He nudges my nose with his and rests his weight on top of me. "No. You're the only person I've ever told."

"Ever? You didn't even tell your senior pastor? What if she had accused you of trying to start something with her?"

"That was a risk I was willing to take to protect her from humiliation. I figured I'd defend myself if the situation arose, but there was no point in telling someone about an experience that clearly embarrassed us both."

"You're too good."

"Sometimes I'm not." He wiggles his eyebrows. "Sometimes I'm very bad."

"Twice in one night?" I question his advances.

"Who says you can't be spontaneous in a bed?" he quips.

COFFEE RUN

When I woke up in the middle of the night to do one of my obsessive clock checks, Brice wasn't in bed. The bathroom door was open, the room beyond dark and empty. I reached over to his side of the bed to feel the sheets, which were cool. Next, I checked the baby monitor, which was on, volume up, but silent. I listened for sounds coming from Max's room but heard none. Other than the oddity of being in bed alone, it felt like any other 2 a.m. in our house. When I strained my ears harder, though, I heard it drifting up the stairs, the tapping of Brice's fingers on his computer keyboard.

Ah. *Middle of the night inspiration*, I thought, finally able to relax, turn over, and settle back down to sleep.

Now, at a more decent hour, he's lying on his stomach, his head turned away from me, softly whistling in his sleep. I have no idea what time he finally returned to bed. I give him a quick kiss on the back of his neck before heading toward the shower. It may be Saturday, but the majority of the occupants of this house don't give a crap and will be up, expecting their breakfasts, any minute.

Downstairs, still damp, my hair in a towel, my body in a robe, I scramble some eggs for the twins and inhale the aroma of brewing coffee. While transferring the eggs to some plastic bowls, I stop and sniff the air.

"Ew," I say out loud. "That smells gross." I walk to the coffeemaker and wrinkle my nose at it. "You stink," I tell it, lifting the carafe from the element and putting my nose next to the spout.

Brice, dressed for a walk (no jogging allowed yet) and holding both twins, chooses that moment to enter the kitchen. Max is right behind him, his bare feet slapping against the hardwood.

"I'd ask what you're doing, but maybe I should just let it go," Brice says, loading the infants into their high chairs for feeding and lifting Max into his booster seat at the kitchen table.

"Smell this," I demand, thrusting the coffee in his direction. "Does it smell off to you?"

"Does coffee go off?" he asks while complying with my request. "It smells fine to me. More than fine." He opens a cupboard to get a mug and holds it out to me so I'll pour some for him.

As the steam wafts around us, I cough. "Oh. That reeks!"

He shoots me a dubious look. "You're weird."

"It's all skunky."

Taking a huge drink and swallow, he sighs contentedly. "It's excellent. Here, Max," he says, sliding in front of the toddler a plastic bowl of oatmeal with two triangles of toast stuck in the center. "Eat up. Then we'll go for a walk." He nods at the twins' breakfast on the island. "Hand me one of those bowls, and I'll feed Squeaky."

We let Max control the conversation for a while, which

means that we recite our ABCs and count repeatedly to seven (that's as far as he gets before he starts skipping around), as we shovel finely chopped, yellow egg bits into babies' mouths. Brice, feeding the more avid eater, reaches the bottom of his bowl first, deposits the last spoonful into Harris's eager mouth, and lifts his arms over his head, mimicking the noise of an enthusiastic crowd.

"And the winner is: Harris! By"—he leans over and peeks at the contents of the bowl in my hands—"four bites!"

"You're a dork."

He lifts his coffee mug and smirks at me over the rim. "Jealous."

"Can you drink that somewhere else? It's seriously turning my stomach. I don't know how you can drink it."

"It tastes the same as it did yesterday. And the day before. And the six hundred days before that. Your sniffer's the one with the problem." In spite of his claims, he moves to the other side of the kitchen, where he rinses Harris's bowl and puts it in the dishwasher. Then he keeps his distance.

I sniff Brooks's breakfast. "If my sniffer's off, then this would smell bad, too, and it's fine. It's only the coffee that stinks. Maybe your nose is dead."

"You know that's not true. You tease me about my hypersensitive schnoz all the time."

Steering clear of him and his stinky brew, I slide Brooks's now-empty bowl down the counter toward Brice and skirt the long way to get to the fridge, where the boys' bottles are waiting.

When I have the two infants settled on their backs in their playpen, I coax them to hold their own bottles and say, "I'm throwing out that coffee and buying a different brand. I can't drink that skunk juice."

"Well, I can." He drains the last of the coffee and places his mug in the dishwasher. Grabbing a to-go mug from the cupboard above the coffeemaker, he says, "Before you go tossing out a perfectly fine pot of grog, I'm taking some for the road. You about done over there, Stink?" he inquires of Max's progress.

"Ah done!" Max answers, pushing away one triangle of toast and several remaining bites of oatmeal.

"You can take that toast with you," I say to our eldest son as I sit at the island, "since your dad's in such a hurry."

"I'm trying to remove my skunky self from your presence," he says, opening the garage door and setting his travel mug on the top step. Closing the door, he returns to the kitchen and dumps the contents of the coffeepot down the drain. "There. Better?"

"Yes. Thank you."

"I'd come over there and kiss you, but I'm sure my coffee breath will make you want to puke."

"Get over here," I demand, laughing.

He does a silly jog around the island and kisses my smiling, upturned lips.

"You taste fine," I reassure him, my eyes still closed.

"It's nice of you to use your lying skills to spare my feelings."

I laugh, open my eyes, and push him away. "Go take your walk. Do you need me to grab some shoes for Max?"

"Nah. It's warm enough out there already. I'm going to put him in the stroller. We'll walk to the store and get you some better-smelling coffee. You want your usual: triple espresso, volcanic temperature, ultra-tall, skinny latte with a cherry on top?" He shoots me a wink as he sets Max down on the kitchen floor, handing him his uneaten wedge of toast.

"Not that, but my usual would be nice. Thanks!" I resist voicing my worries about him having to cross a busy street to get to the store with the Starbucks inside.

Brice opens the garage door, and Max runs through it.

"Careful on the—"

There's a sickening sound of hands slapping on concrete, but before I can rush to the door to check on the reckless little one, he calls out, "I okay!"

Brice shakes his head and waves me away. "He's fine," he reassures me. "See you in a few." As he swings the door shut behind him, I hear, "Stinky! Stairs. How many times are you going to bite the dust before you remember to go slow? Lemme see those hands. Stings, huh?"

Shaking my head at the two of them, I say to the youngest trouble makers, "That'll be you in a few months, so don't go looking all smug."

Brice is gone a long time. A long time. Long enough that I start to get twitchy, and my stomach ties itself in a knot the more minutes pass by with no sign of his return. Finally, despite the knowledge it might annoy him (and the regret I still feel for the message that probably sent him into the path of a car, even though he's been careful to never bring that up to me), I text him, *Where are you?* and nearly instantly receive the reply, *On the way, with your coffee.*

As if the effing coffee was my biggest concern.

When he and Max burst through the front door less than ten minutes later, I expect to hear a story about running into someone from church at the store or a detour they took in order to more fully enjoy the beautiful summer morning, but I get nothing. Max is animated and keeps saying something about "Boons!" but Brice is oddly subdued.

He hands me my coffee with a quick brush of his lips to my forehead and mutters something about putting the twins down for their morning nap on his way to the shower.

I blink, slightly confused by his mood shift, but Max is still yelling about balloons and pulling on my hand, trying to lead me to the back door, so I leave Brice to his shower and follow Max to the backyard, where he points to the sky and repeats, "Boons!"

Sure enough, a fleet of hot air balloons floats overhead.

"Oh, wow! Balloons! Look how pretty they are!"

While Max hops around the backyard like a drunken, pajama-clad orangutan on a stick horse, I take a distracted sip of the coffee Brice brought me—and nearly spit it right back out again. *Oh, my.* It takes a concerted effort, but I manage to swallow the foul-tasting, lukewarm liquid, with the back of my hand pressed to my mouth.

"Ick!" I put the cup on the patio table and step away from it. If I didn't know him better, I'd say Brice put a dog turd in there. Just to be sure, I edge closer to the table, open the lid on the cup, and look down into it while holding my breath. There doesn't seem to be anything unusual about it. Except that it tastes like ass. I replace the lid and push it away from me with the tip of my index finger, as if the cup is full of a poison that can penetrate the cardboard.

Meanwhile, Max is still singing the praises of the hot air balloons and shouting out their various colors. I distractedly encourage him, repeating after him. "Purple, red, blue, yellow. Yes. Very good."

After a few minutes, the balloons drift from sight, and I worry that Max will have a meltdown, but he simply turns his palms out to me and says, "Ah gone! Boons!"

I marvel at his good nature but don't question it or give him time to reconsider. Instead, I change the subject, glad for a distraction. "Let's play with the ball, then."

We're kicking the large, red, rubber ball back and forth when Brice enters the scene.

"Daddy!" Max shouts, as if he hasn't seen him in hours. "Stinky!"

"Kick da ball," Max demands, nudging it lazily in Brice's direction.

He complies halfheartedly before saying, "All right! You and Mommy go ahead and play. I'm going to work in my shed." As he crosses the yard, he walks backwards and asks me, "You good? How was that coffee?"

I don't have the heart to tell him the truth or that I suspected him of dunking a dog turd in it, so I merely smile and nod, "Yeah. It was fine, thanks. Are *you* good?"

He makes a big deal of unlocking the shed, not looking at me, "Yeah. Fine." Before ducking inside, he shoots me a smile, repeating, "Just fine. I'll be in for lunch."

I stare after him for a few seconds, but Max doesn't let me ponder the situation for too long. "Red ball!" he cries, sending it sailing toward my stomach.

I catch it with an "Oof!" and laugh. "Wow, Bud! That was quite the kick. That foot may make you famous someday. Or at least win us some family kickball games against your cousins."

We return to our kick-fest, which is pleasantly mindless, until Max tires of the repetitive game and runs to the back door. "In, in!" he chants, his little hands working uselessly against the stiff doorknob.

"Hang on," I request as I put the ball away and hurry to open the door for him. "Shh... Your brothers are sleeping. Wanna watch Elmo and build with blocks?"

"Yes!" he whispers emphatically.

"You get the blocks. I'll turn on the show."

We each busy ourselves with our respective tasks, and soon we're settled on the floor, building a plastic masterpiece with Elmo shrieking at us in the background. It only takes a couple of episodes before Max begins rubbing his eyes and getting frustrated when the blocks don't fit together the way he thinks they should.

"Okay, okay. Let's clean up and get some lunch," I suggest calmly. "You've had a busy morning."

While I make Max a peanut butter and jelly sandwich and cut up some strawberries and bananas for him, I keep an eye on the back window, looking for Brice. Finally, as I'm setting a sippy cup of milk in front of the two-year-old, I see the shed doors swing open and hear them clunk closed. After a few seconds, the back door opens and shuts, and Brice strides into the kitchen, holding aloft my takeout coffee cup.

"You left your coffee out there. And it feels full."

I blush and stammer, "Oh. Uh. Yeah. I guess I got so into playing with Max that I forgot about it."

He sighs and rolls his eyes, "Well, there goes four bucks down the drain."

I intercept the cup before he can take it to the sink and pour it out. "No. I'll, uh, reheat it. Or something."

He wrinkles his nose. "It's been sitting out in the sun on the patio table. It had milk in it. You'll get sick."

Relieved that I don't have the option of pretending to want it, I wince. "Sorry. I did drink *some* of it," I say truthfully, dumping it quickly into the sink so he can't tell how little that "some" was.

I don't want to tell him my favorite coffee in the world made me want to barf. Not only will he be annoyed that he went to the trouble—and expense—to get it for me, but he'll inevitably ask me a bunch of questions regarding my sudden aversion, and I don't have any good answers. Yet. I plan to check WebDoctor while Max is napping and the twins are busy with their tummy time.

Unfortunately, I can't stop thinking about the thirty-something mom at church who was recently diagnosed with pancreatic cancer. Rebekkah Ursery revealed to Brice while he was sitting with her during her chemotherapy that she first knew something was wrong when she could smell bad things that no one else could smell. Do I think I have cancer? No. But I can't think of any other explanations, either, since my medical knowledge is so limited. And her story is just so fresh in my mind.

Settled down at the table with sandwiches, Brice and I say a quick prayer over our food. Glancing at the clock on the microwave, I note that I've let the twins sleep too long for their morning nap and may have ruined my chances of them taking a decent afternoon nap.

"I'll entertain them, if you want a break," Brice offers tersely between bites.

"It's not about needing a break. I hate when they get off their schedules. I wasn't paying close enough attention to the time."

Again, dismissively, he states, "I'll figure out a way to squeeze in a cat nap with them," as if it's that easy.

I can tell he's in "fix it" mode, though, so I don't contradict him. He'll find out soon enough.

"Whatcha workin' on in the shed?" I ask aimlessly, simply trying to make conversation.

He shrugs. "Nothing specific. Just goofing off. Trying new things."

"Using your dad's stuff that your mom gave you for Christmas?"

"Yeah. His jigsaw's a lot fancier than mine. And I'm trying to think of ways to use the die cutter."

Not at all versed in woodworking, I can only nod and make encouraging noises, so when he says no more, the topic dies a stilted, uncomfortable death.

Max, obviously thinking it's time to inject some action into the meal, pushes away his plate, nearly sending it to the floor. Brice snatches the edge of it, but that only turns it sideways, dropping strawberry slices and sandwich crusts onto the tile.

"Max Augustus!" he snaps. "Why'd you do that?"

I stand and come around the table, bending down to pick up the fallen food. "Because he's two. And tired," I answer for him. Tossing the scraps into the trash, I go to the kitchen sink, where I dampen a paper towel.

When I return to the table, father and son are staring each other down. Max blinks first. And bursts into tears.

"Daddy mad me!"

Brice closes his eyes and sighs. "I'm not mad at you, Stinky. Just... annoyed."

"Daddy 'noyed!"

"Daddy's annoyed at a lot of things since you got home from your walk," I mutter as I wipe Max's hands and work around his tears and snot and gaping mouth. I lift him from his chair and swing him onto my hip. "Let's go take a nap."

"Wait," Brice calls after me. "What's that supposed to mean?"

I ignore his question and continue upstairs, where the twins are awake and becoming unhappy about it. Their cries blend with Max's.

"It's okay," I soothe him. "Daddy doesn't like messes,

that's all. When you're finished eating, you just have to tell us. Don't push your food onto the floor."

He nods and rubs his eyes with his fists while I change his diaper and contemplate changing him into real clothes. His pajamas are still relatively clean, so I leave them on. Everyone needs a jammies day now and then. Even little boys.

After hoisting him into his crib, I lean over the rail and stand on my tiptoes to reach his forehead with my lips. "There. Now take a nap, and everything will be better when you wake up. I'll make grumpy Daddy take a nap, too."

Again, he nods solemnly, snuggling up to his favorite blankie.

Outside his closed door, I take a deep breath before heading to the room next door, where I can already hear Brice dealing with the twins. I pause in the hallway.

"Guys, guys. Really. It's not the end of the world. I can only change one diaper at a time. I'm good but not *that* good. Squeaky, you go second. I know, it's not fair that Screamy always goes first, because he's so loud, but that's how life is. Normally, the squeaky wheel gets the grease. In your case, screamy trumps squeaky. Here. Drink this bottle while you wait." The squeaks stop, replaced by loud sucking. "Go easy, now. That thing has to last at least two minutes. Brooks continues to fuss. "Now, you. If I give you this bottle while I change your diaper, will you be still and drink it? You're a kicker. I don't like holding your kicking feet while I try to wipe your dangly bits. That's how little boys get hurt."

I push my fist against my mouth to stifle my giggles.

"Okay, here. I'll take it away if you kick, though. Don't try me."

The crying stops. Into the relative quiet enters the sound of diaper tabs rasping. I take this as my cue to enter.

"Everything okay in here?"

Brice noticeably goes from warm and light to chilly and curt. "Fine."

I take over Harris's diapering duties, finishing at nearly the same time Brice fastens the last snap on Brooks's outfit. Without a word, he leads the way from the room, down the stairs, and into the kitchen, where he already has bowls of strained veggies waiting.

"Yum. Peas!" I say to Harris, strapping him into the high chair next to his brother's. I'm glad I got the easy baby to feed this meal.

About four spoonfuls into the meal (two for Brooks), Brice clears his throat. "I don't appreciate when you talk to me through our children. You have a problem with something I've done or said, you say it to me."

Ignoring the dictatorial tone with which he's delivered this edict, I reply calmly, "I was trying to calm him down."

"While sending me a message."

"What happened? This morning, you were in a good mood when you left for your walk. By the time you came back—after what seemed like forever, by the way—it was like you were a different person." I dab at Harris's face with his bib, which he tries to eat. "Is this about the coffee?"

He snorts. "I don't even know the 'this' to which you're referring, so how could it be about the coffee?"

"Is it because I texted you to see where you were? You were gone a long time. I was starting to worry. I can't help it." I feel my blood pressure rising as I defend my fears. "Once you get a call like the one I got, you never take for granted that your loved ones are safe."

After muttering to Brooks something about just eating the peas, he says, "It wasn't about the text."

"Are you sure? Because I didn't give a damn about the coffee."

"Obviously. You let it go to waste."

"You *are* pissed off about the coffee."

"I wasn't until you didn't even drink it. If I knew you weren't going to drink it, I would have saved myself the trip into the store."

"I had every intention of drinking it! I told you I appreciated the effort you took to get it. But I didn't ask you to do it. You offered."

"Whatever. This is dumb. I don't give a dang about the coffee."

"Then what's the matter?" I start listing possibilities, hoping he'll accept one of them. "Are you tired? You stayed up really late. Why didn't you sleep longer this morning?"

"I got plenty of sleep."

"Did you bump into someone at—"

"Maybe I pushed myself too hard during the walk," he posits. He closes his eyes, takes a deep breath, reopens his eyes, and continues feeding Brooks.

"Did you try to jog?"

"I didn't try to jog."

"Is it your leg? Your hip?"

"For crying out loud!" he explodes, making both babies flinch.

Harris gives a gigantic frown and looks like he's considering crying but settles for accepting the next spoonful of peas I offer him. Brooks isn't as forgiving.

As he wails, Brice talks over him, "It's not any one thing, all right? It's discouraging when something as simple as a walk to the store for coffee ends up being so draining. That's it. I'm sorry if I seemed to be taking it out on you when I got home. I tried not to. I tried to keep it to myself and leave you out of it. But you won't let it go."

He tilts his head and says to Brooks, "Dude. I'm sorry. Here. You want more peas?"

The infant immediately proceeds to sputter the mouthful he's offered back into his father's face.

Brice blinks and reaches for the dish towel draped on the oven handle. "I deserve that," he mumbles.

I silently thank Brooks for his act of defiance. Finished feeding Harris, I calmly take his empty bowl to the sink, drop it with a clatter, and silently exit the room. This is me, letting it go. And taking my husband up on his earlier offer to entertain the twins for the afternoon.

23

HYPOCHONDRIA

*A*ccording to WebDoctor, I'm going to die. Yep. Should not have plugged my symptoms into that damn symptom checklist thingy. But I really had nothing better to do. I was too angry to nap, so I got out my phone, flounced onto our bed, and dialed up the trusty Internet doctor. Dumb. Dumb. Dumb.

I went there with one symptom in mind: aversion to smells—and tastes, I suppose—that are usually pleasing to me. But that didn't yield any results other than "pregnancy," and it's not that, because I'm taking those magic little pills that make that worry a lot less of a worry. And I had a period recently. At least, it felt pretty recent (let's face it; it feels like it's always my Bye Week). And it's not that, because it *can't* be that. Can't be. Mustn't be.

Anyway, I know what it feels like to be pregnant, and suddenly hating the smell of coffee isn't it. I wish it were that simple.

So I changed my original symptom description to "smelling strange smells" and started perusing the other suggested symptoms, and the more I thought about it, *Yeah, I have been fatigued lately. And yeah, I do get a little nauseated sometimes and don't have much of an appetite. And you know what? I have had more headaches lately.* And I kept adding more and more symptoms, narrowing down the list of possible conditions until the only things on the list were either things I could readily rule out (the aforementioned) or things that could kill me. Pancreatic cancer. Acute kidney failure. Chronic kidney disease.

By the time Brice pokes his head in our room, I'm practically drafting what I want on my tombstone (*Can I legitimately say "Loving Wife and Mother?"*). When he sees I'm awake, he comes further into the room.

"The boys are all sleeping. I'm going to run to the church for—"

Clutching my phone, I stagger from the bed, grasping at his white t-shirt to establish my balance when dizziness overtakes me. *Dizziness. Add that to the list.*

"I'm sorry," I say miserably. "I don't want to fight with you. Life is so short. And I'm sorry I took it personally when you were quiet when you got home. I should have known you had your reasons." He opens his mouth to respond, but I keep going, clinging to his neck. "No. Listen. I… I'm sorry I didn't drink the coffee you brought home, but it made me sick, too. And I usually love that coffee. I think there's something really wrong with me." Now I thrust my phone into his face.

He pulls back his head and tries to focus on the screen. Eventually, he gives up looking at the device while I'm in control of it and takes it from me. "What's this?"

"WebDoctor. I put my symptoms into this computer thing, and these are the things I might have."

He squints at the list, blanches, then furrows his brow as he reads aloud my self-reported complaints. "Fatigue, nausea, strange smells, headaches, muscle weakness, nose-bleeds, lower back pain, and dry mouth? Really?"

I hedge, "Well, it was only one nosebleed, and it was probably because I hit my nose on the kitchen cabinet door when I was hurrying to grab a glass of water before work. But I've been dizzy, too. Sometimes."

He flattens his lips together in a straight line, then says, "I see. Well, what about this condition? It's not fatal." He points to "pregnant" on the results list. "And it seems to cover more of your symptoms than the others."

"It's not that one," I assure him. "I know that for a fact."

Accepting my confident claim, he sighs and hands my phone to me. "Okay, but it's probably not any of those other things, either."

"What if it is, though?"

On a sigh, he says, "I'll tell you what you have."

"What?"

"Three very young children."

"No, really!"

"What even brought this on?" He advances farther into the bedroom, disengaging himself from me, and opening his side of the closet.

"I'm freaked out that I suddenly hate the smell and taste of coffee."

"It's odd," he concedes, "but you never liked it before we had kids. Maybe you're just sick of it." He pulls a short-sleeved black shirt from its hanger, inspects it for cleanliness by sniffing it and giving it a once over, and shrugs it on over his t-shirt.

"All of a sudden?"

He raises his eyebrows at me. "Maybe. I don't know. Here's what I do know: that online tool is a hypochondriac's dream. You can't trust anything it tells you, especially if you're feeding it misinformation."

"What?"

"You can't count a nosebleed brought on by blunt trauma as 'nosebleeds,' plural, as in, 'chronic,' as in, 'a symptom of something bigger.'"

I click the "x" to take it off the list but add "dizziness" to the queue. "There. It still says I could have pancreatic cancer."

Buttoning his shirt and crossing to his dresser, he smiles indulgently over his shoulder at me. "I don't think you have pancreatic cancer."

"Rebekkah Ursery probably didn't think *she* did, either," I say quietly, sitting on the edge of the bed.

His hands falter at his throat, where he's inserting his clerical collar. After a lengthy pause, he closes his dresser drawer and turns to face me.

"She told you she smelled weird things," I remind him. "That was the first sign something was wrong."

"'Weird' as in, 'not detectable to others.'"

"Still," I persist.

He laughs. "Not 'still.' It's different."

"You're going to feel bad for making fun of me if I turn out to be right."

"Hon, I think you've had a rough day."

"One argument with you doesn't make for a rough day. That's a pretty normal day. You're projecting. *You've* had a rough day. Mine's been fine, other than finding out I may be dying."

Sitting down on the bed next to me, he puts an arm around my shoulder. "You don't really think you're dying, do you? I mean, really?"

"Maybe," I say, waffling. "I wish you'd at least consider the possibility."

"I don't want to consider the possibility! Ever."

"That doesn't mean it's not possible."

Suddenly, he pulls his clerical collar out and tosses it toward his dresser. He misses. He unbuttons his shirt and balls it up, throwing it toward the hamper. Again, a miss.

"What are you doing?" I ask.

"Well, I'm definitely not leaving my dying wife at home to go to work on my day off." He puts his hands behind his head and falls backwards onto the bed, staring up at the ceiling.

"There's no need to be patronizing," I say with a sniff.

He pulls on the back of my t-shirt until I stop resisting and take up a position next to him, my hands folded on my abdomen, like I imagine they'd pose me in my coffin. I count beams on the wood-slatted ceiling while we lie in silence for a while.

Finally, he asks, "Are you quite done?"

"I'm going to make an appointment with my doctor on Monday. I want them to do some blood tests."

"You do that," he encourages. "Until then, can you forget this crazy Internet Physician—or whatever it's called —app? I can see where Rebekkah's case may make anyone more aware of their mortality, but suddenly not liking coffee —while a huge bummer—is not a death sentence."

"I know."

"Good." He seems poised to say something else, but at the same time, hesitant.

I'm not sure I want to encourage him to speak if he's going to continue to mock my health worries, so I stare at the ceiling and feed my morbidity by imagining what his and the boys' lives would be like without me.

I've come to the awful realization that if I die in the near future, the twins will probably never remember me, when he blurts, "I ran into Matt Benson at the store."

"You what?" I shoot into a sitting position so quickly that I nearly knee myself in the chin in the process.

He remains reclined, affecting nonchalance. "Actually, he ran into me. We ran into each other."

He looks decidedly guilty, which is mystifying, but I'm too distracted by all the questions swimming in my head to analyze the root of his guilt. "How— I mean, you've never met him. How did you know what he looked like?"

"Well, I Googled him, of course. After you told me about—well, you know. Everything."

"You Googled him."

"Yeah. You know, just to see what I was up against." He half-smiles so I know he's kidding... somewhat. Sitting up, he scratches his head. The front of his shirt still bears some evidence of Brooks's lunchtime tantrum.

"You're not up against anything!" I wrap both of my arms around his one arm and squeeze tightly.

Rolling his eyes, he says, "The crazy thing is that the best picture I found of him online was from the article the newspaper ran, thanks to you."

I wince. "Yeesh. Bad coincidence."

He nods. "Yeah. And that picture didn't do him justice. Why didn't you mention how young he is?"

"He's not young! Not any younger than us."

"He looks a lot younger than I feel."

"Wait a minute! Go back. So, you walked into the store to get my coffee, and you bumped into him. Or he bumped into you. Or whatever." I shake my head, trying to picture it. "What happened?"

"There was a guy in line in front of me at the coffee

counter. I didn't pay much attention to him, because I was entertaining Max so he wouldn't get restless while we waited. Then the guy turned around. And we were looking right at each other. And I instantly recognized him. And it was obvious he knew who I was."

"How?" I wonder aloud before remembering, "Oh… he said he saw you on TV after the tornado hit the church."

"Yeah, well, I'm sure he Googled me at some point, too. Don't you think?"

"I don't know what reality-challenged people do in their spare time. I guess looking up spouses of women they fancy themselves in love with would be one way to kill a few hours, when you're finished cutting out individual letters from magazines to use in creepy shrines. Or ransom notes." I free up one of my hands to place on my churning stomach. "So, okay. You see each other, you recognize each other. Then what?"

Brice takes a deep breath through his nose and stares into space, as if he's watching a movie of the encounter and describing it to me. "He looked terrified. I'm not sure how I looked, but I felt… naked."

"Naked?"

He nods. "Yeah. I don't know how else to describe it. Exposed. Embarrassed. Ashamed."

"That doesn't make any sense."

He shakes his head, like he's trying to clear it. "I know. I thought I'd be angry. I wasn't, though. It was so weird." He blinks. "I've imagined over and over what I'd say to him if I ever had the chance to talk to him. Or what I'd do to him. But never did I think I'd stand there, feeling like a sad, pathetic fool."

I don't even know what to say to that, so I remain quiet, letting him talk it out, waiting for him to finish the story.

After a sigh, he says, "Anyway, there were people in line behind me, but there was no way I was going to be able to simply step up and give my order, like the man who had disrespected me in the way he had wasn't standing right there. I couldn't ignore his presence. And he wasn't ignoring mine. But I could tell he was just as at a loss about what to do. One thing was for sure, though. He was choosing 'fight,' not 'flight.' I had to acknowledge that."

"You think he wanted to fight you?" My eyes nearly pop from my skull as I try to imagine this.

He laughs. "No. I just mean, he wasn't running away."

"Oh. Whew."

"You know I wouldn't fight him."

"Of course." I chuckle nervously. "Just making sure he didn't try it."

He returns to watching the scene unravel in his head. "Anyway, I got out of line, and I said, 'Hey. I don't believe we've officially met, but you tried to steal my wife.'"

"No, you didn't!" I gasp.

He laughs. "No. I didn't. I actually said, 'Hi. You may not know me, but I know *of* you through my wife, Peyton Northam, at Eye Candy.' He kind of grunted a response, still looking like he was going to drop his drink and crap his pants. So I held out my hand for him to shake and introduced myself, like we were truly just two guys with a mutual acquaintance. Then I introduced Max. It was surreal."

"Ya think?"

Smiling, he puts his arm around me and hugs me harder to his side. "But you know what? I knew it was the only way to handle it. If you'd seen his face… I felt sorry for the guy!"

"I feel sick."

"It was really okay, hon."

"I'm so glad I wasn't there!"

"Oh, me too! That would have been ten times worse. But you know what? It would have been okay, too. It would have worked out."

"I live in fear of running into him. Before his little parking lot confessional, I *did* run into him at the store, and I have a really hard time going in there now, worried I'll bump into him again. I guess he lives around here? Or maybe that store is on the way to someplace he goes all the time?"

Brice snorts. "Hon."

"What?"

He looks down into my face, his eyes sparkling. "Do you know how many grocery stores there are in this town? They're third in number only to churches and Chinese restaurants."

"So?"

"You think it's a coincidence that you bumped into him at *that* grocery store? Or that I bumped into him, for that matter?"

I sigh. "I know you don't believe in coincidence."

"I'm not talking about divine providence here. He obviously knows where *you* live. He knows the stores you frequent."

After an audible gulp, I whisper, "Like stalking me?"

I can tell by his smile that he's not worried, so I relax. "There you go with the dramatics again. I don't think it's as serious as stalking. He's infatuated, setting himself up to have encounters with you."

Sounds like stalking to me, but I don't argue, because I'm feeling too lightheaded to do so. "Please. Continue with your story. I don't feel well."

Having mercy on me and honoring my request, he says, "When I apologized for missing his show—"

"*You* apologized to *him?*"

"Yeah. I mean, I would have been at his opening—and you would have, too—if I hadn't gotten myself run over."

"You're amazing," I marvel under my breath, making it sound somewhat like an insult.

"Anyway," he says through his laughter, "when I apologized, he relaxed. That's when he knew I wasn't going to say anything about what he said to you. I don't know. Maybe he thinks I don't know. Either way, he loosened up somewhat. But I could see the guilt, too. He feels bad." Ultra-casually, he adds, "Oh, and I invited him to church."

"What?!" I say for the umpteenth time. "Do you have any idea how uncomfortable it would be for me if he showed up at church?" The thought of it brings on even more nausea.

"He won't take me up on it." When I look into his eyes as a way of silently begging him to promise me that's true, he adds confidently, "He won't. By now, after inviting thousands of people to church, don't you think I can tell when someone is receptive to my offer? He wasn't." A hint of a smirk peeks through his smile, but he quickly hides it and resumes his typical wide-eyed, innocent look.

"Brice Augustus Northam!"

"What?"

"You're screwing with him."

"I'm doing no such thing!"

"Yes, you are. You know he feels bad, so you're being the bigger man and making him feel even worse." I bestow on him an admiring smile. "Nicely played."

"I'm not playing at anything. I was honestly moved by the Holy Spirit to show him mercy and kindness. And to invite him to worship with us. And receive our forgiveness. And God's."

I scoot away from him. "Oh, my. I don't want to be near you when the lightning strikes."

"Fine. Don't believe me."

"I don't."

He pulls me into his lap. "Anyway, don't you think I deserve a teensy bit of revenge?"

"Oh, so now you're admitting it? Let me go."

He holds me more tightly, a determined set to his jaw. "Never."

I struggle against him for a few more seconds, but I'm no match for his upper body strength, and we both know it. His lips land on the back of my neck and linger there for a few seconds before he pulls away and says, "As soon as he left, and I got back in line, the worst feeling hit me."

"You felt bad for screwing with him?"

"I wasn't." He sighs against my neck, making me shiver. "No, I was mad at myself for letting him off the hook."

I turn sideways so I can look at his face when I say, "I'm proud of how you handled it. Really. All kidding aside. Even if a tiny part of you was enjoying the power you had over him in that moment, you were classy, as usual."

"I felt small. And… and impotent."

Knowing he's being serious, I stifle my urge to giggle at the word.

A trace of the moroseness he's been displaying most of the day skips across his face, only to be replaced by his more natural, peaceful expression. "Anyway, that was macho, petty bull hockey. I know I have to forgive him. I guess giving the appearance of forgiveness is a good start. Fake it until you can make it, or something like that."

"So when you got home, you were still wishing you'd decked him and dumped his coffee over his head, with Max cheering you on?"

Sheepishly, he grins, "Maybe."

I hug him, resting my chin on his shoulder. "I'm so glad you didn't."

"Me, too. I had to think about it for a while, though. I tried to walk it off. Max and I took a few laps around the neighborhood. But then you texted me, and your coffee was getting cold, so I came back to the house, still feeling pretty crummy." He wraps his arms around me, rubbing my back with his warm, wide hands. "It would have been rather rewarding to knock out one of his perfect teeth."

His mention of Matt's pretty pearlies makes me tense at first, but I relax when I realize I feel nothing while picturing that smile. "Right?" I simply affirm my husband's primal urge while continuing to look over his shoulder at our wedding picture on my nightstand.

"I mean, they're unbelievable," he says. "So white and straight! And he was drinking coffee." He trails off, his voice mixed with awe and befuddlement. "How much do you think he spends each year to keep them that white? Do you think they glow in the dark?" Pulling away, he bares his own teeth at me. "Wha' d'ya shink? Whi'e enou'?"

I giggle at him but finally manage seriously, "Gorgeous. You have a beautiful smile, and I love it."

As if to reward me, his mouth and eyes relax into one that lights up his whole face.

Tracing my finger along his cheek, I say, "See? That's what I've been missing since you got back from your walk. I can die happy now."

The frustrated grunt my statement produces from him makes me laugh, but inside, I'm a hundred percent serious.

24

OPEN COMMUNION

I knew there was going to be trouble the next day when Wayne stormed from the sanctuary after hearing Brice's new spiel before the usual Communion liturgy:

"We believe that Holy Communion is the true body and blood of Christ, that it's a Holy Sacrament, that it is the key to our salvation. If you believe this, we invite you to come forward and partake with us. Otherwise, we ask that you refrain until you've sought out either myself or Pastors Laszewski and Anthony for a frank discussion of these teachings."

Brice, Jared, and Wes had been discussing for months how they would phrase the "new" invitation, which isn't really new at all but sounds more all-inclusive and more welcoming. After many drafts, this is what they came up with. And they knew it was going to piss some people off. Hardcore.

Namely, Wayne Long.

That, of course, didn't stop them from doing it. In Brice's case, if he were being completely honest, it may have encouraged him. However, he wasn't the one who suggested the change; that was Jared's doing. He agreed, though, that it was time to modernize things—within the confines of the Lutheran church's guidelines, which Jared meticulously and arduously researched before even considering drafting something more modern. And it goes without saying that they got the Synod's unequivocal blessing.

Anyone visiting for the first time or not having a deep understanding of the church's teachings regarding this practice wouldn't think twice about what Brice said. But every staunch, dyed-in-the-wool Lutheran in the congregation that morning (in both services) sat up straighter and paid closer attention when he delivered those three sentences.

For one thing, *"That's not in the usual script,"* undoubtedly crossed their minds immediately. For another thing, "If you believe this, come forward," doesn't exactly have the "Lutherans-only-beyond-this-point" tone that the former— shall we say, more traditional]—invitation had. Subtle differences in semantics don't get by Lutherans when you're messin' with tradition.

So it wasn't wholly unexpected that Wayne left the sanctuary in a huff without partaking. And while others may not have had the gumption to make such a bold nonverbal statement, I saw the disapproval on the faces of several, some of whom chose to stay in their seats rather than come forward for the Sacrament.

My husband's in for a rough week. At least.

What I don't expect is for Wayne to be waiting in Brice's office when I walk through the door with Max and Brooks in tow.

"Oh. Hey. You," I drop dully.

I only kick myself for a second for being so transparently nonplussed at his presence. After all, what's the point in pretending? I know he's not here for a sweet chat about something relatively pleasant, like genital warts. Even if he were, there's no love lost between the two of us. And much less than he thinks I know.

Remembering in more detail what he and his wife said about me to Jared and Mitzi, I lift my chin while I set Brooks down on the floor to practice his crawling. Max hovers near him, more likely to hurt his little brother by stomping on his fingers than to protect him.

I use supervising the kids as an excuse to avoid eye contact with Wayne when I say, "Brice should be here in a minute. He and Harris are still greeting people. You know, people who stayed for the whole service," I add pointedly.

"I wouldn't expect you to understand," he says patronizingly.

"And why is that, *Pastor*?" His thinly veiled insult motivates me to seek his cocky eye contact, and I see he's looking down his long nose at me, as usual. "I've been a Lutheran my whole life. I know the score."

"So does your husband. That's why what happened in there was reprehensible." He points in the general direction of the sanctuary, through walls and doors and corridors. "And that's what I'm going to say when I report this to the Synod."

"What's this?" Brice asks cheerfully, striding through the door, Harris perched on his arm like a ventriloquist dummy. "Good morning, Pastor! Where's Vivian this morning? I hope she's not under the weather. I heard there's something nasty going around. Summer colds are the worst!"

Wayne ignores the inquiry into his wife's health and repeats his rant about Brice's new "open Communion policy."

Brice wrinkles his nose. "Open Communion? Where? When?"

"Don't play dumb with me. You're a lot of things, but dumb isn't one of them," Wayne huffs.

Smiling benevolently, Brice consults Harris when he says, "Not sure, but I think that was an insult."

I hide my laughter behind my hand at the comically appropriate, drooly grin Harris gives his dad in response.

"Play with your brothers," he tells the infant, placing him on the floor with Max and Brooks.

Wayne, glancing pointedly at me and gesturing toward the jumble of children in the middle of the office, asks, "Would it be possible for us to talk, pastor-to-pastor about this? In private?"

Brice follows Wayne's eyes and hands before going around his desk and sitting down. "Absolutely. You can call Lucy tomorrow and make an appointment, if that would work better for you." Bellying up to his desk, he plunks his elbows on the surface and folds his hands. "Otherwise, if you want to speak to me right now, it'll have to be with present company included."

"I know what you're doing." When all he receives from Brice is an innocent head tilt, he elaborates, "You're stalling. Trying to distract me from the conversation you know has to happen."

"Not at all. Why don't you have a seat?" Brice offers, sweeping his arm in the direction of the sofa.

Wayne ignores the invitation and continues standing. "What I have to say won't take long."

"By all means."

"What you and Pastors Laszewski and Anthony are doing is wrong."

"You'll have to be more specific."

"In the LCMS, which is what we still are, last time I checked, we practice closed Communion—"

"'*Close*,' not 'closed.' But proceed."

"That's bull, and you know it. A door is either open or closed. You can't open the Sacrament to just anyone."

"We're not."

"Could have fooled me!"

"I specifically said that anyone who believes the same way we do about what the Sacrament is and what it does for us is welcome at the table. That's consistent with Lutheran doctrine and Synodical practice."

"You're sliding through a loophole. And sounding like a Calvinist in the process."

"Hey, now!" Brice looks less than serene for the first time in the exchange. He quickly recovers, though, and poses the following question to the retired pastor: "When was the last time you made someone prove to you they'd studied Martin Luther's Catechism and had renewed their baptismal vows in a Confirmation ceremony before you allowed them to take Communion?" He pauses to wait for an answer that never comes. "Exactly. At least this way, we're unequivocally stating what we believe and saying that belief is required at the Lord's table."

I want to add, "Pow!" but keep my lips clamped tightly together.

"Being a member of this church is a requirement you're conveniently forgetting. It's a vital part of the sacred closeness, the intimacy of the practice."

"So, if my mother visits, or your children come to visit, they're not allowed to join us, because they're not listed on our membership rolls?"

Wayne's face reddens, and his turkey neck jiggles. "You're being intentionally obtuse. You know the practice.

Visitors speak with a pastor before the service if they wish to participate in Communion."

"When was the last time a visitor approached you about that? I'll tell you the last time *I* had a visitor ask me. Um, never. And I'm okay with that, for the most part. You know why? Because it's not my decision to grant or withhold God's forgiveness. 'Drink of it, *all* of you. This is my blood, shed for you for the forgiveness of your sins.' I don't recall Jesus saying, 'But only if you have a Lutheran Confirmation certificate hanging around somewhere in your keepsake boxes at home.'"

Wayne levels a long finger at Brice and squints down the length of it. "You've crossed the line this time with your reckless, feel-good disregard for authority. You've crossed it good. And people with a lot more say than I have are going to be upset about it."

"Doubt it."

"We'll soon see, won't we?"

I open my mouth to disabuse Wayne of his notion that anything he'll be telling the Synod will be news to them, but Brice cuts me off.

"No, Peyton. Pastor Long is right to speak to someone at the Synod if he has reservations about Peace's ministry and has questions that I cannot satisfactorily answer."

"But—"

Shooting me a warning look, he stands and shoves his hands in his pockets. Then he turns his attention back to Wayne. "Pastor, I hope you have a wonderful afternoon. Give our love to Vivian." When Brice keeps his hands firmly out of reach, denying Wayne a parting handshake, the retired clergyman gives him a curt nod and walks to the door, stepping over our children on his way.

"I'm sure you'll be hearing from someone before the end of the day tomorrow," he tosses over his shoulder.

"I look forward to it," Brice responds mildly, rocking on his feet.

Neither of us says a word or moves until we hear Wayne's footfalls fade into nothingness. Even then, it's like a bubble of silence has descended over the room, including over the babies, who have ceased their babbling.

Finally Max breaks the spell with, "I waunt wunch."

"I bet Mommy's going to take you home and give you some right now," Brice assures his oldest son.

I loop the diaper bag strap over my shoulder and take charge of one infant, while Brice plucks the other from the floor and shepherds Max toward the door.

Stopping on my way past him as he waits for me to go first through the doorway, I ask, "Why didn't you tell Wayne that you cleared all of this Communion business with the Synod?"

He smiles into my face. "I figured it was probably best that Pastor Long found that out for himself. I'm sure he'll be relieved to hear it from someone much more authoritative than I am."

For the second time in two days, I'm taken aback by my husband's cunning. "Oh."

The playful glint in his eye disappears, replaced by a more determined spark. "Like he said, I'm a lot of things, but I'm not dumb."

"*M*ommy!"

"Angel boy!"

Max, holding a clerical collar against his neck as he runs into the house from the garage, barely slows down to squeeze my legs with his free arm on his way through the kitchen to the living room. From in there, I hear him pulling out what sounds like every toy from the bin into which I've only recently tossed them.

I point to my own neck and ask Brice when he catches up, "Do you know Max has one of your collars?"

Hands full with babies, he closes the door with his foot and replies matter-of-factly, "Yeah. He found it in the back-seat." He raises his eyebrows at me, and I blush, remembering a particularly adventurous evening excursion in the garage and Jeep a few weeks back.

Maybe it was the *time,* I think, but say instead, "Ah. Well, 'Mystery of the Missing Collar' solved, then."

Brice shoots me a wry grin and deposits the twins in their respective chairs for them to assume the feeding position. Looking around at the pots simmering on the stove and the ingredients scattered around the counters, he says, "I wasn't expecting you to be home. Or doing this. What *are* you doing?"

My heart races, but I attempt a casual shrug while he peeks into the living room to check on Max on his way past the doorway. After that tiny detour, he moves through the kitchen efficiently as he performs his usual after-work routine and gets the twins' dinners ready. I observe, interested in the rare glimpse into this part of my family's day.

Pouring two servings of various baby foods from jars onto a divided plate and sticking it in the microwave for a slight warm-up, he raises his eyebrows at me when I still haven't answered his question. "What's up?"

"I decided to take the day off from work, after my doctor's appointment." If I stay calm and matter-of-fact when I talk about this, maybe I can control his reaction, too. Because everyone needs to just keep their wits about themselves.

The microwave beeps, but he ignores it. "Oh? Is everything okay?" Again, his eyes flit around the kitchen. "I mean, what's all this?"

"Felt in the mood to cook," I explain. "And clean." He's going to notice that too, when he ventures into other parts of the house, so I might as well acknowledge it now. I came home from the doctor and threw myself into scrubbing all three bathrooms and chasing dust bunnies from under the beds. All surfaces gleam. The vacuum tracks make the carpeted floors in the bedrooms look like freshly iced cakes.

Mmmm, cake.

"In the mood to cook and clean, but not in the mood to go to work." He chuckles nervously. "So, you're really sick, then?"

Responding to the babies' increasingly impatient noises

from their chairs, he retrieves their food from the microwave and walks around the island, pulling up a stool in front of them.

"So, what's the doctor's opinion of your 'issue'? Or did they only run some tests today?"

I stir the spaghetti sauce that's starting to bubble and spurt, then turn down the temperature under it so the sauce doesn't burn to the bottom of the pan. With a tiny sigh and dismissive wave, I say, "Oh, that. Just one simple test."

"And?"

"I'm pregnant. But whatever."

Brice looks up sharply at me and misses Harris's gaping mouth, stabbing him in the cheek with a spoonful of chicken noodle dinner. While rectifying his feeding faux pas and correcting his aim, he says, "Very funny."

"Well, I'm not joking, but I'm glad you're amused." I lift the lid on the pot of spinach and test the temperature of the simmering vegetable before shaving some butter onto the surface, mixing, and repeating the process.

"So you're not kidding?"

I force myself to look him in the eyes when I say, "No," but I then quickly busy myself at the oven, my back turned to him while I set the preheat temperature for the garlic bread I'm going to prepare next.

"I thought you said you couldn't be. I mean—"

"I was wrong. Obviously."

When I turn around, I see he's robotically shoveling baby food into the boys' mouths, alternating between the two of them. Harris is keeping up nicely, but Brooks has more food on his chin and bib than in his mouth. And he's starting to gag.

"You're, uh, making a mess with Brooks. And nearly killing him."

He blinks and confirms my assertion with his own eyes. "Oh," he mutters. "Sorry, Bud." He mops Brooks's face and gives him a chance to breathe. Harris squeaks impatiently. "You've had your share," he tells the faster eater. As if he understands, the baby shoves his fist into his mouth and sucks contentedly on that while he waits for his brother to finish so they can have their bottles. "Good idea," Brice observes.

And those are the last words spoken until we sit down to eat in the dining room, and Brice says the table prayer. When I open my eyes and unfold my hands, I sneak a peek across the table at him to try to gauge his mood. His face is unreadable as he busies himself arranging food on Max's plate.

"I no yike spittach," the two-year-old informs us, his statement falling on deaf ears. He receives a small spoonful, anyway, along with his spaghetti, meat sauce, garlic bread, and asparagus.

As soon as our plates are full, I clear my throat and ask while loading my fork with pasta, "So, anything new on the Wayne front?"

Brice chews and swallows, glancing at the twins in the playpen on the other side of the dining room doorway. "Uh, no. Well, sort of. Pastor Long made an appointment with Lucy today to come talk to me tomorrow. It popped up on my calendar right before I left for the day."

"That should be interesting. What do you think he wants to talk about?"

"Probably what he found out when he talked to someone at the Synod about… things."

"Do you think it's a bad sign that he wants to meet with you in person? I mean, if he got an answer he didn't like from the Synod, he'd either call you or email you or not say anything at all, right? He's not going to look you in the eye to tell you that you were right." I watch Max pick up an asparagus stalk with his bare hands and munch it, but I don't correct him and ask him to use his fork, because I'm too interested in Brice's answer to bother with a table manners lesson.

"I'm sure he won't be telling me I'm right. But..." He shakes his head as if to clear it. "You know, I don't really care what he has to say. And I'm not going to worry about it. I have more important things on my mind." He gives me a pointed look.

I quickly refocus on my plate. I hate that I'm involved in anything more worrisome than Wayne, but I swallow back the dismay and continue eating without acknowledging his declaration. I don't want to talk about it with the kids around to distract us.

I don't necessarily want to talk about it at all. It's happening; talking about it isn't going to change anything. It's only going to make me think and say things that are pointless to think and say. Moving forward without a bunch of chit-chat on the topic is a much more practical approach. Anyway, I don't even know what to say, because I don't know how I feel about this. "Resigned" is probably the strongest emotion I have on the matter. It's definitely not a bad thing, but I also wouldn't classify it as "great." It simply *is*.

Mercifully, he doesn't push the issue. We spend the rest of the meal confirming why we normally eat after the boys are in bed, as we nag Max about his food intake, get up several times to attend to the twins' fussing, and generally don't get a moment's peace, much less two consecutive bites of dinner. By the time the meal is over, I'm more than happy to give my bedtime kisses and wave the boys upstairs with their father as he and I divide and conquer the evening routine. I choose kitchen cleanup.

About a half-hour later, I'm tossing wet dish towels into the washing machine with a load of whites when a ball of bath towels sails over my shoulder into the appliance.

"Nice shot," I say while pouring in the detergent, turning on the water, and closing the lid. "A buzzer beater."

He gives me a hug from behind and a kiss on my temple. "My specialty, apparently."

I laugh for the first time all day. He turns me around to face him.

In a horrible German accent, he says, "So, it's not a toomah, it's a babeh."

"Yes."

"Beats pancreatic cancer."

"I'm glad you think so."

His smile is much-needed, extra reassurance. "Of course I do!"

I avoid his eyes. "But you said a couple of months ago—"

"I said I'd rather you battle a potentially fatal disease than have another baby with you?"

"No!" I giggle.

"Then enough." He lifts my chin. "Four babies in three years is a little intense, but…"

I groan. "I guess I'll just stay pregnant forever. It's obviously my body's preference."

"Ohhhhh, I think maybe we should shut this factory down, don't you? For one thing, we're running out of bedrooms. Demand is definitely out-pacing supply."

I lead the way into the kitchen, where I aimlessly straighten things on the counter, shooting a glare at the coffeemaker for good measure, as if the small appliance got me into this situation. Restless and fidgety, I wander into the living room. There, I pick up Max's toys for the second time of the day, pausing to look at the pictures on the fireplace mantle, bookshelves, and end tables as if I'm seeing them for the first time. Brice keeps his distance but follows me with his eyes.

When I stray within his reach again, he grabs me, placing one hand on my waist and wrapping his other hand around mine. Swaying to a song that's not audible to anyone but him, he asks, "Remember our first dance as husband and wife?"

I stare at the white square of his clerical collar. "Yes. I was worried about everyone staring at us. Plus, the song the DJ picked was godawful. What was it, again?"

He pulls me closer, so I rest my head on his chest. "I don't remember the song," he surprises me by saying, considering he usually remembers everything (and is pretty proud of it).

Before I can tease him, he expounds, "I was too focused on how happy I was. In that moment. Undiluted joy. Just... filled... with that moment. Thinking about absolutely nothing except that. Holding you, my wife, in my arms. There are so few moments like that in life, ya know?"

"You're going to make me cry."

"So what? I'm used to it. And it's okay." We sway in silence for a few seconds. Then he says, "Anyway, I'd rather you cry about something happy than because you're upset."

I merely nod against him, so he continues, "It's unfortunate, but rarely do we allow ourselves that depth of joy. We might be thinking about how it would be better 'if only.' If only Dad were here, the sun was shining, my feet didn't hurt... whatever. Or we compare it to other happy times in the past, to see if it measures up. Or we think about times in the future that have the potential to be even happier. But I can honestly say I wasn't thinking of a single thing other than how elated I was each immediate second during our first dance."

I see where he's going with this and volunteer, "I felt that way the first time I held Max. And Harris and Brooks."

My tight throat won't let me say more, but I ruminate about how the months of discomfort and angst preceding their births just disappeared that first time I held each of them. And I didn't think about the worry and work of parenting. The happiness I felt didn't allow room for any other thoughts or feelings.

"You'll feel that way again, with this one. It'll be da bomb dot com."

I smile faintly at his dorkiness. "I'm sure."

"You won't be thinking about anything else. It'll be like you and that baby are alone in the room."

"No, you'll be there with us. You're always there with me."

He raises his hand from my waist to my neck, which he gently squeezes. "I'm glad, but I'd understand if I faded into the background, too."

"You don't." I close my eyes, lulled by our rocking motion and his kneading fingers on the tense muscles in my neck. "And I know when I hold him—or her—for the first time, I won't be thinking about the stupid minivan we're going to have to get. Or the hospital bills. Or the dirty diapers. Or the sleep deprivation. Or the gallons of puke we're going to wind up swabbing over the next decade. Or daycare costs. Or college funds—"

"Shhh… You're stressing me out."

"Yeah. Tell me about it."

"God will provide. He always has; He always will."

I know he's right. And for once, it doesn't annoy me.

Okay, I'll admit it. I'm a bit self-absorbed right now. Even more than usual. But I have good excuses. I'm getting used to the idea of the next thirty-two weeks being mostly about growing a baby; it's hotter than hell outside; I'm going through caffeine withdrawals; and Matt Benson's going to have another show in the autumn. Obviously, I'm not involved with it, but it's still going to happen; there's still a chance I'll be seeing him around the gallery; and although I feel better since Brice had his run-in with him, I'm still apprehensive about the first time I see him since his crazy parking lot profession of whatever (I refuse to call that "love").

On the positive side of things, I'm eight weeks along and so far, no puking, no insomnia, no zits, no public emotional outbursts, and no worries. Like I said to Dr. Klein at my first visit last week, "Am I really pregnant?" because other than the weird coffee-aroma issues and the lack of a period, I don't feel like I am.

"You are. Definitely," he answered with a smile. "Each one is different, you know. Maybe this will finally be your easy one."

I hardly dare to hope.

So I blame all of these preoccupations for completely letting Brice's meeting with Wayne slip my mind—until this evening, while staring at pictures of impossibly beautiful, rich people in *Entertainment Weekly*. My thoughts have meandered from plans for Brice's birthday in two days to wondering where I stored the maternity clothes from my pregnancy with Max (the ones from the twins won't fit me… I hope) to the appropriateness—however unseemly—of wearing only a swimsuit from now until October. (I know it would raise a few people's eyebrows, but some would be less shocked than others, considering their opinions of my classiness, or lack thereof.)

Out of the blue, I look up from my magazine and blurt, "Oh my gosh! What happened with you and Wayne when he came to talk to you in your office?"

"Huh?" Brice blinks at me from the opposite end of the couch. We're lounging, our legs bent at the knees, my feet resting on top of his.

I repeat my question.

"That was two weeks ago," he points out irrelevantly.

"Yeah, I know. Sorry I didn't ask sooner, but did I really need to ask for you to tell me?"

He shrugs and returns his eyes to his book of essays written about Martin Luther's teachings. (Yawn!) "It was a non-event. He said he was disappointed with the Synod's support of what he views as counter to the Church's teachings. I told him I disagreed with his interpretation. He disagreed with my disagreement. End of story."

"End of story? Well, what did he say when he left?"

"Something dramatic, like, 'I'm afraid, then, that we're at an impasse,'" he replies in a scarily accurate impersonation of Wayne, which he immediately appears to regret when I laugh.

My laughter quickly stops, though, when I realize, "That sounds ominous."

He licks his finger to turn the page in his book. "Hmm. Whatever," he drawls, sounding as bored with the topic as I would be with reading that book in his hands.

I nudge my toes against his butt, close to his "dangly bits." He flinches and nearly flies over the arm of the couch behind him. His book slips to the floor with a fluttering of pages and a thunk. "What the heck?!" he cries, reaching down to grab my foot.

"Pay attention to me," I demand.

"I am, now!" He grins and squeezes my toes. "Don't make me tickle you."

"You wouldn't dare."

"I will if you pull something like that again."

Back to our original conversation, I ask, "Do you really think he's going to drop it?"

"Haven't heard a peep from him since, have I?"

"I think he and Vivian are out of town again, visiting one of their kids. How many do they have, anyway?" I mutter disgustedly.

Brice raises an eyebrow at me. "Fewer than we're about to have."

I bite my lip to stifle a smile. "Oh. Well, have you noticed they all live hundreds of miles away from their parents? Not that I blame them."

He refuses to acknowledge my uncharitable sniping. "I'm not worried. Pastor Long is by-the-book. If our Communion practices have the Synod's blessing, he'll fall in line." When all I do is glare skeptically at him, he adds, "Anyway, what *can* he do about it?"

I hate to even imagine or suggest scenarios aloud.

Releasing my foot, he drops to the floor next to the couch and creeps toward me on his hands and knees. "Stop worrying about Pastor Long and tell me what you got me for my birthday."

I tap my chin and look toward the ceiling. "Hmm. Let's see… I made you something, but it won't be finished in time for your birthday. Not even close."

Suddenly, he looks worried. "You *made* me something? Like, something crafty?"

We both laugh at the idea of my doing anything that would be considered "crafty." I think most of his laughter is based on relief at my reassuring head-shaking.

I swat at his shoulder. "I'm talking about the baby, you goober!"

He smiles quietly. "Oh. Yeah. That's a pretty great present."

"I know," I reply smugly.

"But I helped with that."

"I guess."

"I might give you full credit if it's a girl."

"Oooh. That's not up to me, though."

He nods. "That's true. Well, I hate to break it to you, but you're going to have to get me something in addition to that, since you really can't take as much credit as you originally claimed."

I narrow my eyes at him. "Danger, danger…"

"Are you trying to tell me you didn't get me anything for my birthday? Because that's fine. I'm thinking of ignoring it altogether from here on out. Now that I'm… old."

"Yes. Thirty-six. Old."

"I have a reconstructed hip and more titanium in my leg than you can find in a shipyard."

Biting on my knuckle to keep from laughing out loud, I keep my watering eyes pinned to his face while he continues, "Before you know it, I'll start analyzing and cataloging my bowel movements—or lack thereof. I'll be taking medication for the arthritis that will set in from these massive injuries. I'll complain of stiffness and soreness after playing outside with the kids."

"Oh, c'mon. That already happens to me, so stop whining."

"Exactly. All the work I've done for years to take care of myself, to thwart the aging process… gone in a heartbeat. I'll never be the same. I'm no better than those of you who have abused your bodies with fast food and booze and your sedentary lifestyles."

"Well, excuse us!" I sneer.

He widens his eyes. "No offense. I'm just saying."

"Simple strategy to prevent what happened to you, Reverend Night Jogger. Look. Both. Ways."

His sheepish grin lets me know he doesn't resent my cajoling. He sighs. "Ah, yes. That old adage. Well, I prefer living on the edge."

"Then you'll have to suffer the cruel effects of age like the rest of us slovenly fools."

"I *will* jog again." I think he means it as a promise, but it sounds more like a threat to me.

Flicking my fingers through the hair on his forehead, I reply, "Sure you will. In a neon green, glow-in-the-dark jumpsuit."

"Rad."

"We'll make it Tyvek, so it's nice and toasty. And fire- and chemical-resistant. Waterproof goes without saying."

"Fancy!" He leans in.

Just before his lips touch mine, I say, "I think I know what I'm getting you for your birthday."

BIRTHDAY FAIL

*B*rice didn't get a Tyvek glow-in-the-dark jumpsuit from the boys and me for his birthday, but he got the next best thing, in my opinion: a treadmill. I know he enjoys running outdoors, but for most of the year, our schedules don't permit him to do it during daylight hours. And all joking aside about the glow-in-the-dark suit, I can't handle the worry I feel at the thought of him jogging in the dark.

I bought the machine secondhand from Lucy, who was complaining about hers being in the way in her small apartment. "I like going to the gym, anyway. It's more interesting than staring at the wall in my apartment while I work out," she explained.

So I asked her what she paid for the treadmill and how much her yearly gym membership was and gave her an offer, which she quickly accepted. Transporting the exercise equipment and hiding it at our house was a much bigger challenge than the price negotiations. But with the help of a few co-conspirators, I got it done.

And I could tell Brice was shocked when it was sitting in

the living room, unfolded and ready for service—complete with a big, red bow on the hand rest—when he came downstairs this morning, one twin on each arm.

"Oh, my," he said with an uncertain smile as he slowed to a stop across the room from it.

"Happy birthday!" I gushed.

"Thanks!" He leaned down and kissed my waiting lips. "Wow. That's... a really nice treadmill."

Max, who had run straight for it when he saw it, pulled off the bow and stuck it to the top of his head. "I a pwesent!"

"One of the best, Stinky," Brice confirmed. "Let's get some breakfast."

I was slightly stung at my husband's less-than-enthusiastic reaction to his gift, but I tried not to take it personally. I recognized that the two eight-month-old babies in his arms didn't care that it was their dad's birthday and weren't being patient about the extended stopover in the living room on the way to that room where all the eating happens.

Now, breakfast is over, and the boys are engaged with their toys, so I lead Brice to the treadmill for a closer look and say, "So? What do you think?"

"It's really nice," he repeats, running his hand along the digital display. "Looks... expensive."

The vice around my diaphragm loosens. "Oh, don't worry about that. I got a good deal. Do you like it?"

He pauses. "Yeah. It's... nice."

Tense again, I state, "You hate it."

"No, I don't! I said I like it."

"But I can tell you don't."

He rubs the back of his neck. "It's just— I— Well, where are we going to put it?"

"What do you mean? Here. So you can watch TV while you walk. And eventually, run."

Looking around the room, he says, "But it's… out here. In the room. Sort of in the way."

I begin to demonstrate folding it and rolling it further against the wall, but he stops me. "Whoa, whoa! Don't do that. It's heavy!"

Rolling my eyes, I nevertheless drop the tread deck and step away from the machine. "You get the idea, though. It folds up when you're not using it."

"That's… great. I—"

"You hate it."

He blushes but laughs. "No, I don't! I think it's… great. I've never used one of these before, outside of physical therapy."

"Just admit you hate it already, so we can get on with your birthday. I took the day off, and everything. I don't want to spend it standing here in front of this— this horrible birthday present, while you pretend to like it." To my irritation, I feel my eyes well. "Damn hormones," I mutter.

Visibly dismayed, he pulls me against his side and kisses the top of my head. "Oh, hon. I don't hate it. How many times do I have to say it? Please, don't cry."

I push my fingertips into my eyes. "I'm not crying because of you. I'm just… crying."

"That doesn't make any sense."

Suddenly I hear Max's voice at my side. "Mommy, Mommy! Wha's a mattuh? Elmo sad?"

Brice lets go of me and ushers Max away. "Hey, Stinky, why don't you stay over here and play with your blocks? Mommy's fine."

I take a deep, bracing breath and smile to demonstrate that Brice isn't a liar. "I'm fine. Just silly."

Max points to me and grins, like my crying has been an elaborate joke. "You siwwy!" he says.

"I am," I say. "So silly. Get started on that castle. I'll help you in a few minutes."

When Brice returns to me, looking miserable, I wave away his concern. "Really. I'm okay. You know, if you don't want to use the treadmill, it's no big deal. I'll use it."

"You will?" he checks, sounding as if I've told him I'd be glad to quit my job and devote my life to taking care of things at home, complete with growing our own food in a garden out back and popping out babies until my ovaries gasp and die, dropping from my body with the last baby.

"Yeah," I lie, already mentally drafting the Craigslist ad for the torture device.

So what if I never use it? He only needs to believe it for the day. I don't want him to feel bad on his birthday. It's bad enough he received a present from us that he doesn't like.

Feeling horrible for that, I impulsively explain the reasoning behind my choice. "I don't want you to run at night anymore."

His face closes off, so I know my admission was a mistake. "What happened to me was an accident. I'm sorry I was such an idiot, but I can't go back and undo it, and all I can do is promise you that I won't be an idiot again. Do I have control over other idiots out there? No. So you're going to have to trust that Someone bigger than you, me, and the idiots has it under control."

"I'm not—"

"Just stop! I've said I'm sorry for what happened. But you can't plan for every eventuality. You can't keep me safe by forcing me to give up one of my favorite things, which is running. Outside. In the fresh air." More gently, he continues, "It's how I clear my head. It's one of the only times I get to be alone, when I do run alone. And you know all this."

I nod, fighting a fresh wave of tears. "I know. Please, stop apologizing. *I'm* the idiot here. I'm the one who sent you on that run all worked up because I was feeling guilty. I'm the one who sent you that dirty text, trying to hurry you home. I'm the one who bought you a gift for your birthday that I knew, deep down, you wouldn't like, hoping that you'd learn to like it, for my sake. It was selfish, like everything else I do."

He abruptly steps away to retrieve Brooks, who's started to crawl towards the front door. I get a quick visual of the other two. Max is dutifully working on his oversized building-block castle. Harris sits in the middle of the living room, gumming a stolen block and staring rapturously into space while drool puddles on the floor between his spread legs. *He must be getting another tooth*, I muse distractedly, making a mental note to watch him for fever. Later.

But now… Now, I need to be alone.

Before Brice crosses the living room to resume our conversation, I walk toward him and Brooks. He prevents me from rushing past him and out the front door by snagging my hand. His grip is light but firm.

"Hey. Where are you going?"

"Outside. I need some fresh air." Even if it does feel like it's fresh from an oven.

"Wait. I want to talk to you."

"Why? So I can ruin your birthday even more? Just let me go outside and get my shit together. Then I'll come back in and we can pretend none of this happened."

He smirks. "What am I, ten? I don't give a fig about my birthday. But I'd like to address some of what you've said."

I shrug off his hand and manage around a sob, "Later,

okay?" on my way out the door. Fortunately, the three children inside make it impossible for him to follow me.

By the time the twins are down for their morning naps and Brice seeks me out on the shady front porch, I've sweated through my cotton cami, but pure stubbornness holds me to the swing. I insisted on coming out here for fresh air, and I'm going to get some fresh air, damn it. Anyway, I deserve to suffer, considering how thoroughly I've screwed up this day so far.

He wordlessly hands me a giant plastic cup of ice water and goes to work slathering sunscreen on Max, who's wearing a pair of swim trunks and babbling mostly incoherently about the "spwinkwer." Then Brice sets up said sprinkler on the front lawn and turns it on, jumping clear of the stream while encouraging Max to run through the cold water, back and forth, as many times as he wants. When Max has the hang of it, Brice returns to the porch, where he dries off his legs and feet with the beach towel he brought out for Max.

After refolding the towel and draping it over the porch rail, off to the side, so it's not obscuring our view of our son, he pulls his phone from his pocket, sits down in the swing, and thumbs at the device's screen. I assume he's reading emails or checking Facebook, so I keep sucking down the water, but after about a minute, he silently passes the phone to me. On the screen is my text to him from that March evening that could have been his last.

Hurry up, Rev Hot Stuff. You don't want me to start without you.

If I weren't already tomato-red and sweating, reading those words would do it.

His eyes on Max, he asks, "Is that the dirty text you were talking about earlier?"

I nod miserably, but since he's not looking at me, I have to follow it up with a soft, "Yes," and take another long drink of my water.

He nods. "Well, I never read it before today, so…"

Nearly squirting water through my nose, I sputter, "B-but it was marked 'read!'" I cough and snort unattractively, trying to clear the water from my sinuses and windpipe. Eventually, Brice prompts me to hold my arms up and pats me on the back, like he would do with one of the kids.

After I recover and can speak, I check, "Are you *sure* you didn't read it? Maybe you've simply forgotten?" I return his phone to him.

He laughs. "Probably wouldn't have forgotten that." He rereads it as if to make sure.

My intestines knot at the only other explanation I can conceive. "When Jared gave me your wallet and phone after I got to the hospital, you had no new text messages. That means *someone* read it."

"Well, it's not the first time Jared's witnessed you talk dirty to me. Probably won't be the last."

"It *will* be the last," I vow. I place my left hand on my blazing cheek.

His smile fades. "Have you thought all these months that it was your fault I got hit?"

I nod wordlessly, moving my hand from my cheek to my eyes.

He sighs and pulls my hand away from my face. "Why didn't you say something before?"

"Because *you* never did. And I figured you didn't say anything, because you didn't want me to think you blamed me."

"I didn't know that was even a possibility."

"Jared told Mitzi you were in a hurry."

"I was, but that's not why I ran into the street."

"It's not? Wait! Maybe you really just don't remember. You don't remember talking to me in the recovery room, either, you know?" I cling to this hopeful thought like a staticky sock in a fitted sheet's corner.

He considers it for a second but eventually shakes his head and rejects the idea. "No. I mean, you're right; I don't remember the recovery room at all, but I remember everything that happened during the run and after the accident, up until they put me out for surgery." Demonstrating, he looks over his shoulder, toward the house. "I was looking over at Jared, who was slightly behind me and telling me a joke. I even remember it—'What do you call a Lutheran midlife crisis? Switching from the old hymnbook to the new one.' I was laughing at it, because it's hilariously true." He raises his left hand and holds it at shoulder height, just out of his peripheral vision. "And I didn't hear the car or see any lights, so I assumed there wasn't a car coming from that direction. But when I stepped off the curb..." He claps his hands together. "Smack. It's as simple as that."

"So it was Jared's fault?" I say with a watery smile.

He reclaims my hand and kisses my palm. "No. It was mine. All mine. Even the driver can't be blamed, because I never looked in that direction."

"They should have had their lights on!"

"Okay, yes. They should have. But they were close enough that I would have seen them if I'd only glanced that way. I didn't. It was my mistake. Trust me."

"I do."

He lets go of my hand and half-stands so he can call down to Max, "You still okay there, Stinky?"

"Yeah!" Max replies, flinch-running through the icy spray. He rubs the water from his face and grins at us. "'Scold!"

"Come on up here when you're done. I'll warm ya up." Retaking his seat, he resumes our discussion as if there had been no interruption. "I feel like you don't trust me. I think that treadmill in there is proof of it. And I don't blame you."

"It's really not that. I'm just scared that something's going to happen again. Not that it's going to be your fault. But that it's going to happen. And what would I do without you?" Overcome again, I have to stop and fix my eyes on my lap.

He kneels in front of me, bringing his face into view, a half-smile on his lips. "I have a good life insurance policy; you and the boys will be fine." When I don't laugh, he clicks his tongue. "Come on."

"I know it's stupid to be worried all the time—"

"No. Fear is real. And it's not stupid. You think I'm never afraid? You think I'm oblivious to all the things that can happen to you and the kids on a daily basis?"

"You never seem scared."

He grabs both my hands in his and rubs the tops of them with his thumbs. "We can't give into it. We can't live in fear. Instead, we need to pray. And do things, certainly, to prevent unnecessary risk—look both ways, wear seat belts, strap the boys in their car seats, take care of ourselves—and each other. And then we need to thank God for every day we make it unscathed through the countless dangers out there. But we have to live."

I nod. "I just want that dreadful feeling to go away. But it's there every time I think about something else happening to you. Or if I think about what *could* have happened to you."

"What can I say? Stop thinking?"

I laugh through my tears. "I'm pretty sure I do for long stretches. I definitely did when I thought that treadmill was a good birthday gift idea. I'm so sorry."

He stands, his knees popping. With a slight wince, he shakes his left leg. "Your heart was in the right place." Backing up, he perches on the porch rail, leaning his back against the column, his right leg swinging.

While I dry the last tears from my face, Max climbs the porch steps and runs toward us, nearly wiping out on the painted wood floor.

"Whoa, Stink," I nearly tumble off the porch swing when I reach out to grab his arm before he goes skidding. Brice hops off the rail and steadies me with a quick hand to my elbow.

Max giggles at the close call. "I fallded!"

"Almost," Brice confirms, grabbing the towel and holding it open. "And you almost took your mom out with you. C'mere and let me snuggle you. Oooh! You're freezing!" Max's teeth chatter while Brice rubs his hair dry and wraps him like a burrito. They settle next to me, and we swing while Max gabs about what he wants to do next.

Brice interrupts his soliloquy. "Since it *is* my birthday and everything, everyone has to do what *I* say."

"Oh, is that how it works?" I sass, knowing full well I'll do anything he wants.

"Yes."

"Birfday?"

"That's right. My birthday. And I say we can only have fun the rest of the day. Starting with going inside, where it's cooler. Then maybe coloring and watching a movie. Then lunch. Then a nice, snuggly nap."

"I not tiwerd."

"Not yet, but you will be, after all the fun we have."

"Daddy siwwy," Max says to me, as if he's telling me for my own good.

"Daddy's smart." I stand slowly to prevent vertigo. "Especially with the 'going inside' part. Let's go."

After turning off the water to the sprinkler, Brice opens the front door for Max, who streaks inside ahead of us. Then he holds the door open for me. As I'm passing, he tugs on my shoulder strap, stopping me.

"I'm looking forward to that nap," he murmurs. "There's no statute of limitation on dirty text messages, right?"

I kiss his nose. "You tell me. After all, the birthday boy makes the rules."

TROUBLEMAKERS

*P*rofessionally, it's been a rough summer for the adult Northams.

Whether Matt has outright told people at Eye Candy about what happened between us—his side of it, of course —or people have simply inferred that something happened based on my determination to never be around when he's expected at the gallery, the result is the same: I'm not getting the plush, tony jobs around the shop anymore. People have chosen sides, apparently, and not many are on mine.

Fortunately, the person whose opinion counts most, Carrie, has been supportive, probably because I came clean with her as soon as I found out about Matt's September show. Matt's popularity with the rest of my co-workers, however, has held more sway than any loyalty they may have had to me at one time, so I've suffered through a fair number of awkward, chilly interactions.

None of those interactions have been with the man himself, miracle of miracles. Maybe by warning me of Matt's visits Carrie's simply trying to avoid a lawsuit, but I guess I don't care what her intentions are, as long as I don't have to deal with him. The bottom line is, she always lets me know when he's expected to be around, as he and Kimi work on the grandiose plans they have for his second show, which I've been sniffily told is going to be "way more epic than his debut." Somehow, I doubt that someone who describes something in such a way could pull that off. But I digress.

The unfortunate result of this tension, however, is that I no longer feel like I'm part of the big, happy Eye Candy family. Unless, that is, I'm the soon-to-be-disinherited, outcast cousin who's only allowed to stick around because Great Granny has a soft spot for me. As soon as Granny kicks the bucket (or I wind up pissing her off about something), I'll be out on my ass. It's a tense situation, one that is extremely unsustainable and certain to end badly. It's simply a matter of "when," not "if."

So I've been keeping my eyes and ears open for other job opportunities in Springfield's growing-yet-still-remarkably-small art community. Unfortunately, not many places are in the market for a visibly pregnant part-time employee who will be taking two to three months off less than a year into her employment.

Also, the aforementioned close-knit nature of the art industry in this town means there's no avoiding Matt forever. My initial impression of him as a hobbyist whose interest in producing art would fade once he realized how much effort is required to maintain sufficient interest in his work was way off-the-mark. He's becoming a popular fixture on the "scene" (if you can call what this town has a "scene"). If I want to continue working with art and artists in this geographical area, there will be no running away from him.

My troubles are nothing compared to Brice's, though. Wayne and Vivian Long (mostly Wayne) are setting out to make the reigning shit-stirring champion (my dad) look like a rank amateur. God love my husband for his blind optimism two months ago, but the Longs have proven him wrong, wrong, wrong time and again since they returned to town in late July after a trip to Disney World with their three children and numerous grandchildren.

First of all, Mr. "By the Book" has been boning up on some chapters from *How to be a Major Pain in Your Pastor's Ass*. He and his wife refuse to take Communion with the rest of the congregation, invoking their right to request private Communion (which is a bit of an oxymoron, don't you think?) in Brice's office whenever he can fit them in. If I were him, I'd make it extremely inconvenient for them, but that's not how my husband works, so he's been accommodating to a fault, oftentimes to the detriment of his own schedule.

As if that weren't bad enough, they've spread the word that this "service" is available, so other members who have issues with the [not] new [at all] way of doing Communion —thanks, again, mostly to the Longs—have been demanding the same treatment. And Brice is obliging them all.

Speaking of demands, Wayne seems to have made it his personal mission to be Peace's unofficial quality assurance liaison, sending any and every church member with a complaint ("No concern is considered 'petty,' in the eyes of the Lord") to Brice, usually in his office for uncomfortable face-to-face confrontations.

These issues vary from objections regarding the lack of variety in the orders of service ("When Pastor Long chose the liturgy, we used to use my favorite order all the time, but now we never do. Why not?") to the quality of lighting in the sanctuary ("Those new compact fluorescents are a joke!

Sometimes it's so dim, I can hardly read the bulletin!") to how many verses of the closing hymn we sing on any given Sunday ("Why is everyone in such a rush to get out of there? If a song has four verses, we should sing all four verses, not just the first and last verse. It's like reading the first and last page of a book and thinking you're getting the whole story. Ridiculous!"). I wish I were kidding.

But wait… there's more! When Pastor Long retired, one of the most popular senior adult Bible Study groups fell by the wayside, as he and Vivian led that group in their home each Wednesday night but would no longer be able to do so regularly, due to their travels. Well, back by popular demand (or so *Wayne* says), they've reinstated the group, only they've moved the meeting night to Tuesday, which coincidentally clashes with the church's weekly evening seniors' social group. When it came down to folks choosing between the social group and Bible study, attendance in the social group fell sharply.

One Tuesday night, nobody except the group's tireless, dedicated organizer, Trudy, showed up at all, and she spent the better part of an hour the next morning in Brice's office, in tears about the scheduling conflict. According to her, the Longs said that Brice asked them to avoid Wednesday night due to mid-week services during certain times in the church calendar. This is true. He did. He's been asking all groups to avoid Wednesday evening activities. Nobody else has had a problem with it.

Except, of course, the Longs. Granted, they didn't tell *Brice* they had a problem with it when he made his initial request that they choose another night. But when Trudy pointed out the obvious issue regarding coinciding member participation between their two groups, the Longs placed the blame squarely on Brice's shoulders. Then they told her the only night besides Wednesday that worked for them was Tuesday, because they have commitments every other night during the week.

So Brice promised Trudy he'd work something out with the Longs, even if it meant allowing them to go back to their Wednesday night schedule. However, when he talked to them, they told him they'd recently joined a line dancing group that met on Wednesday evenings. "As a matter of fact, we'll be taking advantage of the mid-day church services on Wednesdays during the Lenten and Advent seasons, for that express purpose," Wayne explained regretfully.

Brice returned to Trudy with the bad news, offering to sit down with her to figure out a new night for the seniors' group. That's when she got huffy, ranting about "recent unnecessary changes" meddling with her hard work of the past fifteen years. "Tuesday has always been good enough, until now. Do you know how impossible it will be to get everyone in the group to remember a new night? We're set in our ways, you know? And that's not always a bad thing, like you young people seem to think."

Brice came home that night with a headache, went straight to bed, and skipped dinner.

Still, he refuses to badmouth the Longs behind their backs and somehow maintains a positive attitude and a friendly demeanor when dealing with them—or the people they sic on him. He's also ultra-polite, and über-respectful, which makes me want to barf. Not because he's wrong to treat them that way, and not because he's phony—he's not; he's being absolutely sincere—but because they don't deserve it. I think that's his point. He's obviously completely committed to taking the high road with those assholes. (Yes, I said it.)

The most recent snag that I know of involves an audit of the church's financial books, instigated by—you guessed it! —everyone's favorite retired man of the cloth.

Of course, Brice isn't worried, because, "There's nothing to hide. If anything, this audit will be a blessing, because it will highlight some inefficiencies that date back *years* and which I've been trying to streamline since I started here. Finally, we might make some headway. And if we can free up enough capital, maybe we can pay off those construction loans faster. This is a good thing," he reassured me one night last week before bed.

It was the first night so far in this pregnancy that I had trouble sleeping. Because I know by now—and I know Brice does, too, no matter what he says—that anything spear-headed by Wayne Long isn't a "blessing" by any stretch of the word's definition. This is simply going to be the hail in a heretofore inconvenient shitstorm. Not sure how, yet, but it will be. I can feel it.

So when he comes home tonight after a late meeting with the church's treasurer, and his face looks like the face of someone who's on the edge of losing it, I sigh and ask, "What did they find?"

"What?" he replies testily, plopping into the nearest chair that doesn't have stacks of folded clothing in it. "What did who find? What are you talking about?"

"Never mind," I mumble, going back to folding the load of laundry (okay, three loads of laundry. I get behind some-times) piled next to me on the couch.

Changing the subject, I tell him, "I think Max is still awake, if you want to go upstairs and give him a kiss good-night. The twins are long gone."

He says something under his breath that I can't hear, but

when I ask him to repeat himself, he says with exaggerated enunciation, "I'll see him tomorrow."

I keep my eyes on the underwear I'm folding when I say, "You probably had a long, stressful day, so I'm giving you the benefit of the doubt, but you're treading on dangerous ground, Reverend Grump-Ass."

Sighing, he says, "I'm sorry," sounding like he actually means it. "None of this is your fault."

"Damn straight."

He shoots me a tired half-smile and adjusts his head on the back of the chair as if to get a better view of me. "Look at you, all domestic over there, folding my underwear against your cute little baby bump."

"Stop trying to change the subject."

"What was the original topic? I honestly never understood what you were asking."

Since he's making an effort to be more pleasant, I try again. "How'd the meeting go? What did the auditors put in their report?"

"Nothing unexpected," he answers vaguely. "I brought a copy home with me, if you're in the mood for some light reading later. It's on my desk."

"Why don't you give me the highlights?"

"Do I have to?" he whines.

I laugh at the pathetic figure he's cutting over there as he sags further and further down the chair, his butt nearly hanging off the front of the cushion. Eventually, I take pity on him. "No, I guess not. Just tell me if there's anything for me to worry about. You look like there's stuff to be worried about."

"You're going to worry, no matter what, right?"

I shrug. "Probably. But maybe less if you tell me I don't need to."

He snorts. "Since when?"

"Shut up. Are you going to tell me, or not?" Blindly, I toss a ball of socks at him.

He lets them bounce off his head and behind him, with barely a blink. "Tell you what?!"

"Is the church in financial trouble?"

"No!"

"Thank you. That's all I wanted to know."

Around a yawn and while rubbing his eyes, he adds, "That's not what the audit was about, though. It's how we're *handling* the money."

"And?" I set aside the last pair of underwear and lean back into the sofa cushions, absentmindedly rubbing my belly.

He stares at my hands. "We could be doing better. A lot better. And we will. But it's going to take a while, and it's going to take a lot of work to restructure some things. And cooperation from some historically less-than-cooperative people."

I hold up a hand. "'Nuff said. I'm already overwhelmed and bored. And potentially pissed off."

After flapping his lips, he concurs, "Yeah."

When I drag myself from the couch to collect the piles of laundry, setting them in the empty baskets scattered throughout the room, he lifts his head to watch me but doesn't move any other part of his body. "I'll carry those baskets upstairs for you later," he offers faintly.

"I can get them." I cross to the never-been-turned-on treadmill, where I have clothes hanging from its handrail. "You rest. I want to get all these clothes put away so I can relax."

"Are you already nesting?" He cranes his neck and twists slightly in his chair so he can see me behind him.

As if it's something to be ashamed of, I squirm under his scrutiny. "Maybe. Is it a crime to want things to be tidy?"

"Not a crime, but out of character for you. And really cute."

"Stop calling me cute."

"Stop being it."

I roll my eyes as I sweep past him with my arms loaded down with clothes on their way to our closet. When I return to the living room a few minutes later, his chair is empty, and he's stacking the laundry baskets so he can hoist all three at once.

"I told you—"

"Please. "Let me help you so you can get this done faster, and we can spend some time together."

"Oh." Well, who would argue with that? Not I.

I trail him up the stairs after locking up the house and turning off the lights. It's obvious he's exhausted and is ready to call it a night, despite it still being relatively early. I put away the boys' clothes while he takes our basket of socks and underwear into our room. The empty basket is sitting at the top of the stairs when I emerge from Max's room, so I nest the other two inside it and shuffle down the hall to our room.

Expecting him to be in the bathroom getting ready for bed, I'm surprised to see him standing in front of the window, looking out over the front yard and into the street. His right elbow rests in his left hand, his right hand resting on his cheek. He rubs his pinkie distractedly against his lips.

I sidle up to him. "Whatcha lookin' at?" I whisper, peering around his body to get a glimpse through the window.

My appearance seems to startle him from a daydream. "Huh? Oh. Nothing. Just thinking." He shoots me an unconvincing smile. "Tell me about your day." His left arm drops to his side, and his right arm pulls me against his side.

I wrap both arms around his torso from the side and rest my head against his pec. "It was a day. I priced merchandise and loaded photos onto the website. Left work early to pick up the boys and bring them home. Nothing unusual about the evening routine, unless you count doing laundry as unusual."

"I do, for you." He grins down into my face.

I stick out my tongue at him.

"Don't tease me."

As I'm about to give him a witty retort, I feel the flutter.

"Oh!" I gasp, placing my right hand on my belly.

"You okay?" he asks, his brow furrowing.

I nod. "Yeah. I felt something."

Despite knowing he won't be able to feel anything this soon, he rests his palm against my slight bulge and grins. "Really? Aw! No fair."

"Oop! There it is again!" I hurry to the bed, where I lie on my back, pull up my shirt, and drape my legs over the side of the mattress. The twitching sensation is a lot stronger in this position.

Brice joins me, placing his ear against my belly. "I'm not sure if that's the baby or your dinner." After a few minutes, when I'm no longer feeling anything, he raises his head and smiles down at me. "That pretty much made my day. Thank you."

"I'm merely the host," I state dryly.

"There's a baby in there," he murmurs, resting his head against me once more. "That will never cease to be amazing."

I feather his hair through my fingers. "I know."

Lifting his head slightly, he turns his face and places a

kiss to the right of my belly button. "This is what matters. Everything else is relatively insignificant."

"Well, I don't know about that," I hedge, not sure I like the tired, resigned tone in his voice.

"I do," he says with more cheerful certainty. "I really do. God has blessed me beyond measure. Don't let me forget that."

And like that, before I can even jokingly question his need for such a reminder, the moment passes, and he heaves himself from the bed and disappears into the bathroom.

28

CONFRONTATION

*G*reat. I'm coming down with whatever's been going around. It's not flu season yet, so I don't think it's anything as serious as that, but I still feel mighty crummy. I'm actually feeling the worst I've felt in a long time, practically draped across the counter at the gallery, waiting for Kimi to arrive to take over for me. I know I should call Dr. Klein, but I can't seem to muster the energy to get out my cell phone to do it. I have to save every scrap of energy for driving home, anyway.

On any other night, I'd call Brice and have him come get me, despite hating the idea of leaving my vehicle overnight in the downtown parking lot, but he's at the audit findings meeting at church. So are Jared, Mitzi, Wes, Marianne, and Clark. Basically, every member of Peace is there except for the senior pastor's wife. Yeah, I know how that looks, but I had to work. And even if I hadn't, I have an ironclad excuse with this sickness I'm suddenly fighting.

And it did come on so suddenly. I was fine when I dropped off the boys at Peace's daycare. Tired, but that's to be expected when you're eighteen weeks pregnant and chasing after two ten-month-olds and a two-and-a-half-year-old. I mean, I've been drawing on stores of energy I didn't know I had. By the end of a typical day, it's all I can do to brush my teeth and put on pajamas before bedtime, which is usually not too much later than the kids' bedtimes.

Today, though, I hadn't been at work more than an hour before I started to feel hot. And not in a good way. But I put on a brave front for anyone who came into the boutique. Not long after that, the chills and aches started, so it became harder to fake it. Still, I thought I could tough it out. Then the nausea hit.

Carrie's on vacation—the first one she's taken in more than five years—so I didn't want to call and bother her. I resolved to find my own replacement and started down the Eye Candy employee phone list. Call after call either went unanswered or my co-workers had reasonable excuses as to why they couldn't help me out.

My final resort was to call Kimi to come in earlier than her usual start time. Unsurprisingly, she didn't take my calls. I left her a voicemail explaining the situation, and she called me back two hours later, sounding put out. But she agreed to get to work as soon as she could.

That was nearly ninety minutes ago. I'm reaching the end of my shift. Thankfully, it's been a typically slow Wednesday, so I haven't had to deal with too many customers. When the bell over the door dings, it takes a lot more effort for me to straighten to a sitting position but I manage it and even summon a cheery, "Hello!" to whomever it is, praying it's Kimi.

My prayer not only goes unanswered—again—but I quickly realize I'm getting a big, fat "no" from God on another one of my fervent prayers when a shamefaced Matt walks toward me.

"Hey," he returns my greeting, which I wish I could take back.

"What are you doing here?" I ask bluntly.

"I'm a little early for a meeting with Kimi."

"No, I mean *why* are you here? I mean…" I shake my two-ton, feverish head. "Nobody told me you were going to be here today."

He smiles sadly. "Ah. That answers that question."

"What question?"

"I wondered why I never saw you around here anymore, even when I had meetings with Kimi that fell during your normal work hours."

"What do you know about my schedule?"

Leaning against the counter as if we're just two friends shootin' the shit, he pulls a face. "It's not that complicated. And you told me your hours when we were planning my first show."

"Carrie lets me go home early when you have meetings with Kimi," I confirm his suspicion about my having an informant.

I hop from my stool, eager to put more distance between us, even if I only have a couple of feet before I run into the wall behind me.

As soon as I'm pressed against that wall, Matt's eyes flicker to my swollen abdomen but quickly up to my face once more. "Uh, yeah. So. I guess congratulations are in order? That's… great."

"Matt, please. Can we *not* pretend like we're best buds? Because we're not. To be honest, I'm not comfortable being here alone with you."

"I understand." He takes a deep breath. "Please, don't be freaked out, though. I'm not going to— I'm sorry about what I said to you."

"You're not forgiven," I say coldly, a shiver making me quake from head to toe.

"Okay…" He looks more closely at me. "Are you okay?"

"I'm fine." My shaky hand betrays me when I push my hair from my damp forehead.

"Maybe you should sit down."

"Maybe you should wait for Kimi in your car."

I feel bad for a split second at the hurt in his eyes. Then he opens his mouth. "Listen. I know you don't want to see me or talk to me, and I get that. I was a selfish dickhead when I told you how I felt—feel—about you."

I can't suppress the squeak his too-honest clarification elicits.

He presses on, "And when I ran into your husband at the coffee counter—"

"You just *happened* to run into him?" I figure I might as well get answers to some of my questions, since he's here and obviously not planning to respect my wishes that he leave.

Blinking, he replies, "Yeah. Why would I plan something like that?"

"I don't know. Because you were trying to run into me?" That question evokes a decidedly guilty expression from him and an intense queasiness from me. "Oh, my gosh!" I breathe.

"It's not what you think!"

"You're a stalker!" I clutch at the wall behind me to keep my equilibrium while I reel at his confirmation of Brice's suspicions. I'd actually started to convince myself our run-ins with Matt at the grocery store were, in fact, coincidences. I'd expected him to laugh at—or at least do a better job of denying—the idea that he was there with the express purpose of seeing me.

"No, I'm not a stalker. Anymore. I mean, I never was. Not really." He sighs. "Please, don't hate me. I was an idiot. I— I followed you home after I ran into you at the store that time—which was a complete fluke, by the way."

"Oh, God," I mutter, bracing my hands on my thighs and trying not to hyperventilate.

"It was a stupid impulse! And as soon as I did it, I was like, 'What the fuck am I doing?' and I drove off and haven't done anything like that again. I swear!"

I straighten. "I'm supposed to believe you? How do you explain bumping into Brice, then?"

"You got me. I used to frequent places near your neighborhood. You know, just in case. I thought if it was meant to be, I'd see you. After I met your husband, though, I stopped doing that."

"He could beat you up, you know?" I cringe at the middle-school threat, then backtrack. "If he wanted to. But he doesn't. Because he's too damn nice."

"I noticed that. So, he knows?"

Self-righteously, I snap, "Of course, he knows. I tell him everything!" Two can play at this lying game.

He runs a hand through his hair and scratches his jaw. "Meeting him made me feel even worse about everything than I did before. And I already felt pretty bad."

"Not too bad to be lurking around places you hoped I'd be, though," I say caustically.

The corners of his mouth turn down. His eyes droop. "Peyton, I've done some stupid, thoughtless things. I'll be the first to admit it. But there's no point apologizing for how I feel about you. I can't turn off those feelings, just because you don't return them."

"You can at least try. You *have* to try!" Too tired to

remain standing, I return to the stool and slouch against the counter.

Matt respectfully backs away and slides his hands into his pockets. "You're right. And I *have* been trying. I haven't been to that store in months. Or anywhere near your neighborhood. But seeing you today… I realize I've been kidding myself. Your reaction, your obvious hatred for me, is killing me. Because I still feel—"

"Shut up," I beg softly.

"No. I'm going to say to you what I promised myself I'd say if I was ever lucky enough to see you again."

I'm too weak to fight him. Or to leave the room and hide in the bathroom until Kimi gets here. I close my eyes and try not to listen to him, but his words are relentless as they dig into my ears and permeate my brain.

"Your husband— Brice is a hell of a guy."

Oh. I know this already, but I'm pleasantly surprised to hear him say it. *Yes, let's keep talking about Brice.*

"Knowing what he knew, he not only resisted the urge to beat the shit out of me—which is what I deserved—but he was *nice* to me. He invited me to your church. He introduced me to your son, who's beautiful, not that I doubted for a second he would be. He shook my hand. He apologized to me for his accident pulling you away from my show."

I lift my head enough to look at him. "Yeah. He told me all this. And I already know he's the best man on the planet, so…"

"That's just it, though. I love you, Peyton—"

"Stop saying that!" I moan.

"—and that means I want what's best for you. And I'm not it. He is." Dense silence falls between us. After a few seconds, he continues emotionally, "That conversation with him has haunted me for months. I mean, I knew he was a pastor and that you loved him—it was obvious any time you talked about him. Your whole face would light up—but I didn't expect him to be so damn *good*. I was hoping he wasn't as great as you always made him sound. But he is, from what I can tell. If anyone in this world deserves you, it's him."

Nearly delirious with nausea, fever, and aches, I grumble, "Why would you wish someone like me on a great guy like him?"

He laughs. "Oh, Peyton…"

This conversation needs to end. Now. Since he's obviously not picking up on my nonverbal cues, I blurt, "Matt, I'm really sick."

"Morning… er, night sickness?" he inquires gently.

"No. Like, fever sick. And I've been waiting for Kimi for two hours. And I can't handle being here, especially with you, for another minute."

"Oh, my gosh! Seriously? I've been going on and on, and you're over there, feeling like you're going to die?"

"I tried to tell you." My body lists, but I catch myself before falling from the stool.

He comes around the counter and stands next to me. I'm too faint to tense a single muscle in reaction to his proximity. "I'm going to touch you, but only to help you."

"No."

"I don't want you to get hurt. You're not going to be able to stay on that stool much longer."

"I'm fine."

"I'm not falling for that again. You're not fine."

I feel his tentative hands under my arms. His grip firms as more of my weight sags against him. Gently, he lowers me to the floor next to the counter and disappears. He returns with a hand-crocheted throw pillow with the three little pigs on it and tucks it under my head. His fingers trace across my forehead.

"You're burning up."

"You're really good at stating the obvious," I slur.

"I think we should call your doctor."

"He's prolly at the church. Big meeting tonight."

"Is your— Is Brice there, too?"

I nod, letting my eyes drift closed.

"Okay. Your phone…" I hear him muttering and rooting around under the counter. Then I hear beeping. "Hey, Peyton!" he yells, suddenly stern.

"Huh?"

"Stay awake. I think. I mean, I'm pretty sure you should. Oh, fuck. I don't know what the hell I'm doing!"

While I violently shiver, he puts my phone on speaker and sets it on the floor next to my head. I hear ringing, then Brice's outgoing voicemail message. Matt curses under his breath, but as soon as he gets the beep, he says, "Brice, this is Matt Benson. I'm at Eye Candy with Peyton, and she's sick. Really sick. I need you to call her phone back—Fuck this. I'm calling you again." He disconnects and redials, getting the same result.

He tries again.

This time, Brice picks up, sounding annoyed. "Hey, can I call you back? The meeting's still—"

"Brice."

"Who's this?" His tone takes on a wary edge.

"Matt Benson."

"Why do you have my wife's phone?"

"I have her here at the gallery."

"What? Put her on the phone."

"She can't talk to you. She's—"

"Listen here, you sick sonofabitch, you put her on the phone right now. Or so help me God, I'm going to—"

I try to talk, but all that comes out is a gurgled moan.

"Oh, my gosh. Peyton? Is that you? What's happening? What did he do to you?"

"I haven't done anything!" Matt cries. "Listen. Pal. Your wife is sick. And it's a good thing I'm here."

"We'll see about that. You might not think so in about ten minutes." His shaky voice betrays the tough-guy act as just that.

If I weren't so ill, I'd laugh.

"I guess I'll have to take my chances, then," Matt replies, "because I'm not leaving her alone like this, so I'll be here when you get here. You might want to bring her doctor, if he's around."

"I'll call him and have him meet us there." The Jeep's open-door chime transmits shrilly through the phone's speaker, followed by the sound of jangling keys and an engine starting. "What should I tell him is wrong?"

Matt describes my symptoms, and Brice hangs up so he can call Dr. Klein.

Sitting on the floor next to my head, Matt says, "No more Mr. Nice Guy, huh?"

I lick my hot, dry lips and rasp, "He's scared."

"Well, you're going to be fine."

I nod, too drained to argue, even though I'm not sure what he's saying is true.

The bell over the door rings, and Kimi's voice calls, "Hey!"

Matt springs to his feet.

She barely gets out a flirty, amused, "What are doing back there, goof?"

"What the fuck, Kimi?" he explodes. "Peyton's back

here, sick as a dog!" I try not to let his comparison bother me. "She's been waiting for you to take over for her for two hours!"

"What?!"

My co-worker's head pops into view above the cash register. I try to blink a hello to her, since that's the most I can do at this point, but my blink turns into an extended, closed-eyelid… thing.

"Oh, my God!" she gasps. "I thought she was just being dramatic!"

"She's not. She's about to be comatose."

Am I in a coma? Maybe I am. I can't move or talk, but I can hear everything going on around me. It's awful. I wish I could tell them I can still hear them so they'd stop talking about me and saying such alarming things as if I'm not here.

"Well, you know how pregnant people are," Kimi defends herself. "Everything's always such a big deal, like they're the first person in the world to ever be pregnant."

"Could you be a bigger bitch?" Matt asks, wonder in his voice. "Look at her!"

"Well, obviously, I see now that she wasn't being her typical drama queen self."

"Peyton's not a drama queen."

"I can't believe you're defending her. Whatever you did to piss her off almost made Carrie refuse to host any more of your shows. And if it hadn't been for me, she would have blacklisted you because of Peyton's theatrics."

"I would have deserved it."

"Whatever! Everyone likes you more than her, anyway."

"It's not a popularity contest, Kimi. What's wrong with you?"

"What's wrong with *you?*" she counters. "After everything, you still— Whatever." Her voice moves farther away. "I'm sorry I didn't get here sooner. Are you happy now?"

"No, I'm not happy. I'm scared shitless."

"Well, do you want me to call an ambulance?" she asks as if it's the biggest pain in her ass since I called her to come in early.

He pauses. "Her husband and doctor are on the way here. Let's wait. Five minutes won't hurt, right?"

"I don't know. God, she looks shitty!"

"Maybe you should stop talking," Matt says through clenched teeth.

Holy balls, Lord. Make them stop arguing! And if I ever wake up from this, I'm going to pull Kimi's hair. And if Matt weren't such a stalker, I'd think he was a really good guy, based on how he's acted tonight. Well, after he stopped saying uncomfortable things, he turned into a good guy. I'm almost glad he got here when he did. You might know what You're doing, after all.

The bell dings again, and Kimi says, nonplussed, "Over there, behind the counter," as if she's directing a copier repair person to a broken machine.

My sense of smell tells me the person kneeling near me is Brice. Breathless, he says next to my ear, "Honey… Wake up, sweetie. Peyton. Wake up." Cool air brushes the side of my face as he moves his head away from mine. "She's not waking up. God, please wake her up!"

My desire to have him closer to me again prompts me to flutter my eyes open and grunt, "Here." You know, just in case we're doing a roll call.

He kisses my cheek and grabs my hands. "Oh! Praise God! Hon, what's wrong?"

"Sick."

"Yeah. How long have you been feeling bad?"

Math is too hard right now, so I merely shake my head.

"Dr. Klein's on his way. Do you have any Tylenol around here?" he asks the room at large. "I was supposed to ask that right away, and I forgot. Oh, sheesh."

Kimi sighs. "I'll go check the first aid kit. Hang on."

"Hurry!" Matt yells. As soon as she's gone, he says to Brice, "I'm about to hit a woman for the first time ever. I don't know what her fu—effing problem is. Sorry, man."

"Uh, no problem. Can you go wait out front for Dr. Klein?"

"Sure thing."

When we're alone, he helps me turn on my left side and rests his hand against my belly, as if he's testing the baby's temperature, too. "There. Don't worry. Dr. Klein will be here soon."

Kimi returns with a glass of water and two pills. "They're generic, but they'll still work, right?"

"Yeah, thanks," Brice says, helping me sit up. "Just for a second," he assures me when I protest having to move. "You need to take these."

"I'm going out front with Matt," Kimi says to no one in particular, leaving us alone again.

After swallowing the pills and most of the water, I settle on my side, my head in Brice's lap. "Just want to sleep," I murmur.

"Not yet, okay? Let's see what Dr. Klein has to say."

"I'm glad you're here."

"Shhh…"

"Don't be scared."

He chuckles. "Too late."

"Okay. It's all right. Just don't give into it."

29

SECESSION

For the most part, I've been out of it for two days. Dr. Klein reluctantly let Brice take me home when my fever dropped a couple of degrees shortly after taking the acetaminophen, but I had a short deadline for shaking the fever altogether before I would have to go to the hospital. He said as long as I stayed hydrated and kept the fever at bay, he suspected it was a simple virus that would run its course and wouldn't put the baby or me in any danger.

Just a few hours after Brice delivered me home, I woke up in the middle of the night, covered in my own sweat, my fever having broken. Unfortunately, I was disoriented and didn't immediately know where I was or what was happening.

"Get away from me! Where are the boys? I'm not a drama queen!" I shouted into the dark bedroom, struggling against the twisted sheets. "Stop looking at me!"

I figured out I was in my own bed and remembered snatches of what happened at the boutique at the same time Brice sat up and turned on the lamp on his bedside table.

"Honey," he mumbled sleepily, "you're dreaming."

"No, I'm awake," I said, even though it could only serve to add to the confusion.

"Everything's okay." He clamped his hands on my damp shoulders.

I shrugged him off. "Don't touch me. I'm gross." I swung my legs over the side of the bed, but he was on his feet before I could even shake the dizzies.

"Wait. Don't get up. Dr. Klein said you have to stay in bed for at least twenty-four hours."

"That's not happening."

"Peyton, I'll take you to the hospital."

"Are you threatening me?"

"Yes. After all, it's a tradition for you to wind up in a hospital bed at some point during your pregnan—" He sucked in a huge breath. "Oh, gosh. I'm so sorry! I can't believe I just said that!"

"I can't either," I concurred, sitting on the side of the bed, feeling like he'd punched me in the gut.

"I didn't mean… I mean, I wasn't thinking about—"

"I know."

"It's still awful." He crawled across the bed and knelt behind me, wrapping his arms around my upper body and pulling me backwards, taking advantage of the fact that my abdominal muscles are getting to the "virtually useless" stage (which happens a lot faster with me than most women, considering they're not that helpful to begin with).

I allowed him to hug me, because I was still so shocked by what he'd said. His hands moved down to my tummy, which he stroked with his thumbs. His lips pressed against my head, he repeated, "I'm sorry."

"It's okay."

"It's not okay. What an insensitive jackamuffin!"

I laughed at his new word. "I know you weren't including *that* time."

"I definitely wasn't. Still…"

I covered his hands with mine and remained still while his heartbeat slowly returned to normal against my back. Finally, he said, "Now, why were you getting up? I'll get whatever you need."

Listlessly, I answered, "Unless you can pee for me, I think you're going to have to let me out of bed for three minutes. I won't tell Dr. Klein. As far as he knows, you brought me a bowl to sit on."

And for two days, I haven't been out of bed for more than bathroom breaks. My fever hasn't returned, but I've been lethargic and apathetic, bordering on depressed, thanks to what Matt said to me before I faded from our conversation in the boutique.

Of course, only *I* could be depressed about someone telling me he loves me and that not only do I deserve better than him, but I *have* it, in Brice. But that's vintage me. And here's why it's depressing: Brice is so good that even a [delusional] guy who fancies himself as his "rival" can't deny it.

Which leads to the question I've been asking myself for nearly five years now: what makes *me* worthy of Brice?

This constant feeling of unworthiness awaits me for the rest of my life. I know it must sound like the lamest problem in the world, but put yourself in my shoes.

Imagine never winning an argument. Imagine that even on your *best* day, you're not as happy, thankful, diplomatic, or kind as your spouse. Imagine *never* being better than him. At anything (besides complaining or screwing up). Imagine never having better intentions or motives. Imagine never being as justified, because all you ever seem to be motivated by are your stupid emotions and impulses, while he allows

Someone higher to dictate his actions and words. Imagine always falling short. And knowing it. Because you have such a reliable yardstick to measure yourself against. He's lying right next to you in bed every night.

But you love him.

And you wouldn't change him for anything.

You know the change has to come from *you*.

I know the change has to come from *me*.

But I'm no closer to knowing how to make that happen than I was five years ago.

So. I've been hibernating. Hoping the problem will go away. Definitely hoping Brice won't ask me what Matt and I talked about before I collapsed.

No, it's really better if Brice continues assuming Matt discovered me nearly passed out at work and called him right away. I know I'm not going to be saying anything to make him think otherwise.

The mattress bounces behind me. I pretend to still be asleep.

I'm either a bad actress or Brice has no regard for my need for sixteen straight hours of sleep. "Good news. You can get out of bed now. I just got off the phone with Dr. Klein."

I use my most pathetic voice. "Still not feeling great." It's true, after all.

"Maybe I should call him back and tell him that. He said as long as your fever's gone, your energy level should be back up. If not, he wants to know. Could be a sign of something serious."

I sigh. "Fine. I'm up."

He grins at me. "The boys miss you."

"Bull crap."

"The shower misses you."

Scowling, I drag myself from the bed. "Okay. I get it. Moms aren't allowed to be sick."

With a laugh, he replies, "That's not it, at all! You're allowed to be sick; you're not allowed to wallow."

"I'm not wallowing; I'm recovering."

He pushes me toward the bathroom door. "You recover in the shower, and I'll make you a full breakfast."

My stomach growls its approval.

"That's what I thought," he says smugly. "Breakfast is served in ten minutes. No dawdling!"

"Which one is it? Do I stink so much that I need to scrub or do I need to hurry?" I grumble as I wait for the water to reach optimum temperature.

"What's that, my bride?"

"Nothing!" I bellow. "I want my eggs over-easy!"

"Gross!" he calls over his shoulder on the way downstairs.

Almost exactly ten minutes later, I sit at the kitchen table. In front of me sits a plate loaded with eggs, bacon, toast, and "Pancakes!"

"I know you love them."

"Oh, my gosh. I'm starving."

"I bet. You've hardly eaten more than toast for two days."

"I know," I say around a mouthful of bacon. I dip my toast wedges into the runny egg yolks.

Brice looks on, nose wrinkled, upper lip lifted in a snarl. Suddenly, he whirls away from me. "Oh! I almost forgot…"

He sets a steaming coffee mug in front of me. I recoil from it like a vampire being offered a cup of garlic juice.

Holding my breath, I grunt, "Uhn!" and turn my head away.

"Hot chocolate," he says, patting my head and sitting down in the chair catty-corner to me at the table.

I take a deep breath, inhaling the sweet smell. "Oh. Thanks!"

"You're welcome. Hey." He grabs my hand. "I know I was giving you a hard time upstairs, but how are you feeling?"

Chewing and swallowing a glob of soggy, syrup-soaked pancake, I bob my head in a half-nod, half-tilt. "Okay. Weak, still, but I don't feel sick anymore." *And we'll conveniently disregard how I'm feeling mentally*, I add silently.

"Good. Good." He hops up from the table. "Hang on. Dangerous quiet going on in the living room." He trots to the other room, where I hear him talking to the twins in their exersaucers, then quizzing Max about the episode of Dora he's watching. Then he pulls the twins into the kitchen with us and takes a seat with a better view into the living room.

"All right. Better." His feet go up on the chair next to him. "I like to keep my eye on these troublemakers."

"Supervision is good." I try not to worry about what may have happened the past two days to make him so much more vigilant all of a sudden.

It's not that he—or I—are neglectful, but we're not helicopter parents, by any means. We have babyproofing measures in place (light socket covers, cabinet locks, baby gates, childproof doorknob covers, etc.), but the TV and exersaucers see a lot of action. That's because Brice can be in the same room with the children, physically, but be a million miles away, mentally. (Maybe I *am* better than him at some things, after all.)

Now Brice says, "When you're finished eating, I want to show you something." The words are barely out of his mouth, though, before he's on his feet again, lifting Brooks from his exersaucer. "Aw, what the hay? I'll show you now."

He sets the baby on his feet and moves a few steps away from him. "Okay, Screamy. Show Mom whatcha got."

With a gummy smile, Brooks toddles four steps before his forward momentum sends him careening into Brice's legs, to which he clings, his rubbery little hands grasping at the hairs like handholds.

Brice bends over, picks up Brooks, and lifts him over his head. "Way to go! You did it!"

Brooks's belly laugh makes me smile through my proud, happy tears. "So big!" I manage to say. After a quick sip of orange juice, I ask, "What about Harris?"

As he returns Brooks to his exersaucer, Brice chuckles. "Uh, not even close. But it's not for lack of trying. Honestly, I think he's too top heavy."

I hold the back of my hand against my mouth and nose to try to hide that I'm laughing. When I have things under control, I shoot Harris a reassuring smile. "Aw, Buddy, you'll get it. You don't have to be skinny to walk. Look at your mom. Walking for decades now."

He squeals and stomps his feet.

"Good attitude," I approve. "Anything else exciting happen while I was out of it?" I ask Brice, returning to my half-empty plate of food.

He retakes his seat and appears to be considering my question. While picking at a loose string on his shorts, he answers, "Um, let's see… I found a food that Harris doesn't like: beets."

"Yeesh. I don't blame him. I can't believe you even tried to feed them beets."

"I like them."

"You're weird. Next."

"Max found that orange highlighter I was asking you about a while back. His arms are almost a normal color again today."

"He can wear long sleeves to church tomorrow."

"Good plan. What else? Oh, I did some research on minivans and priced a few at some local car lots."

I groan.

"Now, now. I'll drive it, until we have so many kids that we need to commandeer the church shuttle bus."

While I clear my sinuses of the hot cocoa that shoots from my nose, Brice continues, "I actually found a couple of really nice ones."

"No such thing."

"No, really. If I can get a good trade-in on the Jeep—which I should be able to do, since it's in good condition and not that old—there's a black minivan I have my eye on. Leather interior. Heated front seats. Satellite radio. Automatic sliding doors, which will be a huge improvement. Gets better gas mileage than *your* vehicle, too." He shrugs. "Plus, I don't care what I drive. It's something to get us all from Point A to B. As long as it's reliable and safe."

"Call me shallow, because I care."

"Shallow."

I stick out my tongue at him and push my plate away.

"You gonna eat that last pancake?"

"I'm stuffed." My stomach has definitely shrunk during the past two days.

He pulls the plate closer to himself, inspects the pancake to make sure there's no runny egg yolk on it, and cuts into it with the side of the fork. After eating in silence for a few seconds, he swallows before abruptly setting the utensil, tines down, on the plate.

"Let me get you a clean fork," I offer. "That has all my germs on it."

Quickly, he shakes his head. "No. It's okay. I'm not worried about that. I just don't want to eat anymore."

"Is this about your love handles again? Because you don't have any."

He shoots me a weak half-smile. "No, no. It's not about that."

"Is it about the minivan? You're putting on a brave front, but really you know how dorky it is to drive one?"

Rolling his eyes, he rewards me with a laugh. "No! You're going to be jealous of my new wheels, mark my words."

"Then why do you look so pathetic over there, all of a sudden?" I'm afraid I might already know what's on his mind, but I don't want to talk about what happened the other night at the boutique. So maybe if I play dumb, he'll get the hint and resist the urge to ask me about it.

He swallows. "The other night, before Matt called me to tell me you were sick…"

Or maybe not. Damn it.

"I would have called you earlier," I jump in, "but I knew you were at the audit meeting. By the way, what did you do with the kids when you left the meeting to get to me?"

He looks guilty. "I walked out without even thinking about them. I mean, as soon as I got off the phone with Dr. Klein, I remembered, and I called Jared right away to tell him what was happening. He and Mitzi somehow got them home after the meeting. I never asked them how. I guess it doesn't matter, does it?"

I can see he feels bad for not knowing, so I fib, "Nah.

I'm sure Marianne and Clark—or someone else with kids— helped. But does that mean everyone at church knows what happened?"

"You've been on all the prayer lists," is his vague, gently affirmative answer.

I sigh but quickly smile so I don't seem ungrateful. "Seems to have worked."

He covers my hand with his on top of the table and squeezes. "Yeah? Good. Anyway," he continues doggedly, "before I got called away from the meeting—"

"Oh, yeah. How'd the meeting go? I mean, the part you attended. Packed house?"

I can tell he's getting annoyed with my interruptions, but if I can control this conversation and avoid certain discussions, everything will be okay. His potential irritation is worth it to me.

"It was crowded. And it was going well—no surprises, anyway—until they opened the floor to questions and comments, and Pastor Long stood up."

I'm no longer worried we're going to talk about Matt, but I don't relax. "Oh, sheesh. Did he apologize or take any responsibility for some of the inefficiencies in the budget?"

Brice fingers the fork handle, which clinks against the plate. "No. No, he didn't. He, uh, held up a packet of stapled papers and announced that he had circulated a petition and had already received several signatures." He stops, swallowing and fixing his eyes on the partially eaten pancake.

"A petition? About what? Spending ideas? Potential programs?"

Raising his eyes to mine, he answers, "A petition to secede."

"Secede?"

"Break away from Peace and form a new church."

"I know what it means! How many signatures did he have?"

"A couple dozen."

"Oh." I breathe a little easier. "Big whoop. Good riddance. Don't let the door hit ya where the good Lord split ya—"

"It *is* a big whoop. He wasn't just presenting the petition. He was soliciting more signatures from the people attending the meeting."

"What an asshole."

"Peyton."

"No, I'm serious! I'm done with this guy and his shit-stirring ways! And anyway, if he—and a couple dozen other people—don't like it at Peace, then what's keeping them? Nothing. There's no need to sign a dumb petition to let everyone know they're a bunch of whiny, impossible-to-please titty babies!" I push away from the table, collect my dirty dishes, and stomp to the sink.

While I rinse my plate, mug, glass, and utensils and put them in the dishwasher, Brice explains the purpose of the petition, that it's a written account of the specific issues these members have with Peace's current practices. It also serves as a chance for him (for the church) to "rectify" those issues. And finally, if Brice doesn't address the complaints in a satisfactory manner, the petition will go to the Synod as part of the petitioners' application to start a new LCMS congregation.

"Good. See ya!" I repeat defiantly as I dry my hands. "Did he get more signatures at the meeting? Who are we talking about here? Anyone we care about?"

Dismay heavy in his voice, he replies, "He got a few more, yes. And we care about all of them!"

"I don't. If they're going to be ungrateful jerks who don't trust your leadership and can't recognize that you have their best interests, their *eternal salvation*, at heart, then screw 'em!"

"Oh, hon."

"Whatever. Don't 'Oh, hon' me about this. Do you have the list? I want to see it."

He doesn't move from his chair. "I don't think that's a good idea."

"What do you mean? I want to know exactly who we're dealing with here."

Lifting his chin, he says firmly, "*You're* not dealing with anyone. And I think it would be best if you didn't know any names—other than the Longs, who are a given, anyway—because when we resolve this—and I'm fully confident Jared, Wes, the elders, and I *will* resolve it—I don't want you holding grudges against people who are only doing what they think is right."

"Bullshit! This is group-think, plain and simple. And if Wayne wasn't getting everyone in a fucking lather—"

"Come on, now. Please. You're doing it again."

"Doing what?"

"A lot of things. Stressing me out, most of all." He rubs his temples and closes his eyes.

"How am *I* stressing you out? I didn't sign that shitty petition." I cross my arms over my chest and wait for him to explain himself.

"Well, your language, for one thing, is going all through me."

"Sorry!" I say as unapologetically as possible.

"And for another thing, you're making it even harder for me to tell you something I've been dreading telling you for two days, because you're flying off the handle, and I'm worrying about how upset you're getting, which isn't good for you or the baby, especially since you're recovering from whatever that was the other day." He takes a deep breath to fill his lungs and says more calmly and quietly, "Peyton, I need you to support me on this."

"I do! I am! How am I *not* supporting you? I'm ready to go to Wayne's house and rip his da—ang throat out!" I circle the island and table and hug him to my body.

"I need you to support me in the way I need to be supported."

Instead of defensively asking what he means, I wait for him to elaborate.

I almost think he's not going to do so until he turns in his chair, buries his face in my belly and muffles against my shirt, "I need to stay calm and focused and handle this in the way I best know how to handle it." He tilts his head up to look into my face. "I need to know you're okay with that, that you're not judging me for being too laidback or lackadaisical. Because I'm not. On the inside, I'm freaking out, like you. But I can't be that way on the outside. And if you are, it's only going to make it harder for me to maintain the focus I need."

When I open my mouth to respond, he cuts me off. "Just promise me you won't go rogue. Don't get in the middle of this. Don't engage anyone in arguments, thinking you're doing me a favor by saying the things I'm not at liberty to say." He reaches up and puts his hand against my cheek. "I know your heart's in the right place, but it will only make things worse."

"I won't stand by and let someone badmouth you. I can't."

"Nobody's going to badmouth me. This isn't personal."

"Like hell—"

"Peyton. Promise me."

I want to cry at the desperation in his eyes. I want to weep at the hopelessness of his request. But I'm stoic when I say, "I promise. I'll let you handle this your way."

He smiles sadly, and his shoulders relax. His hand drops from my face, his arm circling my lower back and pulling me more securely against him. "Thank you."

I have no idea how I'm going to keep that vow. Oh, well. What else is new?

30

FIGHTING WORDS

*I*t's been an interminable week. I've hardly seen Brice at all. When he's not at work, he's at evening mediation meetings with the elders, Jared, Wes, and a small delegation of the petitioners, led by Wayne, of course. He says they're making good progress on the list of requests (I call them "demands") the malcontents have put before him, but the circles under his eyes tell a different story.

When he's not at the church, he's in his woodshop. He often doesn't come to bed until one or two in the morning. In the morning, when he's getting ready for work, he's not talkative. At least, he doesn't have much interest in talking to the boys or me. I have, however, observed him more than once stop whatever he's doing to close his eyes and bow his head. These impromptu conversations with God concern me, but I don't press him about them, because I don't think he knows I'm watching him and probably wouldn't appreciate it if he did know.

This morning, we got ready for church without saying a word. It was Brice's "off" day, so he sat with me during the late service. Now that the service is over, he's in his office, preparing to lead a meeting about the changes he (and Jared and Wes) will make to appease the petitioners.

My stomach's in knots. And I think the baby can tell how tense I am, because he/she is flipping around in there like a deranged fish.

When I get to the gymnasium, where the meeting will take place, Marianne and Mitzi are already sitting in the metal folding chairs that have been set up there. The elders are wandering the area, some talking to each other, most looking fairly relaxed, although somber. I take this as a good sign, as far as the crisis is concerned, that they're confident this will soon be a bad memory with a happy ending.

It's not a good sign, though, when it comes to Brice's vision for the church. It means he'll be going back on the changes he's made since becoming Peace's senior pastor. It means, in some way, that he'll be admitting he's been wrong.

The majority of Peace's members seem to be supporting him, no matter what happens as a result of these goings on. Even Paul Vitely gave me a supportive hug when I dropped off the boys in the nursery a few minutes ago. For some reason, that made me feel worse.

"I don't know if I can do this," I whisper to my friends as I drop into the empty chair between them and watch the room start to fill. "I don't know if I can sit here and watch Wayne and his puppets undo all of Brice's hard work. And Jared's and Wes's, too," I add quickly, pressing a hand against the side of my belly in a feeble attempt to calm the baby.

Mitzi grasps my hand. "It's going to be okay. Since when have our husbands given up when they've been told 'no' about something? They'll find a way to do the work they've been called to do, after this little hiccup is averted."

Marianne nods. "Yeah. This is about money. It would be a huge financial blow to lose so many members at once. We just need to keep them from leaving and work from there."

Confidently, I say, "It's not about money for Brice. We come from a church that was constantly operating in the red. He doesn't stress about money. This is about so much more than money for him."

"Well, it's about money for the elders and the Board of Directors. Clark says Bill Gregory ran a report that predicted the church's income if the petitioners left, and it's not pretty. I think Clark used the word, 'bleak.'"

I refuse to worry about a silly, theoretical treasurer's report right now. Anyway, judging by the few things Brice has said to me while mediation has been underway during the past week, the petitioners are going to get their way, and we won't have to worry about any "bleakness."

Right now, I'm more focused on the people trickling into the meeting. The proceedings are open to the entire congregation, but it's obvious by where people are choosing to sit who's here because their names are on the petition and who's here simply because the decisions affect the church as a whole. We're like guests at a wedding, the two sides of the "family" separated by the center aisle.

I can hear Wayne and Vivian holding court on their side, their jovial tones making me want to scream. I guess they'd be the pretentious parents of the spoiled-rotten bridezilla. Their "guests" are all the usual, impossible-to-please suspects, and I probably could have named them, even though I've respected Brice's wishes that I not see the actual list on the petition. Seeing them now, though, here in person, I'm not surprised by a single one of their faces.

Before I can dwell too much on my disdain for each of them, Brice walks into the gymnasium and heads straight for the simple wooden podium set up in front of the chairs. A hush falls over the assembly. The elders take seats in the front row on either side of the aisle. Clark half-turns and shoots a smile to Marianne and me. Jared and Wes sit in chairs slightly behind and to the right of the podium.

Mitzi tightens her grip on my hand.

Setting on the podium in front of him what appears to be the original petition, Brice makes some welcoming remarks before asking one of the elders to lead us in an opening prayer.

After the prayer, he says, "Thanks, Russ. And thank you all for coming here and spending part of your Sunday afternoon to hear my response to the petition set forth by a number of you. I promise, this won't take long. Thanks to those of you who participated in the mediation sessions last week, too. This experience has been highly illuminating and educational."

If I didn't know him better, I'd suspect he was being sarcastic, but that's not Brice. Still, his tone is uncharacteristically perfunctory.

He takes a deep breath and reads from the paper in front of him. "The petition states: 'We, the undersigned, wish to draw attention to four basic practices we feel have been neglected and/or disregarded under the current pastoral leadership. We feel these are integral to Lutheran teachings and practice and should be immediately reinstated. Otherwise, the undersigned feel it would be in our best interests to secede from Peace Lutheran Church.'"

He clears his throat. "Now for the requests. 'Number one, reinstate more traditional guidelines for communicants. Number two, require new adult members to attend instruction in Luther's catechism. Number three, refuse Communion to members who are quote, 'not in good standing,' or unrepentant in their immoral lifestyles. And number four, require a congregation-wide vote when making decisions regarding practices that affect the church population at large.'"

He looks over his audience. "I've taken everyone's remarks, questions, comments, concerns, and wishes into consideration. I've met extensively with the church's elders, with Pastors Laszewski and Anthony, and even with some of the other members of the Board of Directors, namely our treasurer, Bill Gregory. I've prayed nearly continually."

Returning his eyes to the podium, he refers to the list of requests. "Having said that, I respond... One, we haven't changed the 'guidelines' at all, so we can't reinstate something we never stopped practicing. Two, we offer adult instruction already and encourage new members who are also new to Lutheranism to take the class. There's no way to force people to do so or to enforce such a mandate. Three, if we refused Communion to unrepentant people, nobody would ever be allowed to take Communion. *And* the whole purpose of Communion is to repent. How counterproductive is it to deny someone the opportunity to repent because *I* deem them unrepentant? Your penitence is between you and the Lord. As is mine. Four..."

He raises his eyes and smiles wryly. "Have you *been* to a voters' meeting lately? There's nothing 'congregation-wide' about them. It's usually me and seven other people going through the motions and making the decisions for everyone. But I'll give you number four, if you'll promise to show up to these supposed congregation-wide votes. The more the merrier. Great. Agreed."

I blink rapidly, and my heart flutters in triple-time as I observe the reaction throughout the room. I can tell by the set of some of the elders' shoulders, and the way in which some of them are whispering to each other that this wasn't the message they had been prepared to hear from their senior pastor this afternoon. Even Wes and Jared look slightly taken aback. I dare not look in Wayne's direction.

Brice comes out from behind the podium and advances down the center aisle. "Basically, you need to be able to trust that Pastors Anthony and Laszewski and I have devoted our lives to *your* lives in Christ. Period. Nothing we do or say is done or said without extensive prayer and meditation, as well as direction from the Synod. I take your salvation as seriously as my own, as seriously as my wife's, my children's. Because we're a family. All of us.

"But *this* is not how a family acts. We don't give each other lists of demands and say, 'Do this, or else.' We don't issue ultimatums. The only thing that can result from an act like that is resentment on one—or both—of our parts.

"I became a pastor to bring people to completion in Christ Jesus. All people. Not just those some of you deem worthy of His love and salvation. Because none of us are worthy. And if we only seek to serve the worthy, then we have to shut the doors. As a called and ordained servant of the Word, I am doing my utmost each and every day for you. If that's not enough, I don't know what to tell you. I'm not going to do less or withhold my service to 'certain types of people,' as your list would demand in several instances. That's not how this works."

He returns to the podium, grips its sides, and leans forward. He licks his lips, breathes in, and continues, "So, I say this with a heavy heart, but I say it with no ill will: if you really feel that this list of demands you've presented to Pastors Laszewksi and Anthony, the elders, and I represents a comprehensive account of all the ways in which we're failing you in your spiritual lives, then you *should* go."

"Whoa," Mitzi breathes beside me.

Marianne stifles a squeak.

I concentrate on staying upright.

He pauses when the whispers and murmurs create a buzz he doesn't want to talk over. After a few seconds, he holds up his hand and repeats, "*If* that's the case, you should go." The room quiets. "You should. Because that's an irreconcilable difference of *conviction*, not only opinion. And that will be a hindrance to your growth as a Christian. If you decide you can no longer abide my leadership, and you choose to leave to join other area churches or start your own church, know that you will be missed. But know also that you go with my blessing and with no hard feelings. You have my sincerest prayers for your continued health, happiness, and spiritual wellbeing.

"If, however, you decide to stay, I praise God for your continued partnership."

Petition in hand, he steps from behind the podium and leans across a row to hand the packet of papers to Wayne. "Here. In case you need to send this to the Synod. Again, I hope that's not the case. And if any of you would like to speak with me privately about these issues, I'd be happy to do so. Simply give Lucy a call during my weekday office hours, and she'll set up a time that's convenient for you. Good afternoon."

With that and a slight nod to me, he strides from the gymnasium, presumably to return to his office, probably locking the door.

I feel about a hundred pairs of eyes on me. "Hi," I mutter. "I, uh… Well. That was interesting."

Without meaning to do so, I look straight at Wayne. To my surprise, he's smiling. The smile morphs into a smirk when he catches my eye.

~

"And then, when you said that thing about none of us being able to take Communion... I— Wow. Did you see everyone's faces?"

Propped on my elbow, I look down into Brice's face. He's prone on the bed, his eyes closed. It's eight o'clock, but he's only recently returned home. The boys are in their cribs, quiet, by all appearances cooperating and going to sleep without any further ado.

In response to my question, he says, "No, I was looking down at the papers." He smiles quietly. "What was everyone doing?"

"Everyone on *that* side of the room—*everyone*—looked like they'd sucked on a lemon."

He chuckles. "I bet."

I scoot closer to him, resting my head on his chest. He curls his arm around me and trails his finger lazily up and down my arm.

"And you saw the reaction when you told them to go. I mean, they couldn't believe it. I think they were expecting you to say yes to all their demands, beg them to stay, and apologize for the error of your ways. *I* was expecting that, actually, based on what little you've said to me the past week." I flinch when his finger rubs too lightly and tickles my upper arm.

He shifts under me but settles again. "Oh, that. Yeah. Well. I was supposed to say yes to everything, but I changed my mind."

"Aren't the elders going to be mad at you?"

"I think it'll be okay, since half of the potential defectors came to my office after the meeting and told me they crossed their names off the petition."

I rise up on my hands and kiss his chin. "I was really proud of you today. I would have been proud of you, no matter what, but I was particularly proud of how you stuck to your guns."

He opens his eyes. "I called their bluff, that's all. And I meant everything I said."

"I know. That's what makes it even better."

After running his hand through his hair, he puts it behind his head. "Yeah, well, we'll see what happens next."

"Whatever happens, I think you're amazing."

"I'm amazingly tired."

I move to roll off the bed (literally). "Oh. I'll leave you alone then," I say lightly.

He holds me in place. "Wait a minute. That's not what I meant."

"No, I think I should go. You've had a big day, Reverend Hard Ass."

He looks chagrined. "Oh, no. Did I come off as a hard case? Because I didn't mean to. I meant to sound exactly how I felt: accepting and loving and gentle and somewhat sad."

"You gave us a dose of tough love. It was totally sexy."

"Oh, man."

"I loved it." I rub against him and grab his lower lip in my teeth.

"Tha's nuh whuh Uh wuh guh fuh."

Releasing his lip, I say, "Mmm… Well, hopefully that's not the interpretation that anyone else had." I toss his collar and get to work on his shirt buttons. "Let's assume Mrs. Whitney wasn't getting all worked up while you laid down the law."

"She likes me; maybe she was."

My shriek of laughter harmonizes with the doorbell.

We freeze.

"Shhh. We're not home," I whisper impulsively.

He laughs but sits up, buttoning his shirt. "I think it's pretty obvious we are," he says. He crosses to the window and looks down on the driveway. "Oh. Fiddlesticks."

"You did *not* just say that. Who is it?"

Turning to face me, he answers with a doleful expression, "Pastor Long."

"Shut the front door!"

"Well, it would be rude not to answer it."

"No! I mean… Never mind. What's *he* doing here?"

"I don't know!"

"Get rid of him."

He finishes buttoning his shirt and adjusts his pants. "I will. I mean, I'll try. Just stay up here and wait for me."

Ha! As if! I wait until he's greeted Wayne and has ushered him through to the living room before I creep halfway down the stairs and sit on a step, where I can hear them.

Brice is explaining, "Peyton and the boys are already in bed. What can I do for you, Pastor?"

"Oh, now, I think first names are more appropriate, Brice. Let's talk man-to-man. That's why I've come here tonight, instead of arranging a meeting in your office at the church. Maybe this is how I should have gone about things from the beginning."

"Perhaps that would have been more prudent, Wayne. But what's done is done. No hard feelings."

"No. You wouldn't have any hard feelings, would you? That's not your style. You're such a good man."

Brice pauses, then says uncertainly, "Thank you."

Wayne continues superciliously, "And you're a good pastor, too, even if I don't agree with your methods, and I think you fancy yourself a maverick. What you lack in wisdom you make up for in enthusiasm." Now he sounds thoughtful. "Of course, things would be a whole lot different if that baby had lived."

Ohnohedidn't! and *What the fuck does he know about—* How *does he know about Secret?*

"Excuse me?" Brice verbalizes my thoughts in a much classier manner.

Dismissively, Wayne says, "Yeah, I know about that. I did some asking around at your former church in Chicago. Wonderful people, by the way. Very forthcoming. Very eager to talk about the sweet story of how you and Peyton met."

His voice full of ice, Brice replies, "If Secret had lived, I'd have four beautiful children, with a fifth on the way. That's the only thing that would be different."

Wayne chuckles. "That's quite optimistic, don't you think? You certainly wouldn't be the senior pastor at a church Peace's size. *We* certainly wouldn't have called you. You'd have been relegated to academia, at best." Sounding regretful, he points out, "Think how tricked everyone will feel when they find out. It really speaks to your character— and your wife's character. Most especially hers. It fills in a lot of blanks. Of course, I wasn't surprised at all to learn about her *history*. It merely confirmed for me what I already knew. With all due respect, she does not espouse the Christian values we must display in our line of work."

"With all due respect, Wayne, you're full of crap. And you should do some self-reflection before you start pointing out the speck in someone else's eye. It's a wonder you can see anything for the log in your own eye. So back the hell off."

Wayne trumpets, "Ah! There's the *real* Pastor Northam. I was wondering when we were going to get a glimpse of him.

Seems I've discovered what brings him out for the world to see. Speak truth about your immoral wife and the dirty little *Secret* in your past—"

"Get out!" Brice snarls.

"Or what?"

"I don't know." He sounds somewhat deflated but quickly recovers with an indignant, "But you have a lot of nerve to come into my home and blackmail me, then insult my wife, then threaten me."

"I'm doing this for the good of the church."

"This is all a power trip, a sick game to you."

"Oh, it's no game at all. I've been trying to find a way to get you to move on while saving face, but if you'd rather do this the hard way, I can tell everyone the whole, sordid story and achieve the same goal. There's an illegitimate child's grave with your wife's maiden name on it that will serve the purpose quite nice— Oof!! Aagh!"

I hold my breath, stand, and lean over the banister, trying to see into the living room. Unfortunately, they're too deep into the room for me to see them from my vantage point. They must be standing close to the fireplace. At least, one of them is still standing. And I think it's my husband.

For a few seconds, the only thing I can hear is heavy breathing, some grunting, and indistinct rustling, but it doesn't take long before Wayne cries in a choked voice, "You hit me! Twice!"

Those four words make me want to dance a jig on the step. But I'd probably wind up falling down. So I refrain from dancing, but I grin enough to light up the dark stairway.

Out of breath, Brice threatens, "I'll do it again if you don't leave right now."

"I'll tell everyone!" Wayne sputters. "I'll press assault charges and report you to the Synod."

Sounding a lot less confident, Brice replies, "Bring it. In the meantime, you'd best find the front door with your one good eye, *Wayne*."

Before I can scamper up the stairs, the two men stride into the foyer. Wayne, slouched, leads the way, one hand over his left eye, his other clutching his gut. Brice is right on his heels, making sure our visitor's leaving.

When Wayne sees me standing on the stairs, he stops and looks balefully at me. I try not to feel self-conscious that I'm wearing threadbare men's pajama pants and a t-shirt that barely covers the bottom of my baby bump. I also push from my mind the knowledge that I'm braless and barefoot. Rather, I lift my chin and straighten my back, glad to be the one looking down at him, for once. I have every right to be here; it's my house. *He's* the unwelcome one.

"Keep moving," Brice growls.

He does, but at the front door's threshold he says over his shoulder, "You should have steered clear of that one. She'll only continue to bring you grief. Nobody ever really changes."

With a mighty heave in the middle of Wayne's back, Brice pushes the pastor out the front door. The last thing I see before Brice shuts the door is Wayne flying through the air toward the porch steps. The door's already closed on the scene when we hear the thumps and grunts that accompany a person taking a nasty tumble down wooden stairs and onto a textured concrete walkway below.

I attempt an admonishing tone when I say "Brice!" but my giggles severely undermine my efforts.

He turns and sags against the front door. "Oh, gosh. That was bad. I shouldn't have done that."

"No. Probably not. But it was awesome!"

I trot down the stairs and meet him at the door, peeking over his shoulder through the peephole. Wayne is up, hobbling to his car.

Turning my attention back to my husband, I tell him, "You're going to be the baddest-ass, minivan-driving, kid-toting pastor in the history of the world."

"Let's hope jail time doesn't precede all that." He slides to the floor. "Oh, Peyton. This is bad," he repeats. "I— I'm going to be in big trouble. I—They're going to defrock me for this!"

I kneel next to him and fan his pale face. "No, they won't. You were justified."

"It doesn't matter." He swallows repeatedly, like one does before vomiting. I know that feeling all too well.

"Are you gonna barf?"

He nods and struggles to his feet. "I think so."

I scoot out of his way and watch as he rushes to the powder room. Then I listen helplessly while he pukes. With detached calm, I realize it's the first time I've heard him do that since our honeymoon, when he was sympathetically sick about my seasickness. When I hear the toilet flush and the water running, I take it as my cue to go check on him.

In the tiny bathroom, while he wipes his clammy face with a hand towel (note to self: toss that in the washer), I inspect his swelling knuckles and ask as I avoid his eyes, "Do you really think you'll be removed from office?"

"Yes."

My tummy lurches, and the baby kicks me, probably in response to my increased heartbeat or adrenaline flow, or something. "Oh. Well, we'll get through it," I lamely reassure him.

"Oh, gosh, Peyton. What have I done?" he moans,

pulling his hand from my grip and shaking it before flexing his fingers and wincing at the pain.

"I don't know. Even at my worst, I've never hit anyone." When he doesn't smile, I motion for him to follow me into the kitchen, where I wrap some ice in a clean towel and nod at his hand. "Put this on your knuckles."

He obeys. Flopping into a chair at the kitchen table, he drapes the towel over his hand, arranges the ice cubes so they're resting over his knuckles, and drops his head into his other hand, propped up by his elbow. "I guess I'll just wait here for the police to arrive. I should probably call the church's attorney. And maybe Clark Pryce."

I pour him and then myself a glass of water from the fridge door. "Now, hang on a minute. What makes you think Wayne's going to tell anyone?" I set the water in front of him, but he ignores it.

"Because he said he would. Because he's obviously been looking for a way to get rid of me since I stepped foot in this town, and now I've given him a perfect, foolproof reason." The anguish in his voice is heartbreaking.

After powering down the entire twelve ounces of water in a few loud gulps, I say around a burp, "Don't do anything just yet. Take care of your hand."

"I need to write a letter of resignation," he says miserably.

Why does that make my heart stop? I should be ambivalent to this idea, considering how intrusive his job is on our life. It would even make sense for me to see this as a blessing. Yes! Free at last! But now I feel like *I'm* going to puke. Because I know it would be devastating to him to not be a pastor anymore. It's his calling, his reason for being. But to throw it all away because of one [really big] moment of weakness?

"Don't do that, either," I say. "How about this? You pray. Really, really hard. You're good at that."

He looks pathetic when he raises his eyes to me and nods. "Okay. Yeah."

"I'll stay up and pray with you, m'kay?" I sit down in the chair across from him at the kitchen table. "We'll pray all night, if we have to."

"You don't have to do that. You should go to bed."

"There's no way I could sleep, so I might as well be with you. We're in this together, Reverend Tough Guy."

*I*t's been exactly one week since the punch-out, and we haven't heard a word about it. Not from Wayne, not from the Synod, not from the cops, not from anyone at church. Nothing. Silence. Life has gone on like nothing has happened. Last night, Brice was finally able to sleep, but he stumbled through his sermon—heck, the entire late service—today. Probably the early one, too.

When the second service was over, and it was obvious Wayne wasn't at church or going to show up to church today, Brice nearly ran to his office to be alone. That left me to field most of the questions and comments regarding his behavior and appearance, but I was okay with that.

"Is Pastor okay? He looks so tired! You know, you two need to get as much sleep as possible now before that new baby keeps you up half the night."

As if we don't already have three other kids who interrupt our sleep for various reasons. Max's new thing is night terrors. I think he's picking up on his dad's anxiety.

"When was the last time Pastor had a physical or saw his

doctor? You know, after you have an accident like the one he had, you're more susceptible to health problems."

Oh, really now? Is that your professional opinion, Wilma, the retired school lunch lady?

"Pastor didn't seem prepared this morning."

Uh, is that a question? Because if not, then I'm going to be on my way.

It's been awful. Just now, though, I overheard someone say to someone else that Vivian and Wayne decided to take a spontaneous trip to the Grand Canyon, "To de-stress, you know? The secession petition was a big strain on Pastor Long."

That information sets me off in the direction of Brice's office, in as close to a run as I get.

When I give him the breathless news, he plops into his desk chair and rubs his forehead while shielding his eyes. After what feels like forever, I see his shoulders shaking and realize he's crying.

I rush to his side. "Oh, honey. It's okay."

"It's *not* okay. This is horrible. I… I need to tell someone what happened. I can't keep this information a secret."

"No, no, no. Yes, you can. Really. It's easy. Secret keeping is something you have to practice, but you can do it. You already do it all the time, when you keep people's confidences."

"That's different! That's about other people. I can't allow everyone here to think I'm a nice guy, when I'm not. I'm a guy who punches people in my living room. With my kids sleeping overhead. And my wife listening on the stairs."

"He said horrible things. He threatened you. He black-mailed you. He admitted he's been trying to sabotage you."

He nods. "Yes. And that makes him not very nice. But I

stooped even lower than his level when I hit him. Twice. And pushed him down my porch steps."

I rush to correct him, "Wait. No. You pushed him through the front door. He's old and clumsy and fell down the steps himself." The skeptical look he shoots me makes me clear my throat uncertainly, but I stick to my story. "You didn't push him off the porch."

Disregarding that, he continues, "I'm supposed to be a man of God."

"You are!"

"I'm supposed to model forgiveness and forbearance and patience and tolerance."

"I'd like to see a man who would tolerate someone saying about his wife the kinds of things Wayne said about me. And Secret."

He pinches the bridge of his nose and inhales a shaky breath. "Oh, man. I snapped. I just... snapped."

"Most guys would."

"I'm not allowed to be 'most guys,' though! How can anyone take me seriously now, when I preach Christ-like behavior to them? How can I take *myself* seriously?"

I perch on the edge of his desk. "Brice. Look at me." He complies. "I'll never forget a conversation between you and me when we were dating. I was, as usual, feeling unworthy, and I made the mistake of admitting it, and you told me that modern society has attributed a lot of behaviors and attitudes to Jesus that aren't necessarily accurate. Or historical. Yes, he was perfect, but he didn't put up with any shit. Okay, you didn't say 'shit.' I'm paraphrasing."

"Obviously."

I can't help laughing at his wry agreement. "Anyway, what I'm trying to say is that Jesus overturned the money changers' tables in the temple, did he not?"

"Yes."

"Well, if Jesus had a wife, I'm not so sure he wouldn't have done the same thing you did, in the same situation."

"Oh, I'm sure," he says, wide-eyed. "I'm absolutely sure. Peyton, that's different."

I wave away his argument. "Whatever. God forgives you. You need to forgive yourself."

He nods thoughtfully, rubs his chin, and says quietly, "I would, except... I can't forgive myself for something I'm not sorry about. That's cheap grace." His eyes puddle again when he states more loudly, "I'm not sorry I did it. I'd do it again."

Sighing, I walk behind him and hug him, placing my chin on his shoulder. "Oh, hon. You're exhausted."

"I'm a failure."

I turn my head to kiss his cheek. "No, you're not. You're human. And you're learning. And growing. Wayne may still report you. Then events will be out of your hands, but if you tell on yourself out of some misguided sense of duty, you won't only be losing your job and giving up your livelihood, you'll be destroying this ministry you've worked so hard, with God's help, to build. And how can you grow as a pastor if you're no longer a pastor?"

He shrugs like a sullen teenager.

"Plus, the fact that you think what happened makes you a failure means you *are* sorry on some level. You *wouldn't* do it again, if you had the chance. And if you could go back and undo it, you would."

He nods, and a tear falls onto his hand. Quickly, he wipes it dry and reaches over his shoulder to grab one of my hands and squeeze it.

With a frustrated grunt, he asks, "Why did he have to bring up Secret? I mean, I was okay until then. I know how he feels about you, and while he's off-base and his state-ments anger me, I can step back and rationalize that they're false. And I know you can easily defend yourself. But Secret, she's off-limits. She—" He pauses to regain control of his emotions. "She was—will forever be—a perfect, innocent, beautiful baby, a child of God, who never hurt anyone. And he wants to use her to destroy me. To hurt you. But she can't defend herself. She doesn't have a choice about being his pawn. And I—It makes me so angry!"

I sniff and blink rapidly. "I know. But—"

I don't have a chance to say anything else, though (not that I have a clue what to say), because someone's knocking on the office door, and I hear Max calling, "Daddy! Wh'are you?"

"Oh, gosh, the kids!" I breathe. I was so intent on rushing here to tell Brice about Wayne and Vivian going out of town without calling the cops—or the Synod—on him that I forgot the kids were in the nursery during church.

While I rush to open the door, Brice turns his chair away from it to compose himself. A nervous couple of teens from the youth group stand outside the office, a twin for each of them, Max hovering near their legs. As soon as the door opens, he barrels in.

"All the other parents had picked up their kids," the teen on the left (Ashley?) tells me. "Pam asked us to bring these guys to you."

I try to laugh it off. "Oh, we were hoping they'd take ours, too."

The girls giggle.

"Sorry, guys. I came up here to tell Pastor something important, and I lost track of time."

"That's okay," Ashley (?) says. "They were being good. Until they weren't being good."

The other girl (I have no idea what her name is, not even a guess) hands me the diaper bag. "I think they're hungry," she says. "We gave them those bottles kind of a long time ago."

I nod and take both twins. "Yep. It's lunchtime. Thanks, again, for helping with nursery duty."

Brice, somehow looking completely normal, appears at my side and relieves me of one of the babies and the diaper bag. "Hey, Ainsley. Hey, Grace."

All right then. Wrong on both counts. Ainsley and Grace. Ainsley and Grace.

"Found out you can skip church when you sign up to volunteer in the nursery?"

They giggle some more, and Grace sasses, "Pastor! We're helping!"

He laughs. "Yeah, I know. And it beats listening to my boring ramblings, huh? You got enough of that the few times I had to fill in for Mr. Eiffler at Confirmation, right?"

"Ummm," Ainsley mumbles, blushing.

"Anyway, thanks for bringing these guys to us. When we tell them to walk here by themselves, they get lost."

"Bye!" Max calls from the office behind us.

"Bye, Max!" the girls say in unison, which makes them giggle again before leaving.

As soon as they're gone, Brice's smile drops from his face, and the lines deepen around his mouth. His eyes take on the dull sheen of someone either feverishly sick or despondent. He sighs and wordlessly leads the way to the car. Max, chattering the whole way, runs to catch up to him. I stare after them for a few seconds before following.

∽

"No, we don't know what we're having. Well, we do. It's a baby, not a puppy. We know that much. But we decided not to find out the sex of the baby before the birth." I trace the wood grain pattern in the dining room table with my index finger as I give this speech for the fourth time today and brace myself for the reaction.

Jen doesn't disappoint. She sputters indignantly on the other end of the line while I hold the phone away from my ear for about the same amount of time it took everyone else to protest our decision when I told them. I should have risked pissing people off by telling them the news in an email. With everything else that's going on right now—or *not* going on, more accurately—I don't need the added stress from a bunch of drama queens.

Brice is so lucky he only has his mom to answer to. And she's cool. We could call her and tell her we're moving to Germany to live like authentic Lutherans, and she'd say, "That's great, kids! Send me some pictures with you guys in lederhosen."

My family, on the other hand, would cry and gnash their teeth and toss every negative German stereotype at us in an effort to change our minds. Then, when that didn't work, they'd pile on the guilt so high that we'd need an extra suitcase to carry it with us across the Atlantic. Everything's such a big deal with them.

For instance, now, on ultrasound day, you'd think the fate of the free world hinged on whether our child has a vagina or a penis—or at least, our prior knowledge of it. Jen's simply the latest person berating me for being so "selfish."

And maybe it *is* selfish. But on the way to the appointment today, I realized that if I saw another penis on an ultrasound screen or in a picture, I'd probably cry so hard that the technician would worry about my health and sanity, *and* he or she would judge me for caring so much.

Brice was waiting for me in the clinic's parking lot, and mustering as much enthusiasm as he's capable of displaying lately, he said, "This is it!" as we hurried toward the shelter of the building, out of the cold, autumn wind.

I waited until we were standing in front of the elevators to reply flatly, "I don't want to know."

"Now, when you say you don't want to know, you mean…"

"I don't want to find out today if the baby is a boy or girl," I said more plainly.

"Are you sure? Because this might be our only chance. I'd hate for you to change your mind in a few days… or weeks."

"Are *you* going to find out?" I asked, already doubting my decision.

He snorted. "Not if you're not. I don't want that kind of pressure. I'd spoil the surprise in a matter of minutes."

"Well, I don't want to force you to wait."

We stepped into the elevator car, and he pressed the button for the floor we needed. "I think waiting will be fun, but I didn't want to suggest it, because I thought you wanted to know ahead of time."

That's when I told him about my penis fear. To his credit, he tried valiantly not to laugh. He succeeded for about three seconds. But it was good to hear him laugh. I hadn't heard that sound in more than a week.

"I know, it's dumb and shallow," I said as the doors opened onto our floor.

"No. No," he tried to save it. "Not either of those things."

"Yes, it is. I should be happy with whatever we're having,

and blah, blah, blah, but I'm sick of being so outnum-bered." I gave my name to the receptionist, and we sat down in the waiting room.

"I think that's fair. But what's my excuse? I want a daughter, too, but I can't give the 'outnumbered' excuse."

"Well, every guy wants a daddy's girl."

"That's not true. My dad told me more than once that he was glad I was a boy, because he was scared to death of the thought of trying to raise a daughter." He brushed some imaginary lint from his black pants. "I'm not, though. I think it would be... incredible."

I choked up but sniffed away the tears. "It's settled then," I said in a no-nonsense fashion. "We'll save the big reveal until delivery day, when we'll be so full of joy that there won't be any room for disappointment if Dr. Klein says, 'It's a boy!'"

He grabbed my hand. "I like that idea. Everyone's going to hate us, but who cares? I'm starting to get used to that, anyway."

That statement pushed both of us into contemplative silence. It's not even true, anyway. Nobody hates him. Well, maybe the Longs, although they still haven't been in touch to tell us, nearly two weeks after the fisticuffs in our living room. But nobody else seems to hate Brice, either. Not even the few secession petitioners who are following through with their original intentions have been necessarily hateful. They're simply... leaving.

No, I think the person who hates Brice the most right now is Brice.

Pulled back to the present by the lack of sound I'm hearing through the phone's ear piece, I put it against my head. "You done?" I ask Jen.

Sullenly, she replies, "I guess. It's just—"

"Seriously? I thought I could count on you to be one of the only people not to bust our balls about this."

"Sorry. You're right. It's your choice."

"That's right."

"It's annoying for the rest of us, who would like to purchase things ahead of time, but it's not about us."

"Exactly. I was an idiot to tell everyone the date of the ultrasound, but I did, so I knew you'd be waiting to hear."

"Self-absorbed much?"

"Am I right, though?"

"Yes." Her tone is grudging. "I've been holding my phone ever since I thought you'd be home from your appointment. Which was hours ago, by the way."

I ignore her prompt for an apology. I've been busy talking my family down from the ultrasound ledge, finishing out my shift at work, and suffering through another hectic evening routine—without Brice, who's at work late… again.

"Can we talk about something else? I'm sick of this topic." I focus on a food stain on my shirt while I effect a nonchalant tone. "What's new with you and Lurch? Er, I mean, Wes?"

She sounds equally and purposefully casual. "Nothing much. We've talked a few times on the phone. He wants to Skype, but I don't know."

"Why are you so hesitant?"

"I don't know," she repeats unsatisfactorily.

I sigh. "Is it because he's so intense?"

"No."

"Is it because he calls you Jennifer?"

"No."

"Is it because you can't cuss around him?"

"A little. That's part of it. Not because I have to use bad words. That's not it. It's… It's part of a bigger issue. I feel like I can't completely be myself around him. Like I'm constantly weighing my words, worried I'm saying something wrong. Or bad. Or that he's thinking I'm a bad person."

"I remember those days," I say. "Trust me; you're not going to shock him with anything you say."

"I don't know…"

"He's hung around *me* a few times, remember?"

She laughs. "You *are* pretty bad about putting your foot in your mouth."

"Yeah. So, don't worry so much. Be yourself. If he doesn't like you for yourself, then what's the point?"

There's a shrug in her voice when she says, again, "I don't know. I like him, that's all. And I want him to like me."

It takes a heap of self-control for me not to tease her about sounding so vulnerable and pathetic. I know she must hate sounding that way; I know it's taking a lot of courage for her to admit she feels that way. And I've never heard her sound like this, so I have to say, I'm thrown.

Instead of giving her a hard time, I say honestly, "I think he really likes you, too. The real you, not the you-that-you-think-he'd-like-more-than-the-real you." The garage door buzzes to life, letting me know Brice is home.

"Whatever. I don't want to get my hopes up."

"And Skyping would get your hopes up?"

"Maybe. It's like a date, you know?"

I laugh. "No. It's really not. And it's sad that we've come to this as a society."

"It's the closest thing we have," she snaps defensively, "considering how far apart we live. And that's another thing. Long distance relationships suck so hard. Not that I think we have a relationship. Or will have one. I don't want to get too far ahead of myself."

Now, I can't resist. "Oh, my gosh! Jen. Are you listening to yourself? You sound like… like *me!*"

I'm relieved when she laughs at me—and herself. "Oh, shit. I know! What's happening? Is this what pastors do to people? Turn them into spazzes so prayer is their only hope?"

We giggle about that for several minutes, doing our best pastor impersonations, until Brice pokes his head into the dining room and asks, "What are you doing?"

Feeling guilty for making fun of him behind his back, I lie, "Nothing. Just talking to Jen about… stuff."

"It sounded like you were using that voice you use when you're imitating me in a story."

"Paranoid!" I raise my eyebrows at him.

He shrugs, then stands expectantly in the doorway, looking excessively somber, even more so than he has been lately. "I need to talk to you."

I tamp down the panic and say to Jen, "I gotta go. I'll call you tomorrow. Or something."

She immediately picks up on my change in tone, sobers, and asks, "Is everything okay?"

"Fine," I most likely lie. "Call Wes."

Before she can object to my bossiness, I hang up and turn all my attention to Brice. "What's up? You're scaring me. That look on your face—"

"Pastor Long is dead," he says bluntly while leaning against the doorframe.

"What do you mean?"

"He's gone. I mean, you know… Passed on." He widens his eyes and winces.

"Wha—How?!"

It's been days since Brice hit him and shoved him, but were Wayne's injuries severe enough to kill him? Was he that frail? He didn't seem to be, but... *Is my husband a murderer?*

As I start to hyperventilate at the idea, Brice begins, "His daughter called me and said it happened while he and Vivian were hiking at the Grand Canyon—Are you okay?" He rushes to my side and rubs my back. "Honey, what's wrong?"

"I— I— I—" I instinctively clutch my belly.

"Are you having contractions? What's the matter? Talk to me!"

I shake my head and manage to sputter, "I'm fine. Just... relieved."

"That he's *dead*? Oh, hon, that's not nice."

I shake my head again. "No. That you didn't kill him. Paper bag!"

He stares at me for a few seconds but when I gesticulate wildly to urge him into action, he hurries into the kitchen and returns with a paper lunch sack. As I breathe into the bag, he chuckles sadly. "Wow. You thought my hitting him killed him?"

More in control of my breathing, I move the bag to the side of my face and say, "Or when you pushed him off the porch."

"*You* said I didn't push him off the porch; that he tripped and fell."

"Whatever. It was on our property. And I thought— Oh, just tell me what happened," I gasp before returning the bag to my mouth.

With the crinkling paper as background music, Brice tells me that Iris called him right as he was leaving for the evening. She said early yesterday morning, Wayne and Vivian were hiking one of their favorite trails at the Grand Canyon when Wayne collapsed. He was gone before the paramedics could reach them. The coroner's report says it was a stroke. Vivian's on her way back to Springfield with Wayne's body, as we speak.

"Oh, man. Is Vivian okay?" No matter what our differences, I can't help sympathizing with any woman who's lost her husband. I can't imagine losing mine.

"In shock," Brice answers. "That's why Iris was calling me. She also needed Wes's phone number so she could get started on funeral arrangements. I guess Vivian was lucid enough to specify that she *didn't* want me to perform the service."

"Do you think Iris—or anyone else—knows about… you know?" I nod toward the living room where the clergymen's cage match happened.

He sighs and runs his hand through his hair. "I don't know. She was so upset about her dad that it was hard for me to tell. I mean, she would have said something, though. Right?" Before I can answer, he shakes his head as if to clear it. "Never mind. I mean, whatever. I mean, I shouldn't be worried about that right now. The man is dead."

"Ding dong," I mutter.

"Peyton, seriously!"

I snap, "You know I joke when I'm uncomfortable, and I'm uncomfortable, okay? I mean, it sucks to be glad that someone's dead. And I'm glad. I can't help it."

Rubbing the back of his neck, he says, "Well, it's sad. I feel terrible. Not glad."

"Good for you! We always knew you were better than me."

"Anyway, this doesn't mean anything. Vivian could still report me to the Synod or the elders. Or the cops, even. Or she could say Wayne's injuries led to his death." He plunks into a chair. "The right thing to do would be to resign."

"Not that again!"

"Not 'again'; 'still.' It's too late for me to make it right with Wayne, but a man of integrity would make it right with Wayne's wife and family."

"Brice—"

"No, really. I have to do this." He hops up and moves toward the kitchen, the garage door his apparent destination. "Iris is waiting for them at the airport. I'm going to wait with her."

"No, that's not—"

"Yes. Please, Peyton. This is hard enough. I know what the consequences could be. I know how it could affect our whole family. I'm scared. But I have to do this. I can't keep my position if it means living with this, like this. This week has been awful. And now he's gone, and I feel worse somehow."

I heave myself from my chair and walk to him. Grabbing his hand, I kiss his cheek while I squeeze his fingers. Quietly, I say, "All right then. I understand. But hurry back. Don't make me wait and wonder what happens."

RESOLUTION

*I*t's late. It's really late. Despite my request, Brice is making me wait and wonder. I'm having Braxton Hicks contractions from the stress. I've envisioned so many things happening.

1. Vivian took one look at Brice at the airport and had security arrest him.
2. Brice never made it into the airport terminal, because he forgot to look both ways when crossing the taxi line.

Okay, I've only envisioned those two things happening. But I've pictured them in my head about a thousand times, so many times that I'm sure one of the two has actually happened. Especially the more time goes by that I don't hear from Brice. Of course, if he were in jail, he'd have used his phone call to call me. He *better* use his call to call me. That leads me to imagine:

1. He was arrested for assault and battery—or

worse—and used his one phone call to call Jared.
Or Wes. Or Clark.

Before I can become too enraged by that scenario, my phone jumps to life on the couch cushion next to me. I fumble for the device with my clumsy sausage fingers, finally managing to hit the button to pick up the call, which the phone says is from "Lurch's Mobile."

"Oh gosh, what happened?" I immediately ask. No need for idle chit-chat.

He pauses, then answers in his typical flat-line tone, "Pastor Long passed away."

"I know that!" I snap. "Fast forward a day and a few hours. Where's Brice?"

"Yes, that's why I'm calling you. He can't get away, so he asked me to give you a call."

"What do you mean, he can't get away? Because he's in jail? Or surgery?"

I hear Wes inhale as if to say something, but he stops short and asks, "Are you okay?"

"I'm fine. Well, not really. I'm worried about my husband, who left hours ago and hasn't called me to let me know he's okay." The dam breaks. "I'm so worried, Wes!" I blubber. "I'm worried, and I'm having contractions—but don't tell Brice that, because they're not real ones." I force myself to stop talking and take a deep breath. Meekly, I finish, "I just want to know what's going on."

"Okay… Um… Well, don't be *worried*. There's no cause for that. We're at the Longs' house, and Pastor's been behind closed doors with Mrs. Long and Iris for a couple of hours now."

"Oh, gosh!"

"Pardon?"

"Nothing," I say with a hiccup. "Do you know what they're talking about?"

"No! I'm not eavesdropping!" he replies huffily.

"I didn't say you were, but—"

"It's obviously something private. They didn't even want me in there. I've been out here in the living room, texting Jennifer the whole time."

I wipe my face on my sleeve. "Oh. Really? How's she doing? Are you guys going to set up a time to Skype—Wait! I don't really care about that right now. No offense. I just want to know if Brice is okay."

He sighs. "Yes, he is."

"You probably think I'm nuts," I mutter. "I sort of feel nuts, but he makes me worry."

Wes assumes his most hypnotizing tone when he assures me, "He poked his head out the study door a few minutes ago and asked me to call you. He said don't wait up. Everything's fine."

I deflate on the couch, tipping onto my side like one of the poor cows the young people in this area terrorize by pushing over in their sleep. "You could have led with that, Wes," I grumble. "I mean, really."

Defensively, he responds, "You're the one who was acting so crazy. I had to make sure you weren't, well, having a baby, or something."

I laugh, which makes him chuckle, too. "Sorry. How did Brice look when he told you to call me?"

I can hear the wrinkle in his nose when he asks, "What do you mean? Like, what's he wearing? Or...?"

"No! Did he look happy, sad, worried?"

"What's all this 'worried' talk? Do you know something I don't know?"

"No!" I immediately reply. "I'm a worrier, that's all. And

I tend to project that on other people. Like Brice. Sometimes."

I'm thankful he lets it go and returns to my original question about Brice's supposed frame of mind, "Well, a guy died, so he didn't look happy. But he didn't look any of those other things, either. Just tired, I guess. You know, I'm tired, too," he unexpectedly vents. "I'm supposed to be the one in there, since I'm performing the funeral service. I would have waited until tomorrow if I'd known they only wanted to talk to Brice— er, Pastor Northam."

"You can call him 'Brice' to me," I tell the assistant pastor. "Well, hopefully they won't be too much longer, right? And the good news is that Jen's a night owl, so she won't mind texting with you until then. Or I can talk to you, if you want."

Reverting to his usual self, he stiffly replies, "Uh, no thank you. I simply wanted to relay Pastor Northam's message. Good night."

"Good—" But he's already gone. And now there's nothing for me to do but wait for Brice to get home.

Oh, and ride out these eyeball-bulging contractions.

Jingling keys. That's the first thing I hear. Then hard-soled shoes on hardwood floors. Then what sounds like a tongue clicking once, followed by, "Oh, hon," murmured from above.

I sit up, rubbing moisture into my eyes so I can see the bemused look on Brice's face when I blink into the soft light of the living room.

"You were supposed to go to bed after Wes called you," he states with a small smile.

"You were supposed to… whatever…" I trail off, too sleepy to come up with a decent retort.

He seems to know what I mean, anyway, because he replies, "I know. I'm sorry I was gone so long." He plops onto the cushion next to me, bouncing me hard enough that I have to brace myself against his arm to stay upright. "I don't even know where to start."

"Are you going to prison? Let's start there," I suggest.

He laughs. "No."

"Are you resigning? Are you going to be asked to leave? Are you going to be… defrocked?"

"No, no, and no. Unless you're volunteering to do the last thing."

My head snaps around to look him in his gleaming eyes. "How can you joke about that?"

He shrugs. "I'm happy."

"I see that."

"I don't know if I have the energy to tell you everything right now, though. I want to sleep, for a very long time. Preferably after…" He reaches for me, sliding his hand up the front of my shirt.

I swat him away, "Brice! What the fuck…?"

"Well, you know I don't like calling it that, but okay. Just this once." He resumes his previous advances until I jump from the couch and retreat to the fireplace, putting the coffee table between us.

"What's going on? If you're not too tired to do *that*, then you're not too tired to tell me what's happening."

He rolls his eyes, sighs, and sits normally on the couch. "Fine. But, you know, it's been a while since I've wanted to—"

"What happened at the Longs' house to make you want to?"

With a disgusted expression, he answers, "Ew. Nothing like that. Okay, here's the gist of it: Wayne's been stealing from the church. Or had been. Or whatever."

My eyes feel like they're going to pop from my head and roll under the coffee table (and I'm not even having contractions anymore, although that may change soon). "Say what?!"

Brice grins and nods, like it's the best news he's heard in months. "Yeah. So, I guess after I… you know…" He nods toward where I'm standing and where he punched Wayne. "Wayne went home, and he and Vivian were going to call the police. But Wayne got a call from Bill Gregory."

"The church treasurer?"

"Yes. Vivian says Wayne immediately left to go talk to Bill—he was vague and said they'd report me when he got back. But when he returned, he was in an even bigger rush, and he started packing suitcases. Big suitcases. He told Vivian he forgave me and didn't want to press charges or make waves at the Synod or at Peace. He said he was sick of all the drama and the stress and needed to get away. He suggested they go to the Grand Canyon for a week or two."

"And Vivian didn't think this was odd?"

Brice snorts. "Of course, she did. But she said Wayne was stressed out, because of everything going on at church—"

"All that stuff was his fault!"

"Yeah, yeah, yeah. Anyway, they drove to the airport to get the soonest flight possible. At this point, Vivian thought Wayne had finally lost it, so she tried not to provoke him. She pretended like everything was normal, and a week into the trip, everything *did* seem normal. She said he seemed happier and more relaxed than he'd been in a long time."

"The hike," I prompt.

"I'm getting there! Sheesh." Brice collects his thoughts and continues, "Okay, yesterday—or technically, the day before, I guess, since it's past midnight now—they ordered a picnic lunch from the hotel and set off, like they always do, right at sunrise. They hiked until noon, then stopped for lunch. At lunch, Wayne dropped it on Vivian that he'd been 'borrowing' money from the church to pay off their credit cards and mortgage, and Bill Gregory, during the audit, noticed the discrepancy. When Wayne met with him, Bill gave him a month to pay it back—or he was going to tell me. And report Wayne."

"So Wayne flew the coop. He didn't have time to press charges against you."

"Right. Well, Vivian said she freaked out when Wayne told her. Actually, her words were, 'I plum fell to pieces.' But you know what I mean. She asked if he could pay back everything he'd 'borrowed,' and he said, 'Not by the end of a month,' so she threatened to divorce him. She feels really bad about that, because... Well, that's when he collapsed."

"Oh, no. Poor Vivian!"

Did those words really just come from my lips? No way. I look behind me, but the only thing there is an empty fireplace.

Brice laughs sadly. "Yeah. Poor Vivian."

"What are you going to do?" I ask.

He shrugs. "The guy's dead. I can't turn him in. Vivian had no idea he was doing it, so it's not like I can turn *her* in. His life insurance will more than cover it. Vivian has promised to cut the church a check as soon as the payment comes through."

"Do you believe her?" I ask quietly.

He nods. "Yeah. I do. If you had seen her... She's like a different person. And Iris. Poor Iris. I remember what it was like when my dad died. That feeling. It's like nothing else. To know you're never going to see that person in this life again. You know, despite what he was to us, that was her dad."

"Where are their other kids?"

"On the way here. They should be arriving at different times during the day tomorrow. The funeral is Monday."

"And Wes is going to do it? Because Vivian's still mad at you for beating up her now-dead husband?"

He rubs his eyebrow. "No, Wes is going to do it, because Wes is good at funerals. Vivian and Iris, both, were forgiving and gracious and understanding toward me. They said… they said—" He bites his lip. After clearing his throat, he continues, "They said the Wayne they knew wouldn't have said or done those things to me. They said he wasn't himself during the past year. Which is why Vivian wanted him to retire, in the first place."

"Do you believe *that?*"

He shrugs. "I guess I have to, don't I? I want to believe it, anyway. It makes it somehow okay for me to keep my secret and Wayne's secret, so that we can move on."

I cautiously approach the couch area. "Do you really think it'll be that easy?"

He grins. "Maybe. Why not?"

"Because nothing's that easy?" I posit.

Brice screws his mouth to the side. "Hm. Well, a guy had to die to get most of this straightened out. I wouldn't necessarily call that 'easy.'"

"Easy for us," I point out. When Brice looks shocked, I laugh. "You know what I mean!"

"Well, maybe we should thank Wayne for taking one for the team."

"You're bad."

"I'm looking at the bright side. Besides, I don't want to be sad today. I'll be sad at his funeral on Monday. Is that good enough?"

"I guess," I allow.

"C'mere," he coaxes.

I pretend it's a major hardship, but I do as he requests.

He pulls me into his lap. "Later, I'll tell you more about what we talked about this evening, the two ladies and I. But right now, I don't want to talk anymore."

I shiver at his breath on my neck. "Oh, okay," I say in a long-suffering tone.

At this point, I don't care if it seems too 'easy.' I only care that God has favorably answered a prayer I've been sending to Him for *months*.

TO "V" OR NOT TO "V"

"*I* feel like everyone was staring at us in the waiting room," Brice whispers two months later while he undresses in the urologist's procedure room.

"Why are you whispering?" I ask in a normal voice.

He stops to consider it. "I don't know."

"Don't want to wake up the nut-kraken?"

"You're hilarious." Holding closed the back of his gown, he sits on the operating table, his legs hanging off the end, his black-sock clad feet swinging a few inches above the ground.

I can't resist laughing at the vision of him.

"Do you mind?" he snaps.

"Would you like me to wait in the waiting room?" I ask hopefully.

Unfortunately, he answers, "No. They'll just stare at you."

Darn. I really don't want to be in here for this, but he's requested my presence. I think it's bizarre and uncharacteristic of Reverend Modesty, but I figure fair is fair, considering the number of times he's accompanied me during exams, procedures, and births.

Now I defend the people with the staring problem in the waiting room by pointing out, "Well, it *is* funny to see a guy here with his ready-to-burst, pregnant wife. I mean, could it be more obvious that we're *done* with this whole reproducing thing?"

"It's none of their business!"

"Did you take that Valium, like they told you to do? You're awfully testy." I snicker. "Get it?"

"I'm hungry," he says, ignoring my fabulous wit. "And nervous. This is going to hurt."

"You do know they're going to numb you, right?"

He shoots me a sharp look. "I heard that's the worst part. They spray this cold stuff down there and stick a needle in your… beanbag—"

"The doctor told us all this in your consultation. Why is this such an issue now? It beats the alternative."

"Clark said it was the worst thing he's felt in his whole life." When I titter, he says, "Yeah, he and Marianne cornered me at church last Sunday. Have you told *everyone* about this?"

I shrug. "Oh, come on. It's a common procedure. It's not a big—"

"It's *private*."

"Why? Because they're *your* privates? Childbirth isn't private, even though it involves *my* privates. I've had other mothers ask me how many stitches I had to have with the twins!"

"At least it was woman-to-woman. You and Jen snickering about it or Marianne reassuring me I can handle it is different."

I tilt my head and give him a pitying look. "Oh, hon. You're so repressed sometimes."

"Just, please, stop telling everyone about it," he pleads. "I have to stand up in front of those people every week!"

"Fine!"

After a short silence, he continues sulkily, "Anyway, apparently, it's not as cut and dried as the doctor would have us believe."

"Baahahaha! Cut and dried?" I cross my legs so I don't have an accident in my pants.

"You know what I mean."

I stand and walk over to him. Hugging him from the side, I kiss his cheek (the one on his face, not the one peeking from the back of his cute little surgical gown). "Hon, you need to relax. It's really going to be okay. I'll baby you for the next two days—"

"Oh, two days? Thanks."

In response to his sarcastic snipe, I remind him, "I didn't get much more than that after birthing two babies within ten minutes of each other, so I think that's plenty of time for you to nurse your nuts."

"Are you going to throw the childbirth thing in my face for the rest of our lives? I don't make the rules, okay? Take it up with Eve."

I return to the chair by the wall and sigh, hoping the doctor arrives soon. The only cure for his bad mood is for the procedure to be over and for him to go through the recovery process and see for himself that it's not a big deal. After all, the guy's had orthopedic surgery and has lived through months of physical therapy and recovery. You'd think he'd be relatively unfazed at the prospect of some crotchal discomfort.

I don't say any of this, though. I know he's going to be

on the receiving end of a fair number of similar exchanges in a few weeks, so I try to be tolerant. Folding my hands in my lap, I avert my eyes from him.

Unfortunately, my gaze lands on the rolling tray of sterile instruments. *What's* that *thing for? Ohmygosh!*

As if equally disturbed, the baby jumps, and my entire belly quakes. Brice catches the movement from the corner of his eye and does a double take.

In spite of his stormy mood, he smiles. "Wow. That was a… what? A hiccup?"

"An earthquake."

He takes a deep breath and returns to grousing. "Where the higgety is the doctor? I mean, I'm freezing! And starving. And I want to get this over with."

"It'll be done in thirty minutes."

"Well, I don't want him to rush," he says, seeming to reconsider his desire for things to be over quickly. "We're aiming for quality work here."

I laugh. "You're killing me. Do you know how many of these he does a day?"

"Yeah. Exactly. I don't want him daydreaming or thinking about what's on TV tonight while he's waving that thing"—he points to the scary instrument that disturbed me a few seconds ago—"around my… you know…"

"Yes, I know. It's such a shame you're the first person to undergo this procedure."

"Hey, it's *my* first time. Better be the last, too."

"That's usually how it works." At the risk of pissing him off further, I rise again and stand next to him. Raking my fingers through his hair, I say, "Now, shush. Rest easy in the knowledge that if you're the first person to die during a vasectomy, your family will be okay. We'll live off the money from the malpractice settlement and Lifetime movie deal, in addition to your life insurance. And I'll sell your minivan, too."

He chuckles, his breath making the front of his gown flutter. "Okay, okay. I get it. I'm being a Jerkasaurus Rex."

"I didn't say that."

"I know I am. And I'm blowing things out of proportion."

"Hey, now. There'll be no blowing of anything for a while."

"Don't remind me," he grumbles. "That's not improving my mood."

"Then let's think of happier things," I suggest. "Like the Bears in the Superbowl. Someday. Before we're too old to care."

He laughs. "Oh, yes. Hmm. Well, I'm probably already too old to care."

"No!"

"I'm just being honest. I only pretend to like the Bears to suck up to your dad. I need all the help I can get with that guy."

"I think that Valium's finally kicking in," I state, taking a seat once more.

He reclines on the table, his legs still dangling. Cupping his hands over his private parts, he says in a dreamy voice, "I've never shaved myself down there before this morning. It's not as bad as I thought it'd be. It's going to be itchy when it grows back, though, huh? Maybe I'll keep shaving it. I hear it makes you look bigger."

Oh, dear. I believe this is going to be his second forgotten conversation in less than a year. At least, I hope for his sake he doesn't remember it. After a few more minutes of waiting, neither of us saying anything (which is probably for the best), he suddenly rockets into a sitting position.

"I don't want to do this."

I sigh. "I know, but we've decided this is the only sure way…"

"No. I mean, I don't want to *do* this." He hops down from the table, pulling off the gown as he steps across the room to the chair where his clothes rest, neatly folded and stacked.

"What are you doing?!" As fast as I can in my weighed-down, clumsy state, I rise from my chair, wedging myself between him and his clothes while glancing nervously at the door.

He stands with his hand on his hip, stark naked except for his socks. I peek down and see he wasn't kidding about the manscaping he performed in the shower this morning.

I repeat more calmly, "What are you doing?"

"Getting dressed," he logically answers, tossing the hospital gown on the floor. "I'm not doing this."

"Yes, you are. You've already put it off long enough, as it is."

He reaches around me, just short of pushing me out of the way in his efforts to get to his clothing.

"Brice," I hiss, "put that gown back on and get on the table. They're going to come in any minute."

"And I'm going to wish them a nice day and leave."

He pulls his underwear up his legs and over his bum, and he's adjusting himself when the room's door swings open.

A short, stout nurse (who looks like she might own a necklace made of patients' discarded parts) stops in her tracks, blinks hard, and clutches his file more tightly to her chest. "Oh. I thought you'd be ready by now."

"Never," is Brice's cryptic reply.

I give her a beseeching look that screams, *"Help!"*

She sets down his chart and crosses her arms over her chest, but she doesn't look concerned. "You don't want to undergo the procedure today?"

He resumes dressing, shoving his feet into his pants and yanking the trousers up his legs. "Nope. Not tomorrow, either. Or the next day. Or ever."

"You'll have to sign some paperwork," she tells him.

If that's the strongest argument she's going to give him, we're in trouble. "Wait!" I interject.

But he doesn't. He pulls his shirt over his head and smooths his hair.

"You're not thinking clearly."

Patting his pockets to make sure he has his wallet, phone, and keys, he shakes his head. "I'm thinking crystal clearly. This isn't what I want."

"What about what *I* want? What we decided *we* want—or don't want, more accurately?"

The nurse rolls her eyes and edges toward the door. "I'll just—"

"No!" I nearly shout at her. "Please. Don't leave. Don't let *him* leave."

She shrugs. "I can't keep him here. He's a consenting adult."

"B-but he's under the influence of drugs!"

Her expression clearly conveys she thinks I'm an idiot. "It's Valium. If anything, he's calmer than he would be without it. So count yourself lucky."

"I *don't* count myself lucky. He needs this operation."

She laughs. "I'm going to go get the paperwork he *needs* to sign before we release him."

With that, she leaves me to deal with Brice by myself.

Lowering his foot to the floor after tying his sneaker, he faces me and grabs my upper arms, bending at the knee to look into my eyes. "Don't look so disappointed. It's going to be okay, really."

Disappointed? Disappointed?! I'm seven months pregnant, unexpectedly so for the third time, and the solution to it never happening again—no other method seems to effectively keep the babies away—is about to be snatched away from me. Disappointed? No, not even close.

Begging. That's my only option here.

"Brice. Please. Don't walk out of here."

"I'm already dressed. Let's go." He drops his hands from my arms and claps them together once, as if it's settled.

It suddenly occurs to me, "You can't go anywhere unless I drive you. And I'm not going to do it. We've talked about this—a lot. It was originally *your* idea."

Smiling, he says, "Yeah. I'm beginning to think I'm not as good at decision-making as I used to be. I'm getting all impulsive, or something."

"Yes!" I grasp onto his moment of clarity. "And this is another poor, impulsive decision. I know you're scared, but we can't let fear control us, right? You told me that. And you were right. Don't be afraid. This is not a big deal."

"It's not about being afraid."

"It's okay to admit it."

"I know, but it's not about that. I—" He laughs, scratches the side of his nose with his thumb, and looks down at his feet. "If I tell you, it's going to sound crazy. It seems crazy to *me*, but I believe it wholeheartedly."

Before I can ask him what could possibly be crazier than what he's doing and saying, the nurse returns, hands him a form to sign, and stands by while he does exactly that, with a huge flourish.

"You're free to go," she says. "Good luck with… everything," she adds with a bemused grin on her way out.

As soon as she's gone, I break down crying. "How can you do this?" I ask him. "You promised you'd—"

He pulls me roughly against him and rubs my back. I want to struggle, but I don't have the strength to do it. I'm so tired. I weakly slap his shoulder while I sob.

"Peyton. Oh, sheesh. Don't cry, please."

"I'll stop crying if you take your clothes off."

He laughs. "Well, if I had a dollar for every time you said that to me…"

"It's not funny!" I push away from him and swipe at my eyes. "I'm so mad at you right now! Well, I'll show you! I'll — I'll get my tubes tied while I'm in the hospital having this baby!"

The pitying look he gives me makes me want to punch him. Then he says, "It's a Catholic hospital; they won't do that."

"A hysterectomy, then. I'll convince them I need it or I'll die. It might be truer than you realize."

He pushes me gently into a chair and sits in the one next to it. Angled so we're knee-to-knee, he grabs both of my hands in his. "I don't think telling you this is going to make you think I'm any saner than you already do, but— When I was up there, on that table, I saw something amazing. And God told me not to have the procedure. At least, not now."

"I hate you so much right now," I half-lie in a dull tone.

"Hear me out."

"Whatever. What choice do I have? You played the God card… again."

He ignores my commentary and plows on, "It's so final. And who are we to make this decision?"

With an incredulous look at his earnest face, I answer, "I'll tell you who we are. We're people with limited income living in an overpopulated world. People who are overwhelmed. And I'm a person who's tired of her vagina feeling like a Pez dispenser. We're also people who have discussed this at length while not under the influence of narcotics and have come to the decision—as a couple—that this is the right thing to do."

"Yeah, I know all those things in here…" He points to his head. "But *this*…" He moves his finger to his chest. "…is saying something else. We have more than enough—money *and* love."

"What about energy? And sanity? I don't have enough of that. I'm serious," I insist when he laughs. "You're feeling really good, thanks to that pill you took with the banana you ate this morning. But I'm not on drugs." I point to my head and chest at the same time. "These two things are saying the same thing to me. And that's, 'Stop! For the love of all things holy, just stop!' God's talking to me, too."

"Do you trust me?"

I roll my eyes. "Most of the time, yes. Right now, not so much."

"I guess the bigger question is, do you trust Him? He's not going to give you—or us—anything we can't handle."

"You wanna bet? You knock me up one more time, and you're going to seriously test that theory."

He couldn't sound more dismissive when he says with a pat on my knee, "All right, then. Let's not close the door yet, though."

I want to slam it in his face. And give him a bloody nose in the process. But what can I say to him? He's not giving in. In this moment, he honestly believes he's some modern-day Moses who's seen a vision of the future.

I wonder how many children were in that picture. And where was I? Because I'm sure I wasn't there. It must be with a different woman. Oh, gosh. Maybe I'm going to die!

And he doesn't want to get snipped, because he wants to have children with someone else someday.

That thought brings on the tears again, but I don't tell him what I'm thinking.

Instead, while he soothes me, I try to pull it together and see the funny side to all this. He's already signed the release papers, after all. Nobody named Northam is getting cut on today. And I'm sure once he sobers up, he'll realize he's made a mistake and will reschedule this whole thing. What's the point in getting so worked up?

"Three years. We'll reevaluate then, okay? I promise."

"Your promises aren't worth a shit," I grumble but smile into his face and say, "Fine. Whatever. You're obviously not going to take 'no' for an answer."

"True." He leans forward and kisses my lips, breaking contact barely long enough to say, "I love you."

I kiss him back while he reaches behind himself, toward the counter, for something. He comes up with a tissue, which he offers to me. I clean my face. When I'm finished, he presses his forehead to mine.

"I love you, too," I return his sentiment. "Which is why you're going to walk out of here alive."

He grins. "We're so blessed."

All I can do is nod.

"Just hold on, and everything will be all right."

The *Secret Keeper* series:

- *The Secret Keeper* (Book 1)
- *The Secret Keeper Confined* (Book 2)
- *The Secret Keeper Up All Night* (Book 3)
- *The Secret Keeper Holds On* (Book 4)
- *The Secret Keeper Lets Go* (Book 5)
- *The Secret Keeper Fulfilled* (Book 6)

The *Underdog* series:

- *Out of My League* (Book 1)
- *Rookie of the Year* (Book 2)
- *Opportunity Knox* (Book 3)

The *Nurse Nate* series:

- *Let's Be Frank* (Book 1)
- *Let's Be Real* (Book 2)
- *Let's Be Friends* (Book 3)

Stand-alone novels:

- *Daydreamer*
- *The Family Plot*
- *Plain Jayne*
- *Quiet, Please!*